Flashman in the Peninsular

Robert Brightwell

This book is dedicated to Fiona Brightwell and Jack Brightwell

Published in 2014 by FeedARead.com Publishing

A CIP catalogue record for this title is available from the British
Library.

Introduction

The third packet in the memoirs of Thomas Flashman is by far the largest, covering his experiences in the Peninsular War from late 1808 to mid-1812. The Peninsular War took place in Spain and Portugal, and this was where Arthur Wellesley, later the Duke of Wellington, made his name fighting the French.

To keep the books a manageable size I have broken it down into two instalments, which both work as 'stand alone' accounts. This, the first one, covers the period from late 1808 to the end of 1810.

While many people have written books and novels on the Peninsular War, Flashman's memoirs offer a unique perspective. They include new revelations on famous battles, but also incredible incidents and characters almost forgotten by history. Flashman is revealed as the catalyst to one of the greatest royal scandals of the nineteenth century, which disgraced a prince and ultimately produced one of our greatest novelists. In Spain and Portugal he witnesses catastrophic incompetence and incredible courage in equal measure. He is present at an extraordinary action where a small group of men stopped the army of a French marshal in its tracks. His flatulent horse may well have routed a Spanish regiment, while his cowardice and poltroonery certainly saved the British army from a French trap.

Accompanied by Lord Byron's dog, Flashman faces death from Polish lancers and a vengeful Spanish midget, not to mention finding time to perform a blasphemous act with the famous Maid of Zaragoza. This is an account made more astonishing as the key facts are confirmed by various historical sources.

I have kept editing to a minimum with a few notes in the text, but more detailed historical information can be found at the end of the book.

As always, if you have not already read them, the memoirs of Thomas' more famous nephew, Harry Flashman, edited by George MacDonald Fraser are also strongly recommended.

RDB

Chapter 1
London December 1808

When I think back to how my adventures started, with most of them there was at least a hint of danger at the outset. When I went first to Spain I was on the run from a gang of ruthless murderers. (See Flashman and the Seawolf.) But the event that led to my second visit, and my longest trip abroad, seemed as safe as you could get. It just goes to show that when fate pulls your string, there is really no point hiding. I mean a poetry recital, even one of Byron's, is not the sort of place that you would expect to lead to blood and bullets. For a start the things are generally damned dull, unless you are of the poetic persuasion, and I certainly wasn't. Waste of paper and ink most of it, but it was not the literature that I came for. I was there to boost my diminished income by preying on the witless fools it attracted.

Carefully I lifted the lid of the box and Lord Hartington leaned over to look inside. He must have been eighteen then, heir to the Duke of Devonshire fortune and full of earnest enthusiasm. His mouth dropped open in wonder.

'So this is weally the head of Chwistopher Marlowe?' he asked in the affected Devonshire lisp. He had spoken in what he thought was a hushed tone, but as he was partially deaf his voice was always much louder than he thought. This enquiry must have carried halfway across the room.

'It is,' I lied, as we both stared at the ivory coloured dome that was the top of the skull. It lay in a velvet lined and artfully antiqued mahogany box.

Hartington slowly reached out his hand to touch it, but then hesitated as though he could not quite bring himself to make contact with the bone. 'Beneath this shell,' he boomed, 'a living bwain gave life to some of the finest literwerwy cweations known to man, Dido the Queen of Carthage, Tamburlaine and of course Doctor Faustus.'

'I know,' I lied again while making a mental note that I really should learn more about the bones I was selling. For it was not the first old bone I had sold recently. There had been the head of Thomas Wolsey and the skull of Thomas Becket, the latter skilfully cut in two and the edges made brittle. Then, finding a gullible and wealthy market amongst the literary young men who surrounded Lord Byron, I had met this with the hand bones of John Donne, the shin bone of Andrew Marvell and now the skull of Christopher Marlowe.

4

'It is a cawapace of cweation,' continued Hartington, his voice now shouting around the chamber and tears of emotion starting to brim in his eyes. 'It is a cwucible of owiginal thought that even inspired Shakespeare to some of his finest works. Why it is ...'

'You want it then?' I cut in, looking over my shoulder to see if anyone else in the room was paying attention to us sitting in the corner. Several people were looking over and grinning, you could not do anything discreetly with Hartington. Just the previous night for devilment I had pointed out to him a pretty girl sitting with her family in the next box at the theatre. 'Chwist on the cwoss would you look at the bweasts on her' he had roared in a reply that could be heard half way across the stalls. The object of his desire went scarlet in embarrassment and her father turned a similar colour in rage.

Most of the others in the room looked away again and only Cam Hobhouse held my eye. He was standing next to woman in a green dress by the window. When he saw me look over he gave a sneering shake of his head in disgust. But then Hobhouse disapproved of most of the happenings at Byron's parties; his demeanour was normally that of a nun in a brothel. He was one of the shrewder members of Byron's circle, but while he disliked me, he would not say anything. Apart from the few wealthy members like Byron and Hartington, they all struggled to keep up with the financial obligations of being in the smart literary set. To some degree they all preyed on the innocence of the rich and the foolish.

We were in a private room in Dorant's Piccadilly Hotel, where Byron was living. There were perhaps a dozen people there: Byron was by the fire talking to a couple of fellows about his latest scribblings, a pair of dandies were playing chess near the window and the rest were scattered on various chairs talking errant bosh about some play or other. Yet this peaceful setting was about to launch me on a chain of events that would see a prince disgraced, appalling atrocities, ingenious courage, knavery, and breath-taking incompetence and cowardice that made even my yellow liver seem brave in comparison.

I know lots of Peninsular officers have published their memoirs of the war and they are full of accounts of lines of British redcoats beating French columns, sieges and long marches. Well there is some of that of course, but I venture to suggest that my experiences were rather more colourful. For example, I saved Wellesley from being captured by being shot in the arse, saw a small private army defeat a

5

French marshal and had my life saved by Byron's dog along the way. I did not even make it to the end of the campaign as I had to reluctantly save the most irritating so called 'Intelligence Officer' the British army has ever recruited. I ended up being hunted in Paris for my pains. Even when I thought I had escaped from there I only found myself in the soup again in another part of the world; but that is another story. And if, dear reader, you have read my previous account (See Flashman and the Cobra), which concluded with me wearing undeserved laurels on my brow, and you are wondering what Flashy is doing pedalling bones, well I will come to that presently. In the meantime the jingle of coins attracted my attention back to the sale.

'You mentioned your man was insisting on cash,' shouted Hartington indicating the plump leather purse he had just put on the table. 'Two hundwed guineas as you asked for Thomas. I would have paid double for it is the most marvellous thing. I will use it as my muse to help me cweate works half as beautiful as his.'

I inwardly winced at selling the skull too cheap, but the ease of the transaction renewed my love of poets, for they were easier to gull than a child. They affected to live in the clouds continually talking of beauty, inspiration and love, while pretending not to be interested in realities like poverty or the provenance of the things they were buying. They wanted to believe the bones were real and so they did. You just had to remember to insist on hard cash for payment as most were hugely in debt.

There was a fashion for old bones then, started partly by Byron. At his home, Newstead Abbey, his gardener had dug up the skull of one of the former Augustinian monks that had lived at the abbey before it was torn down by Henry VIII. Byron had arranged for it to be mounted on a stand as a drinking cup and we had all drunk from it at some of his late night parties. This prompted an interest in other macabre relics, which I was only too happy to fulfil as I needed the money. My half pay as a captain in the 74th Highlanders had been cancelled by the army's commanders the previous year. Their excuse was that it was based on a battlefield commission, but in reality it was part of a cost saving drive as the war with France was proving ruinously expensive. The decision, however, nearly spelt ruin for me as well, for I had borrowed against the income. The kindly Russian Jew I had taken the loan from became as inflexible as a dowager duchess' corset when I tried to renegotiate terms. He also had a couple of vicious East End enforcers to ensure that payments were made.

My only other source of income was the rent from Flashman's Row, the tenement building my father had bought for me in a trust that I could not sell. For any gentleman a job in trade was unthinkable, so the obvious thing to do was to turn the screw on my tenants by increasing their rent. That was when I discovered the skills of the forger living on the second floor. He wasn't a painter, bones were his speciality. He picked most of them up from a cemetery in Shoreditch and then he would make wooden chests that looked ancient to keep them in, with inlaid brass plaques saying things like 'The Skull of Queen Anne Boleyn' or 'The Head of Sir Walter Raleigh'. He tried to sell them to the rich and the gullible, but they were wary about buying from someone who was not a gentleman.

He had offered me 'Thomas Wolsey' in lieu of six weeks rent and that is when I started spending time with Byron and his friends. The fact that they were university graduates did not mean that they were astute; the nobility were not required to attend lectures or pass exams to get degrees in those days. While Byron did read widely in Cambridge, he did not attend a single lecture but was awarded a Master of Arts degree. He and his circle of friends were now living in London and spent most of their time partying, gambling, indulging in fashion and countless other ways of enjoying themselves. I amused them with tales of India and soon found a buyer for Wolsey amongst their wider circle.

Byron himself showed no interest in the bones; he was no fool. He was born into relative poverty until he inherited a fortune aged ten. Oh he was vain, extravagant and selfishly dedicated to fulfilling his own desires, but often you felt he was acting the part he thought people expected from him. For example, most people did not know that he had a twisted right foot and withered calf, which he hid with specially made boots. He boxed for exercise and was a prodigious swimmer. At the time of that party he had recently lost several stone in weight through diet and exercise, while claiming to others that food bored him. I never understood his writing, it seemed endless drivel to me but, while I would like to dismiss him as an effete dandy, I must admit that I liked him. I am happy to sacrifice principles for my pleasure too.

Speaking of pleasure, as I looked up after pocketing the gold I saw the lady in the green dress now staring over at me. The other three women in the room were dressed in a page boy style as Byron liked his women dressed as boys. At least I assumed that they were all women, you could never tell with Byron. The low cut green dress showed a generous top hamper leaving no doubt as to the gender of its owner, and she was a stunner. As I watched she put her hand on Hobhouse's arm and had evidently asked to be introduced, as they walked over.

I stood to meet them as Hobhouse, stiffly formal, announced, 'Thomas, may I have the honour to introduce you to Mary Clarke? You may recall that she is a most particular friend of ...' but he got no further as Mary pushed forward and cut him off.

'Why Captain Flashman, what a delight to meet you. I have heard so much about you and your adventures in India, you must tell me all about them.' I was surprised she knew my military rank as I did not use it with the poets. But before I could consider that further her blue eyes were sparkling at me and she took my arm and steered me away to a small table with two chairs where we could be alone.

We talked for some time and she did indeed seem fascinated by India. She listened attentively to all of my tales, while ordering Madeira wine and sweetmeats from a passing waiter to keep me refreshed. She was, I guessed, three or four years older than my twenty-six years but she was pert, vivacious and quick to ask questions. Sometimes she was almost a little too quick, such as when I mentioned that I had lost my commission. She asked if I knew others that had been deprived as part of the previous year's cost cutting review. I had not mentioned when the commission had been lost. I remember looking curiously at her then but she gave me another dazzling smile, leaned forward giving me a good view of those splendid bouncers and put her hand on my thigh. Conspiratorially she whispered to me, 'So we both have reason to resent the commander in chief's cost cutting then.'

'Why is that then?' I asked distractedly.

'He stopped my annuity as well.'

I raised my gaze back to her face. 'I don't understand. You cannot be army, how did you get a pension?'

'Not army?' she laughed, 'I will bet I have commanded more of it than you!' I looked at her puzzled at that. I had heard of some women serving in the ranks disguised as men, but it was hard to imagine Mary Clarke disguised as a man. She laughed at my confusion. 'In my time half of all the senior officer appointments and transfers between regiments came though my hands, and those that wanted them paid handsomely for the privilege.'

I was still confused for a moment, but then as the realisation dawned I blurted out, 'You were the Duke of York's mistress! I have heard stories,' I continued, 'a year or two ago, that if a man could afford it, then the quickest way to promotion was to pay our commander in chief's mistress. That must have been you.'

'Exactly,' she confirmed. 'The daughter of a printer wielding power in the British army, but now I fear on the way down again.'

'Did you really organise that many promotions?'

'Gawd yes,' she was laughing again. 'Sometimes there would be such a list of names I would pin it on the end of the bed to make sure Freddie did not forget it in the morning.'

'And he always agreed to them?' I asked.

'He did if he wanted his plums tickled,' she said firmly. 'Mary Clarke has never given a refund for services rendered; anyway I was a damn fine mistress to him.'

'I am sure you were,' I agreed imagining her standing over a prince of the realm and demanding he agree to her list before she pleasured him.

'Freddie has never been good with money,' she stated of the man who managed the finances of the British army. 'He can drink and gamble his way through forty thousand a year; I know, I have seen him do it. He cannot stand living with his wife so he has to have his own household as well as funding hers, and that does not come cheap. I ran his household and paid for most of it. I hosted his parties, flirted with his generals and, when he was not too drunk, I tupped him to exhaustion. I did it all without it costing him a penny. I was the perfect mistress!'

'So what went wrong?'

'Some cow with perter breasts and fewer wrinkles.'

'You don't have wrinkles,' I complimented her automatically, but when I looked, apart from a few faint laughter lines, she truly didn't.

'Oh you have to expect that sort of thing eventually. I replaced an earlier mistress and I knew he would find a new favourite sooner or later. There is no point getting angry about it. Leave with good grace and a full purse, is what one Madame told me.'

'And that is what you did?' I asked.

'He promised me an annual pension of four hundred pounds which he paid for the first year, but this year all I have had is excuses; and then he stopped replying to my letters at all.'

'That is shocking,' I cried supportively while looking her over and speculating how desperate she was for cash, for she was a very tidy piece and I had a full purse. You had to wonder what bedroom skills she could employ to have the Duke of York surrender control of the army. I had never been with a royal mistress; you would expect them to be amongst the best in Europe. I was just musing over how they would compare to the oriental arts of lovemaking I had enjoyed in India and thinking back to the exquisitely skilled Fatimah, when I realised that Mary had said something and seemed to expect a response.

'Yes I am sure,' I tried as an all-encompassing answer.

'You were staring at my chest and not paying the slightest attention to what I was saying weren't you?' She gave a resigned shake of the head before continuing. 'I was saying that if I knew any of the more radical members of Parliament I could bring down the government with what I know.'

'You could indeed,' I agreed remembering that in a month with Fatimah I had lost nearly a stone in weight and thinking that an afternoon with Mary would help me keep in capital trim.

'Oh for God's sake!' she exclaimed, although for the life of me I could not see why she was annoyed. 'Come with me,' she said standing and pulling on my arm.

'Where are we going?' I asked puzzled.

'To my room upstairs, it is the only way I am going to get any sense out of you.' Well, I had expected a former royal mistress to play slightly harder to get than that but you don't look a gift horse in the mouth.

As it turned out I can confirm that Prince Frederick, Duke of York was a lucky man to have Mary Clarke as a mistress, for she was a most diverting companion who exercised me thoroughly that afternoon. It was as we were lying together on the bed naked afterwards that she restarted the conversation. She propped her head up on one elbow and reached over with her spare hand and started walking her fingers up my chest. 'Thomas, do you remember we were talking earlier about you losing your commission and Freddie not paying my annuity?'

'Oh yes,' I murmured sleepily. 'Damn nearly ruined me that did.'

'Don't you have other income? Hobhouse implied you did. He claimed you were not a man of letters but a man of bones, although he would not explain the remark.'

Did he now I thought, and mentally marked him down for revenge later as I replied, 'I have some rental income to cover basic expenses but I had borrowed against the army pay and some rather unpleasant people were demanding repayment with menaces.'

'What did you do?'

'I had to borrow some money from my wife, or more specifically my father-in-law as he still pays her an allowance. It was pretty much the end of my marriage.'

'I did not know you were married.'

'We are separated now. We got married on a ship coming back from India. The captain told us that three things wreck a marriage: lust, money and in-laws. Well there was no problem in the lust department but my wife is used to having money and her father hated me. He started to poison her against me the minute we stepped ashore.'

'Well, I don't have a rich father-in-law and I cannot afford to lose that annuity. I have four children to support and anyway Freddie should not be allowed to get away with it.'

'He is the son of the king; no court is going to pursue him for an unpaid debt. Men with far more influence than you have been chasing the royals for money for years.'

'But remember what I told you before; you cannot pursue them in the courts, but you could in Parliament.'

'Why would the government attack the king to get your annuity back?'

'Don't be silly Thomas, it would not be the government, it would be one of the radical members of the opposition. Freddie is praised by the government as an excellent commander in chief. They even repeat his claims that he is encouraging the army to promote on merit. If a radical stood up in the House and accused him of corruption there would be uproar. They could not brush the claim aside without it appearing to be true and so there would have to be a hearing. If I appeared as a witness, then Freddie's reputation would be ruined.'

'How do you get your pension back by ruining the commander in chief?' I asked.

'Simple. I will demand a four hundred pound a year pension guaranteed by a bank from whichever radical who takes the case. They would be famous for bringing down a prince so for them it is money well spent. If the government or the crown wants to pay off the radical and me with new pensions, well I would not mind that instead.'

I suddenly realised that the pretty woman I was lying beside was much more than just a gorgeous body. She was shrewd, calculating and had really thought this through. I lay back thinking about what she had proposed. There had been plenty of royal scandals over recent years but most had been sorted behind closed doors and the facts had been hidden. Some scribbling hack called Nicholas Hansard had recently started publishing a journal of all the speeches and debates in Parliament. If the trial was held there everything would be reported, it would be a sensation. She was right that any radical who took this case on would make a big name for himself.

'I know several radical members of Parliament,' I told Mary.

'Really Thomas, I had no idea,' she replied with what I thought was a touch of sarcasm. Then she added, 'I thought you might have been able to help as you were the only person I could think of who had a grievance against the duke and also had friends amongst the radicals.'

'Cochrane would love this,' I told her, referring to Thomas Cochrane, one of my oldest friends. He was a radical Member of Parliament and through him I knew many of the others. It was with Cochrane that I had been on my first adventures overseas and I had told Mary about some of them earlier that afternoon. He had just lost his court martial for the Basque Roads affair and this would allow him to take his revenge on the establishment.

'You like Cochrane a lot don't you?' Mary looked at me while biting her lip, and for the first time since we'd met she looked uncertain about something.

'Of course, he has saved my life more than once.'

'Then think of someone else,' said Mary quietly. 'The government and the court will take their revenge, not on me for they will see me as some simple money grabbing whore, but on whichever politician makes his name out of this. Mark my words, they will take their time but in the end they will try to destroy him.' That got me thinking, for this idle talk of bringing down governments and princes suddenly was very real and would have very serious consequences for some. There seemed a chill in the air and I got up to stir the fire in the grate and put on another log. As I watched the sparks drifting up the chimney I started to consider what I had got myself into.

One thing was for certain, if I was going to help Mary then I was going to make damn sure that nobody knew about it. I could not afford to be linked to a scandal against the government. For one thing I still officially worked for Castlereagh, the Minister for War, although there had been precious little work of late.

I could think of several radical members of Parliament seeking a name for themselves that would jump at the chance and worry about the consequences later. The tricky bit was finding someone to introduce them to Mary, for that was not going to be me. If the radical politician was going to be destroyed then they might well come after the man who introduced him to the scheme. I racked my brains for some nasty piece of work that I would not mind doing the dirty on. I needed some arrogant braggart who was not smart enough to think things through to see the consequences, and who would claim all the glory for himself. That would keep my name out of the frame, but he would also need to know some of the ambitious radicals. I was on the verge of telling Mary I could not help when a name sprang to mind.

'Sir Richard Phillips is your man,' I announced. 'He is close to the radical set and will probably charge one handsomely for this opportunity.'

'The former Sheriff of London?' asked Mary. 'But is he gullible? Can you make him do what we want?'

'Oh yes. I happen to know that just last month he paid very handsomely for an old skull that someone told him was once that of Cardinal Thomas Wolsey.'

Editor's Note
As far-fetched as this might seem, the more detailed biographical information on Sir Richard Phillips confirms that he did possess a skull that he claimed was Cardinal Thomas Wolsey's, although he claimed he had bought it for a shilling. The Cardinal was chancellor under Henry VIII, running the country for the young king until he failed to secure his monarch a papal divorce from his first wife, which led to Wolsey's downfall and the reformation.

Chapter 2

In the long lonely hours of my dotage I look back on my dissolute existence, and there are some for whom I feel just the slightest twinge of guilt. A Russian countess left naked to face her husband's wrath after I disappeared disguised in her clothes to avoid pursuit; the man whose horse I took near Blood River forcing him to escape a Zulu horde on foot; and the sailor shanghaied to the far east after I stole his papers: these all spring to mind after just a moment's reflection. But what I did to Sir Richard Phillips does not keep me awake one jot. He was one of the most odious men I ever encountered. I have no idea how he came to acquire a knighthood and the honorary title of High Sheriff of London, but I can be certain that it was not through any genuine act of philanthropy.

Phillips professed to be a radical and had published numerous books under his own name on civil liberty and justice. He saw no irony in the fact that he bullied, bribed and blackmailed other impoverished authors to write them for him under his name. I had met him preying on the poorer poets trying to earn money to keep up with Byron's literary crowd. He was a parasite, a blood sucking tick, but ironically given his nature, he did not eat meat out of choice, not even a chicken. He called his diet vegetarian. Making a great fuss about removing 'animal flesh' as he called it from his plate, he then stuffed his face with roast potatoes and parsnips, which had probably been cooked in lard. Consequently I avoided meeting him over a meal. The day after my meeting with Mary I found him in his favourite coffee shop, talking to some thin cove with a sheaf of manuscript. Without being invited, I pulled up a chair at his table.

'I hear word around town that you have bought Cardinal Wolsey's head for just a shilling Sir Richard,' I greeted him, smiling genially. The last time we had met I had been ingratiating myself to achieve a sale, for much more than a shilling. Now I wanted to deliberately annoy him, so that he was more inclined to do me an ill turn. It was not a difficult challenge.

Phillips glanced across at the thin man. 'That will be all for now Mr Edgar,' he barked, passing him back the manuscript. 'Remember break it down, state the obvious and pad it out. You cannot sell a book about the rights of man with less than a hundred pages.'

'Yes Sir Richard,' said the thin man, glancing forlornly at his half-drunk coffee as he gathered his coat and made for the door.

'Was that one of your scribblers?' I asked.

Phillips watched the thin man go and then turned to me with a disdainful glare. 'If you have more bones to sell, Thomas, I am not interested. A friend, who knows Leicester well, tells me that Wolsey's grave in the abbey there has not been disturbed in living memory. So I would like to know how his skull came out of it.'

'The box it came in looks very ancient,' I replied 'Wolsey died two hundred and fifty years ago; who is to say when the grave was plundered? You know he died in disgrace and was not buried in his fancy tomb. The skull was probably taken while the abbey was being torn down.'

Phillips growled an assent that such a thing was possible. Everyone knew that the ornate marble sarcophagus that Wolsey had planned for his own use centuries ago, had four years earlier been used to bury Horatio Nelson in St Paul's. 'So what do you want?' he asked grudgingly.

'I come bearing good news for the radical cause,' I told him cheerfully. 'Do you remember Mary Clarke, the former mistress of the Duke of York? Well, the duke has reneged on his promised annuity to her and hell hath no fury like a woman scorned. She promises to bring the duke down and possibly the government with it.'

'What do you mean?' Phillips asked, his eyes glittering with interest.

'She is willing to act as a witness to confirm that bribes were paid to her for promotions and exchanges in the army and that the prince arranged them as she instructed. She just needs a radical member of the opposition to make the accusation in Parliament that she can then support.'

'Hell's teeth!' cried Phillips looking astounded. 'Which radical is she working with?'

'She asked about Cochrane and I am sending him a note as he is in Scotland at the moment. It will be a week or two before I get a reply, but I am sure he will do it. This will be a perfect revenge after the court martial.'

'It will indeed be the perfect revenge,' Phillips was licking his lips in anticipation and you could almost hear his brain working from the other side of the table. 'You must give me all the details Thomas, for an account of this affair would make a famous book. It would add to Cochrane's fame and of course I would ensure that you got credit too. With an overly casual manner, pretending it was an afterthought, he

15

added, 'Oh, by the way, where is Mary Clarke staying in London? We might need to interview her too.'

I left that meeting feeling well pleased with myself, the first part of the plan Mary and I had hatched together worked perfectly. That evening I received a note from her, still at Dorant's Hotel, to say that Sir Richard had visited earlier in the day. He told her that he had heard she was in need of a Member of Parliament at the radical end of politics to act for her. When she told him that I was writing to Cochrane he warned her that it was likely to be some weeks before Cochrane could act on her behalf and hinted that he might not be that reliable. By happy chance he would be able to introduce her to his particular friend Colonel Gwyllym Wardle, Member of Parliament for Okehampton, who could act immediately and save her waiting for Cochrane's return. Mary allowed herself to be 'reluctantly' persuaded into abandoning Cochrane and I and taking on the team of Phillips and Wardle instead.

Over the next few weeks Mary negotiated her fee with her new partners. When Phillips discovered that she had kept much of her correspondence with the duke and many other influential figures, he promised her that if she handed the letters over to him he could make her rich through book sales. But Mary was no fool and she could see through that as well. So she kept her letters, although she talked about the book as a possibility, but only if she wrote it. To encourage her cooperation they offered her the use of a larger rented house which Wardle agreed to furnish for her. Despite the fact that Wardle was about to prosecute the Duke of York for accepting bribes in exchange for army commissions, he was happy paying what could be seen as bribes to a witness in exchange for evidence. The fool even visited the carpenters to buy the furniture with Mary and agreed with the owner that he would be paying the bill for whatever Mary chose. It may seem a little thing, but it ruined him later.

While all this was going on, the talk in London was of Spain and the war. In fact people had been talking about Spain for nearly a year since Parliament had decided to send the first expedition to that God forsaken country. At the start of the year Napoleon had sent his brother Joseph to replace the unpopular Spanish King Carlos IV. The Spanish had initially welcomed French troops into their country thinking that they were there to oversee the abdication of Carlos IV, and his replacement by the popular heir to the throne, Fernando. When the Spanish royal family was tricked into going to France and replaced

16

with a Bonaparte there was a revolt. A Spanish army had beaten a French force at a place called Balien, which raised expectations across Madrid, Lisbon and London that a combined Spanish, Portuguese and British force could throw the French back.

The first British expedition was turning out to be a disaster. It had started well as the third in command, Arthur Wellesley, had arrived first with the army and in a few days had beaten a French army near Lisbon. But then the two senior commanders had arrived and taken a more cautious approach which resulted in an agreement to provide the beaten French army with ship transport back to France. It also allowed the French to keep their arms and all the property they had looted from the Spanish and Portuguese. The Portuguese in particular were furious at watching their allies act as accomplices in the pillaging of their country. All three commanders were recalled, with Sir John Moore put in charge of the army. By then Napoleon had gathered some of his veteran troops who quickly proved that the Spanish victory at Balien was more down to luck than Spanish judgement. The French slaughtered Spanish armies everywhere they found them. Then the French columns started to close in on the British. After a brutal winter campaign in the mountains of northern Spain, the remnants of the British force were trapped at Corunna on the north west tip of the country. An evacuation by ship was organised for the expeditionary force, but not before Sir John Moore had been killed fighting a rear guard action.

There was therefore already much criticism of the army and its commanders, with all this happening as Wardle, Philips and Clarke made their preparations to discredit its commander in chief. All debate on the war was overshadowed on the twentieth of January 1809 when Colonel Wardle sensationally gave notice to the House of Commons in Parliament that in a week's time he would submit a motion to the House on the conduct of His Royal Highness the Duke of York. All of London society knew within hours, and a week of wild speculation followed on what the accusations might be, some a good deal more colourful than what were eventually presented.

Mary had moved to her new house and I stayed well clear. Rumours that she was a witness for Wardle were already circulating and for anyone with government connections, contact with her was now ruinous. Ministers debated on how they should respond to Wardle but, as Mary had predicted, they decided that to try and block the hearing would be tantamount to admitting the duke's guilt.

The House of Commons was packed on the twenty-seventh of January when Wardle rose to submit his motion. The viewing gallery was also heaving with people and despite getting there early I only just managed to squeeze in. Having played my small part to get the ball rolling, I was keen to see how it turned out. There was an air of anticipation in the gallery such as there must have been in the Roman coliseum before the Christians were fed to the lions. How would one woman's evidence defeat the massed power and influence of the court and the government? Most of the crowd's sympathies were with the radicals, but nobody expected them to succeed.

I craned over the rail to see Wardle make an opening address in which he pretended he was only reluctantly doing his duty. With a barely suppressed grin on his face he fooled no one. The government minister duly responded that the duke had nothing to hide and that this was a vile attack on the royal family. There was a sense of anti-climax as Wardle brought forth his first witness, an old man who testified that he had given Mary Clarke two hundred pounds to secure the exchange of a friend to a more fashionable regiment. Then came the moment that everyone had been waiting for.

'Mrs Mary Clark,' called the master at arms and I was half crushed against the gallery rail, which creaked alarmingly, as everyone in the gallery pressed forward to get their first glimpse of the leading actor in this drama. Mary Clarke appeared in a blue silk gown edged with white fur as though she was going to an evening party. It was a colourful contrast to the dull clothes of the politicians. As she was not a member of the House she could not enter the chamber but gave her evidence from behind a bar at the door. Even some of the politicians were standing up in the benches to get a better view, but she did not seem the slightest bit intimidated. She gave a dazzling smile to the whole chamber and then her eyes scanned the gallery. For the briefest of moments our eyes met and she seemed to give an almost imperceptible nod.

When called upon to give her evidence she spoke with calm confidence, her voice carrying across the chamber. She happily confirmed that she had received the bribe from the old man and passed the request on to the duke who arranged the transfer.

'Was the duke aware that you had been paid to make the request?' asked Wardle.

'Oh yes,' she replied. 'I showed him the two notes for a hundred each and one of his servants got me change for them.' There was laughter from across the House at that, particularly from us up in the gallery. People began to sense that there might be a worthwhile contest after all.

Beleaguered representatives from the government then rose to cross examine her but she answered all of their questions confidently. She teased and flirted with her interrogators and soon had them laughing at her suggestive comments. Certainly Lord Folkestone was so impressed that while she was giving evidence he sent her a note offering her three hundred guineas if she would spend the night with him. Most of the politicians, even on the government benches either knew or suspected that she was telling the truth, but duty obliged them to do all they could to protect the reputation of the royal family and the administration.

The government's case collapsed over the next week as more people gave their testimony. Mary was asked to return to the House twice more and each time gave strong and convincing statements. What really destroyed the government's position was the evidence of one of their own witnesses. He was Mary's former landlord and he had been called to discredit her and imply she was seeing other men at the same time as the duke. But cross examination of his claims led to the discovery of a note that the duke sent to Mary referring to one of the requests, which he was clearly aware of.

The whole affair was the talk of the town for weeks, with all the details in Hansard and repeated in other journals so that everyone knew the intimate details of the duke's life.

A vote was finally held on the sixteenth of March and while government supporters doggedly backed their commander in chief, the public had already made up their minds about his guilt. The duke was forced to resign from the army. Colonel Wardle was hailed as a hero in the streets and seemed to be thoroughly enjoying his fame. But those that the public and the press raise up are often torn down again. Wardle's new high status was built on foundations of sand, as I discovered two weeks later.

It was the only other time I met Mary Clarke. I had been trying to avoid her as word was out in government circles that the duke and the Attorney General were determined to track down and disgrace all those involved in the affair. I had taken a walk down to the river Thames as there had been rumours that the old medieval London Bridge, lined with shops, churches and houses would collapse soon due to flood water carrying down fallen trees which were trapped in its arches. I had bought a news sheet on the way and saw now attention was turning back to Spain and Portugal, with calls from those countries for a new expeditionary force. There was much talk of pockets of resistance and guerrilla armies weakening the French forces, who were reported to be near collapse. A new British army, it was claimed, would provide new backbone to the resistance. There was even speculation on who would command, with Wellesley amongst the front runners.

As I reached the old bridge there was a big crowd looking at the spectacle of the water foaming around the arches but it showed no sign of getting swept away. As I was about to leave, a lady whose face was hidden with a hood, came and stood beside me. At first I thought it was a tart plying her trade but then I heard Mary's voice.

'Hello Thomas, I have not thanked you for your assistance.'

I looked around to check we could not be overheard before replying, 'It is not something that I plan to boast about, but it did seem to work rather well. I hear from Phillips that your memoirs have been written, which will increase your fame even further.'

'They have been written,' she replied quietly. 'But they will not see the light of day.'

'Why not?' I asked, puzzled, for Phillips had been boasting that they would bring down the government and he would soon be as famous as Wardle.

'Because I don't trust either Wardle or Phillips; they are more concerned with embarrassing the government than my interests. Wardle still has not paid for my new house or furniture and now I am being chased for payment. The promised annuity has not appeared and I am sure that Phillips will cheat me on the book proceeds. I have never known such a slippery rogue. And anyway I have had a better offer.'

'Who from?' I whispered back.

'Freddie has offered me ten thousand, plus the restoration of my four hundred pound annuity and new annuities of two hundred pounds each for both my daughters, with all the annuities guaranteed by three other gentlemen including an earl and a banker. In return I must hand over the manuscript and any printed copies of the memoirs as well as any letters I have from him, and promise not to write anything about the duke again.

'By George that is capital!' I was amazed at the duke's largesse. He was certainly doing all he possibly could to limit any further embarrassment. 'Phillips and Wardle will be furious when they find out.' I could not resist smiling at the thought. 'I doubt that they will ever pay for that furniture now,' I added.

'I suspect you are right but Wardle will be ruined if he doesn't. The duke's people tell me that the Attorney General is willing to act for the carpenter at no cost. I rather hope he doesn't pay for he has become quite tiresome. I might have to let slip that the man who accused the duke of sexual immorality has his own mistress above a shop in Sloane Square.'

We parted then with whispered good wishes as Mary saw someone she knew in the crowd. But she was right; Wardle did not pay and consequently was ruined. The public had acclaimed him as a man fighting corruption and vice; when they learned that he had bribed his star witness and as a married man had his own mistress, they felt betrayed and turn on him viciously. But I missed all of that because I had my own problems just then.

A week after my meeting with Mary I received a note sent on behalf of the duke requesting that I attend a meeting the next day with a Mr Tasker at Horseguards, the building housing the headquarters of the army. A request from the duke had to be about the Clarke affair. Had Mary told the duke about my involvement now they seemed friends again, I wondered. If she had what did that mean for me? I spent much of the following morning trying to convince myself I was safe, but there was still a nervous feeling in my stomach as I marched across the Horseguard's parade ground to the entrance of the building for my interview. The clerk at the entrance told me that Tasker was on the duke's personal staff and directed me to the offices that had until a few days ago been occupied by His Royal Highness. It was as I was walking across a large and impressive hall that I heard someone call out my name.

'Ah, Flashman, I had expected to see you sooner but you are most welcome, sir.'

I turned and there was Arthur Wellesley, who had been my senior officer when I was in India, walking towards me and smiling warmly. Given his normal frosty demeanour, this was a rare occurrence.

'Since my appointment to command in Spain was confirmed I have been plagued by various petitioners for places on my staff, most completely useless. But I can certainly use you.'

'Err… is Tasker on your staff sir?' I asked, now quite confused as to what was happening.

'I was sorry to hear about your lost commission,' continued Wellesley as though I had not spoken at all. 'Nothing I could do about that then of course, but I would be most delighted to reinstate you as Captain now. I recollect that you have been to Spain before, speak Spanish and I am sure you told me that your mother was the daughter of a Spanish nobleman. This makes you ideal to handle those Spanish grandees. I need you as a liaison officer on my staff.' I stood staring at him trying to take it all in. 'I know that there would not be as much action as you would like,' Wellesley continued, ignoring my look of stupefaction. 'But it is a vital role nevertheless.' He beamed again and barked, 'What do you say eh?'

'I am not really sure,' I admitted. I had been worried about being prosecuted or disgraced and now I was being offered a job.

'Look, I know you Flashman, you like to get stuck in at the sharp end and probably don't fancy the role of a staff walloper, but your skills with the Spanish commanders will be invaluable early on. Later, when good relations have been established, I will see if we can get you something a bit more exciting to do. Will you join me?' He stuck out his hand for me to shake and I just stared at him. My first thought was how little he did know me despite our time together. The last place I wanted to be in any conflict was the 'sharp end'. If I had to serve then staff officer was exactly the role I would want. But after the debacle of the last campaign I had no wish to go to Spain at all.

'I'm sorry sir,' I replied at last. 'There seems to be some confusion, I am here because I received a request to meet a Mr Tasker.'

'Tasker,' he exclaimed, 'but he is the cove looking into the Clarke business. You are not involved in that are you?'

'Absolutely not. That is why I am here, to make that very clear.'

'So you don't want to join my staff?' he asked, disappointed.

'I don't know if I can until I have spoken to Tasker.' I searched around for an excuse, 'He might want me as a witness or to help with the investigation.'

He looked petulant and disappointed for a moment but then his face became set in its more habitual haughty look. 'If you change your mind let me know,' he said, before patting my shoulder and walking away. I was left standing in the big empty hallway feeling more confused than ever.

Tasker, when I found him in an office adjoining that of the duke, was a stern middle aged man dressed all in black. After I had introduced myself and he had shown me to a chair opposite his desk,

22

he sat down and stared at me. He did not say a word, just looked at me with eyes half shut in concentration as though he could divine my intentions just from my appearance. It was damned unnerving; I could feel the sweat starting to break out on my brow.

'How can I help you Mr Tasker?' I asked to break the silence, but he did not show any sign of having heard me. After nearly a minute had passed, or so it seemed for I did not look at the clock, I began to get angry. I was not here to be stared at like some lunatic in the asylum. It was as I started to get up that he spoke.

'Sit down Mr Flashman. You are here at the express request of His Royal Highness and His Majesty's Government.'

'I don't understand why,' I responded tartly.

'Have you ever met Mary Clarke?' he asked, watching me closely. He was getting straight down to the point and no error. If I had not already been tense with anger I might have shown more reaction. I was fairly sure that no one had seen us together at the river, but several of Byron's set must have seen us talking together at Dorant's Hotel. If I denied we met there it would seem suspicious.

I endeavoured to look thoughtful for a moment, as though thinking back, and then said slowly as though trying to remember, 'I think I did meet her at a party a while back.'

'In December last year,' he said referring to his notes.

'Yes, it could have been,' I conceded.

'We believe that the plot to ruin His Royal Highness' reputation was hatched by the conspirators in December.'

'Well that had nothing to do with me,' I stated firmly, trying to sound outraged. I felt a cold clammy feeling now in the pit of my stomach. 'That was all Wardle's doing and I don't think I have even met that villain.'

'We are taking care of Wardle and we have interviewed Sir Richard Phillips who was also closely involved. Yesterday he sat where you are now and told me that Thomas Cochrane and you were the real instigators of events.'

'That is outrageous!' I exclaimed, standing up again. 'He is just trying to deflect the blame from his own nefarious activities.'

'Sit down Mr Flashman,' said Tasker wearily. 'I have already spoken to Captain Cochrane and he assured me that you have never spoken to him about the matter. I am inclined to believe him.'

'Then why am I here?'

'Because I know that Phillips is not smart enough to think this through, so someone must have done it for him.' He paused and then added slowly 'Perhaps someone who has a grievance against the army, someone used to plotting and intrigues in India, and someone who knows lots of opposition members of Parliament.'

'Or perhaps it was Mary herself,' I countered, having every confidence that the truth would be the one thing he would not believe.

I was not disappointed. 'Clarke's skills, such as she has any, are employed when she is lying on her back,' he snarled. Incidentally he was wrong about that; she had skills in all manner of positions. He added, 'There is no way she could come up with a scheme like this.'

Before I could stop myself I responded 'So it was the duke who came up with idea to take bribes was it?'

Tasker slammed his fist down on the desk. 'That is a slanderous comment and you will withdraw it at once.' He took a breath and calmed himself before continuing, now with a slight smile of triumph. 'You show your true colours now I think. A man with means and motive to do the duke damage; a man who mixes not only with radicals but with poets and degenerates. Was that where the plot was hatched?'

'I have no idea what you are talking about,' I responded coldly

'I have a witness who tells me that you were seen talking to Mrs Clarke at a party given by Lord Byron at Dorant's Hotel. Do you deny it?'

'No, that is the one time I met her, I have already told you that. But there were a dozen people there. I imagine that lots of them spoke to Mary... err Mrs Clarke.'

'Who else did you see speaking to her?' I thought back and remembered Hobhouse's sneering and 'man of bones' comment. The stuffed shirt would be appalled to get involved in a scandal like this, so it seemed an ideal opportunity to pay him back.

'I saw Cam Hobhouse speaking to her at one point.' I paused as though trying to remember, 'Yes, they were talking for quite some time over by the window, away from everyone else.'

'Really, Cam Hobhouse,' he repeated as he wrote at the bottom of a sheet of paper containing what looked a list of names. He looked up again and studied me carefully. 'We will find out who is behind this Mr Flashman, I have been charged by His Royal Highness not to rest until the culprits have been ruined and disgraced. You remain near the top of my list,' he said, tapping with his finger on the paper before him. 'So I suggest you remain close as we might want to question you again.'

I took my leave then and walked back through the hallway thinking through my position. There was no way that Tasker could prove my involvement but I was not naive; I knew how the world worked. He refused to accept that the genuine instigator of the plot was a possibility, so when he failed to find the genuine culprit he would cast around for someone he could blame anyway. He had to have a victim to succeed in his task and he looked a very ambitious man. Some poor unfortunate would have endless interrogations, witnesses would be bribed and eventually charges would be laid. Well, it was not going to be me. As I passed the end of a corridor I saw Wellesley again and an idea occurred to me. If I was abroad I could not be questioned, and if I was back in a red coat under a regiment's colours then clearly I had no grievance against the army and the Duke of York. Wellesley's offer of a liaison job would also keep me well away from the actual fighting. I could spend my time loafing around Spanish palaces, surrounded by dusky court ladies. It was so obvious I was surprised it had taken me so long to think of it. Of course if I had known the horrors that awaited I would have gone straight back to Tasker and confessed everything. Instead I marched towards Wellesley calling, 'Sir Arthur, is that offer still open?'

Editor's Note

The Mary Clarke scandal took place much as described by Flashman. Wardle was prosecuted by the Attorney General, lost the case and was fined. His last recorded action in the House of Commons was in 1811 when he cast a losing vote against the reinstatement of the Duke of York as commander in chief (something which had been intended ever since his resignation.) After the war finished he left Britain to escape his creditors and died in Florence in 1833.

The vegetarian Sir Richard Phillips was also later declared bankrupt although the exact cause of his downfall is not recorded. While he wrote a fulsome epitaph for his tomb, his contemporaries were less kind, one described him as 'a scoundrel…who would suck the knowledge out of author's skulls and fling the carcasses on the dung hill.'

Mary Clarke was ultimately not satisfied with her settlement as in summer 1810 she published a new book on the affair in which she suggested that another royal prince was behind the accusation. The man she named was the Duke of York's brother the Duke of Kent, the father of the future Queen Victoria. Having made enemies of two royal princes she had few friends left and eventually she was prosecuted for libel and imprisoned for nine months. On her release she went to live in France where one of her daughters married a man called du Maurier. Mary Clarke's great-great granddaughter was the novelist Daphne du Maurier, famous for such novels as Rebecca and Jamaica Inn. Daphne du Maurier was clearly fascinated with this era and her ancestor. One of her lesser known works is a biographical novel on her great-great grandmother called Mary Anne. While a dramatisation, it is meticulously researched and includes some of the transcripts of the Parliamentary hearings.

Chapter 3
April 1809

When the first expedition had been sent to Portugal a year before,
dozens of men had drowned while being landed in boats through the
thunderous surf. Waves roll in on that coast as tall as houses and I had
no wish to take my chances with the strong currents, waves and rocks.
I made sure then that I took my passage with Wellesley himself in the
Surveillante, which was bound to dock more safely in Lisbon harbour,
while most of the army landed up the coast near Coimbra. Such is my
luck that the army landed safely without loss, while the Surveillante
was caught up in a massive storm on its first day out and was nearly
dashed on the rocks off the English coast.

I had joined Wellesley and some of his staff in a game of cards that
night to try and pass the time while the storm threw us about. At one
point the ship's captain sent down a message to Wellesley that he
should 'put on his boots and come on deck' as the end was near.
Wellesley coolly replied that he could swim better without his boots
and would stay where he was.

The remark was typical of Wellesley; in a time when sang froid was
greatly admired, his coolness under fire was legendary. The term sang
froid literally translates to cold blood, and his must have been
positively arctic at times, but then others around him were the same.
There was the famous incident at Waterloo when Uxbridge lost his leg.
He just looked down at the bloody wreckage of his limb and exclaimed
to Wellesley, 'By God sir, I have lost my leg', to which Wellesley
replied, 'By God sir, so you have'. Of course we did not have
Uxbridge with us in Spain, or Henry Paget as he was known then. He
was Britain's best cavalry commander and sorely missed, but just
weeks before we embarked he had eloped with the wife of Wellesley's
brother Henry, proving that the sang was not always froid.

You may be wondering how your correspondent was feeling when
news of our imminent nautical disaster was announced to the group.
Well, surprisingly calm is the answer. A short while before, I had
taken a turn on deck and spoken to the sailing master. Whenever I am
on a naval ship I always let slip that I was with Cochrane when he took
the Gamo, and that guarantees me a permanent invitation to the
wardroom and respect from the officers. The sailing master, a wizened
old creature who had forgotten more than the rest of the quarter deck
would ever learn, had confidently told me that the wind was shifting

and we would comfortably clear the rocks, then just a few miles off our bow. He also described the captain as a frightened old woman, who was terrified of Wellesley coming to harm on his ship. Thus, when the news of impending doom was announced I was able to sit back, looking cool as be-damned, and made a tidy sum gambling with my more distracted brother officers.

My calm dissipated somewhat over the coming days, however, as I learned more about the situation we were to face in Portugal and Spain. It did not seem a whit better than that which had forced Sir John Moore's desperate evacuation just a few months before. When we had embarked, the press and all the society talk had been of a spring campaign against overstretched French forces that would see victories and us in Madrid by the summer. But now as I spoke to veterans of that horrendous winter retreat which had led to their evacuation from Corunna just three months earlier, I realised that these plans were hopelessly optimistic. While Napoleon had returned to France, four of his marshals, each with armies of veteran troops, remained in the peninsular. Marshall Soult with twenty thousand men was the only one in Portugal. He dominated the north of the country from the city of Oporto, which he had captured the previous month. In the centre of Spain were Marshals Jourdan and Victor, with nearly forty thousand men between them; while to the north of Spain was Marshal Ney with seventeen thousand men. Against them Wellesley had just twenty-five thousand, mostly inexperienced British troops, plus another sixteen thousand Portuguese troops still needing to be trained. I remember expressing my concerns to John Downie, one of the commissary officers, but he brushed aside my worries.

'You are forgetting about the Spanish, Thomas,' he told me. 'Their guerrilla forces are continually attacking French supply columns forcing the French to use thousands of men to guard them. The Spanish have a new centralised government now, the Central Junta based in Seville, which governs the part of the country not ruled by the French from Madrid. General Cuesta commands a Spanish army of over twenty thousand men in central Spain. He can block any move by the French on Seville and can also attack any army that heads to Lisbon from central Spain.'

'But I thought that the French were beating every Spanish army that tried to stand against them?'

'Nonsense,' said Downie. 'The Spanish held out at Zaragoza for months against a prolonged French attack.' That sounded more like a delayed defeat rather than a victory to me, but I did not say anything as clearly Downie was passionate about the Spanish cause. He must have sensed my doubt though, for after a moment he continued, 'The Spanish armies were poor to start with, but it was all down to bad organisation. There's no central command and a lot of the generals distrust each other. Spanish towns and cities introduced conscription, but they saw it as a means to generate revenue as much as anything. They sold exemptions to all that could afford them so only the poor were reluctantly conscripted and half of those deserted at the first opportunity. They also sold commissions in their local regiments to any that could pay for them so that most of the officers had no military experience at all. But the new Central Junta is putting these things right.'

Other officers were more doubtful about the assistance we could expect from the Spanish. Campbell, another staff officer and an old friend from India, was on the first expedition and he gave me more insight. The real problem, he told me, was that before the French invasion all power was held through three institutions: the court with the nobility, the army and the church. The court was now in exile and most nobles driven off their lands and deprived of their income. The army had been routinely thrashed by the French and had little influence. Only the church still provided leadership at a local level and they had every reason to be hostile to the officially atheist French republicans. Some of the clergy had tried to fill the power vacuum with a bloodlust that made Caligula look like a choirboy. Campbell told me of one Catholic friar called Baltasar Calvo who led a gang of assassins which had killed three and hundred and thirty men, women and children, mostly French civilians. Personally I blame the vow of chastity for these excesses; all that abstinence must build up terrible passions. Mind you, the French did their best to ease those pressures, by raping their way through every convent they found.

For all Downie's assurances, few shared his confidence and the Spanish army seemed so damned amateur. One officer told me a tale of a Frenchman called Rigney. He had been sent to Santander the previous year to arrest a British officer who was reported to be moving into the vicinity. He had only just arrived when the rebellion broke out, making it very dangerous to be a Frenchman in the town. This cool character then masqueraded as the British officer he had been sent to find. He was wined and dined by all the local dignitaries and army officers, who freely shared their plans and discussed their strengths and weaknesses. After a week of this he asked to be taken to see the French lines and then persuaded his Spanish escort to take him even closer at night. You can imagine the Spaniards' surprise when he spurred his horse and charged right into the French encampment, shouting at his compatriots not to shoot. They were probably less surprised when they next saw him riding alongside a French marshal who annihilated the Spanish forces, exploiting every one of their weaknesses.

All this talk shook me up a bit I can tell you. Before we had left I had begun to believe the tales about a resurgent Spanish resistance and over stretched French forces. That was why I had thought I could safely tool around the country as a staff officer. Now it looked as if it might be hot work just to stay in the peninsular at all. I did not want to be seen as croaking, but on the last night aboard as we sat around the big wardroom table with Wellesley at the head I asked, 'Sir Arthur, what do you think will make the difference between this campaign and the one before.' It sounded as if I was toadying and giving him the chance to say 'my command', for the previous expedition had gone down-hill as soon as he was relieved of its control. But I knew my man better than that, for he would have spent months preparing for the opportunity to go back. I noticed other conversation around the table stilled and all looked at him expectantly. I was clearly not the only one seeking confidence in our mission. None of us expected the response we got.

'Hanging some British soldiers,' he barked and glared around the room as though daring anyone to challenge him.

There was a stunned and puzzled silence for a moment until the padre hesitantly spoke up, 'Surely you mean French soldiers, Sir Arthur?'

'No,' he stated firmly. 'When the British army retreated to Corunna, units got separated from the main force and even on the edges of the main company they looted, murdered and raped with the same enthusiasm as the French. That cannot be allowed to happen again and I will hang every last one of them if I have to.'

'But sir,' exclaimed one of the colonels who had been at Corunna, 'the veterans from the last expedition are our most experienced troops.'

'I don't care,' snapped Wellesley. 'Don't you see; the French are under massive pressure because the Portuguese and Spanish people hate them for their brutality and kill the French every chance that they get. There is no central government in either country worth a damn,' he added, glancing at Downie who had evidently been trying to persuade him otherwise. 'It is the people's views that count and if we go around behaving like the French then they will hate us too. The very people we are here to liberate will make our position untenable. On the other hand if we show that we are better, pay for supplies instead of stealing them, if women and property are safe where we dominate, they will support us and redouble their efforts to throw out the French.'

'But our men are the scrapings of jails, poorhouses and the desperate,' protested another officer. 'You cannot expect them to behave like gentlemen.'

'Nor do I,' said Wellesley firmly. 'I know that they are the scum of the earth but discipline, supported by hangings and floggings as necessary, must make sure that they behave better than the French. And I look to all of you,' and here his gaze swept around the table looking us each in the eye, 'to make sure that this is what happens.'

At the time I admit that I thought he was mad if he thought he could stop an army looting a captured city. I had been with him at Gawilghur in India when British and Indian troops had sacked the place. The rape and slaughter there had made a Viking raid look like a Baptist tea dance. I was right about that too for at Spanish cities like Badajoz, when the British and Portuguese army stormed into the streets, they behaved like animals. But I could also see that having the populace on our side would be worth a hundred thousand men. At the end of the day we did not need to behave perfectly, just better than the French, whose army supply system was largely based on plunder. Mind you, it still sounded a tall order; after all, taking myself as an example, even some of the 'gentlemen' did not always behave as such.

Chapter 4

Lisbon, when we finally arrived, looked a bright colourful place from a mile or two out to sea with its red tiled roofs and whitewashed walls. But as we got closer to the harbour the poverty, dirt and then the smell became all too apparent. It was a strange place, the capital of large and once powerful country, but now empty of most of the people of influence. Just two years before, as the French first arrived, all the wealthy merchants, the court and most of the government had sailed to Brazil, a Portuguese dominion. The people who were left were generally those too poor to purchase their passage to the New World, and others who had moved to the city after being made destitute from the French pillaging of the countryside. We sailed into the mouth of the river Tagus and past the Tower of Belém to dock by the Black Horse Square. The citizens were gathered in crowds to welcome the return of their British allies, doubtless wondering if our army would cut and run when the French attacked like we had the previous year.

General Craddock, the commander of the small British force that had remained from the previous expedition, welcomed Wellesley and his officers onto the quay. We were ushered into a nearby palatial building and provided with refreshment, while Wellesley and Craddock retired to the next room to discuss matters in private. Soon afterwards I saw several grim faced officers of the local garrison being ushered into their room and a few of us newcomers began to deduce that all was not well. Eventually the doors of the inner sanctum were thrown open and Wellesley himself invited us in with the words,

'Gentlemen, you had better hear this for yourselves.' We trooped in with a feeling of foreboding and gathered around a large table covered with maps in the middle of the room. 'It seems our Spanish allies have suffered something of a setback,' Wellesley coldly continued after we were all settled. 'Colonel D'Urban, you were there, perhaps you would be so kind as to give my officers a first-hand account.'

'Certainly sir,' replied D'Urban, moving forward to the table and re-arranging the maps. It was the first time I had met Ben D'Urban and I got to know him quite well while in Spain. He was a capable soldier and later administrator, especially in South Africa where they have named a town after him. Now, he briskly directed our attention to a large map showing the fork of two rivers near a town called Medallin. To cut a detailed briefing short, the Spanish under Cuesta thought they could trap and attack Marshal Victor's forces. Cuesta had the

32

advantage of total numbers with twenty-three thousand men against Victor's seventeen and a half thousand, although Victor had slightly more guns and cavalry. The French were trapped in the fork of the two rivers while Cuesta arrayed his army in an arc of four ranks of infantry between the riverbanks, with cavalry on either flank. The plan was to simply march them towards the French.

'What reserves did Cuesta have?' interrupted Wellesley.

'None sir,' said D'Urban awkwardly. 'He thought that as he advanced and the rivers got closer together, his ranks would thicken as his men had a shorter distance to cover.'

Wellesley gave a snort of disgust and continued his interrogation, 'How was he expecting the French to react to his attack? Did you not suggest keeping some force in reserve to address any French response?'

'To be honest sir, I am not sure he had thought that far ahead, and General Cuesta is a very difficult man to give advice to, sir.'

'Dear God,' groaned Wellesley, 'What an ally he is likely to be. Go on then, tell us the worst.'

'Well sir, to start with things seemed to go well with the forward French positions retreating towards their main force and the Spanish advancing steadily. Then one of the French cavalry regiments seemed a bit slow to retreat, and the Spanish cavalry on the left flank advanced to speed them along. The French, who had started to ride away, suddenly turned in the smartest manner and charged at the leading Spanish regiment of horsemen... who seemed to get startled,' he added lamely.

'What do you mean, startled?' demanded Wellesley.

'Well sir, it seemed that some had not faced a charge before and instead of meeting it they turned and tried to retreat through the other Spanish squadrons of horsemen behind them causing confusion.'

'Christ,' exclaimed one of our cavalry commanders as he imagined the resulting chaos.

'So,' continued D'Urban 'one French cavalry regiment succeeded in routing all three Spanish cavalry regiments on that side of the battlefield, and the other French cavalry nearby charged in to support.'

'What did Cuesta do in response?' asked Wellesley.

'He galloped in front of the retreating cavalry to try and get them to rally, but they just rode him down. He was knocked from his horse and trampled by his own side and then by the pursuing French.'

'Is he dead?' asked Wellesley with what seemed a note of hope in his voice.

'No sir, I took a spare horse to him with a couple of his cousins and we managed to get him from the battlefield. He had taken several kicks, but was only badly bruised.'

'So I am guessing that the infantry formed squares against the horsemen and fought their way out?' asked a Scottish infantry colonel.

D'Urban looked exquisitely embarrassed and I guessed we had still not heard the worst. 'Err, no sir. Most of the infantry officers were on horseback and when the Spanish cavalry fled the infantry officers joined them, leaving their men to fight for themselves. The Spanish infantry ran in all directions, with the French cavalry riding among them slaughtering until they were too tired to raise their bloodied swords.'

There was a stunned silence for a moment as we all struggled to take this in. I may be a lily livered coward but I don't think even I would have run in those circumstances. Oh, don't get me wrong – this would not be due to any sense of honour, but sheer practicality. A well organised infantry square is a much safer place to be with rampant enemy cavalry about, than fleeing with a pack of witless fools. You could retain most of your men and your reputation with a fighting retreat. Thinking back to my time with the remnants of the 74th Highlanders in India, I could not imagine running out on them like that; not least because Sergeant Fergusson would have tracked me down and gutted me with his spontoon if I had.

In the British army such brazen cowardice would leave a man ruined. Take it from an expert in these situations; you have to be a bit more creative. Helping a wounded soldier to the rear always looks noble, unless you are the commanding officer. Rushing from the command post pretending you have an important message gets you away quickly, or if things are really desperate – hiding under the corpses and hoping to be left for dead. As I was to discover in later years this last course is not recommended when the enemy are Iroquois warriors with a penchant for scalping, or a certain African tribe who take the wedding tackle from the dead and dying for trophies.

The Scottish infantry colonel interrupted my thoughts by muttering, 'The bastards left their men in an exposed line for cavalry to slaughter. They deserve to be shot.'

34

'The Central Junta has put some of the cavalry commanders in front of a firing squad for cowardice sir.' D'Urban said quietly.

'Good thing too,' muttered Downie, but even he looked shaken at how easily the Spanish had been defeated.

'How many were killed?' asked Wellesley.

'The Spanish lost eight thousand men killed or injured sir, with another two thousand taken prisoner. They also lost most of their cannon. French killed and wounded were less than a thousand.'

'And this was the army that was supposed to block any advance on Lisbon while we advanced to attack Soult in the north,' grumbled Wellesley. 'A detachment of army wives armed with camp kettles and skillets would give more protection.'

'There is still the Loyal Lusitanian Legion, Sir Arthur,' said General Craddock, the Lisbon commander. He did not seem to notice a couple of the staff officers wince as the name was mentioned and turn to look at Wellesley, whose face clenched in icy disdain. 'They only have twelve hundred men,' continued the hapless Craddock, 'but with some Spanish forces they have been holding off twelve thousand French at Almeida for the last few months. We might have had to evacuate Lisbon without them.'

'The Loyal Lusitanian Legion,' barked Wellesley with a sneer, 'is only loyal to its commander, and Sir Robert Wilson is no friend of mine.' I looked up at that for I knew Sir Robert, but a slight shake of the head from Campbell and the venom in Wellesley's voice warned me not to admit the association. 'I would rather have the army wives guarding my flank,' growled Wellesley, before calling the meeting to a close.

Most of the officers took this first opportunity to explore the town and I was joined by Campbell who had organised some soldiers as escort to keep the local beggars and hawkers at a distance. It was strange to be back in uniform again and getting admiring glances from the few half decent looking women on the streets. This time I had a proper captain's commission confirmed by Horseguards in the 31st Regiment of foot. I was only nominally attached to that unit as a staff officer and was excused all regimental duties. With the comradeship amongst the staff it was a bit like rejoining a family as there were several familiar faces, like Campbell, from my Indian days. While I was new to others my reputation for being a cool hand, ill gained though it was, earned me respect. My only memento from those earlier times was my sword, which I had captured, mostly due to luck, from an Arab soldier in India. It was a beautiful thing and while I had been forced to sell the precious stones from the hilt, for various sentimental reasons I could not bring myself to sell the sword itself. It was at my hip then as we strode through the streets and if we had thought that the Black Horse Square was full of poverty and dirt, we soon found that this was in fact one of the smarter parts of the town.

While some officers went to the local taverns and others piled into a whore house that from the outside looked as clean as a Turkish sewer, Campbell wanted to visit a church. It was not my cup of tea but I tagged along as we followed the directions he had been given, The city had been completely destroyed by a massive earthquake and tidal wave fifty years before so most of the buildings were new, although often built of old stone. Here and there were still some ruins or half repaired dwellings, but the church when we found it, was from the outside quite impressive. Inside was a different story; all the ornate decoration had been looted, even the wood furniture had been stolen for firewood, the place was virtually bare apart from a stone altar and a wooden cross.

'Hell's bells,' groaned Campbell looking around. 'I thought Calvinist kirks were depressing places to worship in, but they are positively flamboyant compared to this.'

'It could certainly learn a lot from Indian temples for decoration,' I agreed. There was an archway that had previously housed a door long since torn off its hinges, and beyond it a staircase leading up to one of the church towers. We headed up to see the sights and emerged on a rooftop with panoramic views over the city.

'I take it you know Wilson then,' Campbell said as we stood alone together looking over the rooftops to the countryside beyond.

'Yes, I went on a diplomatic mission to Russia with him a couple of years ago. I found him a pleasant and resourceful man, but evidently Wellesley does not agree. What is this Loyal Lusitanian Legion?'

'It is a private army that Sir Robert set up a year ago in London from the émigrés who fled there from Portugal after the French invaded. They joined the first British expedition to Portugal and were supplemented with British officers who trained the men.'

'Why didn't they evacuate with the rest of the British army at Corunna?' I asked.

'They spent time training and when they tried to join the British army they were cut off by the French. The British officers were told that they could abandon their men and disembark at Lisbon, but they bravely chose to stay with them.'

'Quite right too,' I agreed, remembering the Spanish abandoning their men, but thinking I would have been on the first boat home.

'They decided to hold up in the fortress at Almeida with around twelve hundred men, but they managed to convince both the French and the Spanish that they had ten times that number. Over six thousand Spanish troops, thinking that there was a large British trained force to support them, gathered and garrisoned the nearby town of Ciudad Rodrigo. The two fortresses guarded passes that led to Portugal and Lisbon. Between them they stopped an army of ten thousand French invading the south of the country.'

'So why does Wellesley hate them?' I asked.

'When the Loyal Lusitanian Legion arrived in Portugal, one of their first duties was to oversee the evacuation of the French troops with their loot. Understandably the Portuguese soldiers took it badly and Sir Robert wrote to his influential friends in London complaining about the generals, including Wellesley, who had agreed to the terms.'

'I see. I can imagine that Wellesley would not take kindly to one of his officers complaining over his head.'

'That's the other thing – Sir Robert has never seen himself as under the command of the British army. He has styled himself as a major general and sees himself as Wellesley's equal even though he only has a fraction of the men. He even wrote to Sir Arthur before we embarked with some suggestions for the coming campaign. You can guess how well that was received.' I could; Wellesley must have choked on that advice like a cat with a fur ball. We stood in silence for a few minutes looking at the view; two more ships, one a fast message sloop, were coming up the river. Around the town loomed green hills that looked benign now, but if captured by the French they would make holding the city impossible.

'Do you think that we will be able to stay in Portugal this time?' I asked, voicing the thought that had been on everyone's mind since we had heard about the Spanish defeat.

'Not if we just stay here,' stated Campbell. 'The French will gather their armies together and destroy us. Sir Arthur has to move and fast to attack their armies one by one. Soult is the obvious first target, he is nearest.'

'But he has more men, mostly veterans, unless you count the Portuguese and they are not trained yet.'

'The French might be veterans but morale in their army is low. They have been cut off from other French forces for months now, living off what they can find in the countryside around them, with foraging parties regularly being attacked by guerrillas.' He paused now, staring out into the countryside as though assessing how he would attack it. Then he added quietly, 'I don't mind telling you, Flashman, that I think it will be hot work. If we win it will be a close run thing and men like us will have to show an example to some of the less experienced officers.'

I looked across at him then. His blue eyes were still staring at the fields and with his broad shoulders, lantern jaw and curly blond hair he looked the epitome of the heroic officer. He was the genuine article too. While my reputation was based on lies, misunderstandings and situations where I had no choice; he had charged into breaches like Dick Champion, fought to save fallen comrades and had probably flipped a coin to poor Willie the orphan boy on the way home. When men like him start to get anxious then it is time for us lesser mortals to make sure that they have a fast horse to hand and a clean escape route planned. With that in mind I was looking down and counting the ships in the harbour when I heard more footsteps coming up the stairs behind us.

Two young women stepped through the archway, both respectably dressed but from the worldly way they ran their eyes over us, they were professional women for certain and by far the prettiest I had seen since we docked. Campbell did not even look round at them. His mind was clearly still on the battles ahead as he said, 'It is good to have someone who will not think I am croaking to talk to, Flashman. We are both the same; I was reminded of that on the way out when you took fifteen guineas off me in that card game during the storm. Everyone looked nervous apart from Sir Arthur and you.'

'I was surprised you gave me the money so easily,' I said grinning.

'I can't swim,' he replied, 'drowning is the one thing that frightens me.'

'The one thing...' I repeated in dismay at this brave dolt who thought we were the same. Before I could say more there was a giggle from the two girls who had gone to stand on the opposite side of the tower looking at the town.

Campbell seemed to notice them for the first time. 'I say Flash,' he said, indicating across to them, 'You don't think that they are...' He paused and started to blush before continuing, 'That kind of women.'

Hullo, thinks I, have we found the heel of this Achilles? 'No,' I replied. 'They look perfectly respectable to me. This is probably a popular spot for young ladies to take the air.'

'Yes, quite so,' he agreed, but still looked decidedly uncomfortable.

'Are you married now?' I asked, having a suspicion I already knew the answer.

'No, there was a woman three years ago, but not since then.' He gave an embarrassed grin, 'I wasn't joking about the Calvinist upbringing, it is hard to shake off.'

'You mean you have not been with any woman since then?' I asked, appalled.

'No, not one.'

I was genuinely speechless. This strapping hero could have had any women he wanted and he had forgone them all for three years. I may not be a Calvinist but I could see where my Christian duty lay. 'Do you speak Spanish or Portuguese?' I asked innocently.

'Not beyond the basics,' he replied, 'I have never had the time.'

'I am fluent in Spanish,' I told him. 'I had better introduce us to the ladies. I am sure it is what they would expect a gentleman to do.'

'If you are sure,' he said, going red again. 'I'll stay here.'

I stepped across the tower to do the finest service I have ever done for a brother officer. Campbell evidently did not understand much Spanish or he would have picked up on the astonished gasps of 'tres años!', and been more suspicious of the sympathetic and downright lustful glances they cast in his direction. I explained that he was shy and would never go into a knocking shop and would need to be suddenly brought to the boil in case his Christian principles got in the way. It was soon evident that I was dealing with experts in their field. In exchange for the fifteen guineas that I had won from Campbell during the storm, they offered a respectable house we could use and a guarantee that we would both have a night that we would never forget.

'They have invited us to take afternoon tea with them,' I told Campbell when I returned. 'They are sisters and their parents' house is nearby. As Wellesley does not want us to offend the locals I thought we should accept.'

'If you are sure,' said Campbell, going red again at the thought of it. While the two girls had come up the stairs quite easily, they now claimed that they needed assistance to descend and one linked arms with me while the other grabbed a startled Campbell. On close inspection they were both beauties, flawless complexions of the milkiest coffee, lustrous dark hair and hazel eyes with more than a hint of mischief. The girl held by Campbell affected to stumble twice on the way down forcing him to catch her. He was sweating with repressed lust and confusion by the time we reached the bottom. It took all my self-control to keep a straight face as he asked, 'I say Flashman, are you sure we should be doing this?'

I reassured him and a few minutes later we were sitting in the front room of a very well furnished house making polite conversation with one of the 'sisters' while the other ostensibly organised tea. The second sister returned a few minutes later followed by a girl in a maid's uniform carrying a tray of tea things. One glance told you that the girl was no more a maid than I was. She was blonde for a start, a rare thing in Portugal, another stunner and with a wanton look in her eye that latched straight on to Campbell, whose jaw had started to sag at the sight of her. The second sister winked at me and whispered that it was time for us to leave.

'My companion just wants to show me a portrait of her mother,' I told Campbell over my shoulder, but I was not sure he was paying attention. Once out of the room, my girl closed the door and turned the key in the lock.

'We would not want him escaping too soon would we?' she said with a grin, but it was soon evident that escape was the last thing on Campbell's mind.

After a sudden exclamation of, 'Oh you are pros...' there was giggling from the girls and then, 'Oh God' repeatedly from Campbell, accompanied by the sound of breaking crockery. We listened for a few seconds but then I felt fingers undoing buttons and in a moment I found that I had literally placed myself in the hands of a skilled professional who drew me away upstairs.

Fifteen guineas will buy you a lot in Portugal, and we stayed there for the rest of the afternoon and the night. I recall steak and eggs arriving at one point along with bottles of red wine, but it was hard to enjoy a peaceful repast with the ardent noises coming up from below. With the girls giggling and Campbell yelling, they seemed to be making up for three years in one night. I swear he was howling in Gaelic at one point and another time I heard him roar to one of the girls that he was going to bend her over and ... Well what he shouted was not for sensitive ears, but suffice it to say that it would have made John Calvin choke on his beard.

Chapter 5

I woke up the next morning feeling well pleased with myself. A good
rattle always leaves me in fine fettle. I left the house early and as I
passed the ground floor room I tried the door. It was now unlocked and
the interior looked as if it had been hit by a hurricane. There was a tray
and a pile of broken crockery in the corner, half eaten plates of food
and bottles on the floor, and in the middle of the room was a mound
covered by rugs and a blanket. From it protruded a male foot and two
female calves of different complexions, while a loud snoring emanated
from within. Saint Flashy I thought, your duty is done.

I strolled back to the palatial building that Wellesley was now using
as his headquarters. Apart from sentries, few people seemed to be
about, so I went up to the map room where Wellesley had given us a
briefing the previous day. At first I thought it was empty but then a
familiar voice barked from a corner of the room by the window, 'Ah
Flashman, perfect timing. You haven't seen Campbell in your travels
have you?'

'I have not spoken to him since yesterday sir,' I answered honestly,
if not fully. Wellesley was sitting in his usual plain blue coat at a small
table by the window, reading through a pile of despatches.

'Well help yourself to coffee and join me over here will you, there
is something that we need to talk about.' Once I had settled in the chair
opposite the table he continued, 'You ought to know that I have had a
despatch about you from Horseguards.'

'Really,' I said guardedly; I sensed from the tone that this was not
good news.

'Yes, that damnable fellow Tasker seems to think you are involved
in the Clarke affair somehow. He uses the duke's name to require me
to advise him of anything to support his suspicions. It is a gross
impertinence.

'That is ridiculous sir, I can assure you...' but Wellesley waved my
protests aside.

'Don't worry. I have no doubt as to your innocence. You are not the
only one, there are three other names on the list and I am sure that they
are innocent too. But Horseguards seems determined to get to the
bottom of the matter. They have insisted that I take Sir William
Erskine onto my staff as he is close to certain members of the court.
He is to be an unofficial investigator and I am ordered to give him

every assistance. Do you know the man? No? Well he is a dangerous and volatile fellow, completely mad.'

'Mad sir?' I asked, puzzled.

'Oh, I do not use the term figuratively Flashman, I mean literally mad. He has been committed to an asylum twice already, but apparently that does not stop him serving as a Member of Parliament or as an officer on my staff. I complained about the appointment before we left and I got the reply on a fast messenger sloop that arrived yesterday. Here, let me find it.' He burrowed around amongst the despatches on his desk before holding one up triumphantly. 'Here it is, listen to this – they say that 'he is sometimes a little mad, but in his lucid intervals he is an uncommonly clever fellow'. Then a clerk has added at the bottom of this letter that 'the duke trusts he will have no fit during the campaign, although he looked a little wild as he embarked'.' He sat back shaking his head in despair. 'First my Spanish allies show that they are incapable of any sensible action and now I have lunatics appointed to my staff.'

'Perhaps you could appoint Erskine to Cuesta's staff sir, it probably could not make things worse.'

'Christ knows what those two could come up with if they were put together,' exclaimed Wellesley, 'more training exercises for French cavalry probably.' He looked me in the eye, 'No Flashman, liaison with Cuesta is the job I need you for. After his recent defeat it will be harder than I expected, but I know you are cool under pressure. Compared to India it should be a walk in the park for someone of your abilities.'

'I'll do my best, sir,' I was wondering, not for the first time, if my unearned reputation would be the death of me. The trip to India had nearly seen me eaten by a tiger and blown apart by rockets, but at least here I spoke the language and could lie low if I had to. 'What exactly do you want me to do?'

Wellington leaned over the table, pulling a map from his papers and laying it out between us. He traced his route with a finger as he talked. 'In two days' time I am marching north with the army to Oporto and Marshal Soult. Information we have from deserters is that their morale and supplies are low, so if we can get across the river near Oporto easily we should beat them.' He stabbed the town of Oporto with his finger. 'Then I plan to turn south and try to beat Marshal Victor before he can be joined by any other French forces. I need to beat these marshals one at a time or we will be overwhelmed.' The movement of

42

his finger became vaguer now circling a wide area in the middle of Spain. 'What I need you to do is find Cuesta, see what is left of his army and make sure that he is ready to join me to beat Victor. I doubt his army will be much use but we need all the men that we can get.'

'Where do you think Cuesta is now sir?'

'Craddock has no idea,' admitted Wellesley. 'Many of his men fled north into the hills for protection after the battle at Medellin. I am hoping that they are at least holding the bridge here at Alcantara as that blocks the route straight into Lisbon across the Tagus valley.' As he spoke, he pointed to a town on the map just inside the Spanish border where two rivers joined and then headed to Lisbon. 'Go here first Flashman. If Cuesta has the brains of a woodlouse then he should at least have some forces here who can direct you to him, if he is not there himself.'

'Do I have an escort?'

'God yes, the hills around here aren't safe for a single horseman, there are all manner of villains and bandits around. I can spare you a troop of thirty dragoons. Downie is going with you. He needs to find out what supplies the Spanish can provide as we head south.'

I sat back, and in my naiveté I did not feel too alarmed. Few bandits would take on thirty well-armed troopers unless they were guarding a pay chest, and the alternative was to march north with Wellesley and get embroiled in what would probably be a contested river crossing and battle with Soult. From what I had heard, Soult was a very capable commander and Wellesley was then not yet the proven military genius that he became. I knew better than anyone that his victories in India had an element of good fortune to them. A hardened commander like Soult, with his veteran soldiers, would not make the same mistakes. If Wellesley was beaten we would soon hear of it and would have a clear ride back down to Lisbon, or if necessary we could head further south to Seville, the independent Spanish capital.

'Give Cuesta this letter,' Wellesley continued. 'It details my plans, and I don't need to tell you to make sure it does not fall into enemy hands. Once you have had a chance to assess Cuesta's strength and intentions then I would be obliged if you would ride back and let me know.' That, I thought, could be the tricky bit. I did not want to ride slap into a routed British force and the pursuing French.

'When do we leave?' I asked

'Downie is organising the cavalry escort, they leave from the square at noon.' He looked up and saw me looking thoughtful about my mission and grinned. 'Don't worry Flashman, I know you would prefer to be testing your steel against Soult and his men. But this duty is vital for the next phase of the campaign, taking on Victor and his army. I will make sure you are in the thick of the action when we meet him, have no fear.' You can imagine how reassuring I found that statement, but I managed to sound suitably enthusiastic for form's sake as I took my leave.

I met the escort in the square just before noon. The troopers were led by a Sergeant Butterworth, but there was no sign of Downie.

'He was 'ere earlier sir,' said the dour sergeant. 'Fussin' around about supplies 'e was.' Butterworth looked across at his men who, like the two of us, stood next to their mounts. Judging from the way a few of them were checking saddles and tack they looked experienced men. Butterworth followed my gaze and added, 'Most of us were with the first expedition sir. Got taken off at Corunna, but we had to shoot the horses then and leave them behind. These mounts are a bit green and most didn't eat much on the voyage so some of the girths have had to be tightened. Bit of exercise on solid ground and some grass will see them good again.'

'I am sure you are right sergeant,' I replied, testing the girth on my own horse, which seemed tight enough.

'What ho, Flashman!' A voice called out from nearby, and there walking towards me was Downie, and alongside him a pensive Campbell. This could be awkward, I thought. If there was any justice Campbell should be damn grateful for the favour I did him, but you could never tell with these puritanical types. He could now be wracked with remorse and blaming me for leading him astray. My thoughts were interrupted by Downie calling, 'Are you ready to go? I have got you some eggs.'

'Eggs?' I asked, puzzled.

'Yes, hard-boiled eggs, excellent on the campaign if supplies get low. Lots of energy and they keep well, ready wrapped to keep them clean so to speak,' he laughed.

'Thank you.' I accepted the small cloth sack he offered that looked and felt like an overstuffed scrotum, and from the shape contained half a dozen eggs.

'Don't eat them in the first few days remember,' advised Downie. 'Save them until rations are low.' He turned to Butterworth, 'Now Sergeant, did you sort out some eggs for the men as I asked?'

44

'Yes sir,' replied the sergeant with a stony blank look on his face. 'The men have all the eggs they need.' I looked over the sergeant's shoulder and several of his troopers were now smirking at this response. It was evident that these experienced troopers felt that they needed the advice of the boyishly enthusiastic Downie like a drowning man needs a drink. I turned back to Campbell who, to my relief, grinned at me.

'You knew what those girls were from the outset, didn't you?'

'I don't know what you mean,' I replied, with my best 'butter would not melt in my mouth' expression of innocence. 'The girl I was with was entirely respectable, you would not believe how many pictures of her mother we had to look at, then some of her cousins. By the time we came back, the door was locked and ... well, I am too much of a gentleman to say what I thought was happening.'

Campbell laughed out loud. 'You planned it all in the tower! They hinted as much when I thought I might need to pay them this morning. They told me you had paid for me.' He paused, 'I might regret it when the Christian guilt sets in but right now I think it was the best night of my life.'

'When you are old and grey,' I replied, 'what are you going to remember most, last night or a night on your knees praying?'

'You are right, which is why I wanted to give you this,' he was holding out another cloth bag.

'It's not more bloody eggs is it?' I said, taking hold of the gift. The shape at the bottom of the bag was a tube and when I looked inside I saw a small folding telescope which looked expensive. 'Are you sure? This must have cost a good few guineas?'

'I have another. This was loot from the first campaign, and for the service you have done me you are very welcome to it.' We shook hands, and then with Downie calling that it was time to leave, I mounted up and the column of horsemen trotted out of the square.

There are perhaps four weeks of the year when the weather in Spain and Portugal is pleasant, two in the spring and two in the autumn. Outside of these it is either too cold and wet, or too hot. Sadly, our trip to Alcantara did not coincide with one of those fortnights. Once we had ridden out of Lisbon the countryside rose up in a series of steep hills called the Torres Vedras, the top of most of them hidden by low cloud. We stayed in the valleys following the river, but the ground was wet and boggy and we frequently had to wade through gushing streams bringing rain water down from the hills. There was a steady drizzle of rain for most of the day. I was already feeling cold, soaked and miserable by the end of the first day when we had only reached the end of the large Tagus estuary.

We found shelter for ourselves and our horses in a large barn and the troopers broke down some of the stalls for firewood to make a blaze to warm us up. It was then that Downie and Butterworth started to argue over the route. Both had hand drawn maps, which were by no means identical. On both, the Tagus bent north east like the curve of a bow. Butterworth wanted to follow the river on the grounds that we could not get lost and there would be a lot of settlements along its banks where we could get food and shelter. Downie was for crossing the river on the nearby ferry and taking the 'bowstring' route directly to Alcantara.

'The Tagus spends much of its course in a steep sided valley,' he insisted. 'We will spend ages trying to negotiate side streams and rivers, which after all this rain will be in full flood. My route will be much easier.'

'We don't know that,' countered Butterworth. 'The area you want to cross is blank on both our maps.'

In the end Downie won, mainly because he was an officer and stated bluntly that he was going the way he had chosen and ordered Butterworth to follow him. I did not have strong feelings either way but the experience led to a valuable life lesson, which I will pass on for what it is worth. When dealing with maps containing blank spaces, never trust the navigation to an optimist. They will always imagine that smooth roads and plentiful supplies fill the space, which is never the case. There is a reason some spaces on the maps are blank; it is because people rarely pass that way and most folk will normally choose the easiest route. In my considerable experience of blank spaces on maps, they normally contain impassable mountains, pitiless deserts, impenetrable forest or jungles full of hostile tribesmen. None of these were in Portugal of course, but what was there was just a dangerous.

The journey started off well enough; the ferry took us across the river and we found a road, little more than a narrow track, heading in the right direction. Whereas the crowds in Lisbon had welcomed our presence, as we got further from the more travelled route, the populace were much less hospitable to strangers. We would normally be spotted approaching a village and by the time we got there the doors and shutters would be firmly closed. If we saw any people at all they would be old men and women who would glare at us from the village square with hostile faces. To them we were just soldiers, they did not care about politics or why we were there. They just remembered clearly the ones in blue coats that had travelled in the opposite direction and probably taken anything of value that they could find.

As we were riding through one of these ghost villages, the window shutter in a large house opened slightly and an attractive young girl stared out and smiled at us. I grinned and waved back, but a second later a hand reached out and grabbed the girl by the collar, dragging her out of sight. The unseen pater familia then shouted at the girl and delivered such a resounding slap that several of us winced in sympathy. But it was good to know that not every woman in the region was a raddled old crone.

With all this arctic hospitality, the bread, sausage and other supplies we had brought with us soon started to run out. Late in the afternoon on the sixth day we rode through another seemingly abandoned village, and while not a soul was in sight, a decent sized pig could be seen snuffling around a sty attached to one of the cottages. Our dinner the previous night had consisted of boiled beans, hard-boiled egg and the last of some spicy sausage. I don't know if you have ever camped with thirty men who have only eaten eggs, beans and spiced sausage, but let me tell you after that repast they snore from both ends. I hardly got any sleep and when we threw the blankets off in the morning the stench was truly appalling. I could not go through another night like that, and when I looked around me I saw that most of our number were of the same mind. Nothing was said, but there was an exchange of glances which told me that with one exception, we were planning to have pork for dinner that night. Unfortunately the exception was our nominal commander John Downie. While we were both captains, Downie's commission preceded mine so he was the senior officer. He barely gave the pig a glance as we went past and was prattling on in his usual enthusiastic manner. I can't tell you what he was talking about as I had long since stopped listening.

'What supplies do we have left for dinner, John?' I asked.

'Oh, we have plenty of beans left, no more sausage I'm afraid, but we still have enough eggs to make a meal. It might be our last night together before we reach Alcantara. I am sure we must be close now.'

'There was a pig back there, we could buy it to supplement the rations,' I suggested.

'No, we have brought these supplies with us so we should use them.' He laughed and added, 'I am a commissary officer after all, so I should be making the best use of what we carry.'

'Indeed,' I agreed, thinking a more oblique approach would be required. 'That forested hill up in front looks a good place to camp tonight. It will give shelter from the wind but will not be too damp.'

'Isn't it too early to stop?' asked Downie.

'I think Trooper Doherty is feeling a bit stiff after his fall this morning.'

On cue Doherty, who had been listening to the conversation piped up, 'Ah, yes sir, my side is right cruel sore, so it is.' After a theatrical gasp and wince of pain he added in a brave croak, 'But I could go on sir if we really have to.'

I thought the daft bogtrotter had overdone it but Downie never suspected a thing. 'No, of course we can stop Doherty if you're in pain. I had no idea you had fallen this morning or I would have asked how you were.' He turned to me, 'You are a good man, Thomas, to keep an eye on the men's welfare like that, I should have done better.'

'It was nothing,' I brushed the praise aside. 'Now why don't we ride to the end of the forest ahead of us to see what lies beyond. We can leave the men to set up camp,' and here I looked meaningfully over my shoulder, 'as well as forage anything for the pot.' The men grinned back conspiratorially as I spurred ahead with Downie. In a short while we were winding our way through the forest on the path and I asked about his navigation. 'Are you sure we are near Alcantara? I have lost my bearings a bit and we haven't seen the sun for days with this low cloud.'

'Oh yes,' he looked rather pleased with himself as he added, 'there are signs you can look out for to help when the sun cannot be seen. For example, moss normally grows on the south side of tree trunks to get the most sunshine, so you can use that as a guide.' I had never heard this before but looked around and what little moss I could see was scattered on several different sides of the trunks.

'Do you think it would be a good idea to ask for directions tomorrow,' I asked. 'Just to confirm what the moss is telling you.'

'I suppose we could,' he agreed. 'But I am not sure that I would trust those villagers.'

It would be a damn sight more reliable than your moss, I thought. You will not be surprised to learn that Downie had got it wrong. A few years later I discovered that moss normally grows on the north side of

48

a tree's bark. But an old trapper on the Ottawa River in Canada told me that you have to study a hundred trees to get an accurate indication of north as other things such as the direction of rivers and hills also affect the moss.

We rode back to camp and to Downie's surprise and my delight a pig was roasting over the fire.

'Trooper Chapman caught a wild pig while out foraging,' Sergeant Butterworth explained with a straight face to Downie. 'We can keep the eggs to give us supplies for another day, sir.'

'Yes,' cried Downie, grinning. 'And as it is a wild pig we don't have to pay for it.'

There is nothing like the smell of roast pork to build up an appetite and it was the first fresh meat we had enjoyed in days. A few hours later and we were settling down for the night, comfortably full, when one of the troopers on guard duty warned that a party from the nearby village was approaching. There were about a dozen of them, ten men armed with scythes, billhooks and a few muskets, a priest and an old woman. A number of our men gathered at the edge of our camp to face them, several having taken the short barrelled carbine muskets from the holsters in their saddles first, in case there was trouble. Most of the villagers stopped a hundred yards down the hill and just the priest and the old woman came on. As I spoke the best Spanish, and to stop Downie discovering where the pig had really come from, I volunteered to go down to greet them.

'What can we do for you?' I asked them in a friendly tone. The old woman, who had a spectacularly hairy wart on her chin, glanced nervously to the priest.

'We have come to seek payment for the pig,' he replied calmly, while his eyes darted over my shoulder to look at the troopers standing behind me.

'Did you ask the French for payment when they came this way?' I asked.

'No señor,' the priest smiled. 'The French did not sneak into the village like your man. They marched in, took what and who they wanted and killed anyone that got in the way. You are riding west, to fight the French I think. We hope you will be different. It is a poor village and we cannot afford to lose a pig without trying for payment.'

'Let me have a word with our commander,' I said, before walking back up the hill to Downie.

'What do they want Thomas?' asked Downie.

'It seems that woman's pig escaped from its sty, which was why Chapman found it in the forest. They are hoping we will pay for the animal.'

'But if it escaped we are under no obligation to pay,' insisted Downie indignantly.

'True,' I said, 'but if we don't pay they will think badly of the British army. It would be best to give them something. Haven't you some money from commissary funds you could use?' Reluctantly Downie handed over three small gold coins for the animal and I walked back down the hill.

'Here is payment for the pig,' I told the old lady, pushing a single gold coin into her grubby palm. The priest snatched the money from her but complained,

'This is not enough, it was a big pig.'

'I will give you another coin for some information,' I told him. 'We set off from Lisbon six days ago and we are going to Alcantara. How far off is that from here and in which direction?'

'You have come well south of your route,' said the priest, now looking surprised we were here at all. 'Over the hill the path forks – take the track on the left. Alcantara is still some six or seven days for a man on horseback.'

'Thank you.' I pressed a second coin into the old woman's hand and this time it closed with the speed of a trap before the priest could take the money. I still had a coin left and I held it up to show them. 'Do you have brandy in that village?' I asked.

'No señor, but we have jerez,' he told me, and by the way he grinned and made a drinking gesture I gathered it was good.

'Well, bring enough of it for thirty men and you will have this coin as well,' I told them. The woman said nothing but nodded and her mouth cracked open into a nearly toothless grin. She returned a short while later with two large earthenware flagons of the spirit for the coin. I had been expecting some local firewater but it was remarkably good, brown in colour, as thick as port and tasting like liquid fruit cake.

For me you can forget about White's and the Reform Club; for true camaraderie you could not beat nights like that. Thirty men sitting around a roaring log fire on a moonlit night, full bellies, exceptional liquor and not a damned egg or bean in sight. It was around that very fire that one of the truly insane ideas in military history was born. It followed after some of the troops had expressed surprise that we were

50

now paying villagers for supplies. It wasn't like that during the retreat to Corunna, they pointed out.

'Mind you,' said Sergeant Butterworth, 'things went too far then.' He looked at the others. 'Remember when we rode into that village and found those Welsh troops insensible in the snow. They were surrounded by broken bottles and barrels and had drunk themselves unconscious. We could not rouse them and had to leave them as the French were just an hour behind. Whether they were killed by the French or frostbite I cannot say, but I'm pretty sure that they were dead by morning.'

'D'ye think there are partisans in these here hills?' asked Doherty. 'I mean,' he added, while subconsciously touching his genitals, 'we have the heard stories about what they do to French troops they capture, so we have. Ye don't think they'll do that to us do you?'

'Don't be stupid,' exclaimed Chapman. 'They know we are on their side an' we 'ave our red jackets to show we're British.'

'The French have troops in red coats as well,' said Butterworth. 'Swiss and Hanoverians I think. I saw some in the last campaign. They were in the vanguard of a French attack and some villagers came out to welcome them thinking they were us before they realised their error.'

'Jaysus and Mary,' exclaimed Doherty. 'Gettin' shot at is one thing, but I don't want some bastard to cut my knocker off.'

'Don't worry,' reassured Downie. 'The Spanish are not going to attack their own allies. Flashman and I speak Spanish, we can explain who we are and why we're here.'

'Do you think the Spanish army will be in a fit state to fight?' I asked him. 'After what we heard about the battle at Medallin, it does not sound as if they will be a strong fighting force.'

'I have been to Spain several times.' Downie was staring into the fire as he spoke. 'I truly love Spain and the Spanish people, but in some ways they just seem to have given up. Two hundred years ago they stood astride the world, nearly capturing Britain with the Armada and ruling most of Europe and the Americas. They just do not seem to be the same people now, with no pride or proper organisation. They need something to remind them of what they once were.'

'I heard that the Tower of London sent back to Spain all the weapons they captured from the Spanish Armada at the start of Spanish rebellion,' said Butterworth, who then took a long pull on one of the flagons. He wiped his mouth before adding, 'Perhaps they can fit out a regiment in that clobber to inspire the rest.' Thirty-one people round the campfire roared with laughter at the thought of soldiers dressed in doublet and hose prancing around a modern battlefield. One person was not laughing.

'That could work,' murmured Downie, half to himself.

'You can't be serious?' I asked in astonishment. 'They would be shot to pieces long before they could use their swords and p kes. In any case it would cost a fortune to put such a force together.'

'Maybe you're right,' said Downie. 'Still, it is worth thinking about.' As old Peninsular hands know, Downie did more than think about it and he had the money to see it through. This explains why any portraits you see of Downie normally show him looking as though he was a shipmate of Sir Francis Drake, when in fact he was barely older than me.

I saw his famed regiment two years later while still in Spain. Their attire did do wonders for morale; but for the British army rather than the Spanish. The group I was with fell about with mirth when they saw the regiment, and judging from the morose expressions on the faces of Downie's men, I gathered that this was a common reaction. It was raining at the time and the rest of us were all wrapped up in long greatcoats while the pride of the armada looked frozen in waist length cloaks and stockings up to the thigh. Their conquistador style steel helmets gathered rain water like guttering, and every time they moved their heads water spilled either down their front or their back.

You will not be surprised to learn that their only military action against the French was also a disaster. The French let them get quite close, either because they could not believe their eyes or were too busy laughing to shoot. When they did fire, Downie's men found that their steel breastplates did little to stop a ball from either a cannon or a musket. Their morale must have been low after being treated as the joke of the army for months and after a few volleys they broke and ran. The Spanish never forgot Downie's efforts though, and he was given various honours for his service to Spain, ending up governor of the castle in Seville, but all that was to come.

Chapter 6

The next morning, after all the talk of partisans, Downie decided to send two men ahead as scouts.

'Flashman, I would like you to ride as the forward scout,' he told me as we mounted up. 'You have your telescope and speak the language, so you are best placed to spot any trouble.' He grinned, 'I know your reputation but if you see anything ride straight back. Don't try to take them on by yourself.'

There was no chance of me taking anyone on if I could help it, but all the talk of partisans the night before had left me feeling edgy as well. I had Doherty as my companion the first day and we found the fork in the road that the priest had predicted and made sure we went to the left. We saw hardly anyone, moving from one near deserted valley to the next. At the end of the day and without finding a village, the awful prospect of eggs and beans loomed again, but as we were setting up camp near a stream a gun shot indicated that we were saved from that once more.

Trooper Chapman was halfway up the hillside with a smoking carbine in his hand and a sheep twitching its death throes just a few yards away.

'The sheep 'ad a broken leg sir,' he called to Downie. 'It would not 'ave survived much longer, so the shepherd can't complain. It is a kindness to kill it,' he added. His statement would have been slightly more plausible if there hadn't been the audible snapping sound of a breaking bone as he stood on the creature's leg.

Whether Downie heard the bone snap as well I could not say, but if he did he chose to ignore it. The men were ordered to look out for the shepherd so that we could pay him for the sheep, which was soon skinned and roasting over a fire. Eventually a wizened old man in a sheepskin jacket was seen peering down at us from higher up the hillside. Downie called for him to come down and waved a coin at him, but I guessed that men did not get to be wizened and old in these parts by walking unarmed down a hillside towards thirty gun wielding strangers. Downie made a big show of putting a coin on a rock for the shepherd while he watched. The coin had gone by the morning, but I very much doubt that it was the shepherd who took it.

We carried on in this manner for another two days. On the third day Chapman was my companion and I was getting to know some of the troop quite well. Chapman, I was not entirely surprised to discover, was a thief who had joined the army to escape prison or the gallows. As we talked I noticed that the terrain was starting to change. The ground rose up in steep hills often with the lower levels covered in forest. It was cold but dry and the sun was shining as we rode along a valley close to a stream. Looking ahead the valley bent sharply to the right so I signalled, as I had done now many times before, for the troop behind to stop while we went forward to investigate.

The woods came down close to the path, which twisted and turned so that you could not see far ahead. We stood silently watching for a moment and kicked our horses forward to the next bend. Two hundred yards further on, we stopped again at another turn in the path.

'When I was a burglar,' muttered Chapman, 'we 'ad lookouts, crows we called 'em. Sometimes you could feel 'em watching you and I'm getting that same feeling now.'

We had been down several similar valleys but Chapman was right, my danger antennae were twitching too. I took out my telescope and started to study the sides of the valley ahead.

'We'll not be able to get the 'orses up there,' said Chapman. 'We would 'ave to ride along the valley floor or fight our way up hill on foot.'

He was right, but I could not see anything to confirm my suspicions. I was about to put the glass away and ride further forward when Chapman asked to borrow it. I passed it across.

'I 'ave never used a glass before,' he said as he adjusted the tubes. 'Blimey,' he added, when he got the focus right, 'I can see why you officers 'ave these, you could see a flea wipe its arse with this glass.' He studied the right hand side of the valley while I looked across to the left, content to wait. It was just a split second, but there was a flash of light to the left as though something metal had momentarily caught the sun. Before I could say anything Chapman gave a grunt of satisfaction.

'There is something to the left,' I told him, 'I saw a glint of metal.'

'Aye and there is a bugger in those rocks to the right too. I thought I saw 'im with my eye but he just popped his bleedin' 'ead up to look when I was using this,' he passed the glass back to me. I stowed it in my saddlebag, patted both of my coat pockets to check that my pistols were still in them and had a final look round.

'Let's go back. This has ambush written all over it.' Downie had ordered us to come back if we smelt trouble and that was one order I was happy to obey. It was as we started to turn our horses that the first shot rang out from the trees. We could hear men shouting in the hill above us while further down the path in the direction we had been travelling, several armed men spilled onto the road. Another shot was fired and I heard it ricochet off the road nearby. Our red coats were clearly visible, but so was their purpose and it did not leave scope for negotiation. In a moment the scene had changed from an empty valley similar to countless ones we had ridden through, to one of deadly danger. I needed little encouragement to lie low in the saddle and spur the horse back the way we had come. Chapman was alongside doing the same and the horses were quickly at the gallop. But we had only covered a few yards when there was a splintering sound and a tree started to fall across the path ahead, blocking our escape. They had made a trap and we had blundered right into it. There was still a small gap by the edge of the river and both Chapman and I steered our horses towards it. Now we saw that five attackers were tumbling out of the woods by the tree. They were armed with long handled pikes and axes that looked old, but which would still be lethal against horses and men in a confined space. It was a race between us on horseback and these villains on foot to get to the gap by the river first.

The men by the tree had a much shorter distance to travel and, as another ball whined over my head from the slope behind, I looked over my shoulder to see that there were now twenty men running down the path after us.

'Ride straight through,' I shouted. We were already outnumbered but if the men behind us caught up we would stand no chance at all. Our only hope was to use the momentum of the horses to push our way past.

I realised that we were going to lose the race with the men by the tree. My horse's hooves were pounding the loose stones as we sped along but Chapman pulled slightly ahead. I was happy to let him. One of Flashy's firm principles of warfare is never be first to enter a breach. The first man always attracts the attention of most of the defenders and rarely survives. If Chapman took the brunt of the impact I might be able to slip around. With the horse heading in the right direction I dropped my reins and tried to pull a pistol out of my pocket with my left hand and draw my sword with my right. We were on them in a moment and suddenly everything was chaos and confusion. I had planned to fire my pistol as I approached the gap but the hammer had got caught in the flap of my pocket. By the time I had got the gun clear and thumbed back on the hammer I was at the tree. A man with a pike suddenly appeared to my left with the weapon's point just a yard away from my side. Without hesitation I pointed the pistol at him and fired. The ball smashed through the lower part of his face and he went down reaching for what was left of his jaw and screaming in pain.

There was another man to my right by the edge of the water but if I kept close to the tree top I would get clear. I had spurred my horse to keep going when Chapman's mount reared in front of me. The men had thrown a blanket over its head and it was bucking in panic. I heard the men shouting something about the horses and realised that they wanted them alive, but as the man by the river rushed forward with a big old pistol, it was clear that they were not so protective of the riders. With Chapman's horse wheeling in panic in front of me, my mount was slowing too. My left foot brushed the branches of the fallen tree. Chapman's horse was turning round to the left, while he swung his sword at the men who reached up for his horse's bridle. I wanted to go right to get around him and away, but the man with the pistol was now nearly on me. He held the weapon high in his hand at full arms reach. His body was too far away to strike, but I judged that I might just be able to swing my sword down on the weapon to deflect the shot. Sometimes you just act on instinct; my sword arm swung down with all my strength. But as the blade started to swish through the air I had the awful realisation that it would not meet the weapon in time. I saw his knuckle whiten around the trigger and expected the spring loaded flint to crash into the frizzen on the gun creating the spark that would fire a leaden ball of death into my exposed side.

In the heat of battle with so much going on around you, things sometimes seem to happen in slow motion. As I watched that gun fire it seemed to take a lifetime, but then I realised it actually was firing in slow motion. Instead of the spring loaded flint I saw a clamp holding a piece of glowing slow match moving towards the frizzen. It was one of the old wheel lock weapons, probably from early in the last century. It gave me the fraction of a second I needed. The razor sharp blue Damascus steel flashed in the sunlight until there was an explosion of red as it bit into the man's wrist. I felt the steel jar on bone but the blade kept moving down and suddenly the hand still clutching the pistol was falling to the ground and the man was shrieking as he pulled back, looking at the newly made stump on the end of his limb. Now I could get through and I spurred the horse forward again, but instead of going straight, inexplicably the animal turned into the melee around Chapman. There were still three well-armed men around him and with those odds he was a goner, but if my horse would go straight I could still get clear.

I reached down to grab the reins to pull my horse to the right but the reins were already being stretched to the left. A glance showed that they had become entangled in the tree branches and were pulling the horse in that direction. Frantically I wrenched them free but now my mount had barged into one of the men attacking Chapman, nearly knocking him off his feet. The man turned and glared at me and started to swing round a viciously bladed axe. I stabbed down again with the sword and this time the thin blade went deep into his side, sliding between his ribs to prompt another scream of pain. The man spasmed in agony but my sword was wedged in his ribs and I could not get it back. As he fell the weapon was wrenched from my hand. Then Chapman's horse swung around as the trooper killed the man holding the blanket over its head.

There was just one man left on his feet, but as the blanket slipped from Chapman's mount the animal skittered away as it regained its bearings. The sole surviving attacker whirled around holding a long bladed weapon on a pole. He glared briefly at both of us and then over the tree to where his comrades were still running down the track towards us. They were only twenty yards off now and their approach seemed to give the man courage. He stepped forward to block my escape, holding his weapon high. Chapman was turning his horse and trying to pull the carbine out of its holster in his saddle but there was no more time. My hand was already dropping to my right coat pocket and closing around the familiar pistol butt. Having no time to draw the weapon and risk it snagging, I thumbed back the hammer and fired it from inside the pocket. I was already spurring my horse forward as the man's surprised face looked down at the spreading scarlet stain on his greasy shirt front. Another musket ball smacked into the fallen tree a yard off and the leading men were now nearly at its branches behind us.

'Come on Chapman,' I shouted as I dug in my heels again to make my escape.

We had only galloped another fifty yards to the bend in the track when we met the twenty-nine remaining dragoons and Downie coming the other way. They were in two columns that charged past on either side of us with Downie at the front waving his sword and shouting the hunting cry of 'view halloo' when he spotted the men running down the track after us. Caught in the open, the devils stood no chance and turned to run. Sabres were soon rising and falling with ruthless efficiency. Then as the quickest men tried to reach the safety of the rocks, the dragoons' carbines were firing at a range where even their doubtful accuracy was effective.

Chapman and I turned our horses about and slowly returned the scene of the attack, with me beating out a small fire in my coat pocket on the way. I was very happy for them to finish off the rest without us and the action was all over by the time we were back at the tree. There were a dozen dead or dying on the track in front of the tree now and a similar number on the lower rocks, although screams, shouts and small rock falls indicated that some had made their way further up the hillside to relative safety. The dragoons had taken no casualties and were searching the bodies, but judging from their looks of disgust, finding little of value. Downie was questioning the man I had left with one hand but after a moment he came over.

'We heard a crackle of gunfire and thought you might be in trouble,' he explained, looking very pleased with himself as he wiped his sword blade on a rag. 'They thought you two were alone, they were not expecting us.'

I knew I would be shaking when the shock of the encounter set in but for the moment I managed a surprised grin. 'In trouble?' I queried. 'We were nothing of the sort, were we Chapman? We had just fought our way clear.'

'I would 'ave been a dead man if you 'ad not turned back to 'elp me sir. The cap'n could 'ave got clear away sir,' Chapman explained to Downie, and I thanked my stars that Chapman had not seen me tugging frantically on the reins to do precisely that. 'Instead sir,' continued the hapless Chapman, 'e turned around and charged into the men around me, killing two more of 'em. He killed four of 'em in all, I only got one. Proper killing gennelman 'e is,' he added, with a touch of pride that I was among their number.

I knew an offhand remark would best maintain my reputation as the modest hero, so I grinned and added, 'I would have left you Chapman but I could not remember if you had returned my telescope.' They all laughed at that before Sergeant Butterworth walked over to us holding my sword wiped clean of blood and another antique musket. He held the sword up to me smiling. 'Thought you might want this back sir, it took a good tug to get it out of that pikesman.' He turned to Downie and held up the musket for him, 'Would you look at this sir, it must be all of two hundred years old, plenty of weapons here if you want to start that regiment,' he grinned.

'Yes,' said Downie. 'I was just questioning that man with one hand. He is their leader and admitted that they are bandits and were attacking you for your horses, valuables and weapons as they are in desperate need of all three.' He looked around sadly, 'I suppose we will have to retrace our steps and find another valley if this one is full of thieves.'

'Why can't we go up this one sir? We know where the bandits are now,' said Chapman, gesturing up the hill. 'They won't be bothering us again for a bit.'

'There might be another gang further up the valley.'

'Nah,' grunted Chapman dismissively. 'In London you never get two gangs working the same street, they rob each other's trade.' He looked at us as though he found our ignorance of the workings of street gangs quite astonishing. 'They would either fight each other to own the street or join forces to take on bigger marks or gangs.'

'So you don't think there will be any more along the valley,' mused Downie. He was clearly wondering if he could trust London street lore to apply in a Spanish valley.

'Not a chance,' said Chapman confidently. 'That gang was large for a piss poor place like this so I reckon the bandits in this valley joined together and we just beat 'em.' It turned out he was right. We rode down that valley without any further trouble. We did spot what was presumably the bandit's encampment half a mile down the track, with some children and an old man watching us warily, but we did not see anyone else. At the end, the countryside opened out again into rolling hills, and I felt much safer as any gang of bandits would now see that we were thirty well-armed soldiers and steer clear. But the priest was wrong; it took us another ten days to reach Alcantara.

Chapter 7

We had already established that Downie could not navigate his way out of a grain sack, but now that the chance of ambush had diminished, I was in no rush. As soon as we found the Spanish I would have to head north and if Wellesley had been beaten I had no wish to meet the French coming the other way. With luck, I thought, when we finally found Alcantara there would be a few sleeping dagoes under a tree with all the news. If Wellesley had won, and I'll admit I thought that was long odds at the time, then I would head north in safety. If he had lost then we would head south to Seville and the coast beyond, for Soult was likely to follow up a victory with an attack on Lisbon.

So we meandered about the countryside for days. Heading probably south when it was cloudy, based on Downie's misguided moss principle, and north east when we could see the sun, as even that great booby could use the celestial orb as a guide. I normally had a better idea where we were as I would ask any locals I met when riding ahead as scout, but I only passed the news on to our gallant leader when it suited me. I knew we were getting close when very early one morning we passed an old woman with a scrawny donkey loaded with a bundle of firewood. She was hunched under a load of her own and dressed in black with a matching moustache that would be the pride of any hussar. On enquiry she told us that Alcantara lay just over the hill in front of us. Thinking that we had delayed enough, I passed the news on to Downie. A short while later I realised that we had arrived at exactly the wrong time.

The shooting started when we were halfway up the hill; it was around nine o'clock in the morning. To start with there was the low rumble of cannon, lots of cannon. Then as we neared the top there was a steady crackle of musketry. It sounded as though we had happened across a full pitched battle and Downie was in a fever to get over the summit and join in. We imagined Cuesta and his entire Spanish army locked against a French force. Given the Spaniard's recent performance against the French I was keen to ensure that my horse was not completely blown when we got to the top. There was every chance a fast escape might be required. But what we saw when we crested the ridge stopped us in our tracks. It was an astonishing sight and what followed over the next twenty-four hours was one of the most extraordinary episodes in military warfare. Although for reasons that will become clear, it is rarely mentioned in the history books.

The first thing we saw was the French, and by God there were enough of them. The far side of the valley across the river was covered in blue coated troops. There were thousands and thousands of infantry. Some were in the town of Alcantara, which was on their side of the river, and lining the river bank, but more regiments were still marching towards us from the hills beyond. There were squadrons of cavalry too, wheeling around the town while the boom of guns and plumes of smoke told me that there were at least two batteries of cannon firing from the other side in our direction, twelve pounders I judged, from the noise of their discharge.

Between us and the French lay the river Tagus at the bottom of the valley, fast flowing and deep at this time of the year. This was crossed by a stone bridge directly below us that had a triumphal arch over the roadway in the middle of it. Then there was a sight that got my guts churning and had me looking over my shoulder to see the best route back the way we had come. The smooth hillside we could see facing this massive French advance was completely empty. Not a single Spanish regiment was arrayed on it, no guns were firing and not a horseman was in sight.

'Christ on a stick,' I shouted to Downie, 'they will be over that bridge in no time and with Wellesley up north there will be nothing to stop this lot reaching Lisbon.'

'They must be shooting at someone,' argued Downie. Then he pointed, 'Look there are some people on that bluff.' He pointed to our left where there was a slight prominence overlooking the valley. Men could be seen moving amongst the broken rock that covered the ground. Before I could reply there was the blaring of trumpets as the French launched an attack across the bridge.

From our vantage point high above the battle we watched in fascinated horror as a narrow blue column of men marched from the edge of the town towards the bridge. It must have contained at least a thousand soldiers as it moved forward like a short blue snake across the valley floor. The French guns seemed to go quiet and for the first time I heard the sound that would fill me with fear countless times in the future. The column did not move silently, there was the awful tramp, tramp, tramp sound of two thousand feet, which almost drowned out the beat of the drummer boys. Then on a double beat signal from the drummers a thousand voices would bellow out 'vive l'empereur'. Even from half a mile away it was enough to send a

61

shiver down your spine, especially when there seemed to be damn all between you and this massive enemy force.

But then there was a series of four sharp cracks from the bluff to our left, and plumes of smoke. It was the sound of cannon of smaller calibre than the French were using, six pounders I guessed. My time sailing with Cochrane had taught me to distinguish between the sounds of cannon fire – the bigger the gun the deeper boom it made. But there were only four guns fired from our side and if they hit the French column they made no discernable impact.

'When they get across,' I called, reaching for the telescope in my saddlebag, 'we had better get out of here.'

'Yes,' said Downie. 'We should ride north to warn Wellesley that this force is behind him. This army and Soult's could crush Wellesley like a nut.'

I could not have agreed more. In fact I suspected that Wellesley's nut might already have been crushed by the more experienced Soult without this lot to help. But I had no wish to get caught up in the wreckage, which is why I suggested, 'That is a good idea, but we also need to warn the Spanish. I have a message from Wellesley to Cuesta, so if you ride north, I will take a few of the men as escort and ride south to Seville.'

We were just agreeing on how we would divide the escort as the French marched onto the far side of the bridge. There had been no more firing from our side and now I had my glass focused on the bridge. The front rank of the French column reached the archway in the centre of the bridge. There for the first time I saw some disorder in the ranks as the width of the arch was narrower than the bridge and the column. As they squeezed though the archway their lines became ragged and uneven but still they came on. I caught the glint of gold in the archway, the imperial eagle standard of the regiment.

Then the guns to our left cracked again and this time there was also the whoomp sound from two howitzers. I saw at least one of the cannonballs slash its way through the packed men and then one of the howitzer shells landed amongst them on this side of the arch. I could not see the shell itself from that distance but I saw men suddenly trying to get away from something in their midst. They were too tightly packed for those closest to escape and when the thing went off it flattened a whole group as though they had been swatted by a giant invisible hand. But the blue coated ranks at the front of the column marched on and behind them the now disordered men followed. Just as they came off the end of the bridge and left the protection of the parapet there was furious crackle of musketry.

Only now did we see infantry on our side of the river. There did not seem many of them and they were not standing in ranks. Instead they were dug well in amongst the stone and rock on the western bank. They had been hard to spot amongst the ground cover which was why we had not seen them before. But now the puffs of smoke from their firing gave away their positions, and not just to us.

The French cannon now opened up again, a dozen heavy iron balls smashed into the ground at our end of the bridge. I saw one demolish a hastily built loose stone wall and, judging from the screams, it destroyed some men standing behind it. Another ball hit an angled face of rock with such force we heard the crack and saw the ball ricochet fifty feet into the air. I looked back at the French. Their front ranks had been destroyed by the early firing and a pile of dead and dying lay across the end of the roadway where the parapet stopped. More French were trying to climb over their comrades to continue the attack but despite the best efforts of the French cannon, a steady fire was continuing from the men on our side of the river. The moment a blue coated soldier reached the end of the bridge he was met by a hail of bullets and none were getting away.

I realised now that there were more soldiers on our side of the bridge than I had first guessed. Not nearly as many as the French army but there could be up to a thousand, I thought, as I watched men furiously reloading muskets and passing them up to those with a better vantage point to shoot.

'Who are they?' asked Downie impatiently.

'Some seem to be riflemen as they have green jackets. Wait though, no, they are firing muskets too.' I paused trying to make out a common thread in the uniform of the bulk of the men by the river. The green jacketed troops made up no more than a third of the number, the rest were dressed in a myriad of uniforms or seemed to have no uniform at all. There were some with green uniform coats and red facings of the Spanish army, others in uniform coats that must once have been white, and yet more in brown homespun coats. 'They must be some kind of militia,' I concluded.

Whoever they were they were making tidy work of the French who seemed unable to get past the bottle neck at the end of the parapet. Some tried to drop over the side but either there was a steep drop or the Spanish had men hiding under the bridge, for none appeared on the shore afterwards. The bridge itself was now a tightly packed mass of men. The cannon on our side fired again and both and the howitzers managed to get their shells amongst the men on the bridge. This time the French were too wedged in to move and when the howitzer bombs exploded there must have been terrible carnage. Seeing that they were unable to go forward and were sitting ducks for the guns on our side, the troops on the bridge now started to edge back the way they had come. Those at the front of the column however gave one final effort and with a cry of 'vive l'empereur' they threw themselves forward once more. The French artillery that had managed to reload in time supported them and more balls crashed into the river bank. But it was not enough; a fusillade of musket fire threw the blue coated soldiers back. Now with room to retreat behind them, there was a general movement of the French back the way they had come.

'Well that was right handy work,' exclaimed Sergeant Butterworth riding up alongside us. 'The frogs have lost a fair few men there, sir,' he pointed down at the bridge. Sure enough as the French pulled back, helping some of their wounded along as they went, they left piles of men behind. You could see where the howitzer shells had landed by the clumps of corpses and badly injured lying together. But at the end of the bridge there was a mound blocking solidly the space between the parapet ends, which must have comprised at least a hundred bodies.

'Horseman coming, sir,' called one of the troopers from behind, and looking round we saw a knot of half a dozen men riding towards us from the bluff that held the artillery battery. Two wore the green uniforms I had initially confused for riflemen and the other four wore Spanish cavalry uniforms. Downie and I rode to meet them, leaving the other troopers on the crest of the hill watching the French complete their withdrawal.

'Our compliments sir, Captains Downie and Flashman of General Wellesley's staff,' called out Downie in Spanish by way of introduction to one of the green coated men, who wore the uniform markings of a colonel. 'That was smartly done, sir,' he added, gesturing down the hill.

'I am Colonel Mayne,' the man replied in English with a slight Yorkshire accent. 'Your presence may have helped, gentlemen, as doubtless Victor saw a group of redcoats arrive at the crest of the hill and wondered if reinforcements were on hand. I pray to God that you will tell me his suspicions are confirmed, for we are in a desperate situation here.'

'We have come here looking for General Cuesta,' explained Downie. 'Wellesley has gone north to attack Oporto and he thought that Cuesta would be here to guard the crossing.'

'Aye, so he would if he had a wit of common sense.' growled Mayne. 'So are there no other British forces nearby?' he asked, with a lingering note of hope.

'I'm sorry sir, it is just us with thirty dragoons,' replied Downie.

'Did you say that was Marshal Victor's army down there?' I asked, with growing apprehension. This was the commander who had already thrashed Cuesta at Medallin and who had destroyed the army of Galicia the previous year.

'Aye,' grunted Mayne with a dour sniff. 'Judging from the glitter of gold braid I saw through the glass earlier, I think he is up in the church tower this very moment planning what to do next.'

'But sir,' exclaimed Downie, 'Surely General Cuesta is sending you reinforcements, if he knows Victor is here?'

'Cuesta knows Victor is here all right,' said Mayne, with a look of disgust now on his face. 'Have we not been tracking him this week past and sending the good general daily messages of warning as Victor got closer to the bridge there?' He gestured at the horsemen around him. 'Cuesta has sent me fifty cavalry and claims he can spare no more. They are brave men, but precious little use on horseback in defending a bridge. Quite who Cuesta needs his men to defend against I'm not sure.' He looked at our men back on the crest. 'If you are to help us then I need you to leave your horses behind and man the line opposite the bridge. You will have seen we need every man we can get down there.'

I would have told him to go to the devil, for anyone could see that sooner or later the French artillery would pound that thin line of defenders into submission, and then their infantry and cavalry would storm across and slaughter the fleeing survivors. But that stupid ass Downie got in first, piping up like the head boy on school trophy day. 'Oh yes sir,' he gushed, 'we would be happy to help. We have our orders but clearly stopping Victor getting through must take priority.'

'Wait a minute,' I exclaimed, as this was getting out of hand. 'With respect sir, surely you don't expect to hold the French off indefinitely? If they don't pound you into submission now they will come across at nightfall or try to outflank you. May I ask how many men do you have down there?'

'We have around eighteen hundred,' Mayne replied. 'Twelve hundred of those are from the Portuguese Idanhia Nova militia regiment. Not all of those soldiers had muskets but I see that situation is being addressed now.' We looked down and the haphazardly dressed soldiery were picking over the dead at the end of the bridge, looting the bodies and helping themselves to muskets, cartridge boxes and other equipment. We were close enough to see the flash of a knife that one of the militia used on a wounded Frenchman, who had presumably objected to being robbed. 'The other men, dressed in green, are from my regiment, the Loyal Lusitanian Legion.'

I looked up at that. 'Is Sir Robert here then?' I asked.

'Major General Wilson,' Mayne corrected me, 'is away at the moment, but messages have been sent to him and he will bring whatever force he can as soon as soon as possible.' Mayne looked at me curiously for a moment and then added, 'Are you acquainted with the Major General?'

'Yes sir, I had the honour to serve with him in Russia a couple of years ago. But unless he arrives in the next hour or two with several thousand men and more artillery,' and here I gestured at the empty countryside we had just travelled through, 'I still don't see how you can hold that bridge for more than a few hours. They have thousands of men over there.'

'Aye,' said Mayne grimly, 'ten thousand infantry, fifteen hundred cavalry and twelve cannon to be precise. But you are right, it is a desperate situation, which is why if the worst happens we have placed a mine under the bridge to blow it up.'

Even Downie now seemed to realise how precarious things were. 'But sir,' he replied, 'they could attack Lisbon or Wellesley's flank if they get through. Surely the safest course is to blow the mine now as no help seems likely?'

Mayne took a deep breath while staring at the bridge; he had clearly been pondering this dilemma for a while. 'You may be right,' he conceded at last. 'But that bridge was built in the reign of the Roman emperor Trajan, it is nearly two thousand years old. It is the only bridge across the Tagus in the area. When Wellesley comes he will need it to advance into Spain. I want to preserve it if we can.' Well, I thought, this was madness of the first order. After all an appreciation of history has its place, but that place is in a museum or gallery. When preserving some old Roman bridge starts to put me in the path of thousands of murderous Frenchmen things are going too far. I realised that I would have to gammon the old fool into blowing that mine or Downie would have us manning the breach in some desperate last stand.

'Sir, I know that in Almeida you deceived the French into thinking you had ten times your number,' I said to Mayne. 'But that was in a fortress with walls unknown men could hide behind. Here there are no walls – they can see exactly how many men you have.'

For a moment Mayne did not respond. He stared over my shoulder to where Butterworth and the other troopers were letting their horses graze on the sparse grass. Then a slow grin spread over his face and he looked at me. 'Really, Captain Flashman, after what I have heard about Sir Robert's Russian adventures I would have expected you to show more ingenuity.' With that he reached into his pocket, pulled out his telescope and started to scan the route we had come from.

'What are you doing sir?' I asked him, puzzled.

'I am watching Wellesley's army march towards us! We are standing on our wall young man, standing on it right now,' he repeated.

Downie and I looked at each other dumbfounded. Was the old bastard mad, I wondered? We looked in the direction he had pointed his telescope and of course there was no one there; Wellesley's army should now be a hundred and fifty miles away in Oporto. 'I'm sorry sir, I don't understand,' admitted Downie.

Mayne looked at us and grinned again before resuming his inspection of the phantom army. 'You gave me the idea. When considering your strategy you must always put yourself in the enemy's shoes,' he said. 'They know Wellesley has landed, that is why Victor is here. They have assumed he will take on Soult first so Victor is advancing to take the British army in the flank and capture Lisbon. But what if Wellesley has humbugged them and is coming after Victor first. The last thing Victor wants is his army divided by a river with a narrow bridge if Wellesley and his larger army come over this hill. He would not want his men on this side of the river at all with Wellesley in the area – he would want them on the other side. He could then sit back and watch the redcoats try and cross the bridge, and slaughter us as we have them in their attacks.'

Wellesley arrived in Alcantara half an hour later. Through their telescopes the French saw a man wearing a plain blue coat and black bicorn hat arrive on the ridge top, accompanied by several British staff officers. Wellesley was seen to stare at the French positions through his telescope, including the group of French officers in the church tower that were returning his inspection. He then pointed out various positions to his staff officers on a map he pulled from his saddlebag. Colonel Mayne was seen rushing to meet the general, saluting and pointing out his own defences. Most ominously from the French perspective, the front of a column of British infantry could be seen as it marched up to the ridge crest. Wellesley noticed and ordered them back down the far side of the hill out of sight. He could be seen gesticulating to other hidden men to stay back and then he sent the staff officers riding in both directions along the ridge crest to ensure that the British soldiers stayed on the other side of the ridge, out of sight and out of reach of enemy cannon.

Even if I say so myself, it was a fine performance, for it was me in that plain blue coat and bicorn hat. I have acted a few parts in my time but rarely one with so much at stake. I don't know where they found the blue coat, but the bicorn hat was from the Spanish cavalry officer. It had been adorned with gold braid but that was stripped off to form epaulets for my new staff officers, troopers Chapman and Doherty. The infantry column was made up from Sergeant Butterworth and the rest of the troop, without their horses and with their sword belts and helmets, replaced by infantry packs, muskets and shakoes lent by soldiers of the Loyal Lusitanian Legion. Downie, as their officer, rode at their head. Even close to they looked quite convincing, and from a quarter of a mile away I was sure that those watching from the church tower would not spot anything wrong.

It was strange looking through my telescope at the tower and the gold braided figures inside it. Victor must have known about the Legion's deception at Almeida. You could almost sense him wondering if we were bluffing and whether he dared to call that bluff. Mayne invited General Wellesley to join him in his headquarters by the Legion's cannon, so I allowed myself to be led in that direction. Once out of sight of the enemy I slumped in relief, but the deception seemed to have worked. The enemy guns had not fired for nearly an hour now and looking down, their infantry did not seem to be preparing another attack. We celebrated our success with a glass of brandy. While Mayne claimed that he had always known the plan would work, I noticed that his hand shook slightly as he poured the strong spirit. It was rough local firewater that made you gasp. As it was burning my throat Mayne talked about what he thought would happen next.

'Victor thinks he has seen the British advance guard and will assume that the British army is strung out on the road behind. It would be reasonable to expect it to take the rest of the day for the army to gather on the reverse slope. But tomorrow they will expect an attack and if one does not come they will get suspicious again. We have bought ourselves a day, two at most. He may well be sending scouts along the river looking for another bridge or a boat to see precisely what is on our side of the hill. When he does realise he has been tricked we will hold out for as long as we can. If we have to, we will blow the mine. Then we will retreat six miles down the road to hold another bridge at a place called Seguro and try and hold him up for a day or two there. Sooner or later Wellesley will come and we will not be bluffing, but we need to buy him all the time we can.' He looked at Downey and added, 'In the meantime I would be grateful if you would take your dragoons dismounted down to the riverbank. The presence of your red jackets will give the militia confidence.'

Downey of course agreed and even I thought it would be reasonably safe for the rest of the day. Not a shot was being fired now by either side. An unofficial truce had come into effect between the two armies. The French looked as if they had swallowed the deception or were not prepared to risk challenging it for the time being. Certainly it would take someone on a fast horse and a boat at least a day to get on our side of the river to see what was behind that hill. I was back in my red coat and it would have been bad form to run out on them immediately. I thought I would stay for the rest of the day and then in the evening I would insist on taking my message on to Cuesta. In hindsight it was a huge mistake.

Chapter 8

As we walked down the little valley beside the bluff towards the river I began to feel a strange sense of foreboding. I tried to dismiss it as we turned along the bank towards the bridge; I put it down to the hundreds of enemy troops who stared curiously at us as we approached. At the river we could see how tall the bridge was. It had to be, for the river was a fast flowing torrent fifty feet below us in a ravine with steep rocky banks. You could not see the surface of the water unless you leaned right over the edge of the bank. The first two arches of the bridge on either side were over this sharply sloping land, only the central two spans were over the water. The arches were huge; it was a tall and graceful structure and astonishing engineering for its time.

The troopers were back with their original weaponry of their carbines and sabres but Downie and I just had our pistols and swords. When we reached the bridge I saw that the green jacketed troops were sorting the French bodies. The dead were being piled into a rampart across the end of the parapet while those still living were being deposited on the bridge itself. French soldiers under a flag of truce were carrying them away. The militia were all grinning at us and some were even cheering and shouting 'Ingles'. It may not have been just the enemy we had fooled about the presence of a large British force. It all added to the deception, I thought, and we were just introducing ourselves to the English commander of the green jacketed troops, Captain Charles, when all hell broke loose.

To this day I am not sure what gave us away. Perhaps Victor had an exceptionally good telescope that showed him that a British officer's features were identical to those of Wellesley. More likely he realised that dismounted dragoons were not the obvious reinforcements for the men guarding the bridge if there were regiments of infantry just over the hill. Whatever the reason, he suddenly decided that we were bluffing.

Our first warning was shouting from the other side of the river. The French soldiers helping the wounded on the bridge abandoned their charges and went sprinting back to their side. Captain da Silva, who seemed to be the commander of the nearby militia, was yelling at his men to take cover when there was a rumble of cannon fire. Cannon balls crashed into the hillside, smashing rocks into lethal stone splinters. Men ran for cover as the French infantry on the far side of the river – around a hundred and fifty yards away – let fly, creating a deadly hail storm of musket shot. Muskets were not accurate at that range but they did not have to be when you had a thousand men on either side of the bridge blazing away and flailing our bank with lead. Your correspondent did not hesitate to run a few yards up the slope and hurl himself behind the biggest rock he could see. Unfortunately two militia men were already there, but even in those circumstances rank has its privileges and they grudgingly made room for me between them.

We clung together to keep our bodies behind the stone. It was big enough to stop musket shot and we heard several balls whine away off it, but if hit plumb centre by a cannon ball it would have smashed and take us with it. We lay there for what seemed an age, with the Portuguese muttering prayers for their deliverance and me issuing rather more Anglo Saxon oaths about the French bastards on the other side of the river and the moronic Downie that had got me into this mess.

After a while the musket fire slowed to a steady crackle as the number of potential targets had diminished. I put my head up to see what was happening. A score of bodies were scattered on our side of the river, including a dead dragoon. Many more were wounded though and they were screaming for help. Men ran from cover to drag comrades to shelter and Captain da Silva was yelling for his men to take cover near the end of the bridge to meet the next expected assault. My new militia friends reluctantly obeyed, darting across the hillside, keeping their heads down. This left the rock just for me, and as another cannon ball smashed into the packed trenches of men at the end of the bridge I saw no reason to leave its relatively safe shelter.

From my higher vantage point I could see another French column massing for an attack across the bridge. The French cannon were all aiming for the trenches now and survival in them became a random affair. Cannon balls were smashing through walls and bouncing off rocks, and combined with the constant fire of musketry from the far bank. Now, though, the cannon on the bluff behind us were cracking out. I saw the effect of two of their balls ploughing furrows through the massing blue coated troops at the far end of the bridge. But they just closed ranks again and inevitably the dreadful drum beat started as the vast mass started towards us.

'Vive l'empereur,' a thousand voices roared in unison as prompted by a flourish of the drummer, accompanied by the tramp of a thousand boots on stone. It might not sound much on paper but when you are

71

waiting at the sharp end of a French column it is a terrifying prospect, which is why many of their opponents have fled the field at the sight of them. Certainly some of the militia now started to edge back; they had already beaten one column but there seemed no end to them, and the awful cannon fire that preceded their attacks. Two of the militia threw down their guns and started to run back up the valley path.

'Stop,' roared da Silva, 'you are honourable men, do not abandon your comrades.' To my astonishment they did stop, and after a glance between them they turned and started to walk sheepishly back down the path. Da Silva must have known how shaky the morale of his men was for he stepped out of his trench and stood in front of a waist high rock just a few yards away from mine to address his soldiers. 'You have already beaten one of their columns,' he shouted. 'You know you can beat another. Do you want to go back to your houses like whipped dogs with the French taking what they want from you? Or do you want to show them...' At that point his words were lost in another salvo of French cannon fire. One ball whistled over my head, smacking into the hillside just behind and causing a rock fall that cascaded around me, but I barely noticed it. My attention had been fully taken by the effect of another French cannon ball.

By an awful chance the ball had bounced and taken da Silva in the chest. With his lower half against the rock behind, it had literally cut him in half. His chest and head disappeared in a gout of blood and guts across the hill side, but for a few seconds his bottom half remained standing against the rock. Like me, most of his men stared transfixed by the awful sight. Grotesquely his legs now started to twitch and move of their own accord before sliding down the surface of the rock.

There must have been other shooting going on at the time but I do not remember it, I was just transfixed by that ghastly horror. As the legs finally fell onto the ground the spell seemed broken, not just for me, but for the rest of the militia. We will never know what da Silva was going to say, but his death had the opposite effect of what he wanted to achieve. The two would-be deserters now turned again and started sprinting away up the path, but this time they were joined by the rest of the regiment.

In a moment a thousand men were charging past me down the path away from the bridge, with a handful of the green jacketed troops mixed amongst them. Headlong flight was certainly the order of the day for Flashy now, but as I turned to join them I realised with horror that the last rock fall had trapped my foot. I desperately tried to wrench it free but it was stuck solid.

I needed help and I tried to grab at some of the men rushing past roaring, 'Help me you bastards, I'm trapped,' but they just shook me off with wild panic in their eyes. 'Come back you bloody cowards,' I yelled at their retreating backs. I could not believe it; the yellow livered swine were absolutely leaving me to my fate. Not that I blame them now you understand, why I have done the same a score of times and I would not be here writing these memoirs if I hadn't. But when you are the poor devil being abandoned, well it puts a different perspective on things. In a moment and a cloud of dust they were all past me while I was sitting on the ground with both hands desperately clawing at the slab of rock that held me fast.

Not everybody had deserted me though; looking up I saw that the vast majority of the Legion had stood firm, as had the dragoons. Captain Charles of the Legion was ordering his men to the barricade of bodies at the end of the parapet. I yelled at Downie and some of the dragoons to help me, but they could not hear over the increased fusillade of musket fire as the French shot at the retreating militia.

Oh dear God, I thought, I cannot die here, not like this after all I have been through. For I could see as plain as day what would happen. There were at least a thousand men in that column now marching across the bridge and no more than four hundred now crouched at the barricade. They would be beaten and the survivors would run away like the militia, leaving Flashy trapped and helpless to face the vengeful fury of French soldiers who had lost comrades in the attack.

'Help me,' I roared again. 'Light the mine,' I added as an afterthought, but both calls were drowned out by the double whoomp of the howitzers from the bluff behind.

There is a split second between a howitzer being fired and the shells exploding where you find yourself holding your breath. At least I did then, for never had shells been more important and I think that day, never were they more perfectly aimed. For both landed amongst the crowded mass of men marching towards us. From the hill during the first attack I had heard the screams, but now I was close enough to hear the pitiable calls for help from the wounded. I also heard the roars of rage from the survivors who knew that they would be up against the barricade before the guns could fire again. It seemed to give them extra vigour. If there was an order I did not hear it, but instinctively the French broke into a charge. Yelling and screaming with bayonets to the fore the whole column broke into a run. That's it, I thought, we are done for now.

In their looser formation the French came though the archway at the halfway point on the bridge without breaking stride, and were three-quarters of the way across the bridge when the green coated soldiers opened fire. They had organised themselves into eight ranks of roughly fifty men that stood in a short column at our end of the bridge. Many were protected from the enemy infantry on the far shore by the bridge parapet, and the enemy cannon had ceased firing to avoid hitting their own soldiers. The front rank took aim at no more than a hundred yards and fired. Many of the leading French running troops fell, but before those behind could recover the Lusitanian front rank dropped to their knees and the second rank fired, and then the third and so on. I watched in astonishment as over the next minute eight volleys were fired down the bridge, and against such a tightly packed mass of men they could not miss.

The musket smoke was such that after the first few volleys they were firing blind but from my position, slightly to one side, I could see that our side of the bridge was covered with blue coated dead and wounded. Occasionally a French soldier would charge through several volleys, but then there would be the crack of a carbine as he got close and I saw that the dragoons were stationed on their knees at the front to deal with anyone who got too close with their short range weapons.

With eight volleys fired the Lusitanians now stood to reload. It would have been the ideal time for the French to resume their charge, but they could not see the opportunity through the smoke. Instead a French officer now started to organise the troops into ranks to fire volleys in return. With green jacketed soldiers now standing they made a bigger target and I saw some fall. But just after the French had fired their first volley the howitzers fired again and once more the French troops started to edge back.

It was the finest piece of organisation and volley fire that I had seen, helped a great deal by the fact that the French could not outflank them and were trapped on the narrow strip of the bridge. Through the clearing smoke the Lusitanians saw the French helping their wounded back the way they had come. Grins spread over their powder stained faces and they shouted and cheered their delight.

'Will one of you blighters come over here and get me free,' I yelled as the noise subsided.

'I say Flash,' called Downie, looking up from the rampart. 'I wondered where you had gone.' He paused before adding hastily, 'Obviously I did not think you had run,' while blushing red to prove that was exactly what he had thought.

It took four of the Lusitanians using their muskets as levers to move the rock, but mercifully my ankle was not even sprained. At last mobile again I ran over to where Downie and Captain Charles of the Lusitanians were talking at the end of the bridge. Before I could even say a word there was the roar of cannon from the opposite bank and the renewed crackle of musket fire. We dropped down to our knees to get the cover of the bridge parapet.

'They can see how few we are now,' shouted Charles above the din. 'They are going to pound us until we are too few to defend the bridge or run away like the militia.' He was right. Already two balls had slashed bloody trails through the tightly packed ranks of Lusitanians who were now falling back to the dubious shelter of the shallow trenches.

'Where is the mine?' I shouted, thinking that there had only ever been one way out of this.

'It is under the first arch, but we have to await orders before we can fire it.'

'I have orders,' I replied, while patting my pocket to check that my tinder box was still there, and then I slipped around the end of the parapet and started to slide down the slope.

'Captain Flashman, come back,' called Charles behind me but I ignored him. I knew that if I didn't blow that bridge then we would be pounded to mincemeat, and right now the only totally safe place from the French bombardment was under the bridge itself. But no sooner had I started to slide down the steep hillside than there was a renewed crackle of musketry from the far bank. Looking up I noticed too late that Victor had posted a company of infantry on the very edge of the far bank, obviously with orders to stop anyone trying to blow a mine under the bridge. The wily fox must have guessed that there would be one. If they had used rifles I would have been dead, but even at the one hundred yard distance that it must have been, muskets were not accurate against just one man. Balls smacked into the rocks all around me but it would have taken longer to go back up, so I continued to slide down the hillside until I was level with the first arch. There I saw that Marshal Victor had another surprise planned.

75

The floor under the arch was covered with fuses, either cut or yanked out of the four large barrels of gunpowder that were placed against one of the walls. Of more concern however was the huge soaking wet Frenchman who was straining to push one of the barrels over the far edge of the arch. He must have been well over six foot, a grenadier company man from the look of him and judging from the way he was moving the barrel, hugely powerful. He must also have been a good swimmer to get across the river in the strong current and climb up the ravine.

His only weapon seemed to be a large knife which was resting on the top of a barrel, and I am proud to say I did not hesitate when considering my course of action. If this was a romantic novel I would have called to my gallant foe to give him a chance to defend himself, but that ain't the Flashy way, especially when the cove looked as if he could beat me to a pulp. As I ran through the arch the noise of the surrounding battle covered any sound I made. In any event the great brute was too busy pushing and straining to get his barrel over the edge. He succeeded just as I reached him. As he peered over the edge to see the result of his handiwork, I shoulder charged him in the back to tip him over the edge as well. His flailing arms almost got a grip on my jacket to drag me over too, but I wrenched myself free and with a scream he toppled over the edge. I watched him fall and with a sickening thud he hit a rock head first and then somersaulted a couple of times before splashing into the river. A flurry of musket fire from the opposite bank told me that a company of infantry were defending the arches on both sides of the bridge, but I had just enough time to check that there were no more swimming grenadiers before I ducked my head back into the relative safety of the arch.

Looking around I saw that originally a bundle of fuses had led from the arch up to the roadway so that the mine could have been fired from above. That, however, had been cut by the grenadier. The surviving combined fuse was now much shorter and then it split into four separate strands. It was a matter of moments to push these individual fuses back into the barrels so that they were embedded in the black powder. I just hoped that the remaining three large barrels would be enough to blow the bridge.

The battle was still raging above me with the enemy cannon thundering away. I could hear screams of men as the cannon balls hit home. If I could just blow the bridge then neither side would have a reason to be here, and both could withdraw. Lisbon and Wellesley's flank would be protected and more importantly I would not be killed by vengeful French infantrymen when they inevitably stormed across. I opened my tinder box and struck the steel. The tinder caught first time and with some gentle blowing I soon had a flame. I took a deep breath and yelled, 'I am firing the mine,' but with the noise of battle I doubt anyone heard me. I was not concerned as I would warn anyone still near the end of the bridge when I climbed back up. I touched the flame to the end of the combined fuse and it took with a roar.

There are times in my life when I really should have thought things through a bit more before I took action. Lighting that mine was one of those occasions. To be sure fuses burn at varying speeds, and if that had been a slow burning fuse my plan would have worked brilliantly. It wasn't. The flame took off down its track like a scalded whippet. I stared at it transfixed in horror for a moment as the implications sank in. I would not have time to climb back up the hill and get clear before it blew. To pull the fuses back out of the barrels would leave me back in the soup. I could not stay in the arch and that left only one option – sliding down into the river. A sudden burst of flame from the fuse as it separated to go to the individual barrels seemed to break the spell and spur me into action. There was no time to worry about the company of infantry on the opposite shore, I had to take my chances and get out of that arch. I was out and running down that hill in a heartbeat. I was only dimly aware of the renewed crackle of gunfire from the French bank. I could not afford to look up as I had to concentrate on my footing. One slip and in a few seconds tons of rock would fall on top of me. I was halfway down the hill when I realised that it was taking too long. There was nothing for it but to step out onto a rocky outcrop and just jump into the water.

It was deep and cold and probably saved my life, for it moved me down the stream in a fast current. As I surfaced I was gasping with the shock of the icy water but I was already twenty yards away from the bridge. The mine blew. There was a thunderous roar, a huge plume of smoke and seconds later chunks of masonry were splashing in the river around me. For a moment I was jubilant, I had done it, I had escaped and saved Lisbon and Wellesley at the same time. Then, as the smoke started to clear, I discovered that I had been thwarted by a long dead man called Lacer.

I found out later that his name was Caius Julius Lacer. He was a Roman architect and he built damn strong bridges. As I drifted around a bend in the river I had a last look at the bridge and could clearly see that the end span was still standing. I also got a glimpse of the Lusitanian soldiers pulling back away from the river. I drifted and half waded down the river for a quarter of a mile but with my sword and pistols weighing me down, once any air trapped in my clothes had gone it was impossible to swim and I looked for a place to climb up the steep bank on the Portuguese side.

It was late afternoon when, soaked through and freezing cold, I climbed to the crest of a hill that overlooked the bridge at Alcantara. I still had my telescope in my pocket and while some water had got into the tubes I was able to watch the Lusitanian rear guard pulling back to the next bridge that they planned to defend. They had got most of their cannon away and left just one on the bluff to hold the bridge until they departed. Marshal Victor seemed happy to let them go without incurring further casualties; it was the bridge he wanted, and thanks to me he had it. As I looked down, the first of his troops were coming across and the dead and wounded on the bridge were being carried away. The first French infantry and cavalry were moving across in single file.

They would pursue the Lusitanians I thought and destroy what was left of them at the next bridge, which meant that rejoining those brave green jacketed troops was not for me. My urgent need was for warmth and so I walked half a mile away from Alcantara to an abandoned shepherd's hut, where I soon had a fire blazing to return life to my limbs and dry my clothes. The next morning I expected to awake to the sound of a distant battle but there was nothing. I had slept in the hut and made plans on what to do next. With Soult likely to be holding off Wellesley in the north of Portugal until Victor arrived either in Lisbon or on Wellesley's flanks, going north or west back into Portugal seemed a dangerous option. I could not go east as that was French occupied Spain, so south seemed the best idea. I could get to Seville or Cuesta and while the despatches had been ruined by the water, they would be obliged to help a British officer get to safe territory. But first I had to wait for Marshal Victor's army to get out of the way. Later that day I climbed up my hill again to see how things were proceeding and there I saw an astonishing sight. Instead of proceeding west to capture Lisbon, Victor's men were turning around and heading back the way that they had come. I was amazed, puzzled and proud; against all the odds, the tiny forces of the Loyal Lusitanian Legion, ably assisted by one T Flashman, Esquire, had somehow managed to turn back a French marshal and his army.

The big question that we were all asking over the next few days was why the French had turned back once they had secured the bridge. Some British sources later dismissed the matter by claiming that Victor must have got word that Wellesley had beaten Soult at Oporto, but that doesn't wash. The victory at Oporto and the defence of the bridge at Alcantara both took place on the same day, the twelfth of May. I know French messengers would be better at navigating than Downie, but it must be well over one and fifty miles taking into account the rough terrain and avoiding the partisans. There is no way that they could have done it in much less than four days, even with fresh horses at each stop.

Colonel Mayne suggested that one of the reasons was the heavy casualties that the Lusitanians had inflicted on the French. He estimated French casualties at 1,400, more than a tenth of the French infantry, against which the militia regiment lost around fifty killed and wounded before they ran away, and the Legion had one hundred and eight killed and a hundred and forty six wounded, which still left them over three hundred men and most of their guns to defend the next bridge at Seguro.

I on the other hand have another theory, and I speak with some authority as I was probably the only one watching the French at the bridge on the day they decided to turn around. I saw lots of infantry and cavalry cross that damaged span, but not one of the heavy twelve pounder cannon. There were officers, presumably French engineers, studying the bridge and going underneath where the mine had been placed. I am pretty sure that I even saw Marshal Victor ride across in the afternoon to inspect the damage for himself. I don't think that last arch of the bridge was strong enough to take the guns and Victor certainly would not have wanted to advance without his artillery. My hypothesis is supported by the fact that the damaged span collapsed completely a few weeks later.

It is possible that Soult had been sending messages before the battle with Wellesley expressing doubts that he could defend Oporto, but other messages he sent indicate he was confident he could defend the city. I like to think that it was my forestalling the grenadier from destroying the mine and then firing the damn thing that saved the day. As you will read from the following account, there are not many things that happened to me in the Peninsular that I can take a sense of accomplishment from, but that is one of them. After all there cannot be that many men who can say that they have turned back a French army single handed.

Much later, Colonel Mayne and I were both made Knights of the Military Order of Alcantara by the Spanish, recognising the part we played in stopping the French advance. It is an old order that dates back to the Middle Ages and the battles in the region between Christendom and the Moors. Like most of my foreign tinware and awards it won't get you into Whites or the Reform Club, but I still wear mine with pride.

You will only find passing mentions of the defence of the Alcantara Bridge in many of the history books, which is down to pure spite in some cases. Wellesley never gave the Legion credit for anything and officers writing memoirs in his lifetime took care to follow suit so as to avoid his wrath. Cuesta and the Spanish were similarly furious that the bridge had been blown as it added weeks to communications, although they had only been bothered to send fifty cavalry to help defend it. Equally the French felt that they had little to shout about from the action. Apart from mine, the most detailed account you will find of the action was written by the other man at the heart of it, Colonel Mayne. He has written a very readable history of the regiment including the Alcantara action; although the old bastard evidently resented the fact that I blew the bridge without waiting for orders and does not mention me at all.

Editor's Note
The book Flashman refers to is A Narrative of the Campaigns of the Loyal Lusitanian Legion by Colonel William Mayne. A copy is available to read online at the website of the Portuguese National Library or Biblioteca Nacional Digital. See the Historical Notes section at the end of this book for further information.

Chapter 9

Generally speaking my account of the Peninsular Campaign does not reflect well on the Spanish soldier, so I should make a point of recognising the bravery of the fifty Spanish cavalry that Cuesta had sent to support the defence of the bridge at Alcantara. With Downie and the British dragoons on foot they were the only mounted soldiers covering the withdrawal and by all accounts they fought well, as shown by the fact that there were only twenty survivors.

The Legion cautiously returned to the bridge the day after the French withdrawal. I went down to rejoin them but Mayne was damn cool with me as I had not been given his order to blow the mine. I pointed out that if I had waited, the grenadier would have heaved the entirety of the mine in the river and the whole French army would have been marching to Lisbon, but he took little notice of that. Admittedly six of the Legion had been killed by falling masonry when the mine blew without warning, which partly explained it.

Mayne thought that Victor might now try to attack Lisbon by going further south and passing through the area Cuesta was guarding. Having just escaped Victor's forces once I had no wish to meet them again. I thought that the French would sweep through Cuesta's diminished army like a pack of foxes in a henhouse and we had yet to hear of Wellesley's victory at Oporto. When Mayne asked for someone to take news of our victory to Wilson I jumped at the chance. Not only was I keen to meet my old friend again, but to find him I had to travel west, away from the French. Doubtless because he was keen to get rid of me, Mayne agreed.

This time with a small escort of dragoons I followed the better travelled route along the river. The journey was without incident and we arrived at a town called Tomas on the fifth of June. There we found Wilson and learned of Wellesley's victory at Oporto. When I revealed how Victor and his army had been turned back by the Legion, Wilson was jubilant. News of Oporto was already being circulated around the Portuguese army, and a message about Alcantara was sent to Wellesley so that this could be circulated among the British. Privately Wilson admitted to me that he was sure Wellesley would do no such thing.

It was good to see Wilson again and he told me how victory in the north had been achieved.

'Wellesley managed to find some wine barges and cross the river to a convent on the opposite shore,' he explained. 'They were able to fortify the convent to hold the French off until they had enough men across to attack the town. The French were taken by surprise and Wellesley sat down to a dinner that had been cooked for Marshal Soult.' He gave a shout of laughter and slapped his knee. 'Two famous victories against the French on the same day eh? Napoleon will be furious when he finds out. Mind you,' he added with a grin, 'Wellesley had over twenty thousand men to defeat his marshal. We sent our marshal back with just the few hundred in my regiment.'

A broken bridge was rather a significant factor in our victory, I thought, but I did not say anything as Wilson was in high spirits and there was no need to dampen them. Wilson was the complete antithesis of the man he viewed as his rival British commanding general. While Wellesley was haughty and reserved, planning carefully and moving cautiously, Wilson was engaging and impulsive. He was convinced that a small force, led with daring and reacting quickly to circumstance, could do just as much damage to an enemy as a much larger army. 'A rapier will kill you just as dead as a cannon,' he quoted. 'That is why I must always have freedom to act as I think fit.' He was determined that his regiment would not be absorbed as just another unit in the British army… and particularly not under Wellesley's command.

Within a few days word came through that Victor was also pulling back into Spain. He must have realised that he was probably the next French marshal that Wellesley planned to confront. This of course meant that I could now return to my original orders and visit Cuesta and take information on Cuesta's army back to Wellesley. Despite his dislike for Wellesley or perhaps because of his liking for me, Wilson caught up with me again before I left. 'Be careful of the old fox,' he warned of Cuesta. 'The Spanish Central Junta government does not trust him and he views them as impertinent opportunists. There are various feuds between the Spanish generals and they all hate Cuesta. I would not trust any of them to come to his aid if he was in a tight spot. But on the positive side he has an implacable hatred of the French,' Wilson grinned at me before adding, 'which probably only slightly exceeds his dislike of the British.'

With that endorsement ringing in my ears I set off. The original message I carried from Wellesley had been destroyed by my fall into the river but it was out of date now anyway. I carried despatches from

Wilson and Beresford, the commander of the Portuguese army, to prove who I was and had six British dragoons as escort including troopers Chapman and Doherty. A week later and we found ourselves riding into Cuesta's camp and understanding for the first time the plight of the Spanish army.

The camp was in one of the main passes between Spain and Portugal, an area that in recent years the French and Spanish had fought over frequently. As a result many of the local farmers, fed up with their women getting raped and their crops stolen, had moved on so that most of the farms were abandoned. The few peasants that could be seen still trying to scratch a living from the earth looked dirt poor and certainly not able to support the thousands of men now bivouacked nearby. We crested a hill late one afternoon and got our first glimpse of the Spanish army camp. It was June and the weather was already hot. Before us was a large olive grove and under virtually every tree half a dozen raggedly dressed soldiers could be seen lying in the shade. On the air was the stench of uncovered latrine ditches.

There were no orderly lines of tents or clearly marked regimental areas, in fact there were few tents at all, just the odd scrap of canvas strung up between trees to provide more shade. No sentries were in sight and we were not challenged. The men near us glanced up but showed no interest as we rode past. As we got closer to the centre of the camp, a file of cadaverously thin men could be seen marching along guarding a supply wagon. Their uniforms, such as the scraps of clothing that they still wore could be called that, were torn with some barely decent.

'Jaysus,' I heard Flaherty mutter behind me as they marched past. 'Would ye be lookin' at them. Why their clothes would shame a Connemara tinker.'

My eyes were drawn to a riot of colour under an awning by a huge carriage in the centre of the camp. There, around twenty officers in uniforms of every colour and hue, except French blue, lounged on chairs and benches around a large table. They watched us approach and as we got close one tall thin officer in a green coat languidly got to his feet and walked towards us. On his head he had placed a tall bicorn hat adorned with an ostrich feather plume along the rim. It was by far the grandest thing about him. His green coat was patched on both elbows, the hem seemed to have been burnt at some point, while one leg of his breeches had been torn at the knee.

'Look at his sword,' Chapman muttered to the others. 'The scabbard is covered with rust.' Then expressing what was undoubtedly an expert opinion he added, 'You would not bother to steal that even if you found it on the road.' I grinned. Chapman was right, a man who could not bother to keep rust off the scabbard would probably not keep the blade free of rust, or sharp either. For this officer his sword was just another item of his tatty uniform rather than a weapon. He saw us inspecting him and me grinning and gave a look of haughty disdain.

'What do you want?' he asked, in heavily accented English.

'I come from General Wellesley,' I replied in my fluent Spanish. 'He sends his greetings to General Cuesta. I also have despatches from General Beresford and General Wilson.' He held out his hand and I passed over the despatches.

'Wait here,' he said curtly, and then marched back to the men near the carriage, leaving us sitting in the hot sun.

I decided that I was not going to be treated like some itinerant peddler by a bunch of dagos dressed up like a beggar's circus. 'Water and look after the horses,' I said to Chapman after I had dismounted and passed him the reins of my mount. Then I walked over to the men by the carriage. I was a British officer, damn it, and they needed our help to beat the French. Whether their help was of any use to us was another matter. I looked the men sitting under the awning in the eye, daring one of them to challenge me, but they just glared resentfully back. I reached the table set amongst them and picked up an earthenware jug. Pouring what turned out to be wine into one of the silver beakers on the table, I slaked my thirst and I looked about. Ostrich hat was at the door of the carriage talking to someone inside. I could not hear what they were talking about but after a while ostrich hat turned towards me. Looking mildly annoyed that I was already at the table, he gestured me over to the carriage.

The interior of the coach was dark and gloomy with blinds over the windows to keep out the hot sun. As I reached a door I could see a bed along the far side, strewn with maps and other papers. To my left, in the shadow, a pair of eyes glinted at me; they belonged to an old man who had one leg propped up on the bed. Opposite was another seat facing the general. I guessed that they expected me to stand outside as ostrich hat had done, but to hell with that, I thought. I had spent a week getting here and the old buzzard was not going to simply dismiss me through a carriage door. Stepping up into the carriage I heard a grunt of surprise from the general who put out a hand out to try and stop me,

84

but I pretended not to have seen it. I dropped into the vacant seat, causing the carriage to bounce on its springs. Cuesta winced as the movement disturbed his leg, which I now noticed was bandaged. Then he glared at me.

'Officers speak to me though the door,' he barked. 'Even British captains.'

I decided that now was the time to play my aristocratic card. 'My compliments sir, I am also the grandson of the Marquis of Morella,' I told him. 'Through his daughter,' I added.

'I doubt that,' said Cuesta coldly, 'his daughter is only twelve. I suspect that you mean the old marquis who died a few years ago. I take it then that you are not close to the family?'

'I have not had that honour,' I admitted. In truth I had not met any of them. They had ostracised my mother after she married an Englishman but the association had already saved my life once, when I had been captured by the Spanish back in '01.

'Then perhaps you also do not know that your cousin is the Marquesa de Astorga?' He looked at me with a slight smirk before adding, 'Her husband the marquis is the head of the Junta of Granada and one of the leading politicians of the Central Junta.'

'I am indebted to you sir, I did not know that,' I conceded, still puzzled why he thought that my newly discovered link with the Astorga nobility was amusing. I knew that a marquis was just one rank below a duke and Granada was a province that had largely escaped French occupation. So in theory my cousin should be married to a wealthy and powerful man. I was sure there was something that he was not telling me so I asked, 'Is the marquis a popular leader?'

Cuesta gave a snort of disgust. 'All of the juntas squawk and flap like a flock of hens to be popular with the mob. They confuse popularity with leadership.' There was that smirk again as he added, 'Your cousin's husband is not too big for his boots like some, but he is no leader.' Then he looked me in the eye and asked 'Is your General Wellesley a leader?'

'He is yes,' I confirmed. 'I fought with him in India and I have seen him take on an army five times the size of his force and beat it.'

Cuesta gave a snort of derision. 'I have heard he can lead native sepoy troops against Indian princes. But here he is not fighting elephants; he is fighting the French with their cannon and veteran infantry and cavalry.'

'Sir, he has just beaten Marshal Soult's army of veterans,' I reminded him.

'Yes, but that is just one marshal and most of the veterans got away. There are several marshals in Spain at the moment. What will he do, Captain, when those marshals start to gather their armies together?'

I thought that whatever happened the British were likely to put up more of a fight than his Spanish army and glanced out at them through the doorway of the carriage. It was an unconscious gesture but Cuesta noticed.

'I know what you are thinking,' he said. 'You think that your army is better than mine because it is better dressed and better equipped.'

'No sir, no, not at all,' I lied diplomatically.

'Your army came to Spain before,' Cuesta's voice was rising now as he started to get into a passion. 'They promised to stand alongside the free armies of Spain. We fed your army and prepared to meet the veterans the Corsican tyrant sent against us, and what did the British do?' He was shouting now, 'they ran away and left us. This army did not run away. There were no ships to take us away to full bellies and warm beds. This army fought on, through the winter, facing the marshals of France and their armies alone. When there was no food they fought, when there was snow and ice they fought, when rivers were in flood they fought. And now in the spring you came back from your warm beds and look down on my army because it does not look as smart as yours. Show me your army next spring, if it is still here fighting alongside us, and then you can judge my men.'

There was a long silence in the carriage after that tirade because there was little I could say. The presence of the British had helped persuade Napoleon to reinforce the raw recruits he had initially sent to Spain. As soon as Bonaparte led his veteran troops into the fray the British army had been in retreat until it was evacuated at Corunna. I could have told Cuesta that even counting Corunna, of the battles we had fought with the French we had won two out of three, whereas the Spanish had suffered a long series of disastrous defeats; but that probably would not have helped the mood in that confined carriage. I was on the point of making my excuses to leave when he asked another question.

'Why did Wellesley send you? I have already had another message from him telling me of his plan to join me to attack Victor.'

I guessed that Wellesley must have got impatient when I did not return to him quickly and had sent another messenger. 'He sent me when we landed but suggested that I look for you at Alcantara.' I added with a touch of pride, 'I was there with the Lusitanian Legion when it turned back Victor's attack.'

'They destroyed the Alcantara Bridge,' he said with an accusing tone. 'Spain needs that bridge.'

'Yes sir,' I conceded, irritated that he was missing the bigger picture. 'But we did turn back an attack from a French marshal, who could have swept into Portugal and attacked Wellesley's flank or even captured Lisbon.'

'I don't care about Portugal or Lisbon, I care about Spain and Spain needed that bridge.'

'Then perhaps you should have sent more than fifty cavalrymen to help defend it,' I protested hotly.

'Damn your impertinence,' he snapped back. 'You might be the grandson of a Spanish marquis but you know nothing about Spain or about this war.' He took a breath to calm himself and then continued. 'Only I know how to beat the French, not those chattering fools in the juntas or the self-appointed popinjays that now command the other Spanish armies. I beat the French twice in '95 fighting in the Pyrenees and I will do it again.' It was true, I learned later, he had beaten two French armies then, but they were poorly led revolutionary conscripts. Since then Napoleon had taken over in France with new tactics and strategies. Things were very different now, but clearly Cuesta did not realise that. I held up my hands in surrender, remembering I was supposed to be Wellesley's liaison man with this proud fool.

'You must understand sir that the British want to help Spain and Portugal.'

'Yes. No doubt so you have some ports that you can conveniently flee from when things get tough again.' He gave a dismissive gesture to the carriage door as he added, 'Tell your sepoy general that I would welcome his support when I next attack Marshal Victor.' I took my leave and wandered back to the dragoons. Having heard about the battle of Medallin I had not expected Cuesta to be a good general but I was not prepared for such deluded arrogance. I had seen Victor's army, they were well equipped and well trained. In contrast Cuesta's army looked like a bunch of lethargic, half-starved scarecrows.

'Is all well sir?' asked Chapman.

I looked around to check we were out of earshot of the other Spanish officers and gestured at the surrounding troops. 'He seriously thinks that this rabble can beat Victor and seems to put his previous defeats down to bad luck. He is no friend of ours either,' I added. 'He is very resentful that we evacuated the army last year.'

'Well, we did cut out and run,' Doherty reasoned. 'But we should never have got ourselves trapped in the north of the country at all. Wicked cruel place that was in winter.'

'Yes, but...' I started to reply, exasperated that they were not seeing my point of view, but was distracted when I saw that their breeches were all patched and worn. They were like a spare pair you might keep in a saddlebag; and then I noticed a new gold ring on Chapman's finger. Swinging round to the staff officers under the awning I now saw that two of them were looking a lot less ragged in the breeches department than they had been before.

'We did a trade,' explained Chapman simply. 'I could get a dozen pairs of breeches from the quartermaster with this ring when we get back.' He paused as though he had surprised himself with a thought and then added, 'Will we be coming back this way sir?'

We needed to get back to Wellesley, but on the way out of the valley I stopped a couple of times and spoke to the men dozing under the olive trees. Many had strong regional accents which made them hard to understand, but I divined that most of them were conscripts who had been forced to join the army by their towns or villages to make up a quota. They stayed with the army not out of patriotic duty but because they were peasants with no land who would be arrested if they returned home. Being in the army was marginally safer than roaming the countryside in bandit gangs that were hunted by both the Spanish and the French. When I asked about drilling and training they just shrugged. Many had sold most of their cartridges to local farmers to buy food and so with little powder left they rarely used their muskets.

I won't bore you with a detailed account of what happened over the next two months; suffice to say that Trooper Chapman's travelling trouser emporium flourished, as we did two more journeys with messages from Wellesley to Cuesta. The British army having beaten Soult was now heading south, but painfully slowly as Wellesley would not move until he was sure that he had supplies to feed his men. As June progressed into July the weather got warm and then hot and the road between the British and Spanish armies became well travelled.

It was on one return journey from Cuesta that we passed the Loyal Lusitanian Legion and Wilson waiting on the road for the British advance guard that could be seen coming over the horizon. Wilson explained that he had been ordered to join Wellesley's army by the Portuguese, but he intended to engineer an independent command if he could. He was fuming that it had taken Wellesley a month to march south and he was even then still not over the Spanish border. Wilson swore that he could do far more damage to the French with his own small force. I explained about the shortages of food and medical supplies but he claimed that Cuesta had promised to meet all the British needs if Wellesley only increased the pace of the march. Having seen Cuesta's camp it was a promise that I doubted he could fulfil and I am sure Wellesley felt the same.

As the British advance guards marched to within a few hundred yards of us, Wilson turned to the Legion and ordered them to advance so that they were the lead regiment. This was normally an honoured position because the soldiers were not breathing in the dust kicked up by all those that had marched before. Wellesley rode up with some of his staff officers and Wilson went to report to him, but I stayed close as I wanted to watch this encounter.

Wellesley watched the green jacketed troops marching away in the position of precedence for his whole army and glared at Wilson. Despite the heat of the day I swear that Wellesley's disdainful look would have chilled champagne.

Wilson blithely ignored the hostility as he cheerily greeted his new commander. 'Arthur, it is good to meet you at last. We have not had to wait long for your army to catch up.' I realised he was deliberately riling Wellesley as he added, 'I was hoping that you might grant my Legion the honour of leading the army for the rest of the day.'

Wellesley glared at the backs of the green jacketed troops that were even now disappearing around a bend in the road and turned back to coolly appraise Wilson. 'It seems that it is an honour you have already anticipated, Sir Robert.' He looked up at the sun which was still high in the sky as it was early afternoon. Normally the army would have marched for several hours but now Wellesley turned to his staff, 'I think we will stop here for tonight, have the men fall out.' One of his staff officers opened his mouth to question the decision but a glare from Wellesley froze him to silence.

Wilson just grinned, saluted and rode off after his men, winking at me as he did so. He had achieved his goal: he had nominally joined the British army but he would stay well ahead of the main column and operate as he saw fit. A few days later Wellesley decided to get rid of Wilson by sending the Legion and two Spanish regiments into Spain on what was supposed to be a foraging mission. But Wilson had far more ambitious plans that would come to light later.

Wellesley and Cuesta met for the first time on the tenth of July at Almaraz. It was not an auspicious beginning. I had been sent ahead and was waiting with Cuesta for the arrival of the British party. For all of his disdain of the British, Cuesta was determined to make a good impression. That afternoon he had a regiment equipped with the best clothes and weapons that they could find standing ready for inspection by the 'generale sepoy' as he called Wellesley. Whether Downie was acting as guide again I don't know, but in any event Wellesley got lost and arrived later that night, five hours late. The inspection was much less impressive by torchlight, but Cuesta limped along beside him showing all the courtesy of a Spanish nobleman, which is to say he was a haughty bastard but punctilious in manners.

Marshal Victor's army, now of twenty thousand men, was still isolated from other French forces. The allied commanders wanted to confront him before he could be supported by other marshals, so they agreed to combine their forces to attack him. The British army totalled twenty-two thousand and Cuesta had thirty-three thousand, so the combined army of fifty-five thousand was nearly triple the size of the French force. The British and Spanish armies met on the twenty-first of July at a place called Oropesa.

The British army had, thanks to Wellesley's caution, been reasonably well supplied throughout its long journey, although some supplies promised by the Spanish had failed to materialise. You can imagine the men's dismay when they came across the rag tag Spanish army that made up the bulk of their combined force. If anything their condition had deteriorated since I had first clapped eyes on them. Smartly dressed and well equipped British infantry men struggled to keep straight faces as they marched incredulously through the camp of the scarecrow army, saluting officers that looked little more than vagrants.

But it was not their appearance that most worried the British, it was their fighting ability. Most Spanish weapons carried visible signs of rust and the few Spanish units they saw drilling had British soldiers hooting with mirth. One company of redcoats demonstrated firing three volleys in a minute to some nearby Spanish troops who looked on in wonder at the regimented loading drills. When the British goaded the Spanish into a return demonstration of their skills, the result was pandemonium. The first volley crashed out reasonably well, apart from a handful of soldiers who were just going through the motions having apparently sold or lost all of their ammunition. Then the chaos really began with the officers and sergeants bellowing different commands at the same time. Weapons and cartridges were dropped, one man fainted and several looked as if they had never reloaded their guns before, watching the others to see how they did it. The second volley started in the first minute but was so ragged it stretched into the second and of the fifty men in the company, no fewer than six managed to fire their ramrods across the clearing.

There was debate amongst the British as to whether the Spanish would be a help or a hindrance in battle. What had seemed on paper an easy victory for the allies in reality looked as if it would be a much closer fought affair. To make matters worse, once the armies joined there was also increasing tension over supplies. The Spanish had promised large amounts of provisions but precious little seemed to be coming through. Doubtless some Spanish commissary officer saw the relatively well fed British and decided that the food was more deserving with the half-starved Spanish. A reasonable judgement from his perspective but not from the British point of view, who had no intention of sinking to emaciated ineffectiveness like their allies. Consequently there were stories of the British commandeering Spanish supply wagon convoys that according to manifests were destined for the Spanish army. Having carefully marshalled his supplies to feed his army all the way south, Wellesley was frustrated that the promised Spanish food was not coming through. He and Cuesta argued furiously about supplies although Wellesley denied knowing anything about the stolen convoys. He was lying; I know this because he sent me as translator on one of the raids to ensure the wagon drivers cooperated.

Despite all the friction, excitement was mounting at the prospect of a pitched battle. Many were eager to get to grips with the enemy but you can imagine that it was not an emotion I shared. With the Spanish as allies any battle was bound to be a confused and frantic affair. I was also mindful of Wellesley's 'generous' promise to ensure that I would be given the chance to see some action during the campaign. That was the last thing I wanted, so as the armies joined I made sure I was indispensable as a liaison officer and toadied to both Wellesley and Cuesta for all I was worth. The generals were meeting regularly to discuss battle plans and seemed confident of catching Victor by surprise.

But you do not get to be a French marshal without some strategic awareness and Victor was watching his enemies gather. On the day the armies combined he retreated east, over the river Alberche, and stopped just a few miles north east of a place that was to be made famous by the Peninsular Campaign: Talavera.

Chapter 10

The first planned battle of Talavera is probably unique in the annals of military warfare in that it did not happen because one of the armies overslept!

Cuesta and Wellesley had agreed that they could not allow Victor more time to pull further back and join the rest of the French army. They had to take him on while they had a numbers advantage. Accordingly they drew up a plan to attack him at Talavera at dawn on the twenty-third of July. The larger Spanish army would approach Victor's army from the north west forcing the French to face them in a battle formation, and then the British would hit their flank from the south west. Another Spanish army commanded by a General Venegas was supposed to move in from the south east and attack any retreating French soldiers trying to escape in that direction. In theory it was a good plan and Victor's army would have been trapped and destroyed... but there is a big difference between theory and reality.

On the twenty-second both armies set off in the direction of Talavera, camping out of sight of French forces but within a comfortable early morning march of the enemy camp. I spent the night with the British army, which was the wrong decision. I would have had a much more comfortable and uninterrupted sleep with the Spanish. Wellesley had his staff officers up at two in the morning and the army marched quietly to a position from which they could launch their attack. The Spanish were supposed to leave at the same time but Wellesley confided that he fully expected them to be late, which was why he had set the time to start the attack at six.

'If they are ready to attack by nine it will still serve, it will only take two hours for them to march into position.'

'Do you think that they will put up a fight with the French?' I asked him as we rode along.

'They don't need to fight,' Wellesley replied. 'They only have to look as though they might fight to force the French to form against them. We will do the bulk of the fighting, but if we can catch the French in a flank attack it will give us an advantage.' He gave one of his barks of laughter and added, 'Who knows, if they can see we are winning they might join in.'

'You don't rate their courage then?'

'Oh, Cuesta is undoubtedly brave. He is as brave as he is stubborn, proud, petulant and without a wit of strategic thinking. No, you cannot fault him for courage, but his army is another matter. They are largely ill trained and lacking any form of competent leadership. Speaking of which, ride back to the Spanish camp, will you, and let me know if they are actually moving.'

I found Chapman and Doherty who were now permanently allocated to me as escort riders. With all the supply skulduggery it was not safe even for an officer to ride alone. We swiftly covered the three miles back to the Spanish camp and, well you can imagine what we found there.

Instead of a hive of activity and marching men, we found that even the sentries were asleep near their braziers and nothing at all was stirring. We rode through the vast bivouac and a few looked up at the sound of our horses but then turned over again. I headed towards the huge carriage in the centre of the camp and there I did find some people awake; a dozen burly Spanish soldiers who had orders to ensure that their general's sleep was not disturbed. Cuesta, obviously expecting protests from the British, had left the men and a harassed lieutenant to keep us at bay. All my entreaties and threats of retribution had no effect. It looked as though we would simply have to report to Wellesley that the Spanish army was still in bed. Then Chapman spoke up.

'Perhaps Ernesto could help us, sir.'

'Who the hell is Ernesto?' I snapped at him, frustrated at my lack of progress with the stubbornly persistent guards.

Chapman shifted awkwardly. 'He is my main buyer, sir.'

I had expected Ernesto to be another commercially minded private soldier but he turned out to be Major Ernesto Caballo and one of Cuesta's staff officers. I realised afterwards that only officers would be able to afford Chapman's merchandise.

'Cuesta does not trust the British,' Caballo told me when we had found his tent. 'He thinks it might be a trap and that you will leave the French to destroy his army. He does not trust anybody. He even thinks that General Venegas will betray him.' Caballo looked me in the eye and added, 'The general is also resentful that the plan was proposed by your Wellesley rather than him. Cuesta is very jealous of your commander and his recent victories over the French.' Well, that did not leave a lot of room for negotiation and it was clear that the Spanish army was not going to move that morning.

We rode back and gave the news to Wellesley. By then it was six in the morning and Wellesley was livid. He had spent the previous day agreeing every detail of the attack with Cuesta and now the Spaniard was just ignoring the plan. More significantly it was only a matter of time before Victor found out how close the allies were to his new position. Wellesley even considered attacking on his own, but a straight frontal assault would see much of the fighting effectiveness of his force destroyed. In the end he called for his horse and went to confront the general. A bleary eyed Cuesta emerged from his carriage and explained that he and his men were tired after the march the previous day. He claimed he had not had enough time for reconnaissance and that he was worried about the strength of the bridge his men must use. In the end he promised that they would be ready to attack tomorrow. Mañana, he repeated, as with considerable self-restraint Wellesley walked away without striking the old fool. They both knew that the French would not still be there mañana.

People think that wars are conducted by generals, but sometimes, by chance, a common soldier can alter a campaign. Such a chance came later that day. After his return to the British camp, Wellesley discovered that the French army was pulling back again, and the opportunity to attack Victor on his own had been missed. He came to a decision; he would advance no further into Spain until the supplies promised by Cuesta were provided. It was simple retaliation and I was sent back to Cuesta to deliver the ultimatum. This time he did see me and brooded over the message. He must have realised that if relations broke down completely with the British then the Central Junta would probably seek to relieve him of his command. In the end he decided that a conciliatory gesture was necessary and ordered his carriage to be driven to the British camp. Just outside the British lines, the coach stopped again and his horse was brought forward. Cuesta was sixty-eight and had not fully recovered from being trampled by his own cavalry earlier in the year. Now he had to be lifted into the saddle, but he was determined to make a more martial appearance on horseback to the British than appearing in his coach.

We trotted slowly through the British army, Cuesta quiet and sullen, wincing occasionally at the pain being in the saddle gave him. The redcoats, deprived of a night's sleep and an easier battle than what would now inevitably follow, glared back mutinously. It was as we were approaching Wellesley's tent that a voice called out above the low murmuring from the other soldiers.

'You're a bluidy coward,' shouted some unknown Scotsman from a group of men to my right. 'An' your whole bluidy army couldn't fight its way oot of a stale puddin',' he added. The fellows around the heckler started to jeer the Spanish commander. While Wellesley undoubtedly agreed with the man, he could not permit such a lack of respect for an officer. He glared at the men while the nearby provost sergeant shouted for the culprit to be arrested. But it was too late, the laughter and jeering soon spread around the troops surrounding Cuesta.

'What did that man say?' Cuesta demanded, glaring suspiciously at the men around him.

I had suffered enough of the old general's surly ways and was tired through lack of sleep too. There are times when diplomacy requires tact and evasion but I decided that this was not one of them. 'He shouted that you are a coward and that the whole Spanish army are cowards,' I told him bluntly.

Cuesta stopped his horse and stared at me as though I had slapped him around the face. Then with a look of fury he wheeled his horse around and returned in the direction of the Spanish camp. The humiliation of being mocked by the common soldiers of his allies must have burned Cuesta through that night. In contrast it gave those same allies much amusement and the man who had shouted the insult was quietly reprieved. The effect of that soldier's words was not seen until the next morning, when the Spanish army finally marched.

It was good to see our allies moving, even if it was a day late. The problem was that no one knew where they were going or why. As it turned out Trooper Chapman was surprisingly informative on that point, having done some last minute business with his buyer before the Spanish departed.

'Ernesto says that Cuesta is determined to show us that he is in command. The old general is marching after Victor on 'is own and 'e thinks that we will have to follow and support him.'

'But Victor has thrashed Cuesta before,' I protested. 'And as well as Victor there are other French armies gathering out there under Napoleon's brother, the new Spanish king. He has Marshal Jourdan with him who can bring the army stationed in Madrid, why – between them they must have nearly fifty thousand well trained men.'

'That Spanish general called Vinegar...'started Chapman.

'General Venegas,' I corrected.

'That's 'im. Well he is supposed to be tracking the king and stopping the French armies joining up by drawing one of them away.' Here Chapman leaned forward conspiratorially. 'Ernesto says that

General Vinegar cannot be trusted and that Vinegar hates Cuesta and would like to see him get a proper spanking from the French.'

'Why would one Spanish general want to see another defeated?'

''Cos then General Vinegar would be the top Spanish general of course,' said Chapman, looking at me in surprise as though it was obvious.

'The treacherous bastard,' I said in disgust. There were rivalries in the British army of course, but I doubted that anyone would go so far as to engineer the defeat and destruction of a British army to secure promotion. They would never get away with it for one thing, with officers regularly writing to friends in Parliament. Wellesley was frequently getting enquiries from politicians at home questioning his decisions based on information they had received from friends.

I passed on this information to the man himself when we rode up to the top of a long ridge outside Talavera, from where we could watch the Spanish advance.

'Where did you hear this?' Wellesley asked.

'Oh, I have my spies amongst the Spanish staff officers,' I said airily. 'I have not forgotten from my Indian days with you how to build connections amongst our allies.'

'Quite so,' Wellesley grinned, 'and from what you told me before you might even be related to some of them. The head of the Granada Junta wasn't it?'

'That's right, I will need to try and find the time to meet him at some point. He might be a useful connection for us.' We both paused at the top of the hill looking down at the long dusty column of men stretching off towards the horizon in front of us. 'I take it we are not going to follow Cuesta as he hopes?'

'God no,' said Wellesley. 'If he wants to stumble blindly into a French army he can do so on his own. No, when we face the French we will do so on ground of our choosing. Let them come to us. We will be outnumbered and will need a good defensive position.'

'Where do you have in mind?'

Wellesley looked around. 'I have been thinking that this place would serve me well. This high ground dominates the plain in front. To our right, between here and Talavera there is that broken ground with olive groves that will break up any enemy advance.' I looked afresh at the countryside around us, trying to see it from a general's perspective. To the east, from where the French would come, there was a fairly flat plain, with just one smaller hill. Between that hill and

97

the one we stood on a stream ran north to south through this potential
battleground but it would be no obstacle to troops.

'What would the odds be?' I asked anxiously.

'Oh, two to one against us,' Wellesley grinned and slapped me on
the back. 'But after our time at Assaye against much higher odds I
know you will not worry about that. In fact with the Spanish gone I
can release you from your liaison role to see more of the action.'

I sat on my horse reeling for a moment at this very unwelcome turn
of events. Assaye had been a damn close thing and we had only won
because the enemy cavalry had refused to participate in the battle. I
doubted that the French cavalry would be so obliging. Wellesley had
been lucky then and it seemed to me that he was getting dangerously
over confident now. I needed to get my safe liaison role back and fast.

'What about General Vinegar... I mean Venegas,' I said, getting
flustered as I pictured myself in the outnumbered front line of an
infantry regiment in the coming battle. 'Surely if the French attack us
then he might be a useful ally?'

'Oh, I think we could fight just as well without the Spanish, they
are unreliable and if they panic it could spread to our men.'

'I see sir,' I said thoughtfully. 'Obviously I am with you, but some
of the men have not fought against such odds and we are facing
veteran troops too. Would Parliament not expect you to pull back to
preserve your army? We are bound to take a lot of casualties which
will make it almost impossible for us to beat another army without
reinforcement.'

'No, if we retreat the French will just come after us and it will be
Corunna all over again. That is not going to happen under my
command. Here the men are well equipped, fresh and fighting on
ground of our choosing. It is our best chance of success.' He paused,
thinking a while, before he went on. 'But you are right, if this war goes
on the French will keep throwing armies against us. It would be good
to have a strong bolt hole we can go back to in the winter to preserve
our forces.'

'You mean a strong fortress?'

'Possibly, it would have to be a huge fortress and on the coast so
that we could keep it supplied. It is something to think about,' he
mused before turning away. It seemed to me a strange thing to ponder
about, as there was only one huge town on the coast of Spain or
Portugal that could easily be defended against the French, and that was
Cadiz on the south coast. We had a British force there already, helping

the Spanish. But if the British army went there too, the French would simply be able to bottle them up together and have the rest of the Iberian peninsula to themselves. Of course back then I had no idea of the scale of Wellesley's ambition.

I spent the next day in something approaching a mild funk. For the previous two months I had strenuously avoided any danger or risk. I had naively expected this to continue as the war went on, with me leaving the fighting to other chaps. Now, out of the blue, I was being promised a leading and undoubtedly near fatal role in what was to be a death or glory battle against overwhelming odds. The enemy this time were no gutless Pindaree horsemen in India or Mahratta warriors, but the veteran French troops with whom Napoleon had beaten the armies of Italy, Austria, Russia, the Low Countries and Prussia. Their marching columns had smashed their way through all who had tried to stand in their way. I was pretty sure that a line of redcoats commanded by me was not going to succeed where so many other more valiant souls had failed. I spent that evening desperately trying to come up with a plan that would keep me safe while retaining my ill gained credit. I failed, but it did not matter, for in the morning I found I was saved.

Cuesta's army had not just found that of Marshal Victor, but also the force commanded by King Joseph Bonaparte as well. As suspected, the Spanish General Venegas had made little or no effort to keep the French armies apart and it was only due to Spanish luck and French incompetence that Cuesta's army avoided battle and annihilation. The Spanish were pulling back as fast as they could to rejoin the British at Talavera, which meant that I was liaison officer again. I thought I could be pretty sure of one thing: when the allied army was beaten, the Spanish would not be the last to retreat. When they ran I would make sure I was liaising with them for all I was worth, preferably on the fastest horse I could find.

Messengers from Cuesta had arrived that morning to advise that the Spanish were coming back, and by the evening the dust that their army was producing as it retreated could be seen as a low cloud on the distant horizon. The following day Wellesley called for me to join him for a ride to greet our returning allies. He had already sent forward a British division to help cover their retreat. It was the twenty-seventh of July, the day that a battle would start which would win Wellesley fame and fortune; but not before his life would be saved by my right buttock.

We splashed through the little stream that ran north to south through what would be the battlefield. It was called the Portina and at that time of the day it was still crystal clear. Then we rode past the long straggling line of Spanish infantry coming the other way. By mid-morning the sun was already baking hot and many looked as though they had not stopped marching all night. Their faces were coated in dust and sweat and as soon as they reached the stream they fell out to slake their thirst, so that for several hundred yards on both sides of the Portina, men were on their hands and knees drinking and filling their canteens. The Spanish army was strung out over several miles and towards the back we saw the lumbering carriage used by Cuesta. Wellesley and I turned towards it but when we were a hundred yards off the old general looked up and saw us coming. With a scowl he leaned forward and pulled a rope that dropped a blind over the window. It was clear he did not want to talk.

'Well, that is not exactly hospitable,' I said wryly.

'It must be embarrassing for him to come back with his tail between his legs after advancing in high dudgeon before,' explained Wellesley, in a more understanding tone than I expected. 'I will speak to him when we are back in Talavera, but now I want to get to the top of that tower.' He gestured to a fortified farm house on a slight ridge half a mile ahead of us. Most of the farm house was hidden behind a wall but a three storey tower could be seen protruding above it. 'We might be able to see the French from there,' he called spurring his horse forward.

A few minutes later our horses' hooves were clattering noisily over the stone flags in the farm's courtyard. The farm had been abandoned by its owners but there were plenty of people about, for this was the temporary headquarters of the brigade that Wellesley had sent forward to cover Cuesta's retreat.

'Welcome to the Casa de Salinas, sir,' shouted Colonel Donkin, who commanded the men occupying the farm. It was now noon and the sun was fierce. Most of the men were resting in whatever shade they could find. There was precious little of that in the courtyard but the land surrounding it was covered scrub with olive and cork trees, some pines and holm-oaks. As we had approached from Talavera, we could see a cluster of British soldiers with their jackets off under most of those trees, resting in the sun. Some had tried to get to their feet and pull on their uniforms as we had approached while others remained asleep, but Wellesley affected not to notice the undress of his army.

'Can you see the French from the tower?' he now asked Donkin impatiently.

'Oh, yes sir, they are three or four miles off but showing no great enthusiasm for an advance. They seem to be waiting for other troops to join them.'

'Excellent, it will give us more time to organise the Spanish. Come on Flashman,' he added over his shoulder as he strode towards the farmhouse. I followed him up what seemed a very rickety ladder until we got to the equally rickety platform at the top of the tower. It was a loose plank floor which creaked and moved under our feet. I was not sure it would hold the weight of two people but Wellesley was unconcerned as he levelled his telescope on the far eastern horizon.

'Ah, there they are.' He gave a satisfied grunt before adding, 'It seems to be only Victor's men at the moment. What do you think?'

I dutifully got out the telescope that Campbell had given me and scanned the distant blue coated figures. It is hard to count a distant army as different units take up varying amounts of space; cavalry are normally well spread out while infantry march in long compact columns. I halved the force I could see and then quartered and 'eighthed' it, and then tried to approximate the number in that group to get to the total force. I thought that there were around two thousand men in the eighth but more were still coming down the road. 'Around twenty thousand so far,' I suggested. 'Either Victor's men or the other half of the army under the king.'

'No, it will be Victor, he would beat us on his own if he could. Joseph would be more cautious and only come this close if he had his entire army, in case we attacked him.'

'We are not going to attack them, are we?' I asked, alarmed at the thought.

'No, we'll let them come to us and meet them on our chosen ground. Anyway, the Spanish do not have the energy for another march now.' He settled himself in the corner of the tower where he could steady his telescope against one of the pillars that held up the little wooden roof. I shifted again uncomfortably and heard a piece of wood snap under my foot. That was enough for me. I made my excuses and got back down the ladder of the tower.

It was not just a concern over its structural safety but my guts were rumbling too – not due to fear but because I had eaten too many figs for breakfast. I needed to obey a regular call of nature so I strolled out of the courtyard to find some privacy. The gate faced towards Talavera and most of the nearby trees and bushes were already occupied with sleeping men who would not welcome me squatting amongst them. My need was not urgent and I considered waiting until we got back, but Wellesley could be some time yet, so I strolled along the outside of the courtyard walls until I was on the eastern side. A couple of men strolled along the parapet inside the wall on look out. One was a big burly sergeant who nodded at me in friendly greeting, he could no doubt guess why I was there.

Safe in the knowledge that the French were still miles away I stepped into the undergrowth. Twenty yards in I found a nice secluded spot out of view of the farm with a thick trunk of a cork tree I could rest against while doing my business. I unbuckled my sword and propped it against a tree, lowered my breeches and squatted down. There are few things that could be a more everyday occurrence for all mankind. There I was, minding my own business, when suddenly the world was turned upside down.

It was the suddenness of it that left me stunned, one moment I was lost in thought, completely relaxed and feeling secure, and the next I was in mortal danger. I like to think I have danger antennae which have saved me more than once, but this time they let me down utterly. I had just finished wiping myself with some dry grass when a movement caught my eye. I looked up and there, not ten yards away, a man was stepping out from behind a tree and starting to run to another tree nearer the farm. He had taken four or five paces when he saw me and froze in shock. He was not the only one recovering from the encounter as my jaw was gaping as well, for he wore the unmistakeable uniform of a French infantryman, a voltigeur or skirmisher.

I swear we must have stared at each other transfixed for a full second before everything happened at once. Simultaneously I heard a musket shot and felt a searing pain in my right buttock. The voltigeur started to swing his musket round on me, but stung by the pain in my arse, I was quicker. The times that husbands have come home unexpectedly and I have had to leave a lady's company in a hurry, pulling up my breeches on the way, served me well now. Right hand reached out for sword belt, left hand pulled up breeches so that I could run and I was off, shrieking my bloody head off.

'Ambush! Help me,' I bellowed, as two more musket balls whizzed over my head from behind. I snatched one glance to my left and saw more blue coated movement between the trees, but I could not look longer as I had to concentrate on where I was going. 'Help me,' I yelled again, but now the courtyard wall of the farmhouse was in view, ten feet of white washed stone wall with several surprised heads peering over the top.

You might not think a man with a wounded buttock could leap up a ten foot wall, but it is surprising what you can do with bullets whistling over your head and French infantry men with sharp bayonets on your tail. There was not time to run around for the gate, and without thinking I just hurled myself up the wall underneath the watching figures. Two strong hands reached down, grabbed me under the arms and hauled me over the top. One of my rescuers and I tumbled to the ground on the other side and I saw that it was the burly sergeant who had nodded to me on the way out.

'You seem to have upset them sir,' he said, in a slightly accusing tone as muskets now started to crackle steadily on the other side of the wall.

'Oh Jesus, I have been shot,' I gasped. Landing on my back had turned the pain in my right buttock from what had been a dull ache into a sharp pain.

Without ceremony the sergeant rolled me over and then gave a derisive snort. 'That's just a flesh wound, I have had worse shaving.'

'Then you must be damn clumsy with the razor,' I retorted through gritted teeth, wincing in pain. 'Has the ball come out or is it still in my arse?'

'Get away with you. It's just a graze, the ball barely creased your skin.' I reached gingerly down to feel for myself and he was right. There was just a deep groove on the edge of my buttock, and judging from the blood on my hand and breeches it was bleeding profusely. Before I could do any more Wellesley ran out of the door of the farmhouse.

'Ah, there you are Donkin,' Wellesley called to the colonel who seemed slightly confused by the sudden turn of events. 'I would be obliged it you would get two companies in skirmish order on either side of the road back to Talavera, and the rest of the men into column of march. There don't seem to be that many of them but we don't want to be trapped here.'

'Yes sir,' Donkin looked slightly relieved at having the responsibility for making decisions taken away from him. He turned to his major, 'Carter, you heard the general, two companies, skirmish order, quickly now.'

'Two companies, on both sides of the road,' Wellesley corrected, before turning and noticing me still sprawled on the ground. If I had hoped for any sign of gratitude for alerting him to the ambush I was to be disappointed. 'Flashman, what are you doing lying on the ground, we need to get moving.'

'I have been shot. I am wounded,' I replied holding up my blood smeared hand.

'Oh, that is just a flesh wound,' he said dismissively. 'Get a move on man. You don't want to be taken prisoner do you?' For a second I felt hurt at his lack of interest. If I had not stumbled into the ambush the French would have had more time to encircle the farm and trap us here. Then the sergeant next to me suddenly snatched up his musket and fired at the top of the wall. There was a shriek of pain and looking round, I saw a Frenchman who must have been hoisted up by his mates on the other side slump back, his face a bloody ruin. But already three more heads were appearing over the wall and two of them got off musket shots into the courtyard before dropping back out of sight.

'Fall back,' the sergeant was shouting, 'they will be over that wall in a minute.' He turned to me, 'Come on sir, you had better get on your horse or they will do a better job of shootin' you.' He was right. The noise of battle on the other side of the wall was rising steadily; there seemed to be a lot more Frenchmen out there than either Wellesley or I had seen. I staggered over to my horse doing up my breeches and putting on my sword belt as I went. If I did not get moving quickly a wounded arse could be the least of my problems.

By the time I reached the courtyard gate there seemed to be a pitched battle around the entrance to the farm. The French pushed in from both sides, while the outnumbered, redcoats in the skirmish parties tried to hold them back to give the rest of the regiment time to gather and order themselves. The surrounding trees came right up to the edge of the road and battle seemed to be raging all around me. I did not hang around; drawing my sword I laid my heels into my horse's flanks and we sprang forward.

While being on a horse in battle gives you the advantage of speed and a better vantage point, mounted officers always attract enemy fire. As soon as I left the shelter of the courtyard walls I heard balls whizzing around me and I hunched down low in the saddle. Wellesley was some fifty yards ahead organising two more companies into ranks to cover our retreat. I had nearly reached the dubious shelter of the line of redcoats when, bursting out of the trees from my right, ran an unarmed and hatless young British soldier, screaming as though the hounds of hell were on his tail. Without looking where he was going, he ran right in front of my horse; it reared up and I only just stayed in the saddle. As the hooves came back down they connected with a sickening thud to the skull of one of the two blue jacketed pursuers that had followed the British soldier out of the trees. I barely had a glimpse of the second man before he was on me, but his momentum gave him little chance to avoid the sword point that I instinctively twisted in his direction. He ran straight onto the wickedly sharp blade and screamed in agony. Wellesley looked round to see a relieved British infantryman picking himself up unharmed from the dust and the gallant Flashy waving a blood-stained sword, with two dead foes at the feet of his still lively horse.

'Well done Flashman, this is more your style, eh?' he grinned at me before turning back to organise the men. It never ceases to amaze me how an ill gained reputation can stick to a man. Even as I watched, the infantryman was running back to his mates and gesturing over his shoulder at me. Doubtless he was telling them how that big bugger on a horse had just saved his skin. The horseman in question was at that very moment saving his own precious skin by getting back behind the line of British infantry, which was at last now giving fire at any Frenchman that showed himself, while the rest of the British marched in a straggling column back to Talavera.

There must have been more French than Wellesley thought for we lost four hundred men in the withdrawal. Many of them had a rude awakening from their siesta with a French bayonet in the guts before they knew a battle had even started. Once in possession of the farm, which must have been their objective, the French seemed content to let us escape. They did not realise that they had nearly captured the enemy commander.

I was amongst the first back to the British lines and with my now blood soaked breeches and blood-stained sword; I looked the proper wounded hero, a part I played modestly with anyone I met. I noticed on the way that Cuesta had arrayed his men directly in front of the British positions rather than in the gap that Wellesley had left for him, but I left the commanders to liaise directly over that while I went in search of a surgeon. When I found one, a dour Scotsman smelling of spirits, he was as unsympathetic to my plight as everyone else. I was to discover as the campaign went on that just about any injury short of a ball in the chest or the loss of a limb was viewed dismissively as a flesh wound. You were only properly wounded if you lost two limbs. Lose just one and they would still see you as fit for light duties.

The sawbones did at least clean the wound and bandage it, then with a battle in the offing I had no choice but to change my clothes and return to duty. When I got back to the lines I found the Spanish in their appointed place on the British right, and Wellesley in a foul temper.

Chapter 11

'I literally had to go down on bended knee to that stupid fool,' he raged. 'It was the only way I could get them to occupy their place in the lines. I could not have them in front of us – they would have broken and run through our position causing chaos.'

'Well at least they are in place now, sir,' I said, to placate him. I glanced through the flap in his campaign tent to see if anyone outside was listening to this outburst, but Wellesley was not done.

'And do you know what that treacherous snake Wilson had done?' he fumed. 'Instead of foraging for supplies, he has waited until all the available French army are marching on me and then he has set off to liberate Madrid. He is just fifteen miles outside of the city now and if I win the battle you can be sure that he will be in Madrid to take all the glory.' I struggled to hide a smile, for I had been wondering what Wilson had been up to. It was a typically audacious Wilson move to make the most of the small force at his disposal. Wellesley gave a brief snort of satisfaction before adding, 'Well, I have ruined his plan. I have persuaded Cuesta to order the Spanish regiments with him to return. I have also written to Wilson too asking him to re-join the army, but if he chooses to disobey the French are welcome to him. God damn it,' he exclaimed as he slammed his fist on the table, 'what chance do I stand with allies like this?' It was a rare display of emotion from a man like Wellesley who was notoriously cool whatever the circumstance. But we were alone in his tent and he had shared his feelings with me once before in India, when we discovered we were sharing the same mistress. There was a personal bond between us that just occasionally allowed him to share frustrations that he could not share with others, such as his colonels whose confidence he had to retain.

'Will the French attack tomorrow?' I asked, as it was now mid-afternoon. Suddenly the prospect of battle was imminent, with all its dangers, and I realised that in the next twenty-four hours thousands of men were going to die.

'They are getting in position now so they may start the battle today.' He clapped me on the shoulder, 'I am sorry Thomas,' he said, making a rare use of my first name, 'I know I promised that I would endeavour to get you some action, but I need you with the Spanish to try and stop them doing anything stupid.' He gave one of his barks of laughter, 'After all you have accounted for two of the French already this afternoon, you must not be greedy.'

'That is all right, sir,' I agreed, doing my utmost to look disappointed, when in reality I could have kissed him with relief. 'Although stopping the Spanish from doing anything stupid is a tougher challenge than halting a French column single handed armed with just a toothpick.' We laughed then, little knowing how prophetic my words would be.

'Well, you have already stopped a French column armed with nothing more than a slow match,' he reminded me before wishing me good luck.

Before joining our newly returned allies I rode to the top of the hill occupied by the British to get a better view of the battlefield. The French were now clearly in view, thousands of them pouring on to the plain opposite in long blue snakes of men, almost obscured by the dust kicked up by their march. They seemed to be arraying themselves across our entire front, but with a concentration in front of the British positions where the ground was more open. Looking to my right I could see some of the Spanish regiments. They were already in long and slightly dishevelled lines that stretched from the British right to the outskirts of Talavera itself. The ground they stood on was an extension of the plain, but the land in front was broken by occasional trees and bushes that would disrupt the advance of any French forces. Not that it would disrupt them for long, and looking around I did not fancy our chances for victory in this battle. If the Spanish were to face the brunt of the French attack then they would break for certain. Then the French could surround the British on this hill and beat them into submission from all sides. On the other hand if the French attacked the British, we only had the numbers to fight a defensive battle and our allies would be of little help.

Defeat then looked certain to me and one reason I had gone to the top of the hill was to look for likely escape routes. The obvious one was to head for the town of Talavera. Protected by the town walls there was a bridge that led over the Tagus to relative safety from the French. The problem was that this route was too obvious and I knew that in the panic of defeat, the roads to and through Talavera and over the bridge would soon become blocked with terrified soldiers fleeing the French, who would be hot on their heels. Allied soldiers would be fighting each other as well as the French in their desperation to get over that river and the slaughter in the town would be appalling. That

108

would be no place for me, especially as I had the advantage of a good horse under me. Instead I looked to the west and south west, there good roads would take me back to Portugal and safety. With the French concentrating on Talavera – where an army and its loot would be trapped – few, I thought, would waste their time with a pursuit west. But speaking to other officers, such as Campbell who I found also wandering around on the hill top, I found that they were much more optimistic.

'You should have seen us when we took on Soult's men,' he told me. 'We soon sent them packing and I see no reason why we cannot do the same again. We have a good position here and our men are fresh. The French must have been marching for days to get here. They are tired and many of their supplies will still be on the road behind them.' I was feeling quite buoyed until he added, 'You just make sure that the Spanish stand firm, because if the French outflank us we are done for.'

Later that afternoon, with that peal of doom still playing on my mind, I finally turned my horse down the hill towards the Spanish lines. The only positive I could find in the coming disaster was that at least the Spanish would not be slow in breaking. With luck I would be several miles west of their positions before the French over ran them.

The Spanish camp was dominated by the huge black coach and the angry old man who had been lifted into a chair on its roof. From there he had a commanding view of the battlefield and he was staring out over the terrain with a telescope. I rode up and reported my presence but he barely glanced down at me, grunted, and then continued his inspection of the distant enemy. I was about to ride away again when I found that a young Spanish lieutenant was holding the bridle of my horse.

'Excuse me, señor,' he stammered hesitantly, while glancing nervously up at the general, 'but all officers apart from the cavalry must surrender their horses.' For a second I stared down at him in astonishment and then I remembered that this was one of Cuesta's measures to stop his officers abandoning their men. Glancing around, I could now see a cluster of staff officers on foot a few yards away from the carriage, all glaring resentfully at me.

Damn them! I am a British officer, I thought to myself indignantly, not like the Spanish who run at the first opportunity. Then I remembered that the reason I particularly needed my horse was so that

I could indeed run at the first opportunity. Well, British bluff and bluster was required here and I could provide that in spades.

'What the deuce? How dare you man?' I roared at the unfortunate lieutenant. 'I am a British officer and we do not run at the sight of the enemy. Unhand my horse.' With that I kicked my heels and wrenched the leather from his hand as the horse trotted forward.

The other Spanish offers were gathered in groups behind the long line of infantry that faced the French. In contrast, British officers would normally sit on horseback in front of their men to demonstrate leadership, until the need to fire required them to stand behind. I steered my horse towards a gap between the regiments and then rode out to stand twenty yards in front of the Spanish line. I was thus the closest person to the enemy in the entire Spanish army; but don't get me wrong – it was not a great act of courage on my part. The closest enemy I could see ahead were a troop of French dragoons around five hundred yards to my front. That was twice the effective range of a rifle, never mind the wildly inaccurate carbines that the dragoons would carry. I knew I was perfectly safe, but it looked good. As I stared casually around I saw that Wellesley had come down the hill to view the Spanish and was watching me from a distance. He saw me glance at him and he gave a short nod of approval.

What happened next? Well, over fifty years later I am still not sure, but I will tell you as best as I can remember. If it had not been seen and reported by various people including Wellesley himself, well I doubt you would believe it happened at all. It was an incredible chain of events.

It started with a single shot that came from the dragoons. I am sure it was not aimed at us, it was probably a signal shot to attract the attention of some messenger threading his way through the trees beyond our sight. There was some muttering from the soldiers behind me but nothing more might have happened had my horse not been startled. It was probably stung by some insect and it skittered sideways, breaking wind with a sharp crack as it did so. There may have been a couple more signal shots from the dragoons, but I cannot be sure because having got my horse back under control my attention was taken by the ranks of men behind me.

'They are shooting,' called a voice. 'Fire!' shouted another while further back another voice was yelling 'Don't shoot, don't shoot.' That last voice was nearly lost in the noise of thousands of men preparing to discharge their muskets. There was the rattle of equipment and the jingle of shoulder strap harnesses, and down the long line thousands of muskets were being levelled towards the distant enemy, notwithstanding the fact that one T Flashman Esquire was sitting plumb in the way. I did not have time to get back behind their lines and for a moment I stared, mouth agape, as at least four regiments seemed about to open fire on an enemy they could never reach. The click of hundreds of muskets being cocked shook me from my brief reverie and I had just time to throw myself onto the hard ground before the first guns fired. Mercifully the kick of the musket will typically raise the barrel slightly which is why experienced men will always aim low on their target. I am alive today because the Spanish infantry were not experienced. The volley rent the air above me as I pressed myself into the ground. Some balls were close enough to make a buzzing sound like an angry hornet as they whizzed over my head. The noise from the volley was almost deafening, and with no single word of command it seemed to go on for nearly a minute, rippling slowly down the long line of men who fired simply because the men next to them had done so.

The infantry were quickly hidden by a huge bank of gun smoke punctuated by the odd flash of orange as those slow in preparing to fire let off their charges. Then the screaming and shouting began. I could not see what was happening beyond the gun smoke, and the continued crackle of gun fire from the ends of the Spanish line obscured the words, but I distinctly heard someone screaming about treason and treachery. For a moment I wondered if I had somehow missed an approaching enemy force that they had been firing at, but when I twisted around the French dragoons were still where I had last seen them, only now they were all staring in curiosity at the Spanish lines.

I didn't understand what was happening at the time; I only pieced it together later by talking to some of the survivors. Many of the Spanish infantrymen were survivors of the battle of Medallin where they had seen countless comrades slaughtered mercilessly by French cavalry. They were terrified of the horsemen, whom they called devils. They did not understand how an infantry unit could form a square to fight them off. They were so inexperienced that most had not fired a large mass volley before and the combined noise had frightened them. With the bank of smoke obscuring their view of the distant enemy, many had convinced themselves that the devil riders were now attacking and at any moment would spring through the smoke to wreak more death and destruction. With this fear and ignorance it did not take much for a few people to start to panic and run, with the fear spreading until it was a stampede.

I knew nothing about this at the time, of course. All I noticed then was that the firing from the men directly behind me had stopped and then there seemed a lot of shouting. I gingerly raised my head. I was unharmed but the same could not be said for my poor horse, which had served me well since we had landed in Portugal. It was lying dead on the ground with half a dozen musket ball wounds in its side. From halfway down its chest a musket ramrod protruded, fired by some incompetent soldier who had forgotten to remove it from the barrel. Fear was quickly turning to anger now. I had nearly been killed and I had liked that horse, which had cost a good few guineas. I turned and marched towards the Spanish lines determined to vent my fury on the first Spanish officer I found. The smoke was already clearing as I walked through it but as I reached the other side I stopped again in astonishment. Where there had just moments before been some two thousand Spanish infantry, there were now none. The last of them could be seen fleeing either side of Cuesta's carriage while the old man raged impotently at them from its roof. He had a smoking pistol in one hand and a man lay dying on the ground near one of the wheels. As I watched he now hurled the fired pistol at another man while roaring that he would have them all shot. He was positively weeping in rage and frustration.

I don't know when I have been more shocked or disconcerted. A coward like me relies on there being people braver than them around, if for no other reason than to put up a rear guard action to allow me to slip away. I realised with alarm that I was an amateur in poltroonery compared to a Spanish infantryman. Not only had they beaten me to the off but they had shot my mount so that I could not overhaul them as well. I heard a voice shouting behind me, a single French dragoon officer was cantering towards me. He stopped some two hundred yards in front of the allied line and as I turned to face him I noticed some of the remaining infantry start to edge back at the presence of this single 'devil rider'.

'Hey Engleeshman,' he shouted at me in English. 'What 'appened?'

The officer had asked me in my language, so I responded in kind with a Gallic shrug and a shout of

'Espagnol,' as though that explained everything. Well it was the only explanation I had. The French officer guffawed with laughter and returned to his men.

I glanced across to where I had last seen Wellesley. He was still there and watching the Spanish troops with a look of disgust. I walked across to him and by the time I reached his horse he was staring back at the retreating men through his telescope, his lips tightened into a thin angry line. I scraped my foot to attract his attention and his cold blue eyes blazed down at me.

'Christ Flashman, I had no idea they would be this bad. Do you know what the cowardly dogs are doing now?' Without waiting for a reply he continued, 'A good number of them are currently looting our baggage. The rest have run straight towards Talavera, doubtless shouting that we have been defeated on the way. Good God man, how am I supposed to win a war with men like that?'

'I am not even sure what set them off.'

'Your horse skittered about. Maybe they thought it had been hit by a French bullet, a four hundred yard carbine shot,' he snorted in disgust.

'Yes, they killed my bloody horse,' I complained indignantly.

Without another word Wellesley walked his horse towards the big black carriage and the old man who was now being helped down from its roof. 'General Cuesta, I would be obliged if you would supply my officer with another horse to replace the one your men shot.' He paused, staring about at the remaining Spanish infantry that stood either side of the gaping hole in the allied line. 'I take it that you have reliable troops that you can use to make good your defences?' he asked icily.

Cuesta was a proud man and you could see that he was mortified with anger and shame. As his feet landed back on the ground he turned to one of his officers, 'Fetch Captain Flashman the best horse owned by those officers that ran.' He turned to look up at Wellesley but could only hold his gaze for a moment before looking back down at the ground. 'I swear to you, sir,' he spoke quietly in almost a whisper, 'that I will decimate those regiments that ran. The Romans used to kill one man in ten when a legion broke and I will do the same. They will not shame me again.' He paused, taking a deep breath to calm himself, and then added, 'Yes sir, I have enough men to fill the gap. They will not run again.'

I am not sure that any of us actually believed that last claim but Wellesley nodded curtly and turned his horse back to the British lines. As he left he called over his shoulder, 'Report to me when the line is secure, Flashman.'

A short while later I was the new owner of a chestnut thoroughbred and the gap in the Spanish lines had been filled by more nervous Spanish troops. Meanwhile, Cuesta had sent two cavalry regiments to drive back as many of the deserters as they could find. It was getting dark now and I had no intention of spending the night in the dubious shelter of the Spanish forces. If the French attacked their resistance would melt like butter in a hot pan. Instead I opted for the relative safety of the British lines. It was a decision that nearly got me killed; but which may have also changed the course of the war.

Chapter 12

A small British encampment had been built at the western foot of the large hill that dominated the British part of the lines. Having reported to Wellesley, who was dining with some of his commanders, I found myself a billet in one of the tents and settled down for the night. Others fussed writing letters, sharpening swords and otherwise preparing for the battle that was expected to start the following morning, but for once I managed to get some sleep. As dusk had fallen the bulk of the French army, commanded by the new Spanish King Bonaparte, could be still be seen marching over the horizon. No one expected to fight before dawn and this certainly included the officer commanding the troops that were supposed to be the front line of our defence on the hill. Without orders or warning the troops behind him, he marched his men down the slope to more comfortable ground to sleep during the night. What no one seemed to have anticipated was Marshal Victor's ambition.

Victor had not faced British armies before and his confidence must have been buoyed by his easy victories over the Spanish. He did not want to wait for the king and to share the glory; he wanted the victory all to himself. So as darkness fell he ordered a division of his army forward to capture the hill. Once that was in his hands he could dominate the surrounding country, forcing the British and Spanish to withdraw. Victor would be victorious again.

It was hot and airless in that tent, making me toss and turn on the camp cot. I slept fitfully and was slowly awakened by a sound similar to crackling wood in a fire. It took me just a second to realise what was happening and another second to decide on action. The sound was coming from the top of the hill and in the moment I listened, it got louder. I knew instantly that the French were attacking and if they had caught our army half asleep they were bound to succeed. The battle was lost almost before it had begun. But on the positive side, darkness would cover my escape. I was up in a moment, buckling on my sword belt, grabbing my saddle and out of the back flap of the tent while my two tent mates were still rubbing their eyes and peering through the front flap towards the sound of firing. It was a masterstroke but for one small detail… I emerged slap in front of Wellesley marching with a group of staff officers towards the sound of action.

'Ah, Flashman,' he called grimly barely giving me a glance. 'Leave your saddle man, you will not be able to ride in the dark up there.

Come with me.' He turned to General Hill walking beside him, 'So is your division at the top or not?'

'I thought it was, sir,' said the harassed general, 'but Campbell here says he saw some of them camped at the bottom.' I looked around and Campbell was weaving his way through the group towards me.

'It looks as if they have caught us on the hop,' he whispered. 'The best I can tell there is only one regiment on the hill top, and they probably thought that they were the second line of defence and did not post pickets.'

'Good God,' I replied, appalled. 'We are starting to make the bloody Spaniards look professional.' I must have spoken too loudly, for Wellesley wheeled round on us.

'When you two have quite finished gossiping I would be obliged if you would get to the top of that hill. Tell whoever is in charge of our forces to hold for as long as they can and one of you report back to me what is happening.'

'Right away, sir,' answered Campbell, grinning. He seemed delighted to have been ordered into whatever horrors awaited in the darkness, while I just managed to nod my assent as my mind whirled for a way out.

'I will go as well, sir,' said the general, 'I have sent my adjutant to bring my men forward.' I noticed that he walked towards a tethered horse, but he was a portly man who might never have made it to the top otherwise. Campbell was already pulling at my arm.

'Come on Flash, this could be our chance to save the day.' He was already jogging up the bottom of the slope and with Wellesley and the rest of his staff watching, I had no choice but to follow to maintain my reputation as the fearless Flashy. 'Race you to the top,' called Campbell over his shoulder. 'The loser buys the winner breakfast.'

The fearless lunatic seemed to think he was going on some school cross country run rather than into a pitch black battlefield. But there was nothing for it but to shout back, 'I want eggs and bacon and none of your Scottish porridge rubbish.' There was a chuckle from the watching staff at this bravado as the gallant heroes disappeared from view into the darkness. Little did they know that once they were out of sight the 'heroes' behaved rather differently. While one continued sprinting like a highland red deer into the maw of death, the other slowed to a walk and took careful stock.

Battle was still raging at the top of the hill and it looked like we might be holding out. There were regular shouts of 'fire', crashes of volleys and the muzzle flash from lines of musket barrels. Then there were responding shouts of 'tirez', and volleys from the French. Perhaps, I reasoned, it was just a probing attack or an effort to ruin our sleep before the battle next day. In which case, I could not be found by others shirking at the bottom of the hill, as reinforcements would be coming up any minute. I needed to get nearer to the top but I would be sure to get nowhere near the actual fighting. In the darkness I could easily be shot by friend or foe. I climbed steadily up but stopped again when I judged I was three-quarters of the way to the top. The flashes from the musket muzzles were ruining my night vision and making it harder to see what was around, but I sensed the British were starting to fall back. The situation was confused as while I had heard the order 'fall back' given once, subsequently I had heard 'fix bayonets' shouted as well which normally preceded an advance. At one point I thought I saw someone crouching on the ground ahead of me, but when I advanced cautiously with pistol drawn, I discovered it was only a bush growing up against an outcrop of rocks. It seemed as good a place as any to wait until the situation resolved itself.

Then I did hear stones moving on the hillside above me; someone was coming directly down the hill in my direction. I transferred my pistol to my left hand, quietly drew my sword with my right and hunched down in the shadow of the rocks. I wanted to see who it was before I revealed myself. He was nearly on me before I could make out what he was – a very young British officer. He yelped in alarm when I rose up from the ground in front of him.

'Calm down youngster, I am Captain Flashman of General Wellesley's staff,' I told him as I sheathed my sword. He only looked around fourteen and I wondered if he was running away, not that I would have blamed him if he was. 'What are you about then?' I asked sternly.

'Please sir,' he gasped back, 'I'm Ensign Thompson of the King's Hanoverians and my colonel has sent me to find General Wellesley to report that we are hard pressed and need reinforcements, sir.' He waived a paper in front of him which was clearly a message from his colonel. I realised in a moment that this was a stroke of luck and that breakfast could be mine after all.

'I will take that,' I said taking the despatch. 'Tell your colonel that General Wellesley orders that he should hold out for as long as he can and that reinforcements are already on the way to him. Can you do that?'

'Oh yes, sir,' the boy piped, his eyes gleaming at the importance of his role. Without a second's delay he had turned on his heel and was sprinting back up the hill. I grinned in the darkness. Campbell would be up at the top of the hill by now and blundering about trying not to be shot by either side until he could make contact with the Hanoverian commander. Meanwhile I could now return to safety with the Hanoverian's despatch. If we retook the hill then I would enjoy the breakfast, if not then I would make sure I was long gone by dawn. I had only taken a few steps when I heard some more people running down the hill behind me. I shrank back into the shadows again as a precaution, but the clattering footsteps resolved themselves into a British officer on horse. I showed myself as I realised it was the portly general in command of the men who should have been guarding the hill top. I had expected him to rein in, but if anything he was urging his horse faster into – on this terrain – a reckless speed. The general was hunched down in the saddle and his jacket was torn. His horse reared slightly at the sight or smell of me and the general glanced with wild eyes in my direction.

'Flashman,' he shouted at me. 'The French have taken the hill. Run man, save yourself.' With that he plunged on speeding ever faster down the hill. Well you don't need to tell me twice to save myself. I had already turned and run a few paces back down the slope when there was a fusillade of shots from my left, and from out of the gloom came French infantry. I was so shocked I did not look where I was going on the rocky ground; a stone moved under me and I crashed down amongst the rocks. For a moment I think I blacked out. I came to with a stabbing pain in my skull and a trickle of blood from a cut on my forehead that must have hit a sharp edged stone. But I had no time to worry about that. I watched in horror as more and more French troops appeared in front of me. They were concentrating all their fire and attention on the fleeing general on horseback, and none seemed to notice me as I lay prone between the rocks. It was now clear that as well as sending men over the top of the summit, Victor had also sent men around the sides of the hill to flank any relief party. He was no slouch that marshal.

Well, he had truly stuffed my goose as I now could not go down or up without encountering French troops. The best course seemed to be to hide out until the situation was clearer. Running around in a battlefield at night was near suicidal. At worst in the morning I would be forced to surrender to the French, but with luck the British would retake the hill or I could slip away. Slowly I turned around and crawled back to the bush in the outcrop of rocks. Carefully I wriggled between the bush and the rocks until I was hidden from view.

For half an hour I lay there listening to the tide of battle. I had a stabbing pain from my head wound and a continuing dull ache from my grazed arse, but at least I was still alive. I heard the Hanoverians break and run past my refuge, and their shouts of alarm as they retreated slap into the French further down the hill. Then I listened as French infantry followed them down the hill to prepare to face a British counter attack, which from the sound of drums and bugles in the camp below was gathering. For a while all was quiet, I seemed to have the area just below the hill top all to myself. Gingerly I got to my feet and peered over the rocks. There was no one around on the hill above me and I began to wonder if there was a chance to slip away. The moon was now shining through a gap in the clouds and while my bush was well leafed I wondered if it was thick enough to hide me in daylight.

Then I heard two voices talking in French, and as I peered cautiously around the bush I saw two French officers heading straight towards me. I ducked back and crouched down again in my hiding place. I was sure that they had not seen me, they were talking in conversational tones, but still they came closer, heading directly for the bush. If they did see me through the branches in the moonlight then there was no room for me to draw and swing a sword. I drew one of my pistols but they were now so close that they would hear it being cocked. I froze as they walked right up to my bush and stopped. They were no more than three feet in front of me. I thought they must have seen me and my body clenched expecting steel blades to probe at me through the branches.

In the event something entirely different came through the branches, as two streams of piss splashed the ground near my feet. I realised I had been holding my breath for the last few moments and now I allowed myself to breathe silently through my mouth, which also helped me avoid the smell. Only then did I start to pay attention to what they were saying.

'I expected the roast beefs to put up more of a fight,' crowed one.

'Their general is used to fighting native armies, perhaps they do not attack at night,' said the other.

'Whatever, the marshal will be delighted to have beaten them before the king's or Soult's armies get here.' I pricked up my ears at that. Everyone thought that Soult was still licking his wounds after Oporto in northern Spain, now it seemed he was closing in on Talavera.

'Yes,' agreed the companion. 'Beating the army that defeated Soult will give him more pleasure than anything. The Emperor is bound to reward him well.' He paused as a renewed burst of volley fire sounded from the bottom of the hill. 'It sounds like the roast beefs have not given up after all,' he continued. 'We had better get back.' There was a pause as they buttoned themselves back up, and then I could hear the slow tramp of their footsteps and the murmuring of their continued conversation as they moved away.

My mind was whirling; if I was to get away I would need to find out where Soult was so that I did not stumble into his forces in error. The whole area would be swarming with the French soon and that thought made me realise that what I really needed was a French uniform. I spoke passable French, not as a native, but as they had so many nationalities in their army I could pretend I was a German or Hollander. As long as they did not have someone of that nationality to hand I should get by.

There have been times when I have doubted the existence of a supreme being, but at that moment I was given conclusive proof of the existence of a deity as my prayers were immediately answered. No sooner were the thoughts out of my head than I heard a distant whistling.

I poked my head up over the stones for the noise was coming from the east, from where the French had attacked. I could not make out the figure at first but now I could hear footsteps over the stones. Then the whistling stopped.

'Colonel Dreyfus?' a voice called out in French nervously. 'Major Calvet?' he tried again. There was no answer and the whistling resumed. I realised that he must be whistling to ensure that he did not take the soldiers he was trying to find by surprise and get shot by mistake. He was getting closer now and I saw he had a sword at his hip rather than a long musket over his shoulder which meant he was an officer. That was ideal as in an officer's uniform I would be less likely to be questioned when travelling on my own. He was even around my size, but I judged a few years younger, possibly in his late teens. I ducked down as he got closer; he seemed to be walking directly towards me. He came to a sudden stop and I heard the whistling stop again as he muttered to himself, 'Ah it is just a bush.' He must have seen the dark mass of foliage in the gloom and come this way to investigate.

I realised now was my chance. He was turning to walk around the stones I was hiding behind. I stood up and was just able to reach out and grab his trailing ankle before he realised I was there. He gave a slight wail of alarm before he crashed down heavily into the rocks. I was up and on him in a second. I rolled him over and knelt with my knee on his chest. I had my sword drawn and against his throat.

'Silence,' I hissed at him in French. 'I have already killed three Frenchman tonight; don't force me to make it four.' I must have been a frightening sight for half of my face was covered with dried blood from the cut on my head. The whites of his eyes shone back at me in the moonlight as he froze in terror. He had thought that the hillside had been cleared of enemy troops and now he had been captured by what he believed was a ruthless British killer. 'Now listen to me carefully, boy,' I told him, as I noticed that he was so young he had barely started shaving. 'I want to know about Marshal Soult. I know some things already, so if you lie to me I will kill you, understand?'

The boy nodded, as far as my sword blade would permit.

'Right, now where is Soult?'

The boy licked his lips. 'He is coming from the north, monsieur.'

I pressed the blade more firmly against his neck and whispered sternly, 'I know that, but where is he now?'

There was a gulp and bobbing of his Adam's apple before he replied, 'I think he is near Plascencia.' I had not been expecting that. Plascencia was a town in a mountain pass nearly a hundred miles to the west. It meant Soult would soon be between me and the relative safety of Portugal. If the British army stayed north of the river Tagus then it would be trapped between Soult in the west and Victor and King Bonaparte in the east. If I was to escape I needed to get south of the Tagus.

'How many men does Soult have?' I asked harshly.

The boy twitched in alarm. 'I do not know monsieur, truly I do not. I only know what I hear from other officers. They say that Soult will help trap your army if it escapes but I do not know how many men he has.'

The boy was clearly telling the truth and he had already told me all I needed to know. 'All right, I am going to let you sit up. I want you to take off your coat and leave it on the rocks behind you. If you try to pull a knife or a pistol I will kill you, understand?'

The boy nodded. He was not going to cause any trouble, he was desperate to live. He wriggled out of his coat in a moment.

'Now undo your sword belt and leave that behind.' The boy complied again. I flicked my sword point back up the hill in the direction from which he had come and said, 'Now get out of here.' He scampered up in a moment and was away, leaving me with what I wanted. I shrugged off my own coat and picked up the blue one, and then I paused. The noise of battle from the bottom of the hill was getting louder; I could hear orders being shouted in French and English now. It was clear that a counter attack was underway and there would be an awful irony in being killed by my own side in an enemy coat. I dropped back into my little gap between the rocks and the bush holding both coats. I had already sat there during the defeat of the British. Now I would stay there until it was clear who had won the day and come out dressed accordingly.

When you are in the heat of battle times flies, but when you are hiding uncomfortably behind a bush listening to one, it seems to take for ever. God knows how long I crouched behind that stinking foliage. Sometimes I thought the battle was ebbing away, indicating the French were winning, and sometimes it seemed to be coming closer with the British having the upper hand. Only when I started to see some French soldiers run past my hiding place going back up over the hill was I sure that the British were regaining the hill. Gradually the noise of regular crashing volleys become louder and I peered down the hill into the darkness for signs of the battle line coming my way.

The French broke in a sudden rush; from one or two stragglers there were suddenly dozens of blue coated troops running up the hill and past my position. Then I could see more troops marching in solid ranks coming up behind. Salvation in the form of a company of redcoats was marching towards me, they were set to pass either side of my hiding place, and I would emerge and be safe again.

But of all the stupid luck, a French officer and his sergeant started to try and rally their men right in front of my bush. The officer called for his men to stand and a sergeant next to him was bellowing similar orders. Then other soldiers started to hesitate as they ran past.

'Company, halt,' called an English voice from the red jacketed men below.

With an awful realisation I understood that they were preparing to fire a volley. Eighty musket balls would sweep away the French, but the only protection I had in that direction was a bush. I was listening to the orders of my own firing squad.

'Company, present,' called the English voice again.

I did not have to look to imagine the eighty muskets being raised to the shoulder. I had to act. Frantically I pulled my pistol from the pocket of the red coat and aimed it at the broad back of the French sergeant. I fired at exactly the same moment I heard the English voice call, 'Aim.'

I burst out from the bush, sword in hand. 'Don't shoot,' I yelled, 'I am British.'

The French officer, who had turned to look at his sergeant, tried to whirl back to face the white shirted stranger who had appeared from nowhere. But it was too late. I just jabbed my sword at him without aiming and more by luck than skill I stuck it straight in his throat. More blood spurted in my direction covering my shirt and breeches but I did not care about that. My attention was on the line of men down the hill, with their fingers curled around the triggers of eighty muskets pointed in my direction.

'Don't shoot!' I repeated. 'I'm Captain Flashman, I'm British.' Having just seen me slay two Frenchman in front of them, that was perhaps obvious, but I was taking no chances.

'Company port arms,' the voice called. 'Company advance.' The resumed tramping of British boots was right then once of the sweetest sounds I have ever heard. It was interrupted by the buzz of a ball over my head as one of the French infantry behind me stopped retreating just long enough to take a shot at the man who had killed their officer and sergeant. I was not out of the woods yet, and in keeping with my reputation as a brave and resourceful officer, I felt a gesture was required.

'Come on lads,' I yelled, waving my blood-stained sword in the air. 'Go at them, they won't stand now.'

'Go at them lads,' confirmed one of their officers and with a guttural roar the whole company surged forward passing either side of me. It was a fine sight, men in their familiar red coats with their sweating faces and bayonet points glistening in the moonlight. You may be sure that no one cheered them on more enthusiastically than me, although I was careful not to take a single step further up that hill. Once they had passed it seemed strangely quiet. I looked down on the bodies of the two Frenchmen I had killed, for they were both now quite dead. It had been one hell of a night and I had been just the twitch of a trigger finger away from joining them. I sat down on a rock to gather my thoughts, but before they had even had a chance to rally themselves I heard my name being called.

'Flashman, good God, I thought you were dead.'

I looked up and there was the portly general who had evidently survived his brush with French skirmishers. He was riding back up the hill again and behind him other officers were emerging from the gloom, some on horseback and others on foot. 'I nearly was, sir. Is Wellesley with you? I have news for him.'

'Sir Arthur,' shouted the general, while twisting around in his saddle to shout at those behind him. 'I have found Flashman, he is alive.' Several of the horsemen nudged their mounts slightly to head in my direction, amongst them the familiar tall lanky figure. But it was one of the men on foot who reached me first, as bounding over the rocks came a beaming Campbell.

'Flashman you rascal, the general was sure you were killed or captured and here you are, ready to buy me my breakfast after all. I say, are you wounded?' He stopped in surprise as he notice that the dark stain on my shirt front was blood and there was more caked down the side of my face.

'Oh, most of it came from that fellow when I killed him,' I explained, gesturing with deliberate casualness to the French officer lying near my feet. 'Took a knock on the head though, bullet I think, but it just bounced off my skull.' I was not going to admit to cutting my head falling over, and by now the other officers were crowding round and congratulating me on my good fortune.

'Remarkable, 'pon my word,' called one, 'where is your coat sir?'

'Still behind that bush,' I said without thinking, and Campbell darted into the foliage to retrieve it.

'It is good to see you Flashman,' Wellesley greeted me primly but already his eyes were darting ahead to where his men were securing the crest of the hill.

'I say,' said Campbell emerging from the bush holding up both of my coats. 'There is a French coat back there as well as a British one.' The babble of voices suddenly stopped and people looked to me enquiringly, some I thought with a slightly hostile glare, as though they guessed why I had procured a French coat in the first place. It was certainly not considered seemly to run out on your own side.

'Flashman, what is this?' asked Wellesley with slight distaste. But I was ready with my explanation.

'Well of course there is, you could hardly expect me to join a meeting of French officers in a British uniform.'

'You did what?' exclaimed Campbell, astonished.

'You heard,' I grinned. 'Remember I was recruited first as a spy in India? Well it is an old habit to break. So when I found myself behind enemy lines and a number of Victor's officers gathered to discuss the battle, I found a uniform jacket on a dead officer and stood at the back to listen. Damn good job I did too as what I learned might save this army.'

Most of them crowded round at that, some patting me on the back as they admired my coolness under pressure. Wellesley, I noticed, stayed where he was, watching me with a curious expression which made me a tad uneasy. But I did not get time to consider this as the rest of them were clamouring to know what I had discovered.

'The army you know is out yonder,' I told them, pointing to the eastern horizon, which would soon reveal the combined army of Victor and King Bonaparte, 'is just part of the French plan.' I paused for a second to allow the tension to build, for I was going to milk this for as much credit as I could get. 'We are already humbugged, gentlemen,' I told them portentously. 'For five days march to the west, behind us, comes another French army commanded by Soult.'

There were gasps and exclamation aplenty then. Some were saying they could not believe it, others shouting we would have to beat Victor without delay and yet more counselling caution and a retreat across the Talavera bridge, and guarding the few crossing points of the river Tagus. Above the babble Wellesley's voice cut in.

'Where exactly is Soult now?'

'The French believe he is at Plascencia,' I told him.

Wellesley nodded, showing he thought my five day estimate to be realistic, before asking the critical question. 'How many men does he have?'

'I don't know. They did not mention numbers and I could not attract attention by asking questions or they would have realised that they had a stranger in their midst.'

'He only had around fifteen thousand men left when we beat him at Oporto,' opined the fat general.

'Yes, but there are other French marshals in the north,' said a voice in the crowd, 'such as Ney and Mortier who could have given him reinforcements.' That sparked a new debate before Wellesley cut in crisply.

125

'It does not matter now. What is important is that we have time to beat the French army in front of us. Then we will worry about Soult.' He turned to look at me and warmth broke through his normal cold look of disdain. 'Flashman, once again I have underestimated your resourcefulness. You were worth a regiment to me in India, undermining enemy morale and then letting us into Gawilghur. Now you are saving my army again. I thank you.' His grin widened as he added, 'Now I suppose I should reward you with the thing I know you crave...'

As he spoke I remembered with horror that the misguided fool believed that I wanted a role of action in the heat of the coming battle. Well, I had already done enough, and there was no way I was going into the jaws of death again. I knew just how to get out of it too. All it took was an artful stumble and my hand going to my bleeding head for several people to reach forward to catch me and guide me to a nearby rock to sit.

'I say, sir,' called a major I did not know, although I could have kissed him at the time. 'This Flashman fellow is not well.' He turned to me, 'This cut sir, was it caused by a sword or a glancing bullet?'

I weakly waved the major away as I looked up to Wellesley. 'Don't worry sir, it takes more than a French bullet to stop me.' He looked down at me with a mixture of concern and admiration as I added, 'I will be ready for action in a moment, just feeling a bit dizzy all of a sudden.'

I allowed myself to slump more against the major who was by now standing beside me, and fluttered my eyelids as though struggling to retain consciousness, but I had done enough.

'I am sorry, Flashman,' said Wellesley decisively. 'But you are too valuable to waste against the enemy when you are not in top fighting trim. Major, would you take Captain Flashman back to the surgeon's tent to be examined.' I made a token show of reluctance but the major soon had me moving in the right direction. Wellesley patted me on the shoulder as I went past him. 'You can join me on the hill to watch when you are patched up, but you are not for the front line today.' And this from a man they later called the Iron Duke!

Chapter 13

Initially I had no intention of returning back up that hill, but all of the walking wounded from the night's battle were rushing back up there to regain their places in the ranks. It would have looked strange if the hero of the hour had remained lounging in the surgeon's tent with just a bandage round his head, sipping the surgical brandy. At least I had Wellesley's assurance I was not for the front line, so reluctantly, as the grey light of dawn spread across the sky I set off again. But this time I took my horse. If things went badly I wanted to be sure I could make a fast get away.

Wellesley had organised his forces in a long line stretching from the hill towards the Spanish on the right. The hill was the dominant position and it was at its summit that I found Wellesley and half a dozen of his officers sitting on their horses, squinting into the sunrise to make out the enemy formations. We watched as regiments started to march and form up into three huge columns. Most alarming from my perspective was that they were all forming up on the French right, opposite the hill I was standing on.

'They are Victor's men,' said Campbell to me. He had ridden up alongside when I reached the summit. 'He is readying for an early attack. He failed to take the hill by stealth in the night and now he seems to be planning to take it by weight of numbers and force.' Victor did not know the number of men that opposed him on the hill for there were no British infantry on the facing slope. I had passed them on the way up, a long line of redcoats resting out of sight of the enemy but ready to come over the crest of the hill when called. Looking at the huge mass of men that were gathering across the valley, the line I had ridden through seemed pathetically fragile. Turning to the right I could see the British line extending beyond the hill towards the Spanish position. That thin stream of red coated men seemed no thicker than the ones I had passed and they were in full view of the French. Looking at the men massing against us it was as though we were planning to stop the advance of three whales with a flimsy net. The French had double the number of the British, while our allies seemed literally frightened of their own shadow. I looked for the British horsemen and found them some distance off to the left to forestall any flanking move. The French had cavalry of their own on the wings to counter any move of our horse.

There was a mutter of excitement from the watching officers and someone called out, 'That must be Joseph Bonaparte.' I trained my glass towards a knot of gaudily dressed officers on the hill rising from the far side of the valley. They were too far away to make out any features in my glass, but evidently they were there to order the start of the attack, as almost immediately a signal gun fired. The hollow boom was followed a few seconds later by a rumble of gunfire like rolling thunder, as down the valley over fifty large cannon opened fire. Any rational person with a wit of common sense would be looking to take cover at this point, but not of course a British army officer.

'It looks likely to be a hot morning,' said Campbell calmly, although whether he was talking about the guns or the sun that was only just rising into the sky it was hard to say.

'Oh I say, are those bunting?' called another officer as a flock of birds startled by the gunfire rose up in a large flock from the valley floor. It was the fat general of the night before, Rowland Hill, a kindly old duffer who was known as Daddy Hill to his men.

The hundreds of pounds of iron screaming through the air in our direction were blithely ignored by my brother officers as most of them gazed up at the wretched birds. I stared at them in astonishment. If there was ever a time when I was less interested in flora and fauna, well I couldn't think of it. The first salvo fell well short as the cannon barrels were cold. I saw balls bounce up the slope beneath us kicking up clouds of dust, tufts of grass and turf. I seemed to be the only one watching the fall of shot. As the gunfire of the first salvo died away, the rest of our party engaged in the evidently more important debate of deciding whether the birds were bunting, finches or wastrels.

I stared around me wondering how long this madness could last, but then I noticed that their studied airs of unconcern were, if anything, a little too studied. One officer was choosing this moment to pick lint from his sleeve while another found a mark on the back of his hand fascinating. I knew that I was looking at the insidious influence of British public schools. From the first day, boys are taught that a gentleman should never show fear and certainly not in front of the enemy or the lower orders. With our own men resting in relative safely over the crest it was unthinkable that we should run to cover to join them. Oh no, honour demanded that we sit there like fish in a barrel nonchalantly ignoring the shot coming our way. Rugby school had tried to instil that ethic in me too, but with mixed success. I was careful to keep my credit with those that mattered, but given the chance I would slide out at the first opportunity.

'Do you think they are bunting, Flashman?' Hill was looking enquiringly at me.

'I am sorry sir, I have no idea.' I did not care a fig for the wretched birds; my mind was turning to other more important matters, such as saving my own skin. I glanced down to our right at the long lines of redcoats stretching away to the Spanish position and completely exposed to the French cannon. 'Sir Arthur,' I turned to Wellesley, 'should we not order our men on the right to lie down, they are horribly exposed as they are.'

'Ah yes, Flashman, that is a good idea.' I was already sliding my feet into the stirrups ready to take the order; and thinking that a relapse of my head injury and another spell in the surgical tent was called for, when he turned to a young cornet behind him. 'Mr Darcy, would you give my compliments to Sherbrooke and tell him that I desire his men to lie down until the enemy advance.'

'Yes sir,' the young man threw up a smart salute before turning his horse to carry away my message.

'And wait with the infantry on your return Mr Darcy,' called out Wellesley. Once the lad was out of earshot he murmured, 'I promised his mother I would look after him,' as though an excuse was required for this act of compassion. I glared with a look of jealous venom at the retreating back of the boy, but before I could say any more the first French guns completed their reloading and fired again.

This time many of the French gunners had over compensated for their cold barrels by aiming high. Two balls flew over our heads making a sound like tearing calico. Instinctively several of us ducked our heads. Instead of a single salvo, the gunnery was more ragged now as the French gunners took varying times to reload their pieces. There was nothing for it but to sit there watching the blooms of smoke appear on the opposite side of the valley, and know that each one was sending an iron ball towards the British lines.

As the guns continued I could hear Hill continuing a conversation with Fenton, his aide, and those around him about more bloody birds. 'Guns on skiffs, you say...' he was interrupted by another crash of gunfire. 'What was that?' At this point two more balls crashed into the hillside in front of us sending small stones flying through the air. I did not catch what Fenton said but as the stones settled I could hear Hill exclaiming, 'Well that just ain't sporting, not sporting at all.' This was followed by a rumble of six guns firing together although where those balls went I had no idea. You can imagine how I felt; it was like being the target at a fairground stall and hoping not to be hit. The valley was slowly filling up with gun smoke but through the gaps you could see that the columns had not even started moving yet. I sat there staring to my front and found that I had been gripping my sword hilt so hard that the wire around it was cutting into the palm of my hand.

There was distant shouting from behind me and looking around again I saw that at the bottom of the hill one end of the surgical tent had now collapsed. It appeared that one of the cannon balls which had been aimed high over the hill had smashed into the tent on the far side. It just went to show that cannon fire was a damn random business. A few moments ago I had been fervently wishing I had stayed in that tent and now I saw that I might have been killed if I had.

As the second salvo died away, giving us a moment's peace, Hill turned to me again.

'Flashman, Fenton here tells me that in North America they use two inch guns loaded with shot and mounted on skiffs to hunt ducks. They push them through the reeds and blast the birds. Now tell me, that ain't sporting is it, what?'

I came within an ace of telling the old fool that I did not give a damn for his bloody birds, but then I managed to pull what shreds of reserve I had left and turned to him. I even managed a grin as I replied, 'At this moment sir, I do have some particular sympathy with the ducks.' There was a chuckle at that but before anyone could say more the fastest French guns opened fire again. The French gunners were getting their aim in now and one of the first balls pitched right in front of Hill's horse, and then twisted away to pass in a blur close to Campbell. I knew Campbell was a certifiable lunatic when it came to courage so I did not expect him to blanch, but even he turned to me pale faced and grinned, 'I think I felt the heat of that one.'

My attention though was on Hill. I had seen the look of horror on his face when the ball had first pitched and he thought he was about to die. Belatedly I realised that despite his rambling about birds he was as frightened as the rest of us. I understood now that he had been chattering away to try and distract us. That was why he had kept trying to involve me in the conversation despite my obvious lack of interest. I felt a twinge of compassion for the man. I knew nothing about birds but I thought I would give him something to talk about.

'My Uncle John said he shot a knock kneed knuckle warbler up near Inverness,' I shouted at him over the gunfire. 'Apparently they are quite rare.' Campbell looked across at me and grinned. He realised instantly that I had made up the name of the bird. Fenton, Hill's aide, caught the glance and smiled conspiratorially from behind his general's back

'What kind of warbler?' enquired Hill above the noise. I shouted the name again but the words were lost in the resounding booms of further cannonading. I took a deep breath and shouted it as loud as I could a third time... just as the guns fell silent again. 'A knuckle warbler,' said Hill intrigued, ignoring the fact that I had virtually bellowed the name in his ear. 'How strange, is it a local name do you think?'

'Oh yes,' said Campbell giving me a wink. 'And they are good eating, thighs as big as a chicken.'

'An edible warbler? I have never heard of such a thing,' Hill sounded genuinely fascinated.

'One of my aunts on the Essex marshes used to serve us warbler pie when I was a boy,' said Fenton, joining in.

Before Hill could react to that another officer who had sensed the fun joined in too. 'My wife is very fond of fricassee of warbler.'

'Well I am blown,' muttered Hill as we all agreed that fricassee of warbler sounded an excellent dish. Fenton was struggling now to keep a straight face and was hiding his grin behind a large kerchief that he wiped his nose with.

Wellesley had stayed silent, he generally stayed aloof of pranks by his staff officers. But now he interrupted his surveillance of the enemy and lowered his glass. Glancing across at Hill he gave an indulgent smile and added, 'I think you will find potted warbler very enjoyable. I am most partial to it.'

'Potted warbler,' repeated a bewildered Hill, trying to come to terms with the apparent culinary dexterity of the bird. Fenton behind him was going red in the face as he now seemed to be eating his kerchief to stop himself laughing.

'Well, Sir Arthur,' exclaimed Hill, 'I will certainly try it when I get the opportunity.'

There was a squeaking sound and I thought Fenton was choking. Hill looked round at him and saw his shoulders shaking with laughter.

'Oh I say,' he grinned, 'you bounders have gulled me.' Anything he said after that was lost as the French guns roared again. The six of us sat on that hillside with cannon balls whipping around us while we roared with laughter; at least one of us slightly hysterically. It was not that funny a joke, but it acted as a release for the tension that had been building in each one of us. I don't know about the rest, but I felt strangely fatalistic now as the balls bounced around. I saw one land a few yards short and ricochet away, and I remember thinking that if there had been an ounce more powder in the charge or a gust of wind then that would have been the end of me, dying with smile about edible warblers still on my lips.

That is not to say that I did not breathe a sigh of relief when Wellesley shouted out that the French columns were finally on the move. His next order was for our artillery to be uncovered and to open fire on the slowly moving blue blocks of men. Sacks of stones were pulled away from the front of the gun carriages and they prepared to fire. Wellesley had kept them protected until the columns started to move, as he did not want them dismounted before they were able to whip bloody trails through the columns. I knew that now the French gunners would concentrate on our gun batteries and give us some relief.

As we sat and watched, strangely calm now, the salvos got longer and the gaps between them shorter until the French fire was continuous. It was punctuated by the crashing discharges of our guns from their batteries on either side of the hill top so that it was now almost impossible to hold a conversation. We watched as the French columns slowly crossed the valley floor and I realised that soon matters would come to a conclusion one way or another.

The word 'column' may be misleading as they were wider than they were deep. I estimated each contained fifteen hundred men, being over a hundred and fifty men wide and around ten men deep. All three seemed still to be heading directly for our position on the hill. The French were clearly determined to capture it with its commanding position over the rest of the battlefield. The French marched with the confidence of men who knew that nothing could stop their mighty columns smashing through whatever they were aimed at. These were the veterans that had smashed through the armies of emperors, tsars, kings and princes, even the Mamelukes in Egypt. Some heavily outnumbered redcoats on the top of a hill were not considered a great obstacle. Golden eagle standards glittered along the lines marking out each regiment, and within their mass the drummers beat the pace like the heartbeat of a single huge creature. Then, as I had heard in

Alcantara but now on a massive scale, the drummers would pause and in unison nearly five thousand men would roar out, 'vive l'empereur!'

'Thank Christ I am on a horse,' I thought as I watched them approach, for it seemed impossible that our flimsy ranks would stop them. I even glanced back down the hillside I had climbed to ascertain the best route back. I looked around to see if any of my brother officers were also edging back a little but they were all sitting resolutely on their mounts.

It was one of the heaviest cannonades I have ever experienced. The smoke from the French guns slowly built in the valley until I could barely see the French columns at all. But I could still hear them, and in some ways that was even more unnerving. The steady tramp, tramp, tramp of thousands of boots, the pounding of the drums and then that regular bellow of loyalty to their emperor. It made the hair on the back of my neck stand up, aye and it did every time I heard it over the coming years too. Even the redcoats, sitting and lying on the reverse slope in their long lines, had fallen silent now as they listened to their approaching enemy and tried to picture the scene they would shortly be facing.

As the French columns emerged from the smoke near the Portina stream at the bottom of the valley, the order was finally given for the British troops to come over the crest and form up on the slope. Most companies marched forward in lines but the light companies ran scattered down the hill to disrupt the enemy approach. There was no hesitation but I guessed there must have been some gasps of trepidation when they finally saw the smoke and maelstrom of shot they were walking into.

Somehow the French gunners had seen the British troops move and now all the French cannon seemed to be trained on the men on the slope in front of me, even those to the south which had previously been firing at the redcoats opposite them.

The iron whizzed through the air now like mosquitoes in a swamp. In the first few seconds I saw four balls tear through the double lines of red coated men, smashing bodies and flinging them away like rag dolls. Some cannon balls bounced before reaching the lines and gave the men a small chance to avoid them, while others screamed over our heads. But the French gunners knew their business and most were well aimed.

I saw freakish deaths and miraculous redemptions. One ball bouncing on the ground towards a group of infantry men hit a rock, deflecting it to decapitate a corporal who had been shouting a warning to his men in its earlier path. A sergeant was snatched away but instead of being killed he got up unharmed to find the ball buried in his pack. One young ensign, a boy of no more than fourteen by the look of him, was white and shaking with fear. His captain noticed and walked over to help strengthen his resolve. God knows what was said, but the boy stiffened and stuck his chin up, and then to show his courage he took a few steps towards his men shouting encouragement to them in his piping voice. A few seconds later a ball whipped through the line taking one of the rear file men and the young ensign, smashing them both to a pulp. I reflected that if the lad had stayed quaking where he was he would probably have survived, which shows what courage gets you! Hill must have seen it too, for now he shouted for his men to lie down again to get what little protection there was.

There was the intermittent crackle now of British skirmishers picking off officers and the leading ranks in the French columns as they came into range, before falling back up the hill. I did not have to see them to know that this would be as effective as firing pins at an elephant. The French marched on as though they were not there.

Eventually, when the French soldiers started to climb the slope before us, the cannonade eased as the French gunners worried about hitting their own men. Attention turned now to the battle between the skirmishers in front of the columns. The French had sent out their own skirmish troops to keep ours at bay. The light troops were battling each other but the British were putting up a good defence and falling back in good order. In fact they were falling back too slowly for Hill who feared that they would still be in the way when he wanted to fire his volleys. The French were now half way up the hill and he roared at his light company officers, 'Damn their filing, let them come in anyhow.'

As the last light company troops disappeared into the ranks. The French were just a hundred yards away now. The stamp of their thousands of boots alone was enough to drown out conversation. I saw some of the front ranks grinning at the thin line of men still lying down in front of them, and they gave a final below of loyalty to their emperor, perhaps in the hope of just frightening our men way. It nearly worked with me.

Hill turned to the nearest regiment and shouted, 'Now twenty-ninth, now is your time.' The men of the twenty-ninth rose to their feet and all along the line other regiments followed suit, so that the front ranks of the French must have seen a wall of red rise up in front of them. Then, for the French, the horror began.

The French might have been used to enemies melting away in front of them, but the hard faced men in red showed no sign of going anywhere as they half turned and raised muskets to their shoulders. The crash of the volley was not as loud as I had anticipated and I glanced quickly down the line to see what had gone wrong. I half expected to see streams of men pouring back over the hill and I was ready to join them if they were. But not a single man had moved, and as I wondered what was going on another volley crashed out, well before the first could have reloaded. Then I realised that only part of our line was firing at a time.

Rolling company volleys are a devastating technique, but they can only be done by well-trained troops. The British had practised them well. Every third company along the line fired their eighty muskets at the enemy and then started to reload using the fast drill that was now automatic to them. A few seconds later the next third of the regiment would fire and then after another short delay the final companies, by which time the first company was readying itself to fire again. The end result was an almost continuous hail of lead into the front of the column.

The French commanders had probably expected a single volley and then planned to return fire, having closed the range while the British were reloading. They had never faced anything like this and must have realised with a shock that there was not going to be a lull for them to prepare their men to fire. Not only were the British fast to reload, but they were experienced enough to know to aim their guns low against the French, so that the recoil took the ball into their bodies and not over their heads. Already between the volleys we could hear the screams and yells of the wounded as they were hit or trodden on by the men behind.

The front ranks of the columns were collapsing in waves as the men in front of them fired, but the French still came on. The regular marching was more hesitant and stumbling now as they stepped over the dead and wounded. The range closed to seventy yards and then fifty, but by now there was carnage in the front ranks of the huge columns which were overlapped by the continuous line of redcoats. At that distance a musket ball could easily pass through two or more bodies, and men were being shot down faster than those behind could climb over them. I watched in fascinated horror as the front ranks crumpled and the men behind struggled to get around or over their comrades, with disorder rippling through the ranks. Too late the French commanders tried to get their men to return fire.

The column finally ground to a halt. While the French still outnumbered the British, only their front two ranks could bring their guns to bear, and they were also the ones facing the devastating storm of shot from the men in front. I glanced quickly along the line and the other two columns had similarly ground to a halt and one was already starting to fall back. I turned to the men in front of me as a sporadic volley finally rang out from the front of the French column but it seemed to do little damage. Many of the French seemed to have fired wildly just to obey the order as British balls continued to slash through their ranks.

The French could see that they were making no progress and that the British fire was steadily turning their front ranks into a blue coated rampart of dead. With no sign of a let up in the steady barrage of lead, some of them now started to edge back. Suddenly the edging back broke into a run, and like a dam breaking, the rear files of the huge columns were hurtling back down the hill as fast as they could go. Ironically it was this sign of their breaking that gave the French the respite from volleys that they wanted. Not that it did them much good.

'Cease fire,' called British officers and sergeants down the ranks. Then after a brief pause came a new order, 'Fix bayonets.'

Even if the front French ranks did not understand the English, there was no mistaking the portent of eighteen inches of cold steel being attached to every musket in front of them. The screams and yells of the many wounded were now augmented by yells of panic as the front ranks pushed desperately at the men behind them to get away from the onslaught they knew was about to be unleashed on them. The rest of the French column had broken before the order to charge was given. With a roar the redcoat line sprang forward at the survivors. Some of the French whose muskets were still loaded tried to make a stand half way down the hill to cover their retreat, but a third of the British were also loaded and the rest had their blood up. A red coated tide swept down the hill driving all before it and in a matter of moments the hillside was ours.

As you can imagine I was jubilant, if not a little awestruck, at the devastating firestorm that had just been delivered. Like the French I had not seen anything like it, and for the first time I began to understand why some of my brother officers had more confidence in our success. Our charging infantry stopped at the bottom of the hill; the French side of the valley was still wreathed in artillery smoke and who knew what horrors waited there. The officers, conscious of the gaping hole left in our lines, urged the men back up the slope to fill it again. They were worried that French cavalry could swoop forward and cut up the redcoats who were scattered out of formation, but none appeared. The cannon fire did not even resume, and as the French had disappeared into the smoke on their side of the valley, our guns stopped too. We listened for the noise of more marching men but all we could hear was distant French shouting.

After such a deafening cannonade and then a battle, the relative quiet – with just the odd groan or whimper from the wounded – seemed almost eerie. Hill had ridden forward to congratulate his men as they climbed back up the slope, while Wellesley kept glancing up and down the line to see if the French were preparing to attack somewhere else, but all was still. Slowly the smoke began to thin in the valley and we could see that there was no movement in the French lines at all.

'Surely they will attack again sir?' one of the staff officers asked Wellesley.

'They will certainly try something,' he said. 'Hello, what is this, a flag of truce?' I looked, and about a hundred men could be seen coming forward, but they were unarmed and not in any military formation. They met Hill on the slope and he sent them further up where they began to collect the French wounded. More French soldiers could be seen now gathering by the Portina stream where they filled canteens and drank the water. Our soldiers watched enviously, the sun was climbing high in the sky now and the morning was already warm. They had been biting down on cartridges and spitting the balls into the muzzles of their guns as they loaded; the salty gunpowder had made their mouths dry and their own canteens were empty. It was evident that the French had not sent nearly enough men to collect their wounded, so now some British soldiers were allowed to leave the line to help carry the French wounded down the slope to the stream. Once there I noticed they did not rush back up and were busy drinking their fill and trying to talk to the French soldiers around them.

There was no formal truce, but it was unofficially understood all along the line that hostilities had temporarily been suspended. Men who had previously been trying to kill each other now worked together to bandage wounds and carry those that needed help. There followed one of those curious incidents that are hard to understand by those who were not actually there. The British soldiers still on the hill had watched the French, and their comrades who had helped them, drinking and filling their canteens from the stream while their own throats burned. They must have appealed to their officers to be allowed to get water themselves. One British captain released his men to go down and the French soldiers made room for them. In a moment the whole British line had been released. Soon the former enemies were helping to haul bodies out of the stream and pointing out the clearest flows of the precious water.

There was a strange camaraderie between the common soldiers of the French and British armies. This was the first time I saw it but it continued throughout the war. Soldiers in both armies were in a strange country with different customs and a local language that they did not understand. They were there reluctantly, through conscription on the French side, and poverty and dubious recruitment practices on ours. They both had a healthy respect for the others' abilities. I know many of the redcoats rather envied the French their revolution, which they imagined would take them out of poverty. They all knew that unlike the British, the French had banned flogging in their army and that many of the French officers had been promoted through the ranks. Redcoats with nothing to lose thought that the French model was modern and enlightened and only fought against it because they were ordered to do so. The French who had lived through the harsh realities of the revolution were more pragmatic about it, but they were still committed to their cause and their emperor. They in turn envied the British, particularly the supply system which kept the redcoat reasonably fed, while for the most part the French were left to fend for themselves.

We watched as infantrymen reached across the stream to shake hands. Having slaked their initial thirst and filled canteens, thought seemed to turn to the common language of trade. Packs were being emptied of spare loot, food and drink, and exchanged for items that could not be found in their own army. Some French officers were drifting down to the stream now and I suddenly found Campbell had ridden up alongside me as I had been surveying the scene.

'Let's go down,' he suggested, nodding at the détente below us. 'There will be no more fighting here for a bit.' I nodded in agreement; anything that kept those bloody cannon quiet was good for me. Having seen the French soldiers from a distance more than once, I also was curious to discover what they were like when they were not trying to kill me. We walked the horses down, dismounted and let our mounts drink their fill at the stream too while we refilled our canteens. Soldiers from both sides had now cleared the bodies from the water but in places it was still decidedly pink with blood. A French voltigeur pointed out to us the fastest flowing part of the stream where the water was clearer. He was in the act of trying to exchange a small gold crucifix for some thick leather boot soles, a bottle of rum and a leatherworking needle.

'It eez from a nun,' the voltigeur explained, shaping a buxom hour glass figure with his hands and giving the British sergeant he was trading with a knowing wink. He could not have said anything better to peak British interest for there was great fascination about nuns among the British army at that time. While nuns were familiar to the Catholic Irish troops, for the Anglican British they were a strange foreign concept. Most had never seen one, as when soldiers were in town the convents were firmly locked up and guarded. Lascivious rumours had been spreading for weeks amongst the British army that if young women from good Spanish families became too promiscuous they were shut away in convents to protect the family honour.

Most soldiers believed that if they could only get into one of these places to liberate the girls, the women would be so grateful that they would satisfy every depraved need as a reward. It wasn't just the common soldier who believed this fantasy either. A few weeks previously a major from the medical corps had launched a 'rescue' attempt on a nearby convent, enthusiastically supported by a number of dragoons. As the terrified women ran around screaming inside, the gallant heroes attacked the door with axes and bawled up reassuring endearments that the girls would soon be under their dubious protection. They were in the act of fetching a cannon to blast the door when the provosts finally forestalled the onslaught.

'You have seen the nuns then?' asked the sergeant, his voice hoarse with desire.

'Of course,' said the voltigeur, 'I took zis from ze neck of ze pretty one myself.'

'And it is true then that they are willing?' asked the sergeant again, thrusting with his hips to make it quite clear what he meant.

The voltigeur looked puzzled for a moment and then laughed. 'Zey stop screaming after ze second or third man has raped them.' The British sergeant looked disappointed. Not, I suspected, at the act of rape for when looting a captured town they showed little restraint, but at the thought that the convents were not full of willing and eager women. I looked across the stream and saw that a French lieutenant, also watering his horse, had been eavesdropping on the same conversation. He turned to me and grinned.

'Are you shocked at the behaviour of the French army, Captain?'

'Not at all,' I replied, thinking back to the capture and looting of Gawilighur I had witnessed. 'I have seen our army behave in the same way in India.'

'But perhaps you think men and women of the Christian cloth should be protected yes?' he asked in well-spoken French. 'I did before I came here, but it is a barbaric place. With my own eyes I have seen the bodies of four of our dragoons that were beheaded by monks. Tricked to enter a tower one at a time by an altar boy with a large gold cross. Once they stepped through the door....pffft.' He finished the sentence by gesturing across his throat with the flat of his hand. 'When we realised what was happening we threw the monks from the top of their own tower.'

'It is a brutal country,' I agreed.

The French lieutenant nodded to the south where the Spanish army, who had not so far been attacked, held the Talavera end of the line. 'Do you trust your Spanish allies?' he asked. I gave a non-committal shrug, judging it would not be wise to admit I was half Spanish myself. 'Remember they were our allies before, a few years ago.' the lieutenant continued. 'They welcomed our troops into their country when we entered last year and then when our men were well dispersed and off their guard they attacked.'

While true the Frenchman's description left out some key facts. The Spanish people had welcomed the French troops when they thought the French were supporting the replacement of the unpopular Spanish king with his Spanish son and heir. They had revolted when they discovered that the French had imprisoned their king and his heir and replaced them with Napoleon's brother.

'Do you know what they did to our sick soldiers at the hospital in Manzanares?' the lieutenant asked. 'They killed every single one, but not quickly. Some were even boiled in oil so their corpses were all shrivelled up. One had been hauled with a rope up a chimney and a fire lit underneath. When we got there we found bits of bodies everywhere. You might think we are cruel, but you wait until they turn on you.'

The voltigeur, who had been listening to our conversation, now turned to the British sergeant and gestured down the hill at the Spanish. 'Zey shoot then zey run away, yes?' He had clearly heard about the debacle of the previous day.

'They run like frightened jack rabbits,' agreed the sergeant. 'No bleedin' use at all.' He gestured back over his shoulder at the British baggage camp where the wives and other camp followers awaited the outcome of the battle. 'Our women make better soldiers than them.' We all laughed at that and having seen some of the formidable army wives in the camp, I thought he was undoubtedly right.

The conversation was interrupted by a trumpet call and the sudden drumming of horses' hooves.

'What is going on up there,' asked Campbell, pointing to a troop of French dragoons that were riding down the French side of the valley and dispersing to shout out something to the soldiers gathered at the stream.

'It seems we are to attack again, gentlemen,' announced the French lieutenant as drums on the French side now started to beat the recall. All along the line the blue coated men started slowly to pull back to their side. The lieutenant saluted, 'You should have at least half an hour before our regiments are ready.' Having remounted his horse he turned with a grin and added, 'I wish you good fortune in our coming victory,' before riding away back up the hill.

'Cheeky bugger,' Campbell muttered. 'We have beaten them back once already.' He slapped me on the back before adding enthusiastically, 'We'll do it again and then ride to break them, eh Flashy!' Men on our side were also starting to walk back to their former positions on the hill. Looking down the stream where moments before there had been hundreds of men, there were now just a few stragglers of both sides taking a last chance to loot the dead before rejoining their comrades.

Campbell had spurred his horse into a trot, apparently eager to get back into action, but I did not have the stomach to follow suit. I had used what little resolve I had facing that onslaught of artillery and the risk that at any moment the French columns could burst through that seemingly fragile thin line of red coated killers. It takes courage to ride into danger once, but having relaxed by the stream I was damned if I was going to stare at those distant cannon and await their random charge of death a second time.

141

Chapter 14

The French were gathering again on the opposite side of the valley from the British position, and I glanced back across to where the Spanish infantry stood, untested, in their wavering lines. That is the place for me, I thought. My resumption of duties as liaison officer was long overdue and I knew just how to achieve it. I made a point of stopping half way back up the hill in front of Wellesley and studying the Spanish lines through my glass. From where he was I could see that Wellesley did not have a direct view of the entire Spanish line and he was too busy looking to his front to worry about them. Then I rode up alongside him.

'The Spanish seem to be moving men about at their end of the line,' I lied. 'They may be planning to advance and attack the flank of the next attack. Is that what you ordered, sir?' I asked sounding slightly surprised.

'Damn them, no!' Wellesley glanced towards the Spanish but found, as I knew he would, that his view was blocked by the curve of the hill. 'If they attack they will just get in our way and then when they retreat they could break up our line. Flashman ride down there, will you, and tell them that under no circumstances are they to attack.'

It took a superhuman effort but I think I actually managed to look disappointed as I acknowledged the order; I turned my horse to safety down the reverse slope of the hill.

'Never mind Flash, you had enough action last night you know,' called Campbell consolingly at my crestfallen face. You stupid brave ass, I thought as I rode away. It would be a cold day in hell before they got me back atop this hill with the French still on the other side of the valley. My heart was singing as I rode down the slope. I was away from danger and on a strong horse if I needed to make a fast escape. If the French did attack the Spanish then I could guarantee plenty of confusion to cover my hasty withdrawal. I had not even reached the bottom of the hill before the first French cannon boomed to signal the resumption of the bombardment. Even though there were now thousands of tons of rock between me and the guns, my spine tensed at the memory of the danger, and in sympathy for those poor devils I had just left behind.

I took my time getting back to the Spanish and could follow the now familiar stages of the battle from the noise alone. The cannon bombardment continued as I walked the horse slowly around the bottom of the hill. Then the British guns commenced firing, which indicated that the large French columns were approaching, and finally the French guns stopped as the French gunners were worried about hitting their own side. When I reached the edge of the hill the rolling volleys began. From that distance they merged into a continuous crackle of musketry. I knew that it would be devastating the blue ranks in front but this time the French must be prepared. I listened for some new tactic that would cause the volleys to falter and signal a change in our fortunes. I craned to look around the hill to see the action but it was taking place on the forward slope, out of my view. Then the British guns did stop, but after a slight pause as bayonets were fixed, the silence was replaced by a now familiar roar and I could picture that red line surging forward to bring more death and destruction to the enemy.

I slumped slightly in relief as I had feared the French would employ a different tactic rather than one that had failed already. Little did I realise that the critical moment of the battle was just about to happen. I trotted on towards the Spanish, confident of victory. Their lines would give me a better view of what was happening in front of the British. Soon I could see the blue jacketed men streaming back over the Portina stream. But I realised now that the French had kept two huge columns of men back from the attack. One of those untouched columns watched impassively from the far side of the Portina as their beaten comrades rushed back towards them. It was at that moment that the British nearly lost the battle.

Previously, the British had pursued the enemy as far as the stream, but no further. Now I saw that a large formation of redcoats, the guards division as it turned out, had crossed the water and pursued the enemy up the far slope. In the distance there was the sound of trumpets indicating that our cavalry were charging the northern end of the enemy lines. For an instant I was jubilant: after taking punishment in a defensive position for so long, we were finally going on the offensive. But I had forgotten that we were outnumbered two to one by experienced troops, and in the twinkling of a sabre the balance changed again.

While I could not see them from my vantage point, the French infantry at the northern end of the battlefield was swiftly assembling in square formation and putting up a robust defence against our cavalry, supported by horsemen of their own. But what I could see were the two huge French columns, each at least two hundred men wide and several ranks deep. One now calmly took aim at the hundreds of British redcoats running up the hill towards them. It was almost the reverse of the situation on our side of the valley earlier in the day; only the French dispatched nearly half of the men facing them with a single devastating volley. Before the survivors could recover, the first massive column of blue coated men started to advance. They were aiming for the large gap that had been left in our lines by the guards division. If they got through it the battle would be lost. The second column also started moving, aiming for the weak spot where the Spanish and the British lines joined. I realised that the French had planned a new strategy after all; a trap, and we had walked no charged, right into it.

Trumpets urgently rang out to recall British troops to the lines but the survivors would not be able to fill the gap they had left. The British units south of the guards' position now started to move north to close the breach the first column was aiming for. What Wellesley could not see from his position was the new gap that this opened up between the British and the Spanish, which the second French column was now marching straight towards.

The Spanish troops who had been next to the British watched white eyed as their allies left them.

In a matter of moments it seemed that defeat had been snatched from the jaws of victory. I watched transfixed as imminent disaster unfolded before me and did not notice the other rider come along side until he spoke.

'I have what your Wellesley calls reserves this time,' said Cuesta with a touch of pride in his voice, as though he had just learned a new trick. I looked around and he sat there, his eyes shining with excitement as he stared at the advancing French, gauging how long they would take to reach the allied lines. Now I noticed a thin column of men running at a steady pace behind the Spanish lines and heading towards the newly created gap. Cuesta saw where I was looking and added, 'They are some of my best men.'

I watched them come on. They looked like the usual half-dressed Spanish scarecrow soldiers to me, only now their faces were covered with a mixture of sweat and dust as they were made to run in the fierce heat of the day. At the speed they were going they would make the gap in time but many would be blown when they got there. I looked around again at the vast French formation coming towards us, and if anything, the direction had shifted slightly to hit the British line at its thinnest point. This meant that only its southernmost end would be opposite these Spanish reserves. Given that the last time I had seen Spanish troops shoot they had run from their own volley, I could be forgiven for thinking that these now winded troops were unlikely to stand in front of the onslaught heading towards us. The doubt must have shown in my face.

'Don't worry Captain, these are tough men from the mountains, they won't run.' Cuesta gestured over his shoulder before adding, 'They know what would happen to them if they did.' I looked behind him and the two aides who had ridden up with Cuesta edged their horses to one side to give me a better view. On the ground, well behind the Spanish line, some two hundred men sat in the dirt in just their shirts and breeches with their hands tied behind their backs. These were the two hundred prisoners from the men who had run, who were to be executed after the battle. But the thought must have played in Cuesta's mind for suddenly he reached across and patted me on the shoulder. 'Come Captain,' he said, 'we will stand behind them and strengthen their resolve.'

It was the last thing I wanted to hear. I had been about to suggest that I return to Wellesley to let him know about the Spanish reserves. It would have been a journey that would have taken me back to the rear ready for a quick escape if the battle went against us. But Cuesta knew as well as I did that I could not reach Wellesley before the French column reached the allied line, and supporting that line was the most important thing. I glanced desperately around for another excuse and saw Sherbrooke, the general commanding the southern end of the British line, look over and wave at me. 'Well done Flashman,' I heard his voice call from the distance. The fool must have thought it was me who was organising the reserves. I cursed under my breath, I could hardly be seen to abandon them now. Cuesta had already spurred his horse forward and the two aides had ridden close up on either side but he waived them back. Their role was to help the old general stay on his horse, but he evidently did not feel the need of them at the moment. In fact the prospect of battle seemed to have taken years off the old warrior. I had no alternative but to kick in my heels and follow him.

The Spanish troops got into their new position quickly. To be fair to them they looked a lot less winded than I would have done, running half a mile in that sun with a full pack and musket. The French troops were now at the bottom of the shallow valley crossing the Portina stream. This gave the French gunners a clear line of sight on the

145

British line, which instead of lying down as before, now stood erect, receiving the last few strugglers of the guards division that had managed to retreat back to their lines in front of the French. Orders were shouted down the Spanish line as soldiers straightened their files and checked their flints and priming, ready to face the onslaught in front of them.

The British soldiers the Spanish reserves had joined with glanced across nervously. They were obviously concerned that if the Spanish gave way the edge of the column would wrap around their flank. I nodded in greeting to the captain of the nearest British company who saluted back. Then I noticed his eyes move to the Spanish men and his lip curled in contempt. I followed his gaze and was surprised to see that the first company in our line had fallen to its knees.

'Christ on his bloody cross, where the hell did he come from?' I had muttered this to myself but had spoken in Spanish and now I heard Cuesta chuckle beside me.

'I take it from that blasphemy that you are not a Catholic, Captain. I would not let the good father hear you say that, he does not approve of Protestants.'

'But where has he come from?' I asked again, looking at the thin priest sitting astride an equally scrawny donkey. He was dressed in white robes and was flicking holy water from what looked like a small gilt bucket and making the sign of the cross at regular intervals towards the kneeling men. In front of him walked two altar boys in spotless white surplices, one carrying a large cross while the other combined leading the donkey with swinging an ornate incense burner.

'Believe me,' said Cuesta with feeling, 'the good father often turns up when you least expect him.' The little procession was moving briskly along the line and it would be touch and go if they reached the end of the reserves before the French got there. The priest seemed unconcerned at the French marching towards him. I did not see him glance back once and the little party also ignored the resumed cannon bombardment. As the pious procession reached the end of one company, orders were given and the men rose to their feet, and the next company dropped to its knees. It was as the second company knelt in unison that I saw something that will stay long in the memory. A rock just in front of the altar boy with the cross suddenly shattered; stone fragments shot everywhere. Amazingly no one seemed to be hit. More significantly, the cannon ball that had shattered the rock was sufficiently slowed down to be seen as it bounced low over the kneeling men, close enough to take off one of their battered shakos. If the men had been standing at least two would have been killed as it had passed at chest height for a standing man. There were muttered prayers from many that witnessed this apparent act of grace. I noticed even Cuesta crossed himself next to me. I glanced across at the British company captain who had also seen the incident, he just grinned and shook his head in resignation.

This distracted the men momentarily from the approaching French, but now the blue coated men were climbing the hill towards us and the French cannon fire petered out as their own men obscured their aim. I could see now that only the left hand three companies of the Spanish would face the French column and the fourth would be able to fire into its sides. The others could fire but the range would mean that they would do little damage. Officers were running about the first three companies, trying to compact hours of drill on how to achieve effective company volley fire into a few short minutes. The French were just a hundred yards off now and I expected the British to open fire. They stood in a long unwavering line with muskets to their shoulders pointing at the French, but no order came. Ninety yards and still no order. The Spanish in front of me were swaying nervously as they held the long muskets towards the enemy, but not one fired prematurely. You could see the faces on the French clearly now and pick out the buttons on their coats. They came with bayonets fixed as though planning one volley and then a brutal charge through the fragile thin allied ranks.

Eighty yards; the French could cover that ground running in less than twenty seconds and I was licking my lips to give the order myself when finally the British opened fire and the Spanish followed suit. Every third company fired. The Spanish had seen the British volley fire earlier in the battle and understood the benefit of the rolling volleys. Only the first and fourth companies fired and I was pleased to see that the men had aimed low. Men were falling all along the French front rank but their comrades stepped over them and kept on coming. Seventy yards and as the first companies reloaded furiously the second companies fired. Whole files of men seemed to go down but still they came on. Dear God, I thought, they are not going to stop this time and at any moment they will be released into a charge. The third companies fired and at sixty yards almost every gun seemed to find a mark. The French were struggling to get over their dead and wounded now and at last their line started to falter. The British first companies were ready to fire again but many in the first Spanish company were still struggling to reload.

The British first companies fired but there was only a faltering fire from the Spanish. I saw several ramrods arc through the air as men fired before they had finished reloading. Two struck the French line like arrows in some medieval battle, but others waited until they were loaded and along the Spanish line there was now a steady continuous crackle of fire. It did not sound strong but combined with the crashing regular volleys from the British it was enough. Several groups of French burst from the front of the broad column and tried to charge across the remaining fifty yards to the British but they were brought down by concentrated fire from the volleys which also lashed at the men behind.

I looked along the line to see how the first French column was progressing against the recently closed gap in the British line. Already it was pulling back and I suspected that the French in front of us saw that too. Some of the French, sensing that the attack had stalled, tried to return fire but the effect was nothing to what they were receiving. I saw half a dozen of the Spanish troops fall but in front of us there seemed almost a rampart of French dead and wounded now blocking their advance. The fourth and fifth Spanish companies started to cheer; they could see the side of the column and noticed that some of the rear French ranks were now starting to pull back down the hill.

'Fix bayonets,' came the call from the British and all down the line steel glittered in the sunlight as the long blades were attached to hot barrels. The order was passed down the line to the Spanish troops. Some of the Spanish soldiers looked round at Cuesta, scarcely able to believe the command. Many were terrified of the devil soldiers in blue who had beaten and butchered them time and again.

'Yes, go on,' roared Cuesta to his men. 'We are winning, you are beating the French.' Almost hesitantly at first the Spanish reserve regiment moved forward. I noticed that the rest of the Spanish line stayed rooted to the spot. The reserves may have advanced cautiously to start with as though believing this was some kind of French trick to lure them in, but when they saw the British start to reach and kill the French stragglers they suddenly started running in earnest. It was as though only then did they believe that they were actually allowed to overcome the French. The Spanish excitement was not limited to their reserve troops. Cuesta grabbed my arm and pointed. 'Look Captain, they are pulling back. See, they are withdrawing their guns.' He was right. The nearest French artillery battery was starting to limber up its guns and I could see harnessed horses being gathered up to carry them away.

All along the line, the French were now in full retreat. They were not waiting for the bayonets but hurrying back to get across the Portina as fast as they could. There were trumpets from the north as British cavalry once more surged out to harry the French flanks, and that caused Cuesta to look to his own horsemen. There were two huge formations of Spanish horse guarding the right hand end of the allied line. He drew his sword and pointed it at the distant gun battery, then raised it and brought it flashing down. The meaning was clear across the noisy battlefield. The cavalry commanders were evidently watching as trumpets sounded immediately and the horsemen started to move forward. Some French cavalry moved to intercept, but as I watched the Spanish horsemen split into two with one arm aiming to block this advance and the rest spreading out and increasing speed towards the guns. It was smartly done and I had to admit that shooting some of the cavalry officers after the debacle at the battle of Medallin seemed to have done wonders for their professionalism.

Before I could reflect further Cuesta was grabbing my arm again. 'Come on Captain, to the guns.' The mad old bastard spurred his horse forward. It was a quarter of a mile to the guns and the ground in front of them was littered with French wounded and survivors heading to the rear. For a moment I hesitated: if the damn fool wanted to get his head shot off by some vengeful French infantryman he could do it without me. But if that did happen questions would be asked and many would have seen me with the general before he advanced. As I watched, the French cavalry seemed to be turning back in the face of the Spanish horsemen and I thought that Cuesta would probably angle his charge to join the other Spanish cavalry running to the guns. Reluctantly I dug in my heels and followed him through the new gap at the end of the Spanish lines.

He was already riding through the French stragglers and most of the French soldiers heard the horses coming and got out of the way, but a few who were still loaded gave fire. They could see Cuesta was a senior officer from his age and the gold braid on his uniform; the balls must have whistled about him. I deliberately held back a bit. The lunatic could attract all the fire as far as I was concerned, so that the French soldiers would not still have loaded weapons when I went over the same ground. I saw one of his aides take a bullet in the arm but the old general was untouched. He was waving his sword around and roaring his head off as he charged on. He nearly toppled from his horse at one point when his mount stumbled over an unseen corpse in the long grass, but his unwounded aide helped prop him back in the saddle.

Once we were through the main French line I rode up alongside him. 'Look at them run!' he shouted at me, his eyes wild with delight. This normally stiff and proud man was lost in the joy of victory. After years of crushing defeats, injuries and humiliations he was finally beating his arch enemies again. In his enthusiasm he was still racing directly towards the enemy battery rather than angling to join his horsemen.

'We should join your cavalry, sir,' I shouted at him.

'Nonsense, I want those guns, look they are getting away.'

A quick glance showed that the French were succeeding in getting one or two of the lighter guns away, but they were not moving fast enough from my perspective. I calculated that we would reach the battery just before the rest of the Spanish horsemen and I did not fancy our chances. Four men, one of whom was wounded and another a half mad near septuagenarian, against a battery that still held nearly a dozen guns and their crews was long odds. The emplacement was a hive of activity, some of the gunners deciding that the situation was lost were streaming out of the back while others tugged furiously on trace ropes and straps to attach horses to the guns and get them moving. But as I thought of hanging back again, to my horror I saw that some brave souls had abandoned thoughts of retreat and were loading several of the pieces with canister. One was pointed in our direction.

With a sickening lurch of fear I realised that I was now trapped in what seemed a suicidal charge. I could hardly turn round and abandon the general with at least half the British and Spanish armies watching us hurtle across the battlefield. My reputation would be ruined, but more importantly I would probably still be dead, cut to pieces by French canister. The only option was to press forward to get into the gun emplacement before they could fire and hope to survive the resulting melee until the rest of the Spanish horsemen arrived.

The last hundred yards of that charge seemed to take for ever although it could only have been a few seconds. Cuesta and the aides were slightly out in front; I was hunched down low in the saddle, reins in one hand and drawn sword in the other. The Spanish cavalry, seeing our charge had picked up speed. They now seemed set to enter one end of the battery as we crashed through the other. But my eyes were locked on the crew of a French twelve pounder. I could see the gun captain screaming at his men to work faster as they rammed down the metal canister of shot that would spread a devastating spray of death when fired. At the same time he was pricking with a needle through the touch hole to pierce the cloth bag of the powder charge. We were still fifty yards off when he pushed down the quill of finely ground powder through the hole he had made, which would fire the charge. For a brief moment our eyes met and for a split second I thought I was looking at my executioner. Then he looked down and I saw fear cross his face; something had gone wrong. I never found out what it was, but he needed another second to fire that gun and he did not have it. I was now almost up to the muzzle, but Cuesta's horse was already jumping the protective ditch in front of the guns and the general's sword was swinging down on the gunner's head.

Cuesta might have been sixty-eight but there was nothing wrong with his sword arm. It split the gunner's skull in two, spraying blood and gore all around him. I was clearing the ditch now and my horse's hooves knocked down another of the gun crew coming at Cuesta with a musket. For a second the emplacement seemed full of the French gun crews and I thought we were lost. One lunged at me with a bayonet but I stabbed at him with my sword. I had been aiming at his throat but I caught him across the ear instead and he went down clutching his head. Then, where there had been nothing but French, suddenly the area was full of Spanish horsemen charging from the other end of the battery. The air was alive with whoops of victory from the Spanish riders, screams and shouts from the French … and one Englishman swearing on all that was holy that if that crazy old bastard tried to get him killed like that again he would murder the general himself.

Cuesta was unrecognisable from the proud arrogant man who had angrily ordered the execution of two hundred of his own men. Now he was wheeling around on his horse in the centre of the battery, waving his sword around in delight, a danger to friend and foe alike. When some of his men pointed out that some of the captured guns bore markings that showed they were formerly Spanish, he shouted his thanks to the heavens and then looked round for me. He rode up so that our horses were nose to tail and flung his arms around me so that his sword blade was waggling dangerously close to my head.

'Thank you,' he said. Then gesturing to the northern side of the battlefield where the British were still streaming forward, he repeated it. 'Thank you, you have given me a victory I never thought I would see.' With that he leaned forward and kissed me on both cheeks. I was only slightly more surprised than the goggling cavalry officers.

Chapter 15

'Did he kiss you as well?' I asked Wellesley as he returned from
Cuesta's camp later that afternoon.

'Mercifully no he didn't,' Wellesley grinned wryly. 'He had
recovered his normal demeanour by the time I saw him.'

'But he was still grateful for the victory, surely?'

'Oh he was grateful; his men were full of your death or glory
charge for their guns, some of the few we captured. I suspect that by
the time Cuesta's despatches reach Seville it will be his victory rather
than mine. That is why I sent for you, Thomas. I would be obliged if
you would ride to Seville and take my account of the battle to the
Central Junta. Be a first-hand witness as to what actually happened. I
am content for the Spanish to take some credit, but if our part is not
recognised, the Spanish may think we do not merit further supplies.'

'Certainly,' I agreed, and my heart soared. We were not out of the
woods yet, Soult was closing on our rear and there was still a sizeable
French force to our front. Now I would be spared the next
engagements and instead was ordered to spend time in the salons of
Seville countering misleading gossip.

An environment where a cake fork was the most dangerous
implement of war sounded just the right place for me and I was
certainly not going to be in any hurry to rush back. 'Surely after his
previous defeats,' I continued, 'no one in Seville will believe that he
beat a French army twice the size of the Spanish one without our
help?'

'Oh, he is back to his old irrational self. He will probably claim it
was an act of God. I spent most of my time with him trying to deter
him from shooting people.'

'Who did he want to shoot?'

'There were his two hundred prisoners; I persuaded him to reduce
the executions to forty. He agreed to that readily enough. But then one
of our picket officers arrived in his camp to complain that Spanish
soldiers were roaming the battlefield shooting French prisoners and
wounded.'

I was genuinely shocked. There was, and as far as I am aware still
is, an unwritten code for warfare. At that time it was probably at its
zenith. The earlier British meeting with the French over the Portina
turned out to be not unusual for that campaign. Captured officers
would normally give their parole, a promise not to escape, and then be

held in loose confinement until an exchange could be made. It was not unheard of for officers to be invited to dine at an enemy mess. I have seen a blind drunk artillery major carried back to our lines by four French gunners after he had overindulged on French hospitality. There were even understandings amongst common soldiers, for example when opposing forces were camped close together. Sentries standing guard between two armies would not be shot at. I have heard tales that they would even share duties so that they could take turns having a sleep, waking each other up when officers inspected.

In all cases, prisoners were treated fairly and wounded treated as far as medical provisions allowed. Both the French and the British soldiers saw each other as professionals. It was not simple charity; given the randomness of war, you never knew when you might need such courtesy yourself. 'What did you do?' I asked.

'I told him it had to cease at once, of course. But as a precaution I have sent three companies of guards to the southern end of the battlefield to protect the wounded. Cuesta tried to justify his men's actions by saying that the French shoot Spanish brigands and guerrillas on sight.'

'But Cuesta is a professional soldier, surely he knows better.' I was starting to feel slightly ashamed of the Spanish half of my ancestry.

'Yes, but in the winter a lot of Cuesta's men go up into the mountains where they can more easily defend food supplies from the French. A lot of them live amongst the brigands and have seen the massacres. But don't worry, I have been very clear that I will not see this victory dishonoured.'

He ran his hands through his hair and he suddenly looked very tired. He had not slept for two days. He had marshalled his forces to fight a prolonged battle, placated allies and now instead of resting, his mind was already turning to the challenges ahead. 'Sit down, Thomas,' he gestured to a campaign chair near the door of his tent and turned around. I heard the clink of glass and a few moments later he sat down beside me and passed me a glass of brown liquid. 'Try this, it is a local brew, but very pleasant.'

I sipped; it was the jerez drink that I had first tasted in the mountains a few months ago with Downie. For a moment we sat in silence staring at the unlit brazier outside the tent and feeling the warming effects of the spirit.

Now that I knew I would not be required for the next battle I felt able to view the situation more objectively. I wondered if this was actually a victory at all. I already knew that British casualties, dead and wounded, were around five thousand men which was a quarter of our force. The French had lost a similar number but they still had around forty thousand men left to our fifteen. The Spanish had lost around a thousand and so had over a thirty thousand men left, but they would not withstand a full French onslaught on their own.

'Was it a true victory or a pyrrhic one?' I asked quietly.

Wellesley considered the question seriously for nearly a minute before he replied. 'Well, we will certainly present it as a true victory to Parliament. I need victories to keep them funding the campaign. The Spanish will proclaim it as such as well; they have had little to celebrate recently. But the French will not retreat far. They will want to hold our attention while Soult closes in on our rear. Then they will have us trapped.'

'What will you do?'

'I need to give the men a day to rest, and tomorrow I am expecting three thousand men from the Light Division as reinforcements. Then Cuesta will stay here to deceive the French into thinking the whole army is still resting. He can look after our wounded too. But I will take the British and we will try to beat Soult at his own game. He only had around fifteen thousand men when we threw him out of Oporto. If he still has that number then we should be able to beat him, especially if we can catch him off guard.'

'You will lose more men fighting Soult. How many more battles can you afford to win and stay in the field?'

'I don't know,' he sighed. 'Right now I am forced to fight to survive. Despite what Cuesta thinks, we are in no state to attempt to drive the French out of Spain. We will need to pull back into Portugal or south of the Tagus to allow our wounded to recover and more reinforcements to arrive.'

Even that downbeat assessment turned out to be optimistic, but we were not to discover that for a few days. In the meantime the battlefield of Talavera had one more horror in store.

After sharing half a bottle of jerez I made my excuses and left. I was dog tired, it had been a long and exhausting two days. The sun was still up, it was late afternoon but I was ready for a siesta. I found my tent and must have fallen asleep as soon as my head hit the bag of spare clothes that served as a pillow. I was soon in a fitful doze. Of all things I dreamt of Christmas, the smell of roasting pork, the crackle of flames in the hearth and the excited squeals of those playing games. That was until I was rudely awakened.

'Thomas,' Campbell was urgently shaking my shoulder. 'Come on, the battlefield is on fire! The wounded are being burned alive.' Wearily I swung my feet to the ground as those facts sank in. There was still a smell of smoke and roasting pork in the air but with revulsion I realised that it was the smell of roasting human flesh, and the excited squeals in my dream had been the screams of dying men. You could not see the battlefield from the camp which was behind the hill the British had defended, but plumes of smoke rose into the air from its southern end. One look at the horses tethered in lines by the side of the camp told us it would be better to go on foot. They were already being made uneasy by the smell of smoke and were pulling anxiously at their traces. We would struggle to ride them towards the flames and then find a secure place to tether them. Campbell and I followed a trail of other officers and men running around the edge of the hill to see how bad it was. I was puffing to keep up but the sight that met me as we rounded the bottom of the hill left me gasping for breath in shock.

You may have seen paintings of hell in a gallery, but I think in that moment I looked directly upon it. The shallow valley in which the battle had been fought had originally been covered in waist high grass. It was bone dry as it had not rained in weeks, and while swathes had been trampled flat by the movement of horses and columns of men earlier in the day, the majority was still upright. Many of the wounded had already been moved, particularly those in the flattened areas that had been easy to find, but many others remained. These had either been wounded during the routing of advances where the fighting spread over a wider area or, in the case of some French wounded, they had crawled into the long grass to escape vengeful Spanish infantrymen after the battle.

A cinder from a campfire must have been carried by the freshening wind into the grass. That same breeze had fanned the flames so that they covered the southern end of the battlefield, and were advancing like an army of demons northwards. Figures could be seen silhouetted against the blaze, some darting forwards looking for the wounded and others helping to carry them out of the path of the inferno. The screaming and wailing from those still trapped in the path of the blaze was pitiable. Smoke was drifting up the valley too but it was not too

156

thick and it did not block out the awful sight of one poor devil staggering in front of the flames with his clothes ablaze.

'Come on Flash, let's help get them out,' Campbell was already darting forward. As you know, I am not one to willingly leap into danger, but we were well in advance of the fire and the cries of those in its path appealed to anyone with an ounce of humanity. I followed him in and in a few moments we had found a British infantryman dragging himself along with a broken leg. We had him up between us in a trice and soon had him deposited in the relative safety of the rocky ground at the bottom of the hill where other wounded were being gathered.

Back we went, but the smoke was getting thicker now, and we both paused to tie neckerchiefs around our faces. I thought we had time to save one more person and we both scanned the ground as we spread out to find one. Voices were calling out in all directions, some for help, and others guiding the rescuers. I heard one voice nearby and thought I had spotted its owner but a gust of smoke obscured him. I pushed forward blindly towards him but fell over a body instead. The voice was still calling, 'Help me, help me, I am over here.' It was tantalisingly close and I pressed on this time on my hands and knees so that I could see. I had lost track of Campbell but now I heard his voice.

'Here you are laddie, I've got you.' Then he called out to me. 'Flashman, where are you? I have found one, see if you can get another and let's get back.'

'I'm here,' I shouted back. I stood and headed blindly in the direction I had heard his voice. I stumbled ten yards and then twenty before I realised that I must somehow have walked past him. It was getting uncomfortably hot now. My eyes were streaming with the smoke and it was starting to burn in my throat. 'To hell with this,' I muttered to myself as I decided it was time to get out of there, with or without a wounded person. I had lost my bearings blundering about but I would let the heat guide me. It now seemed strongest on my left side, the flames had been moving from south to north, so if I kept them on my left then I should come out roughly where I went in. I staggered forward, half running, to get away from the smoke which came and went in sudden gusts. Suddenly I saw a flicker of flame ahead of me and now I realised that there was as much heat coming from in front as from my left. I was starting panic. The fire seemed to be on at least two sides, but I had the presence of mind to drop to the ground where the smoke was thinner to try and get my bearings again. On my hands and knees I took big gulps of the cleaner but still hot air as I stared ahead. There was a roaring wall of flame ahead and looking to my left I could see the dull glow of yet more flames. I took a deep breath, turned to my right and ran as fast as I could.

I must have run twenty or thirty yards in that sprint. I was holding my breath to avoid breathing in the thick smoke and had my eyes shut to stop them stinging; there was little I could see if I had them open. I remember my foot kicked against one body as I went, but it made no noise and I did not stop to investigate. I was just about to drop to the ground and take another gasp or two of the cleaner air when I cannoned into someone else. We both crashed down in the dry grass and from the muttered cry of 'merde' I gathered I had hit a Frenchman. I squinted at him through watering eyes. I thought he was an infantryman to start with as he had a musket, but then I saw the sword at his hip and the bloodstains down the lower half of one leg and realised that he had been using the longarm as a crutch. I staggered back up to my feet and looked back over my shoulder; the flames if anything seemed even closer despite my running.

'Please monsieur,' the Frenchman held up an arm in a desperate appeal for assistance. Tears were streaming down his face, more through the smoke than emotion, and he was gasping for breath. It was a sight to make your heart melt. An appeal to Flashy when he is running for his life is normally a forlorn hope. Not that I am kept awake by the grabbing hands and pleading faces I have ignored in my long and ignoble career; it would have been a lot shorter if I had heeded them.

I remember hearing what sounded like a volley of musket fire somewhere behind and realising that it must have been a cartridge pouch on a corpse's belt catch fire. There were still distant screams and yells for help but fewer now, unless the roar of the fire was drowning them out. No, I decided, I would pull this fellow to his feet so that he was no worse off than when I found him, but then he would have to fend for himself. I reached down, grasped his hand and pulled. As I did so I happened to glance over his shoulder and there was a sudden gap in the smoke. Through it not much more than twenty yards away, for a brief instant I could see people standing on the rocks at the bottom of the slope staring at the fire. They were hard to make out in the rippling heat haze but one seemed to see me and point.

Relief surged through me. I was saved, and as I had been seen with the Frenchman I could hardly abandon my charge now. With safety in sight I helped him climb up onto my back and staggered forward to where I had seen the people. The frog was gasping his thanks in my ear but I just concentrated on putting one foot in front of the other without stumbling over the rough ground. The heat down the left hand side of my body was almost unbearable now, at least the Frenchman kept the heat of my back. I could see little snakes of flame moving through the grass as though they were trying to cut me off but they were still small enough to stamp my way through. Suddenly I felt hands helping me. The Frenchman was lifted off my back and strong arms helped half carry me out of the smoke. The next thing I remember I was sitting on the rocks at the bottom of the hill with a crowd of other men and Campbell was next to me handing me his water bottle.

'Good grief Flashman, I thought we had lost you there. The wind is whipping the flames up the valley and several of the rescuers have not got out. They were asking me where I had last seen you and suddenly there you are staggering out of the flames with a wounded Frenchie on your back.' There was a wall of flame and smoke some fifty yards in front of us now; while it was giving off some heat, the wind was blowing most of it away from us towards the north.

'Well, I could not come back empty handed,' I gasped, after the cool liquid had soothed my throat. My clothes were still smouldering in some places and I patted out a trail of smoke coming from my coat hem. But while my uniform was hot I knew enough to play things cool to maximise my credit. I passed the canteen to the French officer who now lay on the rocks beside me. 'Anyway,' I added, gesturing to the Frenchman, 'this chap said if I rescued him he would introduce me to his sister.' The men around guffawed at that.

'Did those French gunners offer their sisters as well?' asked a voice in the crowd. 'Is that why you charged their battery virtually single handed with just an old general and his aides for support?' Men were slapping me on the back now and murmuring 'good show' at me and I realised that my reputation had grown more than I thought. Half the army had seen Cuesta's mad charge and, given the reputation of the Spanish for cowardice and mine for pluck, most seemed to have thought I was behind the move. As we had captured nearly a battery of guns this was no small feat, and now just a few hours later they had seen me stagger out of an inferno rescuing a wounded enemy officer. Even the Frenchie had no idea that I had been on the verge of abandoning him before I had seen safety through the gap in the smoke.

'Alas, monsieur,' he said to me quietly now as the others started to drift away, 'I have no sister or I would have been happy to introduce her to such a courageous enemy.' He reached out his hand to shake mine. 'My name is Jean Lacodre,' he said wincing in pain as his other hand clutched his injured leg. He then grinned as he added, 'but my father is an organist. When he learns you have saved his son's life if you are ever in Paris he will give you a concert, possibly in Notre Dame itself!'

'Thank you,' I replied, 'but I have no plans to be in Paris any time soon.' It is strange how fate works, the twists and turns of various threads come together when you least expect them. I had replied lightly without giving it any thought but little did I realise that three years later I would be in Paris and that brief conversation would save me from years of captivity or worse.

Chapter 16

The next morning after a fitful sleep the golden dawn revealed a nightmarish scene. The shallow valley that the battle had been fought over was now burned black and scattered over it were charred corpses, twisted as though they had died in agony. Some undoubtedly had, but Campbell told me that dead bodies also twist in the flames as muscles contract with the heat. He related a tale of his grandfather who had fought with the English at Culloden, sixty years before. His ancestor had helped gather the bodies of the defeated Scottish highlanders and Jacobites, many of whom he had known. They were piled together on a pyre and set alight. The body of one of the old Campbell's neighbours had suddenly sat up in the flames and pointed at him; the old boy had nearly died of a seizure.

As if the sights weren't bad enough, there was also the regular crash of musket volleys through the morning as Cuesta executed his forty prisoners in front of his whole army. While this had been designated a day of rest by Wellesley before the British turned around to face Soult, the area seemed to be a hive of activity. The dead were being gathered in one area. Elsewhere the surviving wounded were also being gathered and many taken by cart to the town of Talavera where buildings had been commandeered by the surgeons as sick bays. As well as carts for the wounded, supply wagons beetled about with ammunition, spare flints, rations and everything else the army would need for the march ahead. I had expected to be leaving that day but Wellesley had been too busy to write his despatches. He called me into his tent late that evening to hand over his reports on the battle for the Central Junta. Another officer was taking copies of these to Lisbon for the British government. It was too late to leave then in the dark so we both arranged to depart in the morning. I would head south to Seville while the rest of the British would march west to face Soult. Cuesta would stay in Talavera, giving the impression to Victor's army that the whole allied army was still there.

I was awoken before dawn the next morning by shouts rousing the British army so that they could cover as much ground as possible in the relative cool of the early morning. As I prepared my own equipment I watched as the first regiments formed up and started to march away. They were each followed by a pathetic straggle of wounded men still able to walk. Some had arms in slings, others hobbled slowly on crutches and I even saw two men who had been blinded in the battle being led by their fellows. Cuesta had promised the Spanish would look after the British wounded and some fifteen hundred British were in their care. The redcoats, however, were deeply suspicious of the attention that they would receive, so any who were capable of marching in some manner, generally chose to do so. Despite the discomfort, they would rather stay with their comrades even if a battle waited at the end of the journey.

I mounted up and headed south. There was no need of an escort as the road between Seville and Talavera was packed with civilians and soldiers generally heading in the same direction as me. I fell in with some Spanish cavalry officers who had been ordered by Cuesta to detail the Spanish side of the victory to the Central Junta.

In the first few towns we passed the inhabitants sought reassurance that the battle had been won, as earlier refugees and fleeing soldiers from the first day of the battle had insisted that the battle had been lost and that the French were on their tail. It was a hundred and fifty miles to Seville in a straight line, but with hills and mountains in between, the actual road distance was closer to two hundred and fifty. As no one rode through the midday heat it took ten days to reach the independent Spanish capital. Unknown to me, much had been happening during that time to the British, which I should probably recount here.

On the day I left Talavera, Cuesta received a despatch from one of the guerrilla leaders warning that instead of the expected fifteen thousand men, Soult had a command of fifty thousand. Wellesley's own fifteen thousand would stand no chance against this force. Cuesta sent a message just in time which allowed Wellesley to retreat south of the Tagus where he could use the river to help protect his force. The dark suspicions of the British wounded were confirmed when Cuesta then immediately abandoned them in order to retreat himself, ultimately also going south of the Tagus. There, the allied army stayed in relative safety guarding the few bridges across the river, while the French dominated all the land to the north, including Talavera.

I knew nothing of this as I rode south. If I spared a thought for Campbell and the others who I believed were marching to battle, it was not for long. For once I was in the vanguard of those bringing the news of Talavera, I found every town and village we passed through wanted to enjoy the victory. After a series of crushing defeats they were desperate for something to celebrate. I found glasses of jerez and other local brews pushed into my not unwilling hands at every settlement. I was drunk most of the way, which was why the journey took so long, but I did not care. I had come to Spain on the promise of a quiet staff job and to escape royal scandal. Instead I had faced ambush, intrigues, nearly been killed by my own side as well as the French, not to mention the death or glory cavalry charge that had come within an ace of seeing me blown apart. Hell, I deserved some rest and relaxation, and if the rest of the army wanted to throw itself against one French marshal after another until it ceased to exist, well it was nothing to do with me.

I was therefore hung over and feeling somewhat belligerent when I finally crested a hill and saw Seville spread out before me. The skyline was dominated by the huge tower of the cathedral, which was across a square from the royal palace which housed the Central Junta. I rode slowly down along the river and acknowledged the shouts of 'bravo' from some of the citizens who recognised my red coat. Most buildings in the centre of the city had Spanish flags flying from them and preparations seemed underway for a major celebration. Clearly some diligent swot, who had not stopped to get drunk at every town he passed, had brought news of the victory before me. It was as I reported to the secretary of the Central Junta that I discovered the news of Soult's larger force and the plan of the allies to retreat south of the Tagus, abandoning the hard won battleground of Talavera.

'But please señor,' the little clerk had wrung his hands as he appealed to me, 'you must keep this information secret for another day. The Central Junta want to celebrate the victory before it is known that the army has been forced to retreat.' He pushed a colourfully engraved pasteboard card across the table. 'You are of course invited, as a representative of our honoured allies, to a celebration ball this evening here at the palace.'

'I suppose I could do that,' I agreed, wondering if my constitution could stand another night of celebration.

On leaving the palace I rode across the square past the cathedral towards a broad thoroughfare that seemed to be lined with places of refreshment. I realised I was hungry and was just looking for a vacant table in the shade of the big awnings that had been put up to protect the patrons, when I heard my name being called.

'By Jove,' called someone incredulously. 'I say that is Flashman. Flashy, over here!'

I turned, trying to place the familiar voice, but probably would not have guessed that its owner would be in Seville in a month of Sundays.

Sitting at a large table in front of the grandest café was a man dressed in an immaculate lancer's uniform; it was Lord George Byron.

Editor's note
Astonished as Flashman was, Byron's biographers confirm that he was in Seville at this time. He had arrived in Lisbon a few weeks previously and was travelling south via Seville to Gibraltar where he joined a ship to take him on his first 'grand tour' of the Italian states and Greece. His timing was such that he followed the news of the victory of Talavera, so while he did not attend the ball at Seville, he did attend the celebrations at Cadiz.

I stood and gaped for a moment. As if a military Byron there in the Spanish independent capital was not surprising enough, there beside him was a sunburnt Cam Hobhouse in a plain brown broadcloth suit. Sitting next to them was a dour young woman dressed in a modest black gown with a large medal hanging round her neck on a ribbon. Behind their table the stone flags were covered with a pile of luggage and what looked like an old grey fur rug. I was not the only one staring; there was a good sized crowd of nearly two dozen looking in curiosity from the street. I dismounted shaking my head with disbelief and, handing my reins to a waiter, I pushed through the crowd to meet them.

'What on earth are you doing here,' I asked, while shaking hands with Byron and Hobhouse and bowing in greeting to the lady in black who just scowled in return. 'And why the uniform?' I asked, gesturing at Byron's lancer fig. 'Surely you have not joined the army?'

'Of course not,' said Byron, smoothing down a crease in his britches. 'But it does look rather fine on me, doesn't it? I thought a military look would be appropriate given our army is here as well.' He gestured at the people watching, 'I'm not sure whether these people have come to admire the cut of my clothes or because they have heard of my poetry but they have been watching for the last half an hour.

I glanced at the spectators and most seemed to be staring at the woman, but they were not uppermost in my mind. 'Yes, but why are you here?' I asked again.

'Ah well,' said Byron, 'it is the strangest thing. All London society is currently gossiping over what scandalous behaviour I must have committed to make leaving the country necessary, when in fact we had to leave because of Hobhouse here.'

'We don't need to bore Thomas with any of this,' said Hobhouse, looking mightily embarrassed. Then in a desperate attempt to change the conversation he added, 'Were you at this big battle at the place called Tala… something?'

'Oh no,' I said, grinning at Byron. 'I would not be bored at all. I would be intrigued to know what Cam has done to merit your voluntary exile.'

Byron patted Hobhouse on the arm, 'It's all right, we know Flashman, and he won't tell anyone.' He turned to me before continuing. 'It is quite incredible. The Duke of York has somehow become convinced that Hobhouse was in league with Mary Clarke in plotting his downfall. Some of his people have been asking questions all over town trying to put a case together, suggesting that Clarke seduced Cam to be the brains behind the scheme.' As he spoke, Hobhouse's already red face was flushing a deeper crimson, while I could not resist giving his normal pomposity another tweak.

'My stars,' I looked at him in feigned admiration. 'There was me thinking you were a bit of a dull old stick and all the time you were ploughing that prime furrow.'

Hobhouse puffed himself up like an outraged bullfrog. 'I can assure that I have never ploughed… I mean I have never been with the lady. I only met her once.' He paused, a brief look of dark suspicion crossing his face, and then added, 'actually I think I introduced her to you.'

'I think you did,' I agreed, smiling with what I hoped was a look of angelic innocence. 'That is the only time that I met her too. But what makes the duke think that you are responsible? It is such a shame I have not been in London or I could have stood as a witness for that meeting.'

Hobhouse looked mollified. 'Thank you Thomas, an army witness would have been helpful; it might still be helpful if they hound me again when we return. I have no idea why they picked on me. They kept saying that they have a witness who claimed to have seen me plotting with her. The duke's people are busy ruining Colonel Wardle and seem determined to find another victim in London that they can pin this on. That is why we had to leave to go on this wretched tour.'

Byron grinned at me again. 'As you may have detected Thomas, Cam is not enjoying foreign travel!'

I felt a certain vicious amusement as Hobhouse took this as a cue to grumble about filthy hotels, the heat, appalling food and what he referred to as a barbaric and superstitious populace. He had always looked down his nose at me, and it gave me some pleasure at seeing him being brought down a peg or two. If he had known that the man who had named him and thus forced him to exile was sitting across the table he would have been livid. Had we been alone I would have been tempted to tell him just to see his reaction. Instead I interrupted his diatribe on all things Spanish and Portuguese to mention that I was half Spanish myself.

'Then you have my deepest sympathies,' he said cuttingly. 'The sooner we are safely on the British warship that is taking us to Rome the better.'

'You should be careful what you wish for,' I told him. 'I spent a year with the Navy in the Mediterranean and unless you have a liking for storms, salted meat and ship's biscuit full of weevils, I think you will find the food a lot better here.' His red face took on a tinge of green at the thought. I turned to look at the scowling woman in black, who had still to speak a word. She might have been pretty if she bothered to smile but she just looked away. I turned to Byron and gestured towards her, 'Who is the lady?'

'Ah,' said Byron, who then pointed at a priest standing nearby in the watching crowd. 'Her name is Señora de Aragon; the priest there brought her over to sit with us. He told us all about her. She is also known as the Maid of Zaragoza. After praying for help, she was able to turn back a French advance single handed and saved the city for the Spanish. I am thinking of including some verses about her in my new work.' I glanced across at the priest, who looked pleased with himself as he heard his tale recounted to another British soldier. He appeared less happy when I turned to the woman and spoke to her in Spanish.

'The priest says you prayed for help, stopped a French advance single handed and saved the city of Zaragoza,' I told her, not bothering to hide the disbelief in my voice.

The woman looked briefly surprised that I spoke her language before replying quietly, 'The priest is a lying, cock sucking bastard.'

I grinned; clearly she was not the devout woman that the priest had described. 'Were you even at Zaragoza?'

'Oh yes, I was there.' She glanced resentfully at the priest, 'With a man called Raul, not my husband. But now I am famous my husband has made these priests my guardians and they watch me like a hawk.'

'So what happened in Zaragoza?'

'Raul was a gunner and he was defending one of the bastions of the city. I had gone there with some apples for him and his crew when the

French attacked. They came storming up a breach, Raul and his men were desperately trying to load with canister shot to sweep them away when the French troops shot at them. Raul fell and most of the other men he was with ran away. I was not praying, I was crying when I ran forward to hold him, but he was dying. As he saw me he held up the burning slow match and urged me to fire the gun. I did it for him.' She paused as though remembering the moment and then continued briskly. 'The French had not expected a girl to fire the gun and the canister shot tore through them taking half of them down. Raul's men heard the gun and looked back to see me standing over it. They found their courage, came back to finish off the rest and the French attack failed.'

'So you were a hero and they gave you a medal?' I pointed to the one hanging over her chest but she just gave a scornful laugh.

'Raul was the hero, with his dying breath he wanted to kill the French. The church and the politicians want to use me as an example, but I had left my husband who beat me and took my child to live with another man. The church spread tales that my husband was at the gun, but he was not even in Zaragoza. They say my son died before the siege but he died of a fever while I was being held a prisoner afterwards. Every night I see the face of the French soldier who refused my pleas for a doctor or medicine and let my son die.' She paused with tears showing in her eyes before adding in a quiet whisper, 'One day I will find him and kill him.'

'What did she say?' asked Byron, who had sensed her emotion in the story. I recounted the tale to him and he sat back even more impressed. 'I will certainly include her in the work now. That is a far more passionate tale than the one the priest told.'

I turned back to the woman; without the scowl she did look pretty. She seemed shapely too although the black gown fastened up to her neck did her no favours. She saw my look and returned my appraisal.

'Were you at Talavera?' she asked. 'Did you see the Spanish charge to capture the guns that everyone has been talking about?'

'I was in the charge,' I told her, and was rewarded with an appreciative smile as I added that I had been just a yard behind General Cuesta when he entered the battery.

'And who are these?' she said, gesturing at Byron and Hobhouse. 'They have far too much luggage to be real soldiers.' I explained that Byron was a poet and for devilment told her that Hobhouse was a surgeon who specialised in treating the clap. This earned him a withering look before she poured scorn on the idea that anyone could earn a living by writing poems. She held up her medal and exclaimed that real men had to show courage with a sword or a gun and not a quill. Before I could explain that Byron earned little from his poems and much from his massive estate, the man himself interrupted.

'What did she say Flashman? She seemed very passionate about something.'

'Oh, she says she does not like the look of Hobhouse, but she was very pleased that you were going to include her in one of your poems.'

'Really?' Byron looked absurdly delighted at my gross misinterpretation. He reached across and patted her hand. 'I will make your story live for ever in poetry,' he told her pompously. Then he turned to me. 'What did she say about the medal? Was she given it for saving Zaragoza?' But before I could answer he was distracted a disturbance in the crowd. A carriage was pulling up with two saddled horses tied to the back. 'Ah, here are our horses for Cadiz.'

I was struck by a flash of inspiration, 'Yes it was for Zaragoza,' I guessed. 'But she is on the verge of having to sell it,' I told him. 'The priests take what little money she is given, and she wants to return to the war. She really needs someone to give her some money when the priests are not about.'

Hobhouse looked at me with open suspicion but Byron, having given the priest in the crowd a dark look, turned to me with the solution I had been hoping for. 'You will be in Seville for a day or two. Here, take this purse and I would be obliged if you would get it to her somehow.' He pulled a leather purse from his coat and passed it to me across the table. I picked it up – it was impressively heavy – and dropped it in my pocket. Byron was giving the woman a final look of inspection, taking in the drab black garments she wore. 'Make sure she gets some better clothes, Thomas,' he added. 'Maybe a soldier's uniform if she wants to fight.'

Hobhouse turned to look at their baggage, but now he turned to Byron with what I thought was a cunning smile on his face. 'Perhaps Thomas could also look after Viriates; we have to find a new home for him before we board the ship.'

I was sure that Hobhouse had guessed that the woman would see little of the money, and anything he was pleased about was probably bad news for me. 'Who on earth is Viriates?'

'Didn't they teach you anything at Rugby?' asked Byron with a grin. 'Viriates was a famous leader of the Portuguese, or Lusitanians as they were then. He beat several Roman armies before he was murdered by assassins.' As he spoke I realised that a long dead chieftain was not the Viriates in question. For Hobhouse had poked what I had taken to be an old fur rug in their luggage, and the thing had moved. It uncoiled itself from the bags and sat up beside Byron's chair staring suspiciously at me. Even sitting, the beast's head was taller than Byron's, who now noticed its presence and reached from his seat to pat the animal. 'Ah, here he is, Viriates. He is an Irish wolfhound. They were given by Irish chiefs to honoured guests apparently, but this one was sold to me in Lisbon by a soldier from the Connaught Rangers. He is a good companion, but not particularly bright, he does not know any tricks.'

Having just accepted a purse full of gold I could hardly turn down the dog. Hobhouse gave a smile of triumph as I accepted the end of rope attached to its collar. 'The bloody animal also has fleas and some disgusting eating habits,' he grumbled. Hobhouse glanced round at Byron who had now got up and was talking to the carter about loading the luggage. 'And if you try to lose him,' he added quietly, 'and deliberately leave him tied up at an inn, the bloody creature will chew through the rope and track you down over several miles.'

I could not help but grin, anything that annoyed Hobhouse was all right in my book. Byron had always been fond of dogs. I had heard him say that he wanted to be buried with a dog called Boatman that he had been forced to leave behind when he went to university. When Cambridge University had said that under their rules students were not allowed to bring dogs to the college, he bought himself a brown bear to spite them, as bears were not mentioned in the rules, and kept the creature in the stables.

With much hand shaking, back slapping and exclamations of undying friendship, Byron was soon ready to leave. 'Good luck Thomas,' he called. 'When we are back from Byzantium we must meet again in London and exchange tales. You can bring Viriates with you.'

He and Hobhouse rode out of the square with their baggage carriage following on behind. Most of the crowd stayed to watch the woman, which confirmed my suspicions that she had been the attraction in the first place. She was a fine looking piece, I reflected, and in a proper gown instead of the dour black smock she had on, I was sure she would certainly turn heads. As I sat down at the table again something I had in my pocket dug in my ribs. As I reached in to remove it I saw the priest coming forward to reclaim the woman. She scowled at him malevolently.

'Apologies sir,' said the priest in English to me, 'but the lady must now come with me.'

I had finally dug the thing out of my pocket and I saw that it was the pasteboard invitation for the ball that evening. 'I was wondering,' I said in Spanish, looking at the woman, 'if the lady would like to accompany me to the celebration ball this evening?'

Her face lit up with a smile for the first time and she nodded. But before she could say anything the priest gave an exaggerated gasp of astonishment. 'That is impossible sir,' he spoke again in English so that she could not understand. 'She is a married lady and it would be most unseemly. She has been placed by her husband into the care of the mother church. She could not possibly attend the ball without her husband.'

'Nonsense,' I replied again in Spanish so that the woman could follow the conversation. 'She has told me she left her husband over a year ago. She was allowed to defend the city of Zaragoza and beat back a French attack without him so I think she can be trusted to attend a ball without his company. In an event to celebrate victory over the French, I can think of no better companion.'

'It is impossible,' said the priest stubbornly now in Spanish, and he started to pull on the woman's arm to get her to rise.

I rose to my feet as she wrenched her arm out of his grip. 'You listen to me,' I told him in my most officious manner. 'I am General Wellesley's personal representative, an officer and a gentleman. I have asked the lady to the ball and she has accepted. That is an end to the matter unless you want me to take this up with the president of your Central Junta, who I am meeting later. The Junta is looking for British support, so I do not think they would want General Wellesley's representative insulted. I rather think that they may also want the heroine of Zaragoza at the ball too.'

The priest's eyes glittered dangerously as he weighed likelihood of my words. But then he gave a grim smile of satisfaction as though the battle was not over yet, but he was grudgingly conceding the first engagement. 'You can collect her from the convent opposite the cathedral.' With that he pulled again on her arm, getting her to her feet.

'Wait,' I said. I turned to the lady, 'Madam, I am Captain Thomas Flashman but I do not yet have the honour of your first name. I cannot call you the Maid of Zaragoza all night.'

She smiled hesitantly. 'I am Agustina,' she said, and then more confidently, 'I am Agustina de Aragon.' With that the priest led her away.

I should mention at this point that Byron was true to his word and did dedicate two verses of his epic poem Childe Harold to Agustina's exploits. It is his usual turgid flowery nonsense of course, as you can see for yourself. I got my grandchildren's governess, Miss Tuttle, to scour through it to find them. The poor woman is quite besotted with Byron even though he is now long dead, and was beside herself when she discovered that I had known him and the subject of these verses:

LV
Ye who shall marvel when you hear her tale,
Oh! had you known her in her softer hour,
Mark'd her black eye that mocks her coal-black veil,
Heard her light, lively tones in Lady's bower,
Seen her long locks that foil the painter's power,
Her fairy form, with more than female grace,
Scarce would you deem that Saragoza's tower
Beheld her smile in Danger's Gorgon face,
Thin the closed ranks, and lead in Glory's fearful chase.

LVI
Her lover sinks - she sheds no ill-timed tear;
Her chief is slain -- she fills his fatal post;
Her fellows flee -- she checks their base career;
The foe retires -- she heads the sallying host:
Who can appease like her a lover's ghost?
Who can avenge so well a leader's fall?
What maid retrieve when man's flush'd hope is lost?
Who hang so fiercely on the flying Gaul,
Foil'd by a woman's hand, before a batter'd wall?

Chapter 17

With Agustina gone I settled down to finish the bread, olives and some spicy sausage left on the table, washing it down with a jug of good red wine. The great hound sat beside me and fixed me with a brown eyed stare, probably in the hope that I would give it some sausage. But I was hungry too, so all it got were the two rough end pieces of the meat, which it gulped down with barely a chew. After varying degrees of refreshment, man and dog sat and surveyed each other. He was a tall, lean brute, but despite what Byron had said, I thought there was a calm intelligence to him.

'Viriates,' I said thoughtfully. The dog's head twisted to one side slightly at the name and I will swear that he cocked a single shaggy eyebrow at me. Not another word was said, but I sensed without a shadow of doubt that we were in unison in thinking that Viriates was a ridiculous name for a dog. He had been an army dog before and I wondered what his previous name had been. Soldiers were not that imaginative with dogs' names and I had known several just called 'dog'. There was another name popular at the time, partly because it was an abbreviation for Bonaparte and partly because it related to a dog's favourite food. Looking at this animal, whose haunches and even some ribs were visible through its skin, it seemed particularly appropriate. 'Boney,' I tried, and was rewarded with a wag of his tail and the opening of his mouth to reveal a smiling crescent of sharp white teeth.

A short while later, Boney and I were exploring the narrow streets of Seville's Jewish Quarter in search of lodgings. Despite the name, there were few Jews in residence as most had been expelled or forced to officially renounce their religion during the Middle Ages. Several doors had already been slammed in our faces when we found the gateway to a courtyard of a large guest house. The stout surly woman who managed the establishment was another to refuse my request. The city was already packed with soldiers and politicians, she told me. But this time, before she had a chance to slam the gate shut, Boney sprang forward, wrenching the rope attached to his collar out of my hand.

'Hey, what is going on,' shouted the woman, she fell back against her gate to avoid the charging animal, who gave a short bark of excitement. The swinging gate revealed a filthy stable yard with a pair of mules tied under an awning in one corner and a cart and some bales of hay in another. Two large rats could be seen between some barrels in the middle of the courtyard, and too late they noticed the grey shape leaping towards them. There was a squeak of alarm that was truncated by the audible snap of jaws. Boney, dropping the first rat, reached the second with a single bound. He snatched it up, shaking it to break its neck. Then with a sickening crunching noise he seemed to swallow it in two gulps before turning to find his first victim.

'Bravo,' shouted the woman in appreciation before turning back to me. 'Señor, your dog, he can stay.' She paused, looking me up and down and appraising what she could charge before adding, 'And you too perhaps.' She eventually found me a room on the top floor of the house. It was comfortable apart from the summer heat, but everywhere was hot in southern Spain in July; well almost everywhere. I did not have to share with Boney as I found him residing with the owner in a much cooler parlour on the ground floor. It was poorly lit with shutters keeping out the sun while allowing a breeze, but I could clearly see the dog stretched out across the cold stone flags that made up the floor. He had a pail of water set for him at one side and the woman cooing over him and feeding him bits of stale bread. The damned creature even noticed me looking in through the door and its mouth lolled open into one of its canine grins.

That evening, after persuading my landlady to leave my dog alone long enough to press some clothes, I finally presented myself at the door of the small convent opposite the cathedral. It was a small miserable place that looked more like a private house, but they still took over a minute to answer my knocking. When the door finally opened, there was the priest I had seen before, with a look smug satisfaction on his face.

'The lady has been prepared for you,' he intoned pompously. 'And while I believe that a British gentlemen would only behave with the utmost honour and integrity,' he managed to say this in a way that implied he actually believed the exact opposite, 'duty requires me to protect the lady's honour with all the resources at my disposal. Brothers Joseph and Antonio will therefore escort you throughout the evening.' He gestured at a middle aged monk and a younger novice who had appeared at his shoulder. He paused at this point, looking at me as though he could guess my intentions. Well, he was bang on the money so far, I had little honour or integrity but if he thought he was entrusting an innocent lamb to a wolf, well he was wrong there. For I knew rather more about women than him and Agustina was no lamb. Quite what she was at that moment though was hard to tell, for when the priest and monks stood back a figure dressed entirely in black emerged. If you imagine a nun in mourning with a black veil over her head then you pretty much have the picture. Only the medal still hanging around her neck gave any flash of colour. I had been expecting this and had prepared for it, but I did not want the priest to know that, and so I reacted indignantly.

'Good God man,' I exclaimed. 'That veil is so thick there could be another of your damned monks hiding in that costume and I am not taking one of them to a ball.' Agustina reached down for the hem of the heavy lace veil, and ignoring a shout from the priest to leave it alone, she pulled the front up over her head.

'I am sorry señor, they forced me to wear this and even held me down while they sewed the veil into my hair.' Her eyes were red and she looked sad and forlorn. If I had harboured any doubts about the arrangements I had put in place they melted at that moment. 'You do not have to take me to the ball dressed like this.'

The priest gave a smile of triumph, but it was short lived as I reached for Agustina's arm to guide her through the convent door. 'Nonsense, I would still be delighted to take you to the ball,' then in a lower voice that only Agustina could hear I added, 'don't worry, everything is in hand.' As we reached the square instead of turning left towards the palace we turned right, and then into a street lined with cafes and shops, near the place we had first met. We walked briskly and I glanced over my shoulder to see the two monks hurrying to catch us up. They were still several yards behind us when we turned again to enter a small discreet establishment. Most businesses were closed with many of Seville's tradespeople attending the celebrations themselves, but the door to the dressmaker's shop opened instantly to my knock.

'Hello, dear,' the portly shop mistress greeted Agustina, 'It is an honour to have you in my humble establishment. Come along, we will soon have you sorted out.' She was interrupted as the two monks burst in behind her. 'Ooh monks,' she said gleefully, before giving me a broad wink. 'We don't get your sort in very often. Lucia, could you attend to these gentlemen?'

From behind a screen stepped a well painted professional woman with a predatory smile. But it was not her face that you noticed first, for she was wearing nothing but a very low cut scarlet silk bodice and the shortest of petticoats. She had a body that could have brought a regiment to a halt in that outfit and to use her on two monks seemed almost cruel. They stood frozen in eye bulging, slack jawed astonishment as she slowly walked forwards giving them plenty of time to take in the view.

'Hello boys, is there anything I can do for you?' she asked, cocking a suggestive eyebrow. By Christ she was a comely piece and I realised that Agustina had disappeared with the owner out to the back of the shop without me even noticing. The younger monk seemed transfixed while the front of his robes showed that with one significant exception he was frozen with lust. The older one licked his lips as he surveyed the bounty before him. I was clearly not the only one to be considering the possibilities. The whore, for that was undoubtedly what she was, reached forward and grabbed the tent pole that had appeared underneath the young monk's cassock. 'Do you want me to help you with that?' she asked, laughing. The touch seemed to break the spell and with a shriek the young monk leapt back as though her hand had burned him through the rough cloth. Muttering a garbled prayer in Latin he flung himself out of the door. With a last reluctant look, his colleague followed. The woman laughed and shut the door behind them. As she turned around she noticed the effect that her appearance had had on me and giggled. 'Don't worry señor,' she whispered, nodding to the back where Agustina had gone. 'From what I hear she is very good at firing off big guns.' The scarlet temptress disappeared into the back with the other women while I was left to wander around the front of the shop alone.

I had found the dressmaker that afternoon on the way from the café where I had met Agustina to find some lodgings. It had been obvious from the priest's reluctant agreement to allow Agustina to attend the ball that he would do what he could to ruin the evening. I had been sure he would find her the dowdiest dress. I had not anticipated the nun's habit though and I had been expecting priest to come himself as escort. When I had looked in Byron's purse I had found even more money than I had guessed at from the weight and I was curious about the girl. Even in the loose black gown there had been a lithe body evident and she had a pretty face when not scowling. She undoubtedly had courage and spirit and I wanted us both to enjoy the ball. So when I saw the dressmaker sitting outside her shop making delicate stitches through a blue silk gown in the bright sunlight, I decided to make some preparations. Most of the seamstress' clients were the better off courtesans of the city who had little love for the church. Everyone had heard the story of the Maid of Zaragoza and the woman had seen Agustina several times so was able to guess her size. She made clothes to order but had several overdue for payment that she could offer. It would do her business no harm for the Maid to be seen in one of her creations, although the amount she charged seemed eye-wateringly steep to someone who had never bought a gown before.

A very long hour later the amount paid was worth every penny. Agustina stepped out from behind the curtain at the back of the shop and looked stunning. The scarlet assistant, now properly dressed, was still fussing with Agustina's hair, now artfully piled on top of her head, while the dressmaker was beaming with delight. I had paid for a red satin gown but Agustina was wearing the pale blue silk dress I had seen being made that morning. 'This one looked better,' the dressmaker explained. Agustina herself appeared as though she was still in a state of shock from seeing herself in the mirror. She walked hesitantly towards me, clearly unfamiliar with the size of gown that now surrounded her legs. When she reached me she grabbed my arm tightly and whispered her thanks as though at that moment she could say no more.

We walked back through the square to the palace. The monks were nowhere to be seen but the smartly dressed British officer and radiant beauty on his arm gathered envious glances from nearly all we met. Agustina was barely recognisable from the modestly dressed woman the priest had paraded in the town that morning, although she had kept her medal, which now dangled below a generous glimpse of cleavage. It was at the entrance to the palace that we found the cleric and two chastened monks awaiting our arrival. Even then we were almost up to them before the priest recognised us. His draw dropped briefly in astonishment at the transformation in Agustina, while the lustful look she was given by the two monks should have cost them a month of Hail Mary's at their next confessions. I gave the priest no opportunity to intercept us and pressed on through the gate, waving the invitation card to one of the flunkeys.

The party was in full flow when we arrived, and there seemed a sense of urgency to the celebrations as though more than a few people knew that while we were rejoicing a victory, more bad news was in the offing. The palace itself dated back to the Moorish rulers of Spain, with exquisitely tiled rooms and courtyards with fountains.

'It is beautiful,' breathed Agustina enthusiastically

'Haven't you been here before?' I asked. 'I would have thought the Maid of Zaragoza would have been a guest of honour.'

'Oh, I was paraded before the Central Junta and given my medal, but then the priests claimed that my husband had placed me in their care. They did not want me talking to anyone and word getting out that I have been with a lover in Zaragoza and not my husband. So I was hustled away again.'

'Have you spoken to your husband? Is he angry about the death of his son?'

'Oh, he was not the father of the child, something else the church would not want you to know. I was wild as a girl,' she smiled and added, 'I still am if I can get away from those wretched clerics. My parents were poor and I was pretty. I soon learned that I could earn money at the gates of the local barracks.'

'I see,' I said, realising that there was much more to Agustina than I had first thought.

'Like hundreds of girls before me I found I was with child, so had to find myself a husband. His name is Juan, he knew I was pregnant but he did not mind. He wanted a pretty wife but there was no affection, he treated me like his personal whore. I was sixteen then and I stayed with him while the child was a baby, but he used to beat me and ... and,' she paused before adding in almost a whisper, 'make me do things that I did not want to do.'

'Don't worry, that is all over now,' I comforted her while wondering what these 'things' were. I knew some soldiers would lend out their wives to comrades for money and suspected that the 'gallant' Juan had seen his young wife as a source of income. He must have known that when she was loitering around the barracks gates, it was not to listen to the regimental band. Still, I was not going to get sentimental for I had been developing carnal thoughts for Agustina from our first meeting, which had only become more inflamed when I saw her in the ball gown. I grabbed another glass of wine for her from a passing waiter and asked, 'So how did you end up in Zaragoza?'

'When war was declared Juan had to spend more time with the army. While he was away I took Eugenio, my son, and ran away. I went to my sister who lived in Zaragoza and that is when I met Raul. I enjoyed being with the soldiers, I used to go up on the ramparts as often as I could. They had even let me fire the gun before.'

At this point we were interrupted by one of the cavalry officers that I had ridden with from Talavera to Seville. He was already drunk, and through glassy eyes gave Agustina an admiring glance before slapping me on the back, causing me to spill half my wine. 'What a night eh, have you heard any news of Soult? Have your redcoats beaten him?'

'Sorry, I do not have any news,' I lied.

'Ah,' he leaned towards me in an effort to be confidential. In a very loud whisper he added, 'I am hearing rumours that you have beaten Soult but others say the whole army is south of the Tagus.'

'Perhaps we will hear tomorrow,' I predicted with a strong degree of confidence.

'Yes, you are right,' he agreed, straightening up. 'Tonight is for celebration.' He pounded me on the back again, this time emptying my glass, before turning to Agustina. 'You should have seen this one at Talavera,' he boomed. 'The general, this captain and two aides charged the French battery without waiting for the rest us. The four of them captured one end of the battery all by themselves. I salute you sir,' he added, raising his own full glass before staggering away into the crowd.

'So you really did charge the battery,' exclaimed Agustina grinning. 'I thought you were lying to impress me before.'

'Lie to impress you!' I gasped in exaggerated outrage while collecting two more glasses from a passing waiter. 'Why would I do that?'

'I wonder,' she replied grinning as she took the glass, and then gave me a knowing look. 'I am sure you would say that you were not trying to get me drunk too.'

'My dear, you have a shockingly poor impression of the behaviour of a British officer.'

'I hope I am not disappointed then,' she said coyly. I grinned back. She was clearly a woman who enjoyed the company of men and must have been frustrated with the nuns, priests and monks who had guarded her over recent months. I flatter myself that I am not bad looking and if she thought I was a hero as well then so much the better. Flashy, I thought to myself, if you haven't bedded this girl by the end of the night, well you are losing your touch. With that thought uppermost in my mind I steered her out towards the large gardens where hedging and arbours offered far more opportunity for intimacy.

The crowd certainly thinned in the gardens but this revealed that our minders had also somehow managed to enter the palace, and the priest and the two monks dogged our every turn so that wherever we went at least one of them was watching.

'What are you going to do?' I asked, gesturing to one of our watchers. 'You cannot spend the rest of your life with them peering over your shoulder.'

'I want to get away to fight. They used me like a living talisman in Zaragoza after the first siege and before the city fell. That is why they helped me escape, but now they are doing the same here. I am paraded around like a holy relic but I want to avenge my son and Raul and fight the French myself.'

'Would you join the guerrillas?'

'Yes, there are already women fighting amongst the guerrillas and most of the bands would welcome the Maid of Zaragoza among their ranks. Now the allied army has beaten the French the tide will turn and we will drive the French from our country. I want to play my part in our liberation.'

I paused, there was a gleam of passion in her eye now that I did not want to extinguish, but I had to tell her the truth. 'The allied army has already retreated south of the Tagus,' I told her quietly. 'It will be announced tomorrow. If they had stayed in the north they would have been crushed between two huge French armies.'

'Oh,' she was silent for a while as she took in this new reality. 'If the combined allied army has to run from the French, will Spain ever be liberated?'

That was a question I had been pondering ever since I had learned the size of Soult's army. It would take years and cost a fortune to get the Spanish infantry to a standard where they could match the French veterans. A vastly bigger force would be required from Britain too and I was not sure if there was the political will or the treasury funds to pay for that. The Navy was the first priority, to blockade the French into submission. The allies could only be sure of beating small French armies. Once the French forces combined, as they would to meet any threat, then the allies would be defeated. It seemed only a matter of time before there was another humiliating withdrawal. Not that I was going to admit that then of course. 'Oh, the allied army will get stronger all the time and the French cannot keep a large army in the field for long, not with your guerrillas attacking their supply chains.'

To my surprise she seemed strangely heartened. 'Yes,' she agreed. 'I need to join the men fighting in the hills. I just have to prove to the priests that I am not a holy relic.' To lighten the mood I took her back to the ballroom and we danced after a fashion, with Agustina struggling with the wide skirts. Having worked up an appetite we

179

helped ourselves to the heaving tables of food and more of the plentiful drink. By then I was feeling well-oiled and as randy as a prize bull before tupping time. From the occasional grabs and fondles she allowed and indeed returned, I sensed that Agustina felt the same. We were both ready to boil but whenever we tried to slink away and find some private place one of those damned clerics would appear.

I was getting to the point where I could have taken her in the middle of the buffet table and the spectators could go to hell, but Agustina told me to be patient. Just before midnight the guests began to disperse. We mingled with a large group of people as we walked out of the gates, to make it harder for the priest and monks to follow us in the darkness. I did not want them snatching Agustina back to the convent before I had the opportunity of having my lecherous way with her. The main square was lit by flickering torches, and while some servants also lit the way ahead with burning brands, it was still hard to make out faces and colour. Several parties peeled away from the main group, and looking over my shoulder I could see the priest and monks spreading out to check out whether we were in those groups. We stayed with the largest crowd, that suited me; once past the cathedral we would be in the commercial district and then on to my lodgings in the Jewish Quarter. I was sure I could shake off any stubborn cleric there. To my surprise as we approached the cathedral doors the bulk of the group turned to go in. I grabbed Agustina's elbow and made to pull her on but she pulled back and gestured back to the church.

'Stay with the crowds, it is dark in there. They are having a midnight mass to celebrate the victory.'

'But I don't want to go to church, damn it!' I growled at her. 'We can have a much better time somewhere else.'

'Trust me,' she whispered, smiling over her shoulder as she let go of my arm and walked through the big cathedral doors. I stood foxed for a moment. The bloody woman was infuriating. I wanted to rush forward, scoop her up off the ground and run with her into the nearby streets. But even at midnight, kidnapping a doubtless protesting woman in the middle of Seville would attract attention and those wretched clerics would soon reclaim their charge. The last of our crowd were moving towards the church doors and I could see the priest in the distance staring about him looking for us. I had no choice but to turn reluctantly into the dark cavernous cathedral. I passed the entrance to the huge Giralda bell tower on my right and moved into the body of the church. The rest of our party had continued to move down the nave towards the altar which was bathed in candlelight, showing that a service was starting. There were candles on stands every few yards down the nave. I stared but I could not see a blue dress among the group.

'Over here, Englishman.' Her voice called from the left and I just caught a glimpse of the light silk of her dress moving between the columns.

'Come back, damn you,' I whispered as I plunged after her into the gloom. 'What in Christ's name are you doing?' I called out quietly when I got to the place where I had seen her. We were at the edge of the huge cathedral with private chapels lining the walls. There were hardly any candles here, just a few on the private altars stopped it being pitch dark. 'What the hell…' I exclaimed as a hand reached out and pulled me behind a pillar. I relaxed as I felt her arms go around my neck and then her lips on mine. 'Mmm, that is more like it,' I whispered to her. 'Now let's get out of here so we can go back to my rooms and continue that line of thought.'

'What is your rush?' she soothed. 'Did you know that Christopher Columbus was buried here before his bones were taken to the Americas? His brother is still buried here.' She looked round as we heard more footsteps. We watched as the priest came in through the same door we had entered. There were candles around the entrance so we could see him clearly as he glanced around. I shrank back behind the pillar but he could not see us in the darkness. Peering round again I saw him genuflect towards the altar and then move forward towards the congregation.

'I don't care about Christopher Columbus and neither do you. Come on, the priest has gone. Let's get out of here.'

I saw the white of her teeth in the gloom as she grinned at me. 'I will have you know that I am a great admirer of people who search for new territories, you never know what they will find.' Before I could respond I felt her hands on the front of my breeches, caressing and undoing buttons.

'You can't want to do it here in the cathedral?' I gasped hoarsely. God knows I am no prude; I have made love in carriages, boats, theatre boxes and on one memorable occasion in the basket of a hot air balloon. But I don't take any thrill from the risk of discovery. More than once I have had to flee, boots and trousers in hand, at the unexpected arrival of a husband. You cannot concentrate fully on the matter in hand, so to speak, while listening out for a key in the lock.

But some women like the spice of danger. I recall Carstairs telling me that Eliza Marchbanks once insisted he take her from behind while she leant out of the window to give instructions to the gardener.

Agustina seemed of the same persuasion and by now her hands were busy exploring left, right and centre, particularly centre. I felt any last inhibitions I had dissolve as she reached up to nibble my ear and whisper, 'If you want me, you have to take me right here.' Almost working of their own accord my hands went on their own voyage of discovery down the front of her gown and she gasped as her breasts were liberated from the fabric. We were both coming to the boil nicely and while we were panting and grunting in pleasure, the sound seemed lost in the cavernous cathedral. The congregation were some fifty yards away near the great high altar and seemed intent on listening to the chants and incantations of the priests.

I was struggling to lift the skirts of her gown – it was like peeling an onion. Every time I got some layers up above her waist I reached forward and found more layers to hinder me. The gathered folds were getting in the way between us and Agustina suddenly turned her back to me. 'Pile the skirts over my back,' she whispered as she bent over some waist high stonework. I did not hesitate, reaching down, grabbing all the cloth I could hold and hauling it upwards. I ran my hand over her bare thigh and stepped up behind her. She gave a deep groan of pleasure as I set to and this time I noticed a couple of ladies in the congregation turn their heads and stare in our direction. They evidently could not see anything as they turned back to the front.

For a while I lost myself in the pure pleasure of the situation, and the regular low groans from just in front of me indicated that Agustina was doing the same. Just as I was thinking that I should enjoy carnal pleasures in church more often, my attention was taken by movement at the altar. A richly dressed priest with a mitre, who I took to be the bishop, was stepping forward and altar boys holding candles and a huge cross were forming in front and around him. More priests were lining up behind and with a lurch of dismay I realised that they seemed to be preparing to move through the church.

'What are they doing?' I hissed at Agustina.

'It is the procession of the cross,' she gasped back. 'They walk around the cathedral blessing it and the congregation,' and as she dropped this bombshell she gave a little giggle.

'They do what?' For a second I was stunned and then I realised that Agustina had known this would happen all along. She actually wanted the priest to discover her fornicating in the cathedral so that he would leave her alone.

For a second I was appalled and it quite put me off my stroke. 'You can't stop now,' she gasped, and she wiggled herself against me in a way that could only be described as sublime. I don't like to be used but by God there were compensations in this case and she was right, I was too gone in lust to stop now. But I was damned if I was going to be caught 'in flagrante delicto' either. I grabbed hold of her hips and pounded away with even more vigour intending to bring things to a speedier conclusion. She gave a slight squeal of delight and the regular groans became faster and louder. Over the top of the piled dress on Agustina's back I saw the two ladies in the congregation look back across in our direction. Several other heads turned too but then the procession started down the front of the church.

An unbidden memory came into my head of my school days and the time a master had accused me of playing pocket billiards with myself in prayers. I well remembered burning with embarrassment but that would be nothing to the scandal of a British officer, Wellesley's envoy no less, caught bulling away at a national heroine of Spain in the middle of a cathedral service. Throughout the long procession down the centre of the church my mind and body toiled to bring satisfaction to us both. Agustina was undoubtedly a prime piece and normally this would not be difficult, but now as I tried to lose myself in the moment my thoughts would be interrupted by visions of laughing schoolboys and sneering masters, which took the edge off, so to speak. Not that Agustina seemed to mind my prolonged performance. Her groaning had got even louder so that she had buried her face amongst the multiple layers of the front of her dress to muffle the effect.

I watched the procession as it neared the church door to see in which direction it would turn. A man with a large cross led the way followed by an altar boy with an incense burner. Then came the bishop walking between four more altar boys all carrying large candles, which illuminated yards all around them. The bishop seemed half asleep, still blessing on both sides even though he was well past where the congregation had gathered. Behind him trailed half a dozen other assorted clerics, with the whole mass chanting in Latin. There was an inevitability to the fact that when the man with the cross approached the door he turned right, in our direction. Flight was not an option. I was now at the point where wild horses could not have dragged me off

Agustina and from the muffled noises she was emitting I sensed she was the same. Tearing my gaze from the procession I renewed my efforts with a desperate urgency. I shut my eyes and lost myself in the pleasure of the flesh.

'Oh God!' Maybe there is something in the risk of discovery after all, for I have rarely known a convulsion of pleasure like it. I had called out in English without thinking and opened my eyes just in time to see the bishop's procession pass by ten yards in front of me. The man with the cross and the altar boy with the incense burner had apparently passed by without noticing us, lost in their own chanting and religious devotion. The bishop, though, had heard my appeal to a higher power. Still looking half asleep he turned and with his hand made the sign of the cross in my direction while muttering a blessing. The young altar boys holding the candles, with sharper eyes and hearing, had also heard me and while their vision must have been affected by the lights in front of their faces, they stared into the darkness with an intense curiosity. Agustina's body shuddered deliciously against me, and I saw her raise her head and emit another deep groan of pleasure that had the two ladies in the congregation look across again with what I thought were looks of naked envy.

There was still a dim darkness around us, but now I guessed that the light blue silk of Agustina's dress could be seen like a cloth cloud in the darkness of the church. Clearly the candle bearing boy on our side just in front of the bishop had the best eyesight as now he stopped in his tracks, his jaw gaping in astonishment. He may have seen me standing behind Agustina, or her breasts as she half rose from the folds of her dress. The boy must have guessed what had been happening for he allowed his candle to droop as the oblivious bishop walked past, his vestments trailing over the flame. The candle holder behind blundered into his colleague and with some heated whispering they resumed their stations, neither seeming to notice a wisp of smoke coming from the bishop's robe. Agustina and I stood frozen as the rest of the procession went past. I had half expected her to call out something to make sure we were discovered but she just stood there, pressed into me and breathing heavily.

For a moment I had thought we would get away with it, but then came the last priest in the procession. It was our old friend. Even though the candles had moved their arc of illumination further down the church, he stared intently into the darkness around us and I saw him stiffen as he seemed to recognise us. 'Bastard,' Agustina whispered, I thought loud enough for him to hear. He stopped and a look of fury crossed his face. I thought he was going to march towards us and throw us out of the church but he reluctantly glanced back to the procession. This was returning slowly to the altar with one of the candle bearing boys now discreetly trying to put out the bishop's smouldering vestments. The priest's mouth set in a grim angry line and he resumed his ceremonial pacing down the aisle, while I sagged with relief.

'Do you feel a sense of release?' Agustina whispered to me quietly.

'I did a minute or so ago.'

'No, no that,' she giggled. 'Although that was good too. I mean I don't think the church will be bothering me anymore.'

'For what we have just done, we could probably be tortured by the Inquisition.' I wanted to feel angry that I had been used, but I was still in that post coitus glow as we separated and adjusted our clothes. 'Let's get out of here.' We moved quietly to the door we had entered through but I could see one of the monks waiting outside. I didn't dare look back at the altar as now we were clearly visible in the candles by the door. If the priest had harboured any doubts that it was us then my distinctive red coat and Agustina's blue dress would dispel them.

'Come along, we can leave by the orangery,' Agustina whispered. As we disappeared once more into the gloom on the opposite side of the church from where we had been, she explained that this huge building, the largest cathedral in Europe, had originally been a mosque built by the moors. Down one side was a courtyard with a fountain where the faithful used to wash, and it was now planted with orange trees. We emerged into the night through a side door and had nearly got to the gate when another figure stepped out to block our way. It was the second monk, but as he raised his arms to stop us a voice called out from behind.

'Let them be!' shouted the priest. I turned and he was striding towards us from the door we had just used, and while it was too dark to see his features his voice was cracking in anger. 'You are a whore and a disgrace to the church and to Spain. I swear by all that is holy that I will see you ruined. And as for you sir, your general will hear of this. I will tell him that you are an abomination to the Catholic church.'

'You are very kind,' I murmured, and smiled at him serenely. There was so little respect for the Spanish amongst the British then that the threat held little danger. British soldiers, even the Anglican officers, did not understand or trust Catholicism. As I had not been caught in the act, if the church did try to spread damaging stories about me most would probably assume that I had been successful in tempting a nun out of a convent.

Chapter 18

The sour news of the withdrawal from the battlefield of Talavera spread through Seville during the morning after the victory celebrations. It left many of those enthusiastic party goers with a bitter taste in their mouth to go with their sore heads. The news was all several weeks old and having been suppressed for a few days, the facts were coming out in the wrong order or being misunderstood. It seemed that Cuesta had wanted the combined allied army to take on Soult on the northern shore of the Tagus, but Wellesley had refused. He was not fighting a battle with a river at his back, heavily outnumbered and with unreliable allies. The British therefore pulled back over the river and effectively forced the Spanish to do the same. Some hot heads thus blamed the British for the ignominious withdrawal. Furious complaints sent by the British about their abandoned wounded got little support. Wiser heads however were starting to realise that this would be a long war, even with the British help.

Various regional junta representatives were summoned to discuss strategy, with many believing that pitched battles between standing armies would not succeed, while the French veterans outnumbered any combined allied army. They pressed instead for more support to the guerrilla forces that harried the French supply lines. The guerrillas were particularly effective in the winter when the French had to disperse their armies to live off the land, and the mountain retreats of the irregulars became dangerous to all those who did not know their way. But in the summer the French would gather forces and attack, not only the guerrillas, but also all those they suspected of supporting them. Little quarter was given on either side.

To a soldier, the guerrilla conflict seemed a vicious war within a wider campaign with many of the fighters originally thieves and brigands or those escaping conscription. But to the Spanish, the guerrillas were at least holding their own against the French, which was more than their army was achieving. Their tactics forced the French to divert thousands of troops from the front line to protect their rear. Agustina was certainly still determined to join them. I discovered this when she asked if the blue silk dress belonged to her. When I told her it did, she asked if I would mind if she sold it. Apparently the dress maker had offered to buy it back and even a fraction of the princely sum it had cost me would get Agustina the horse, weapons and supplies she needed.

So ten days after we first met, Boney and I walked with Agustina to the northern edge of city to see her off. Even dressed in a man's clothes she was a striking figure. She was confident that she could deal with any unwanted attention, but I was not sure that the knife she had hidden up her sleeve would be much use if she had more than one brigand to deal with.

'Don't worry,' she told me. 'I have been living with soldiers since I was fifteen. I know how to get men to do what I want.' Given how she had tricked me into helping her break with the church I could not deny that, but she still looked very vulnerable as she rode away down the road. I thought I would never see her again but I was wrong, for she did know how to manage men. While I had saved her from the church, she saved me two years later from something far worse.

Once Agustina had disappeared beyond a bend in the road Boney and I turned back for the centre of Seville, for I had discovered that I had relatives in town to meet. The gathering of the regional juntas had included the Marquis of Astorga, head of the Junta of Granada and the man who, according to Cuesta, had married my cousin. The marquis had his own small palace in town and now that Agustina had gone I planned to appeal to my cousin's hospitality, and move from my room in the Jewish Quarter to something a little grander. I was certainly in no rush to return to the British army, which according to the latest rumours was shadowing the French as the armies moved along both banks of the Tagus. Somewhere comfortable and many miles from the danger seemed just the place for Flashy.

The palace, when we found it, looked quite nondescript from the outside, just a solid wooden gate in a plain high wall. But I knew that these things were normally built around a central courtyard that could not be seen from the street. The gate was open and some men were unloading some crates from a cart. While there was a guard, he took no notice of me in my British uniform as I stepped inside with Boney in tow. Once in the courtyard I could see that, like all of the best buildings in Seville, the palace had been built in Moorish times. There was a fountain in the centre and an arcaded walkway around each of the three stories to join up the rooms and provide shade. A man who looked like a gardener approached us, but when I explained we were here to see the marquesa he just grinned like a village idiot and strolled off to what looked like a potting shed in the corner. Opposite the gate a broad staircase led the way up to what seemed the grandest floor where I guessed the main reception rooms would be. I decided to climb the stairs to find some major domo who could announce me to my cousin. We entered a vestibule which, with its high ceiling and cold tiled floor and walls, seemed refreshingly cool after the heat outside. Those Moors certainly knew how to build for the climate, but there was still no one to be seen inside. I did not want to roam around the house uninvited so we stepped into one of the reception rooms to wait for a servant to appear. I found a comfortable chair while Boney stretched himself out in the corner, laying his belly on a stretch of the cold marble floor not covered by ornate Arab rugs.

'What are you doing in my house?' The voice recalled me from a snooze, my last night with Agustina having been very draining. Opening my eyes I saw a dwarf in the middle of the room. He was clearly one of those favoured servants kept to amuse the marquis, for he was fitted out in a soldier's uniform, a general's from the frogging and braid. Half of his chest was covered in medals and glittering orders that would have been a magpie's delight. He even had a little sword about the size of a bread knife. I laughed at his appearance which seemed to annoy him, as he puffed himself up with bulging little eyes like an outraged owl. The last dwarf I had seen was a three breasted female one in a travelling show back in London. We had paid a shilling each to view her, and she had been taller than the one in front of me. Hartington had paid an extra shilling to feel her tits and had claimed that the middle one was a false bladder.

'Run along and find your mistress,' I told him. 'Give her my compliments and tell her that her cousin from England has come to visit.' Instead of obeying my instruction the little fellow went red in the face and stamped his foot.

'How dare you speak to me like that in my own house,' he piped. 'Get out at once.'

I sighed in exasperation. Finding dwarfs and fitting them out as generals might amuse the marquis, perhaps they pretended he was a general and gave him some soldiers to order about, but clearly this little chap had forgotten his station. Spoiling servants is all very well, but it doesn't do to let them get above themselves. 'Now look here, my lad,' I told him sternly as I got up and walked towards him. 'You go and find your mistress and be quick smart about it.' I reached forward, grabbed him by the shoulder, turned him around and pushed him back towards the door. He wobbled forward two or three steps but he was still babbling indignantly. So to show him who was boss I helped him on his way by swinging my boot into his arse, which sent him sprawling. But instead of running off to get his mistress, the little squirt had the nerve to turn around and draw his little sword.

'By the saints you will pay for that,' he squeaked, while waving the blade threateningly at my kneecaps. I was just about to fend off the little pest with a nearby chair when I saw that Boney was taking charge of the situation. He had been resting near the door and the dwarf had not noticed the dog when he had walked in to challenge me. I had seen Boney sit up and stare curiously at our little visitor when he arrived. But now as the dwarf was advancing on me with his sword the great hound silently paced up behind him. I'll swear there was a grin on his canine features as he approached. He bent his head down to be close the dwarf's neck and issued a low and very menacing growl. I almost felt sorry for the pint sized generalissimo, for a wolfhound the size of a horse would be a terrifying prospect. He whirled round, gave a scream of fright and took two steps backwards before falling over a footstool. I stood over him with my boot trapping his little sword and Boney leaned down to sniff him.

'I would get up if I were you,' I told him grinning. 'I have seen him catch and eat things bigger than you.' He scrambled to his feet and with a venomous backwards glance hurtled out though the door without saying another word. 'And don't forget to tell your mistress that her cousin is here,' I shouted after him.

I went back to lounge in my chair and Boney returned to a cool stretch of marble floor. I think we were both feeling well pleased with ourselves and confidently expected that my cousin would appear shortly. You can imagine our irritation when the dwarf reappeared, only this time he had two full sized soldiers with him, armed with muskets.

'Shoot that dog and then throw that knave onto the streets,' he shouted, now waving two handed a full sized sword that was the same length as him. The men looked like they were set to obey as well, one hefting his musket to his shoulder while Boney wisely took cover behind a settee.

'Oh, for God's sake,' I exclaimed in exasperation, as the little man had clearly taken leave of his senses. But their weapons were real and it would not do to be shot on the orders of the little squirt. I needed to take a firm hand, so I reached into my coat pocket and pulled out my own pistol. Cocking it I pointed it at the dwarf. 'If either of your men comes anywhere near me or my dog I will shoot your damn fool head off.' The men stopped moving and the dwarf looked at me with narrowed eyes, but before he could react there was another voice from behind me.

'What on earth is going on here?' I turned my head and was so shocked I damn near pulled the trigger and shot the little bastard. A woman was coming through another doorway followed by a maid and the village idiot gardener, who had clearly gone to fetch her after all. While I had never seen the woman before, her face was one I knew almost as well as my own. My mother had died when I was ten, just before I was sent to school. Memories of her now were hazy but I had often stared at the portrait of her in my father's study. The woman now in front of me was the living likeness of that portrait.

For a moment I could not speak at all, I just must have gaped at her in wonder. 'I am your cousin,' I eventually managed to blurt out.

'My cousin?' she queried. 'I think I know most of my cousins, and I do not know you.'

'Hah!' shouted the dwarf triumphantly.

'My mother was your Aunt Maria Luisa, she married an Englishman called Flashman, and I am Thomas Flashman. You look just like her portrait.'

Now it was her turn to be shocked. 'By the saints, you are my cousin then. I never met Aunt Maria but I am named after her. Is she still alive?'

'I'm sorry no. She died fifteen years ago…'

'Never mind that,' interrupted the dwarf. 'This villain and his dog attacked me.'

'Damn it, you little pipsqueak,' I roared at him, furious that he dared intrude in his mistress' conversation with me. 'Hold your damn tongue or I'll…'

'Please, please,' shouted the marquesa, walking between us and holding up her hands. Instead of giving the upstart the thrashing he richly deserved she spoke placatingly to him. 'I am sure that Thomas did not mean to cause offence.' As I goggled in astonishment she turned to me. 'Thomas, perhaps you did not realise that this is my husband, the Marquis of Astorga.'

'Your husband?' I gasped. 'But he is a damned dw…'

'He is the Marquis of Astorga and leader of the Junta of Granada.' My cousin cut me off with a rising voice to drown out any further insult I could deliver. She gave me a warning glare before adding, 'I am sure you would not want to cause further offence to the marquis.' For a second or two I could not believe it, and then I remembered

Cuesta's amusement when he had told me about my cousin. He had made a comment about the marquis not being too big for his boots and suddenly I knew it was true.

'Well, 'pon my soul, no, of course I had no idea,' I blustered. I mean, what do you say when you have just discovered that you have booted your marquis cousin by marriage up the arse in his own house and held a pistol on him. 'I do truly apologise, sir,' I added lamely, 'on behalf of myself and my dog.'

The eyes of the marquis narrowed at the mention of Boney and he glanced round to where the hound sat watching proceedings from behind the settee. I got the distinct impression that the marquis was not the forgiving sort, but Maria swept forward and with her back to me she proposed to him that we must stay with them and join them for dinner. The initial reaction of the marquis to that suggestion was to resume his constipated owl posture, but I suspect that Maria also mouthed something to him that I could not see, for he suddenly deflated and gave her a cunning lustful look. God knows what she promised him – I never want to find out – but it worked, for that afternoon we were installed in very comfortable rooms in the palace and invited to dine.

My suspicions about the marquis' forgiving nature were confirmed later that evening. An hour before I was due to join the party for dinner, a servant arrived with a plate of meat for Boney. I hadn't asked for anything and it seemed surprisingly good fare. Remembering the old adage 'beware of Greeks bearing gifts,' I did not give it to Boney straight away. I took one piece of meat from the plate and put the rest in a cupboard so that Boney could not get it. Then I stepped out onto the balcony and looked down into the courtyard. Resting in the shade beneath our window were two cats. I had first seen them when we were shown to the room. Dropping the meat between the two cats I leant on the balcony rail to watch what would happen. The biggest ginger cat took possession of the morsel. It had obviously had a bad day with the mice for it wolfed the meat down. For a while it seemed fine and I had started to get dressed for dinner when I heard a strange noise and looked out over the balcony again. Now the ginger cat was convulsing and spasming, even three floors above I could hear its groans of agony. As its companion circled it, the ginger cat collapsed onto its side and lay still. I have never really liked cats, but I did feel sorry for that one. It had saved Boney's life.

I took the dog with me when I went to dinner; it did not seem safe to leave him alone. As I came down the stairs I saw a group of uniformed children singing for the marquesa in the courtyard. I went out to join them. The Spanish eat late generally and already some torches had been lit around the courtyard. The dead cat was still in the corner but no one paid any attention to that as the children sang local folk songs and Maria clapped and complimented them. An adult in the same uniform as the children explained that they came from a local orphanage that the marquis and marquesa were kind enough to support with donations.

'Ah, Thomas, you have brought your dog,' said Maria when she noticed me. 'Come and meet the children.' She introduced me as an important officer in the British army, but the children were far more interested in petting Boney. After a two more songs the marquesa handed over a small purse to the attendant and then led me inside to dine. 'Are you bringing your dog into dinner?' she asked.

'It seems the safest course of action,' I replied guardedly.

She seemed about to defend her husband but then her shoulders sagged slightly. 'I have to admit he does seem to have taken against the animal. He does not really like dogs, he much prefers cats. There are two here,' and she waived her hand airily in the direction of the courtyard, 'that he has had for years.' We walked into the dining room and there another shock waited for me, for a second guest was sitting at the table.

'Have we met before?' asked the Bishop of Seville. 'You look familiar, and I never forget a face.' I sincerely hope you do, I thought fervently as I leant forward to kiss the ring he proffered on his finger.

'No, your Excellency, I think it is the first time I have had this honour,' I told him, remembering all too clearly how he had given me his blessing at the moment of climax with Agustina some two weeks before. He had looked sleepily in my direction at the time. If he had seen me he obviously did not recognise what we were doing. But did someone tell him afterwards? Before I could consider this further the marquis strode into the room in apparent good humour still wearing his miniature general's uniform. Having greeted the bishop he beckoned for us to take our places. I sat opposite the bishop with Maria to my left and the dwarf stepped up a small ladder into a specially made high chair to my right.

It was only once we had settled that the marquis noticed Boney, who had lain down in a corner of the room. 'I did not expect your dog

193

to join us for dinner,' he sneered coldly while studying the animal carefully. 'I asked the servants to send up some food for the hound to your room.' He was still looking curiously at the dog as though looking for something. 'Did they not bring it?'

I was almost certain now that as well as ordering the food he had also ordered the poison, but I had just thought of a delightful way to confirm it. 'Thank you sir, it was most generous. But Boney had already eaten today and the meat looked such good quality, I gave it to that man who looks after the orphans.'

'Oh, how kind Thomas,' gushed Maria, but I was watching the dwarf for his reaction.

'You did what?' gasped the little man as colour drained from his face and sweat appeared instantly on his brow.

'I gave it to the orphans,' I said innocently. 'They were very grateful,' I added. 'They were only going to have a vegetable broth tonight until they received the donation. Of course, I told them that the gift was through your generosity.'

'Wasn't Thomas kind dear?' Maria repeated to her husband, smiling encouragingly at him as though this largesse would start to build a bridge between us. 'Are you all right dear? You look a little ill all of a sudden.'

'Excuse me, please,' muttered the dwarf, as he scampered down his little ladder and ran full tilt through the door almost faster than the footman could open it for him. Through the doorway I could hear frantic whispering and orders and then the slam of the great front door as some servant was sent out in a hurry, I guessed to retrieve the meat from the orphanage.

We made small talk until the marquis came back and climbed back up onto his perch. He looked at me suspiciously, weighing up whether I was making a fool out of him or if he was averting the painful death of twenty orphans. The first course came and went with the dwarf twitching every time the door opened to admit a servant. The bishop seemed blithely unaware of the tension emanating from the high chair and asked me questions about the chaplains in the British army. As the second course was served an out of breath and sweating servant slipped into the room and leant down to whisper in the ear of the marquis. Evidently they had discovered that I had not given the meat to the orphanage and now knew that I was aware of the poison. As the whispering continued both the servant and the dwarf kept glancing in my direction, with a growing look of malevolence in the eyes of the marquis.

'Is everything all right dear?' asked Maria, noticing the prolonged conference at the other end of the table.

'Yes, everything is fine,' confirmed the marquis, dismissing the servant. He turned to me and gave me a smile that did not extend to his eyes. 'Well, Cousin Thomas, since our… meeting this morning, I have spoken to someone who knows a little about you.'

'Really,' I said guardedly. You did not have to be a gypsy fortune teller to know that the venomous midget was looking to make trouble.

'In fact that was why I invited the good bishop to join us for dinner, to give my wife a flavour of the family her aunt married into.'

The bishop looked puzzled at this, as we had already established that he had not met me before. But before he could say anything there was a voice from the other end of the table.

'You have not been trying to dig up scandal, I hope,' said Maria warningly. 'Thomas is my kinsman and our guest and I will not tolerate our guests being insulted.'

'Of course not, dear,' said the marquis smoothly. 'Thomas has been mixing in renowned company while he has been in Seville. Thomas, I understand you are a friend of Agustina de Aragon, the famed saviour of Zaragoza.'

'I do know the lady,' I conceded, while taking a mouthful of fish to buy time to consider what more to say.

'And I gather you attended the midnight mass to celebrate the victory at Talavera, with that lady,' continued the marquis, now grinning in triumph. He turned to the bishop, 'Perhaps you remember Thomas there, your grace?' That bastard priest had promised to blacken my name, I thought, and clearly the marquis' men had dug out the story for him. Now he would have his revenge and I could feel the sweat breaking out on my brow as I measured the distance to the door for a swift exit. I tried to swallow down the fish so that I could speak in my defence, but before I could say anything the bishop intervened.

'Yes, that is it!' he exclaimed happily. 'I knew I had seen you somewhere before. You were at that midnight mass for Talavera.' I started in shock and the lump of fish seemed to transform itself into a hard rock in my throat. As I reached for a glass of white wine to wash it down, a sea of differing faces met my slightly watering eyes. The bishop, to my surprise, was still beaming at me happily while the marquis stared at him with incredulity, and my cousin gazed with open curiosity.

'Do you not remember what Thomas was doing in the cathedral during a holy mass?' exclaimed the dwarf angrily.

'Why yes, let me see now,' muttered the bishop, staring upwards as he searched his memory. 'He and a lady…'

'Agustina de Aragon,' clarified the dwarf.

'Yes, yes,' said the bishop, irritated at having his recollection interrupted. 'They were both apart from the rest of the congregation, praying in the darkness.'

'What evidence was there that they were praying?' asked the marquis, sounding like some barrack room lawyer.

'Why, Thomas here called out to Our Lord as I went past. And if the lady was Agustina de Aragon, well she is known to be very pious. I have heard stories that she prayed for strength before she fired the gun at the French that saved Zaragoza.'

'Nonsense!' exploded the dwarf. 'They were fornicating!' There was a gasp of astonishment from Maria's end of the table and a croak of indignation from me before he continued. 'Fornicating in the cathedral during a holy mass – it is the talk of city, the clergy at least. I am amazed that no one has told you about it.'

'Ridiculous,' shouted the bishop back and banged the table with the palm of his hand. 'I am surprised that a gentleman of your standing would listen to such tavern gossip. Do you think I would not notice someone fornicating in my own cathedral?' He paused to take a breath and continued in a calmer tone. 'I may have been brought up in a monastery and know little about fornication but I know a man cannot commit the act while fully dressed and standing behind a lady kneeling in prayer.'

'She was not kneeling, she was…' interjected the dwarf before he in turn was interrupted.

'Please,' shouted Maria to cut off her husband. 'It is not seemly to discuss such things over dinner, especially with the bishop present. But tell me Thomas, why were you and this…lady, not with the main congregation in the church?'

Until now I had been watching the exchange between the bishop and the dwarf in fascinated horror as my reputation bounced between pagan satyr and Christian saint. The bishop had done a far better job of defending my good name than I could have done and I had to think quickly to avoid ruining his fine work. 'Well, I am Church of England you know, not Catholic. It did not seem right to join in a Catholic mass.'

'Agustina is Catholic,' murmured the marquis, loud enough for us all to hear. 'Although by all accounts she was groaning in pleasure throughout the service.' He turned to the bishop. 'Just answer me this please, your grace. Are you absolutely sure that the girl was kneeling when you saw her?'

I held my breath. The bishop looked angry at having his memory challenged, but after a second he said simply, 'Yes.' But before I could expel that breath he continued, 'Well, she may have been leaning over a stone altar rail in prayer.'

'So,' said the dwarf triumphantly, 'the girl was bent over an altar rail moaning, while the gallant Captain here, who you could see was dressed from the waist up, was standing behind her.'

'That is right,' agreed the bishop firmly, evidently still seeing no scope for licentious behaviour in this pose. 'And I distinctly remember Thomas calling out 'Oh God' in English as I went past.' There was a stifled gurgling noise from my cousin, but I could not bring myself to look at her as the bishop added proudly, 'God is one of the few English words I know.'

The marquis sat back in his chair, satisfied at having demonstrated to his wife the character of her newly found cousin. The bishop, meanwhile, appeared oblivious of what he had confirmed and I guessed that not even the marquis wanted to explain the practicalities. I had felt myself colouring at the final clarification and reluctantly turned towards my cousin. To my surprise, she was not looking angry or appalled at my heresy. She might have been shocked, but her face was half covered with a napkin and her shoulders were shaking with laughter. She pulled herself together as the bishop looked at her and then she asked me with a wicked glint in her eye, 'And can you explain the moaning and groaning of your partner?'

I paused for a moment, realising that I was in the presence of a kindred spirit, but equally that I could not say anything that would alert the bishop to his misapprehension. 'Perhaps she was considering the second coming,' I ventured.

Chapter 19

That night, despite the fact that my bedchamber was three rooms away from theirs, I could still hear Maria arguing with her husband over my behaviour. While I could not make out every word it was clear she thought he was a prude and a hypocrite while he accused her of being blind to the faults of her 'mongrel cousin.' Eventually, after much slamming of doors, it went quiet. But I had not been the only one listening and in the morning it was clear that all the servants knew about what Agustina and I had done in the cathedral. I was met with looks of disgust or amusement wherever I went in the house. Maria's maid, Consuella, seemed particularly entertained by the tale from the appraising glint in her eye. I remember thinking that there was one who would not mind a Flashy church 'service', and I was not wrong.

I took Boney for a walk in the cool of the early morning and when I got back I was just in time to see the marquis ride out in his little uniform, perched precariously on a big horse. He was followed by several of his servants and what looked like a cart full of luggage.

'You killed my cat,' he screeched when he saw me.

'With food you gave my dog,' I shouted back while restraining Boney, who looked set to knock him off his horse. The little man glared back wide eyed, with his cheeks puffed in outrage. His arms flapped ineffectually a couple of times and then with a roar of rage he started twitching his little legs to urge his horse into a run. It would have been a more impressive departure if a servant had not had to lean forward with a leather crop to get the dwarf's horse into a gallop. The marquis damn near fell off at the sudden acceleration and I could not help but laugh, which made him even madder. Leading his entourage, he charged past me up the street shrieking insults in my direction, most of which I could not understand.

'I am sorry I have caused problems between you and your husband,' I said to Maria when we met over breakfast later.

'Oh, don't worry, he will calm down. It is a shame your introduction did not get off to the best of starts. Did you really kick him?' she asked.

'Yes, but I did not realise who he was.' I paused, wondering whether it was indelicate to ask the question that was uppermost in my mind. 'If you don't mind me asking, why did you marry a, um...'

'Dwarf?' she said, to cut off my hesitation. 'My father had several daughters and as he is a marquis too we had to marry into the aristocracy, unless we were to be disowned like your mother.' She gave me a sympathetic smile. 'After the French invaded, most of the aristocracy lost their lands and hence their income. Granada is still mostly free and my husband is one of the few aristocrats with money and power. So, as I think you say in English, I drew the short straw.' I laughed at that but she cut me off. 'Please don't think I dislike my husband, he is a good man. He is a popular and effective leader of the Junta of Granada and was nearly elected head of the Central Junta. Those are big achievements given the obstacles he has had to overcome. He gets very frustrated when people look at him and just see a dwarf. If he was full sized there is little doubt that he would be leading the Central Junta now.' Maria looked me sternly in the eye as she added, 'I am proud to be his wife.'

For a second I felt a twinge of guilt about the way I had treated him, but then I remembered that the pompous bastard had ordered me out of his house before enquiring who I was, and then he had tried to poison Boney. 'Where is he going now,' I asked.

'Oh, back to Granada and his harem of cortejo.'

'What are cortejo?' I asked, puzzled.

'You really do not know Spain at all do you?' Maria smiled. 'Before a girl is married she is expected to be chaste and pure. But once married she can have official male companions called cortejo who can take her to dances and other social events if her husband is unavailable. They have a similar thing called cicisbeo in Italy, but in Spain it is very formal. In the past married women used to signal with beauty spots if they were seeking a new companion.'

'You mean these cortejo are official lovers,' I asked, astonished that I had not heard of this custom before.

'Not at all. Cortejo are often churchmen, and they must be of at least equal social standing to the woman. The bishop has accompanied me to some events. But army officers are also popular and many do become lovers, possibly some of the priests too.'

'Do you have cortejo?'

'We both have several. Most of my husband's are in Granada. Here in Seville, as well as the bishop I have an aristocrat army colonel who I go dancing with. As you can imagine my husband does not enjoy dancing, but I like to dance a lot.' There was a warm twinkle in her eye as she uttered the last words and I got the distinct impression that they did rather more than dancing. Until I met Cousin Maria I had always thought that the more lustful elements of my character had come from the Flashman bloodstock, but I was swiftly discovering that the Latin Spanish line had those character traits too.

'What are you going to do now?' Maria asked. It was a question I had been pondering. I could not stay in Seville much longer. For a start I had been superseded as Wellesley's representative, as his older brother Richard had just arrived. I had met Lord Mornington, as he was known, in India and had no wish to meet him again. Not that he would be interested in seeing me; he had left his wife and brought a courtesan called Sally Douglas with him as his official companion. He was besotted with the girl and that scandal must be replacing Agustina's and my behaviour as the talk of Seville.

From what Hobhouse had experienced they were still looking for someone to blame over the Mary Clarke affair, so it would not be safe to go home, even if I could get leave. There seemed little choice but to return to the army. The latest news I had heard was that the redcoats had retreated to the Spanish fortress of Badajoz, while the French had stayed north of Tagus, consolidating their hold on northern Spain. The Spanish army was in disarray after Cuesta had suffered some kind of seizure, blamed on the British refusal to continue fighting.

Winter would soon be coming and the word was that the British would retreat back into Portugal and leave the Spanish to face the French on their own. When I heard that I could not help but remember my conversation with Cuesta in his carriage months ago, when he complained that the British forces had run away last winter while his ragamuffin army fought on. 'Show me your army in the spring,' he had said when I had looked down at the state of his forces. Well, it looked as if history was repeating itself as the redcoats were leaving the Spanish to fight on alone, while they went into safer winter quarters. I could understand Wellesley not wanting to throw his army away in pointless battles and knew that supplies of food were not coming to him in Spain. All the same, the British half of me felt a twinge of shame. I was glad Cuesta had been retired as I did not think I could look him in the eye.

The French war with Austria had recently come to an end. Once a treaty had been agreed, everyone expected Napoleon to send yet more of his trained veterans to complete the subjugation of Spain and Portugal. If the British and Spanish armies could not be organised to fight them together, then surely it would be easier for the French to take on their enemies one at a time. The French would crush the Spanish first as they were nearer, but come the next summer when food was more plentiful, huge French armies would sweep into Portugal and I could not see how the British could withstand them. As it turned out I was both right and wrong, for the big French army did come; but as I was having these thoughts, Wellesley was devising plans of his own.

'Why don't you take me to meet Lord Wellington,' suggested Maria, interrupting my thoughts. 'I would love to meet him.'

'Who the blazes is Lord Wellington?' I replied grumpily.

'Why, don't you know?' asked Maria, knowing full well that I didn't, as she was waving in her hand a local news sheet that had only just arrived. 'Your Arthur Wellesley has just been made Lord Wellington in honour of his victory at Talavera. He is a lord now like his brother, and he is now my equal in social standing,' she added, raising an arch eyebrow.

I laughed. 'Well, if you are thinking of him as a cortejo, you should not have much trouble. He is a randy bastard as I discovered in India.' Of course then she wanted to know all about him. In truth, he is probably what women would call good looking, although he could be a cold fish and damned haughty when it served him.

While Maria denied that she had any designs on Wellington, as we must now call him, as a cortejo, she did not take long to sort out her affairs in Seville and within three days we were heading out of the city on the road northwest. We travelled in comfort in Maria's carriage, which was just as well as British redcoats were unpopular now amongst the Spanish as news of our refusal to fight in Spain spread. I was spat at twice and took to wearing a civilian coat and talking in Spanish as we stopped at places along the way.

Badajoz when we reached it was a huge fortress town, near the Portuguese border on the river Guadiana. It looked impregnable and, as I was to discover two years later, it damn nearly was. The British army was camped in and around the town, and already plans were being made to move further west. But of Wellington there was no sign. He had left some weeks before and no one knew where he had gone, or if they did they were sworn to secrecy. Maria found rooms in the city and I returned to my old friends in the officer's mess. I visited Maria regularly over the coming weeks but I came at night to her maid Consuella more frequently. She was a pretty piece and as I had suspected, she was keen on me. She was an enthusiastic lover too and I often needed a good siesta to recover from a night spent in her small room down the corridor from her mistress.

I was not the only one looking for female company however, for Boney seemed to have become obsessed with a bitch owned by one of the other officers and he could not have made a worse choice. Lots of officers had dogs with them on campaign; Wellington had a whole pack of hunting hounds which he rode with as often as he could, but of course Boney was not interested in any of them. No, he had set his sights on a huge dog owned by a Captain Avery. It was a black and brown monster – I think Avery called it a Rotthound or something similar – he had bought from an officer in the King's German Legion.

Avery called it Brunhilde and claimed it was a killer dog. He planned to release it against the French at the next battle. It was certainly a vicious brute, snapping and snarling at anyone who got within reach. Avery admitted that it had bitten him twice. Many of the officers thought that releasing a dog against the French was against the code of war and quite a few were prepared to shoot the animal before that happened. I agreed with them, not through any scruples of warfare, but because its snapping jaws seemed unlikely to distinguish between British and French. When released it would probably go for the first human it could find, which was likely to be wearing a red coat. Brunhilde gave no quarter to her own species either and when Boney tried to express an interest she flew at him, snarling. Only his speed saved him and still he got a nasty bite on the rump. But if anything this only made him keener, and he could often be found placidly watching her, while she growled back at the end of her leash.

Wellington reappeared in October, but gave away nothing about where he had been, even to his senior officers. 'A tour of inspection' was all he would say, but he seemed in remarkably good spirits given a dire military situation and a disastrous political one back home. He had brought news that the British Foreign Secretary Canning had been shot in a duel by Castlereagh, the Secretary of War and my old patron. Both had survived the encounter. Their dispute was over troops that should have been sent to us as reinforcements. Instead they were sent to the Netherlands on a disastrous expedition that left most of the survivors suffering from dysentery and certainly in no state to be sent on to Portugal. We would be left to fight on without reinforcements but Wellington seemed to have not a care. When I finally introduced him to Maria he greeted her warmly with that familiar leery glint in his eye. I was not surprised when we were both invited to join him and some other officers hunting with his hounds. I was mildly put out to learn that Maria had been invited a few days after the first hunt to join another one without me. Through Consuella I discovered that subsequently Wellington had taken to inviting my cousin on rides with just the two of them alone, and that Maria had returned looking 'flushed and satisfied', as her servant put it.

As I was getting regularly 'flushed and satisfied' as well I supposed I could not complain, and a short while later the whole British camp moved west to Celerico in Portugal. I will not dwell too long on the winter and first half of 1810, for in truth not a lot happened. The British remained in relatively comfortable quarters throughout, well fed and without sight of a single Frenchman. The same could not be said for elsewhere in the Peninsular, as the Spanish faced one disaster after another.

Abandoned by their ally and with nearly a hundred and forty thousand fresh veteran French troops pouring over the border, the Spanish insanely decided that this was the moment to liberate Madrid. They sent two armies towards the capital in a pincer movement with entirely predictable results. Initially they caught some French forces by surprise and pushed them back, but then a large Spanish army of fifty-five thousand men met a French army of thirty-four thousand men at a place called Ocana. The Spanish general left his flank completely exposed on a flat plain, and as a result his demoralised troops faced French infantry to their front and rampaging French cavalry in their rear. Spanish losses, including those captured, amounted to over a third of the army while another ten thousand deserted. The Spanish also lost nearly all their cannon and supplies. Against this French casualties amounted to just a few hundred men. The second, smaller Spanish army of thirty-two thousand men was beaten a week later by a French force half its size. Again divisions were routed and huge numbers of men deserted. The surviving army units fled to the nearby mountains where thousands died over the winter from disease and starvation.

The whole campaign had been a reckless gamble and it left southern Spain virtually defenceless. To make matters worse, the city of Gerona finally fell to the French after a six month siege that had killed two-thirds of the garrison and half the citizens of the town. In response the Central Junta abolished all exemptions from military service and desperately tried to raise new armies. But the people were now on the verge of revolution, and even if the men had come forward there were no arms to equip them.

The French had the Spanish at their mercy, only the guerrillas now offered them any resistance. In January the French swept through Jaen, Cordoba and Granada and by the end of January they were at the gates of Seville, which fell without a fight. Maria had stayed with the British throughout the Spanish collapse as it seemed the safest place. Word came through that the marquis had survived and reached Cadiz; the coastal fortress which was now the only city in the south to hold out against the French.

With Spain subdued it seemed certain that the French would turn their huge army on the British next and the croaking amongst our officers increased. During the march down to Talavera the previous year spirits had been high and many had expected to end the campaign capturing Madrid themselves. Now we seemed to face inevitable defeat and ignominy. Some were pressing for leave and others writing tales to the government of what they perceived as mismanagement and incompetence by Wellington. Well, I had started to croak too as I could not see how we would beat a French army three times our size, but Maria had stopped me.

'He has a plan,' she had told me of Wellington one evening when we were alone.

'Do you know what it is?'

'Yes, but he has sworn me to secrecy. It will work Thomas, trust me. The French will not be able to push the British out of Portugal.'

'Oh, come on,' I protested, 'I am your cousin, we are of the same blood, surely you can tell me.'

'I have given my word,' she said, smiling. 'But I will tell you this: he will use what the French perceive as their strengths against them.'

She was right, Wellington definitely had a plan, but if other officers knew about it then they weren't talking. Even senior officers grumbled that they were being asked to put their trust in unknown phantoms of his imagination. But despite all the griping and groaning and letters from politicians and articles in the press, Wellington remained close lipped and resolute. The only time I heard him refer to the matter at all was when one exasperated officer shouted at him that the French could bring a hundred and fifty thousand men against our force in the next few months.

'The more men they bring the better,' he replied with an enigmatic smile, and then he walked away before the man could ask another question. Whatever he had in mind it was clear that we would be relying on his brain beating French brawn in the months ahead. Having seen the luck he had ridden during the Indian campaign I was not sure if I found that comforting or not, but a strange event a few days later seemed almost a good omen.

With other officers I was staying in a large requisitioned house, which according to rumour was built on an old roman villa. Certainly there was the stump of a roman pillar in the centre of the courtyard that all the rooms faced on to. As Avery was also sharing the building, a ring bolt on this pillar became the mooring point for Brunhilde. The damned creature snarled and lunged at the end of a long rope tied to the pillar, at everyone who entered through the gateway, forcing us all to move around the edge of the courtyard to get to our rooms. One evening I returned to my chamber up on the first floor to find Boney sitting by the window. As usual, he was staring at his heart's desire as she paced around the column outside. He had spent hours intently watching the slobbering bitch prowl about on her rope, but every time we walked past her together she would fling herself at Boney with jaws snapping.

I was quickly getting ready as I was expecting Consuella in a few minutes, and sure enough her arrival was soon signalled by snarling and barking outside. Boney got up on his hind legs with his front paws on the windowsill to watch. Consuella, grinning up at him, edged round in our direction, while Brunhilde ran around the column after her.

I put my arm around the dog's shoulders, which were now at the same height as my own. 'I think I am going to have more fun with my girl tonight than you are with yours,' I told him as I watched Consuella reach the bottom of the stairs that led up to my room. 'You need to forget about that one and find a willing bitch that will not try to take a chunk out of your arse. Now get going, you know I don't like you in here when I am entertaining.'

The dog reluctantly dropped to the floor and padded out of the door as I opened it for Consuella, who patted him as he walked past. We shared a cup of wine and I was just getting her stripped for action when a cacophony of barking came from outside. There were the usual snarling growls from Brunhilde, but this time there were excited barks from Boney too. I tried to ignore it at first; if the daft mutt wanted to risk another mauling that was up to him. I did not see why it had to stop me. Consuella was whispering ardently in my ear and it looked as though my attentions were going to be far more welcome than Boney's. But as I tried to concentrate on matters in hand the continual barking and snarling was a distraction, and then other officers billeted around the courtyard started shouting for me to do something.

'For God's sake Flash,' called Avery, 'pull your flea bitten hound away from Brunhilde'

'Those bloody dogs should be shot,' called another unknown voice.

Reluctantly, I pulled myself away from Consuella and went to the window. I took a deep breath to bellow down for Boney to desist.

'I say Flash, hold on,' called a voice to my right. It was Campbell who was leaning out of the window of his room next door.

'What do you mean?' I bellowed back over the din.

'Look at Boney, he is reeling her in.'

'What?' I shouted back.

'Look at the pillar, man. He has taken her around that column four times already; I swear your hound is deliberately reeling that German brute in.' I looked down and he was right. There were already four tight lines of rope around the pillar and Boney, darting backwards and forwards, was leading her clockwise around a fifth time. To this day I am not certain if what followed was sheer dumb luck or animal cunning, but given subsequent events I am inclined to believe the latter. Certainly there were a couple of occasions when Boney did move half a turn counter clockwise, usually to dart in and tease the German dog. He would spring back from the snapping jaws with ease and then as she strained towards him he would resume his clockwise movement. Apart from Avery and one red faced major who hurled lumps of firewood at them from the opposite side of the courtyard, most of the officers had appeared at their windows and were watching proceedings with open curiosity as it became clear what Boney was attempting.

'Never seen anything like it,' called the man who occupied the room to the left of mine. 'Do you think he actually knows what he is doing?'

I shrugged my shoulders in response and felt Consuella press her naked body up behind mine, so it could not be seen from outside, as she peered over my shoulder. Even she was curious to see what was happening. Avery's plaintive appeals for me to intervene were now met with jeers as the spectators wanted to see what the outcome of this confrontation would be. Some were even wagering on it.

Eventually as her leash shortened to just a few feet, the German dog began to sense her vulnerability. She was panting heavily and showing the whites of her eyes as she struggled against the rope trying to understand what was happening. Boney darted towards her again; she only seemed to know one response to this and lunged forward once more. A few moments later and the Teutonic hound was trapped fast against the stone column. Boney stood in front of her for a moment watching her confusion as she strained to reach him, then with a few eager steps he moved around again until he came up behind his prey. The noise Brunhilde made as Boney mounted her was one of the strangest I have ever heard from a creature. There was an initial snarl as she felt Boney behind her which changed into a yelp of surprise and then a pitiable howl as she understood she had been mastered. The rest was drowned out by a cheer from most of the watching spectators and bellowed threats of a lawsuit from Avery if my dog had whelped a litter on his pedigree killer.

'Now I want you to do that to me,' Consuella whispered huskily in my ear before moving back to the bed.

'You want me to put a rope around your neck and tie you to a pillar?' I asked, grinning.

'Well, maybe we can try that later,' she said as she waved her 'tail' invitingly in my direction.

Chapter 20

Brain might have beaten brawn in the canine contest of wills, but for the British, as spring turned into summer, very little changed. Wellington kept disappearing for his mysterious tours of inspection and rumour had it he headed west when he did so. But while Spain collapsed under French domination the British army continued to sit quietly in its Portuguese quarters. The fighting men found it a huge frustration to do nothing while French marshals routed every Spanish force they could find. We all knew that sooner or later the French would amass their armies and head in our direction in numbers that seemed unstoppable. There had been rumours that Napoleon himself would lead this huge army but he was now distracted with his new Austrian princess bride. Instead, word was that Marshal Massena had been given the command. Son of a shopkeeper, Massena had risen through the ranks from private to become one of Napoleon's most trusted and able marshals. Bonaparte had heaped glory and titles on him in recognition of his victories, he was now also Duke of Rivoli and Prince of Essling, but more worrying from my perspective, he seemed to know what he was doing.

Instead of rashly charging west to beat the British, Massena was systematically destroying all major opposition in Spain first so that he would not be interrupted when he did move on the redcoats. Only Cadiz and a handful of fortresses such as Badajoz were left in Spanish hands, but they were in no state to go on the offensive. Eventually he turned his attention to the northern routes into Portugal which were guarded by the fortress of Ciudad Rodrigo held by the Spanish and Almeida in Portugal garrisoned by the British. The French finally laid siege to Ciudad Rodrigo early in the summer and immediately there was a cry from Spain for us to march to its relief. This was supported by much of the army who were fed up with doing nothing while its allies' forces were picked off one by one. It did no good, Wellington refused to move and the Spanish commander of Ciudad Rodrigo was forced to surrender.

Croaking against Wellington now rose to new heights. Like an African swamp in springtime, nearly everyone was at it, claiming that our gallant commander did not know what he was doing. Of course while most people agreed that Wellington's inaction was wrong, there was no consensus on what he should be doing instead. All sorts of lunatic schemes were discussed, with hotheads pressing for an immediate attack, while some wanted to join the Spanish at Badajoz and others wanted to retreat to the coast. While Maria kept assuring me that Wellington had a plan and all would be well, it was hard to put complete faith into such vacuous promises.

The situation only became worse when the French besieged the British garrisoned at Almeida. The fortress was expected to hold out for at least a month but a day after the cannonade started a French shell ignited a trail of gunpowder that led straight to the magazine. When the news of the resulting disaster came through, many people claimed that they had heard or felt the explosion in our winter quarters. The castle, the cathedral and the whole centre of Almeida was completely destroyed. Hundreds of the garrison were killed and the few survivors had little choice but to surrender.

We were now getting reliable reports of French numbers, they were less than expected but still a formidable force: around sixty-five thousand veteran soldiers were with Massena. Now that Almeida had fallen they were only thirty miles away. Against this the British still had just twenty-five thousand men, most of which had stood at Talavera. The officers who pushed for us to fight pointed out that there were a similar number of Portuguese troops now available which General Beresford had been busy training up over the winter. Robert Wilson had long since sailed home after endless snubs from Wellington but his Legion had been absorbed into this new Portuguese army. While they had been impressive, I also remembered the Portuguese militia at Alcantara who had run away. Wellington ignored suggestions to stand and after some prevarication, ordered a retreat fifteen miles south west to Gouveia. For the first time he seemed hesitant and uncertain. When a man with such immense self-confidence looks worried it is time for lesser men to look for a fast horse and a way out.

By chance just such a way out presented itself. Maria had over the last few months received several messages from her husband. Initially he had been in Cadiz but later he escaped back to his lands in Granada. Since then he had been working with partisans and other groups to plan a route of safety for his wife back to Granada. On the day that we heard of the destruction of Almeida, a pair of swarthy men arrived in the camp looking for Maria. They were her guides to take on her on the first part of the journey, fifty miles south east to Fuentes de Onoro, where she would meet a bigger troop of men to take her over the mountains.

As a British officer I had a duty to the army but as a gentleman I had a duty to protect ladies, especially of my own family. Most important of all, as a man determined to protect my own skin at all costs, I had a duty to get out of harm's way as soon as possible. With my unearned reputation, no one would suspect the gallant Flashy of running out on the army just as it seemed an engagement with the French was likely.

It was fortunate that the guides that the marquis had sent looked a proper pair of cut throats. You would think twice before entrusting an impoverished grandmother to them, never mind a pretty aristocratic woman and her maid carrying jewels and other valuables. When Maria came to take her leave of Wellington I made sure that the villains were on hand and I saw him give them a disdainful glare. While I had my story ready, I did not even have to use it as Wellington had the same idea.

'Do you know those guides your cousin is using?' he asked me quietly once Maria had left the room.

'No sir, and I don't like the look of them above half. I was thinking...' I replied, before he interrupted me.

'Flashman, I think it would be best if you went with them, at least to Fuentes de Onoro. Make sure she is put in safe hands or bring her back. I am very fond of your cousin and I cannot think of a better bodyguard for her. Don't worry, there will be plenty of time for you to get back before we are likely to see action.' One of his aides stiffened at that for it was the first time I think he had referred to any imminent battle, but I was too busy stopping my face breaking out into a relieved grin.

'You can count on me, sir,' I told him. 'I will do my best to ensure that she does not come to harm.' I meant it too; even if I had to travel all the way to Granada, or at least close enough to Granada to get a boat and slip to the British bastion of Gibraltar for safety. For if Wellington was planning a fight then odds of nearly three to one, excluding the unproven Portuguese, did not sound appealing. If by some miracle the British won, then I could slip back down from the hills loudly cursing my luck at missing the fight. On the other hand if, as seemed likely, they were chased into the sea, I would be safely out of it and on my way to safety.

I was feeling well pleased with myself as we slipped away late that afternoon. Never have I escaped action so easily. One of the guides, called Rodriguez, led the way then Maria and I followed. Consuella and the other guide brought up the rear. The guides each led a baggage mule for the small amount of luggage that the ladies were able to bring with them over the mountains. The two guides, despite their appearance, seemed capable men. They treated Maria respectfully as their mistress, although they looked wary of me. You can never be too careful and I made sure that I had a loaded pistol in each coat pocket just in case of trouble. Boney bounded alongside our group, glad to get away from Celorico at last.

'It was generous of Arthur to let you come with us,' said Maria as we rode along the path.

'Well, he wanted to make sure you got through safely. I am to report to him as soon as I am back from Fuentes de Onoro,' I told her. 'But if things do not look safe there I am to bring you back or possibly go further with you as escort until I am sure you are safe.'

'That is very thoughtful of him with a battle coming. He must need you for that as well.'

'Oh, we both want to beat the French but the safety of you two ladies,' and here I looked round and winked at Consuella, 'means a lot to both of us.'

'Still,' persisted Maria, 'Fuentes de Onoro is only two days ride, with luck you will be there and back long before the French attack.'

'I am sure I will,' I agreed, while deciding that whatever we found at Fuentes de Onoro, I would deem it insufficient protection and insist on going further. I turned to the guide, 'Where in Fuentes are we meeting the rest of the escort?'

'We are not meeting them in Fuentes,' the guide replied curtly.

'Really?' asked Maria, puzzled. 'I thought you said that was where we would find the rest of the party.'

'We meet them in the hills behind Fuentes, at an old stone windmill.' I felt the first prickle of alarm at this change in the story and then the guide gave me something I could really worry about. 'By now,' he added, 'the French are probably in the town of Fuentes, so we will have to keep to the hills.'

'They are in Fuentes already?' I asked in surprise. 'I thought they would march from Almeida,'

The guide looked at me curiously. 'They are everywhere east of here,' he stated simply.

I was started realise that my escape might not be as straightforward as I thought. While the French had three hundred thousand men across Spain, I had imagined that there would just be pockets of French to be avoided and the bulk of the populace and the territory would be friendly to Spanish partisans. Now I began to realise that in this area at least, with Massena's army on the move, the reverse might be true. I trotted my horse up a slight incline to get a better view across the hills. We could see for miles, but equally, soldiers miles away would be able to see us.

Rodriguez, seeing me scanning the horizon, grinned at me for the first time. 'Do not worry señor, the French are not nearby.' He rode up alongside so that Maria could not hear the rest. 'When they enter a village they are looking for food, valuables, women, anything they want. They usually burn a house or two to get any villagers to hand over these things. You can see their progress from the smoke.' He was right as we saw the next day, when several plumes of smoke marked the north eastern horizon. By then we had also seen several groups of refugees, hurrying south to escape the French, with small bundles of food and any possessions that they could easily carry. They would often stop to speak to our guides, telling them where they had seen the French forces.

Towards the end of the second day as we were riding higher in the hills, Rodriguez turned to me and asked if I wanted to see Fuentes de Onoro. I rode up with him to the top of a nearby hill, then dismounting, we crept cautiously to the rocky crest. There below us about a mile away was a sizeable town. I took out my glass and studied it. I had never been to Fuentes so did not recognise the buildings, but I did see familiar French troops. There were hundreds of them: an infantry column was marching around the town to avoid clogging up its streets which were already congested with artillery trains and other wagons that needed the smoother roads. Cavalry companies could also be seen patrolling the road in both directions.

'Señor, may I borrow your glass?' the guide asked as I finished studying the scene.

'Of course,' I passed it over. 'Those cavalry patrols, will they come up here?'

'Not unless there is something up here that they want. Small groups will not stray far from the main army unless they have to.' He studied the town for a minute, carefully looking in all directions, and then passed the telescope back. 'Did you see the square to the right of the large church?' he asked.

'No,' I took up the glass again to find it. It took a moment before the scene swum into view. It was a tree lined square but wooden beams had been found and pushed into the branches of the trees to join the gaps between them. Hanging from these beams were some two dozen bodies; the whole square had been turned into a giant gallows. 'Good God,' I breathed. 'Are those partisans?'

'One or two might be,' replied the guide. 'But the French probably wanted to make an example and dissuade anyone from causing trouble. They could be the mayor, someone who did not want his wife raped, or people who just happened to be in the wrong place when they were looking to make a point.'

'You mean that they are killing people for no reason at all?'

The guide gave me a pitying look. 'You British in your comfortable camp have no idea what it has been like in a Spain occupied by the French. This is nothing. I have seen them kill everybody in a village that they suspected was helping the partisans, men, women and children.'

'I have heard stories, but I was not sure if they had been exaggerated. But you have seen it, you say.'

'They do it to cow the populace into submission. But for every person they kill they create more hatred and more partisans. They know that if we find a French sentry on his own we will cut his throat. If we can tempt a small group away from the rest we will ambush them. And the people help us,' he added. 'Children have poisoned their wine, old men and women have stabbed them. Just last week we used a group of pretty girls washing by a stream to tempt a patrol of lancers into a valley. We killed all but two, who we tortured to get information.'

He spoke proudly of their achievements, but for the first time I truly began to understand the brutality of the situation in Spain. While French atrocities might encourage support for the partisans, you could easily understand how partisan activities drove more savagery in the French. If your soldiers were being murdered by men, women and even children you would quickly view all civilians as the enemy. I thought back to that conversation on the boat on our way to Portugal and Wellington insisting that we had to behave better than the French to keep the populace on our side. Now the importance of this was clear. 'Do you know a partisan called Agustina de Aragon,' I asked suddenly, remembering that she had ridden off to fight amongst all this savagery.

'The Maid of Zaragoza? Of course I have heard of her, but I did not know she was a partisan. She is not amongst the partisans around here but there are many different bands. Perhaps she is fighting near Zaragoza.' He started to get up but then he paused and smiled as though he had just thought of something. 'Are you the Englishman that… knew her in Seville?' he asked grinning salaciously. There was no doubt what rumour he had just remembered.

'I did meet her there, yes.' I admitted stiffly, getting up and returning to my horse.

'If you are that Englishman then you are also the one that charged with General Cuesta, yes?' persisted the Spaniard.

'Yes I was,' I conceded, glad that something other than my carnal activities in Seville had been included in the gossip. 'I also fought at Alcantara when we stopped Victor coming over the bridge. In fact I am now a knight of Alcantara as a result.' If you have a title, I thought, you might as well use it. The guide seemed impressed. For the rest of that afternoon we rode together as he told me partisan stories and I told him a suitably edited version of my adventures in Alcantara. By early evening we were riding through a wood in the hills behind Fuentes de Onoro when Rodriguez brought us to a halt again. We were coming to the end of the wood and the guide said that we were close to the windmill.

'We must be quiet now,' the guide told us, 'while we check that the French have not found our men.' He asked me to tie up Boney to a nearby tree so that he did not bound out and give away our position. Then his comrade was sent around the edge of the forest to approach the windmill from a different direction. While he was working his way around, the guide and I made our way up to the edge of the trees where we got our first glimpse of the windmill on the hill opposite, a quarter of a mile away. The ladies had stayed with Boney to make sure he did not bark.

'My friend will approach the windmill from the far corner of the forest,' Rodriguez explained. 'If he pretends to find us by walking back to that corner it is a signal that there is an ambush and we must get away. We might gain a few extra minutes if the French search the wrong area when they realise we are not coming.'

'You have clearly done this before,' I said, while studying the windmill through my glass. I could see no sign of life at all.

'A partisan who is not cunning and careful is soon dead, señor.'

I passed the glass to the guide who studied the windmill and the surrounding area and gave a small grunt of satisfaction as we settled down to wait. A few minutes later his comrade appeared and slowly walked to the windmill. He stopped a few yards from it and seemed to be talking to someone and then he went inside.

'The man must search the building now to check that whoever is there is not being held at gunpoint,' Rodriguez said. 'If any of the French spies in your camp have told them that a British officer and a Spanish marquesa are riding this way, then you would be attractive prisoners so we must be very careful.'

'You be as careful as you want old sport,' I agreed, relieved that someone was being as careful of my precious skin as I was. We watched anxiously for nearly five minutes and then finally the other guide reappeared. After a moment's hesitation he started walking directly towards us, the signal that the rendezvous was safe. The ladies came up at our shout and Maria threw her arms around me and gave me a kiss on the cheek.

'Thank you, dear cousin,' she said, 'for your escort this far, but you had better get back. We have left Boney tied up in the trees. Make sure you write to tell me of your adventures and tell me how I can reach you.'

'Yes, of course, but I should see who is taking you on the next stage of the journey as well. Wellington was very clear that if you seemed to be in any danger I was to continue to escort you further, and the French are still just a few miles away you know...' I would have continued but Consuella now threw her arms around me, kissing me on the mouth, thus stopping any further words in a delightful way. Her embrace was a convincing argument that I should find fault with the new escort at all costs. 'I must speak to the escort commander,' I gasped when my lips were free.

As it turned out that was not difficult to arrange for he wanted to see me too. The partisan coming back from the windmill started to shout that the ladies should mount up and ride up the valley quickly as they wanted to be well away by dark. Then he turned to me and asked me to go quickly to windmill where the commander had messages that he wanted to pass on to the British. Well, that suited me, so I strode up the hill in the pleasant evening sunshine. I still had not seen any of this new escort so there could not be many of them. I would just tell this new commander that my orders were to continue to escort the marquesa until she was well away from French forces. I was rehearsing to myself what I would say as I walked through the little door of the mill. From the bright sunshine outside my eyes struggled to adjust to the gloom of the interior; not that they got the chance, for a moment after I stepped over the threshold the world went entirely black, as I was hit on the back of the head.

Chapter 21

I came to, not for the first time in my life, with aches in my shoulders and wrists which told me that my arms were tied behind my back. I also had a mysterious pain in my ribs, and I gently moved my legs to discover that they were tied at the ankles. When coming to in a potentially hostile situation it is always a good idea to keep your eyes shut and ears open before your captors realise you are conscious. I sensed there were several people around me, one quite close as I could hear him breathing.

'Kick him again,' called a voice, and a boot slammed into my ribs, which explained the earlier pain.

'All right,' I gasped now opening my eyes. 'I am awake.' My vision was a bit hazy after the blow but I could see that I was still inside the dark windmill. There were three strangers in the room, one with the sharp boots standing next to me, one seated on a tall chair nearby and another standing behind the seated figure. They all had big beards and travelling clothes and looked like partisans; but if they had ambushed me I wondered if they were working for the French. At least the French treated the British honourably and I was still in my uniform, so could not be accused of being a spy.

'Why have you tied me up? I am a British officer.'

'Oh, we know who you are,' said the seated man, and I saw teeth smiling at me through his shaggy beard. He spoke with menace and his voice sounded familiar, but I did not recognise the face at all.

'Then for God's sake let me go. If you work for the French, then take me to their commander. If you are partisans then you should know I am here on General Wellington's orders.'

'I do not care about your General Wellington,' said the seated man. 'He has, I suspect, had enough from me already. I know exactly who you are. You are the mongrel fornicator Thomas Flashman. Don't you recognise me?' The voice was familiar and for a second I was puzzled, and then everything fell into place. I should have probably guessed from word 'mongrel', as only one person had called me that in my life, but lying with my face on the floor I noticed something else. Looking across at the seated man I saw he had no feet, or at least, none that reached the floor.

'It's you!' I gasped, looking into the bearded face of the marquis. He had been clean shaven when I had last seen him.

'Yes.' White teeth shone through the beard as he gave me an unpleasant grin. 'I came to collect Maria to make sure that these partisans treated her well, but I had no wish to meet her Lord Wellington. So I arranged to meet her here.' The grin was slowly replaced by a look of sadness as he continued, 'I have missed her all the months she has been away. Someone like you will not understand this, but I am very fond of my wife. We parted arguing over you and that is not going to happen again.'

I felt a chill run down my spine; if he just wanted to warn me off there was no need to tie me up. 'Look, if you just cut me free, I will get on my way back to the British and you and your wife need never see me again.'

'I don't think so. Do you think I have forgotten how you insulted me in my own house, how you mocked me and laughed at me? I have burned to avenge myself on you. Then I heard you were with my wife again, like a festering sore between us. Well, I am going to cauterise that wound once and for all, so that you never bother us again.'

'You can't kill me for God's sake, I'm family damn it. Maria will never forgive you for this.' Then taking a deep breath I yelled, 'Maria, I am in the windmill, come quickly!'

'She is long gone down the valley,' the marquis laughed at the fear that must have started to show in my face. 'And you are right, I cannot kill you. When my wife does discover that you are dead, if she ever asks, I want to be able to look her honestly in the eye and say that I did not kill you.'

'Thank God,' I breathed.

'Oh, you misunderstand me,' chuckled the dwarf. 'You are going to die, just not by my hand.'

'What do you mean?'

'A few days ago some Polish lancers were ambushed near here and the men were all killed or tortured to death. Their commander has sworn vengeance and has been hanging Spaniards ever since. One of my men is taking a message to the commander to tell him that the attack was organised by a British officer, and if he stops hanging our people we will hand him over. Of course the commander will agree, whether he actually intends to stop the hanging or not, and then my man will tell him of this windmill.'

'You cannot do that,' I gasped.

'Of course I can. What is to stop me? You get the death you so richly deserve and I might even save some innocent Spaniards. Have you ever seen lancers fight, Flashman? Their points are razor sharp and they love nothing better than to stick them in a running man. If you are lucky they will run you through, but maybe they will untie your legs and chase you for sport.'

'Please, look, I know we got off on the wrong foot so to speak, but we are on the same side!' I was gabbling but I was desperate as I realised that this pint sized tyrant had carefully planned out my death. 'I am sorry,' I pleaded. 'I realise I was wrong to do the things I did, I apologise of course. I am truly sorry. If you let me go I will put in a good word of you to Wellington. Perhaps he can help you with the leadership of the Central Junta; he would be keen to help both you and Maria.'

As soon as I mentioned his wife's name I saw his face darken and I realised that this had been an error of judgement. 'Oh, I can imagine how keen your commander is on my wife.' The marquis sneered. 'I hear you have been acting the goat with her maidservant too. Well, I hope you enjoyed it because you might get a closer view of your manhood than you have ever had before, soon. When the partisans tortured the Poles, they cut off their pricks and stuffed them into their owners' mouths. That is how they were found the next day. Perhaps the Poles will do the same to you.' He grinned nastily before sliding off his chair and standing on the floor. 'Now it is time for me to get going. But in case my wife ever asks if we parted on good terms, let me wish you good luck for when the Poles arrive, probably around dawn tomorrow.'

'You bastard,' I shouted at him. 'You filthy, stinking, murderous, pint sized little bast…' a boot slammed into my head, roughly where I had been hit before, and the world exploded with a flashing light before returning to blackness.

It was night when I awoke. The door to the windmill was open and I could see stars in the night sky. For a moment I could not remember where I was or why. Then the memories came flooding back, followed swiftly by gut wrenching fear. I could not just lie there waiting to be tortured and mutilated by vengeful lancers. Even if I had to crawl or roll I would try to get into the forest and hide. A second later I discovered that in addition to tying my hands and feet tightly, the rope around my feet was secured to one of the beams in the windmill. I twisted trying to reach my sword to cut the rope but the scabbard was empty. Looking around I could see my sword embedded in the floor a few feet out of my reach. It was glinting in the starlight, a razor sharp blade that could be my salvation if only I could get to it. The gold hilt was valuable but the marquis evidently thought it was worth more to use it to taunt me in my final hours. I managed to sit up and reached around for anything sharp that could cut the ropes, but there was nothing. All I could find was the sharp edge to a wooden beam, so I sat there rubbing the rope around my hands against it. I did not think it would cut through the rope by morning but it gave me something to do and helped keep the panic at bay.

It was not the first night I had spent expecting imminent death, nor was it to be the last. Just a few years ago I had been destined for an explosive execution and I nearly went mad with fear that night. I knew I had to keep busy. I kept rubbing the rope against that beam until my arm muscles burned with the pain. It seemed to be futile I was making no progress at all. When I thought of my likely fate my legs instinctively clamped together and I felt physically sick. I would protest my innocence and try to explain, but would they listen? Surely they would not mutilate a British officer, I tried to reason, but then I remembered that this 'little war' – the guerrilla war – was completely different to the world of regiments and battle lines. There was unlimited savagery on both sides, no quarter asked or given, and if the Poles thought I had a part in it then they would give me what they thought I deserved.

Suddenly I heard a noise. A horse, it was definitely the snicker of a horse outside. Oh, Jesus, were the Poles here already? It was still dark but perhaps they thought it would be safer to travel at night. I strained my ears, I could hear hooves now but only one horse I thought, surely the Poles would come in strength.

'Señor, are you there?' It was the voice of the partisan guide, and relief flooded over me.

'Rodriguez, is that you?' I called, remembering his name. 'Please help me.'

'Come out so that I can see you.'

'I can't. I am tied up in here.' He did not reply but I heard him slowly approach. I thought he was looking carefully through the door before something crashed into the woodwork behind me.

'Jesus,' I jumped, my nerves were already on edge, 'What was that?' I asked, twisting around to see.

'A rock, I had to check you were alone and not being used as bait for a trap.' He was through the door now, a large knife glinting in his hand. He reached me in two strides and bent down to grasp my shoulder. His rough hands went down my arm until they found the rope, and then my hands were free and burning with renewed circulation.

'My feet as well,' I gasped.

'Who did this to you?' he demanded.

'That bloody dwarf,' I snarled.

'But he is your cousin's husband, I saw him greet her.'

'Yes, well, he is no damned friend of mine.' I picked up my sword and put it back in my scabbard. 'Now, let's get of here before those bloody lancers arrive.'

'What lancers? What is going on señor?' Of course then I had to explain what the marquis had organised, as we hurried into the trees. 'I need to get my men away,' Rodriguez said when he understood the situation. 'We were just coming back down the valley after escorting your cousin higher into the hills when I found your horse and dog still tied up in the trees. If the lancers are coming you should go back through the forest. There is more cover and it will take you back in the direction of the British.' He was interrupted by a welcoming bark from Boney, who recognised us approaching through the trees towards him.

'What will you do?' I asked. I had been hoping he would escort me back to the British lines.

'I must find my men. It was my people who attacked the lancers.' He was rushing now, anxious to get on his way. 'If they spread out to look for you we may be able to kill some more. Good luck, Captain, keep in the trees and keep heading west,' he said, pointing me in the right direction. With a shake of the hand he was gone. I was left standing in the forest with my hands and feet still tingling at the renewed blood flow, just a dog and a horse for company and a squadron of angry cavalry on the way. For a moment I had considered joining the partisan gang for safety in numbers. But then I would be drawn into their savage pitiless war; sooner or later they would get cornered and slaughtered. If I could just get away from those Poles who thought I was with the partisans, then even if I was captured by another French unit I would be treated honourably as a British prisoner of war.

I estimated that there was at least an hour or two of darkness, so grabbing the horse's bridle I walked on in the direction the Spaniard had pointed. Unless you want to lose an eye to a low hanging branch or worse, I knew better than to ride through an unfamiliar forest. The foliage was blocking out any light from the stars so that it was black as pitch. We made slow but steady progress. I heard a screech from the undergrowth as Boney tracked down his dinner, but I did not feel hungry, I just wanted to get myself as far away from that windmill as possible. As the grey light of dawn filtered through the leaves I could see more clearly and mounted up. Later, once the sun was well over the horizon, I thought we had covered several miles and at last allowed myself to rest. I breakfasted on wine from my canteen and the food in my saddle bags. We had found a little clearing in the forest and the horse was grazing on the sparse grass. I sat in the dappled sunlight and congratulated myself on my good fortune. I had escaped the Poles and with luck and two days careful riding I should be back amongst the British, where

I would write a very informative letter to my cousin. I tipped the last of the wine down my throat and then out of the corner of my eye I saw Boney stiffen. He had heard something and his head was turned to the west, the direction we were travelling. I strained my ears but at first I could hear nothing. Then faintly on the wind came the sound of voices.

You may have found this yourself, but to me languages seem to have a distinctive sound even if you cannot make out the words. Compared to English, French is a more nasal tongue, while Spanish has rounder tones. This language was neither, it was harsher, more guttural, the only thing similar I had heard was Russian a few years back, when I had been with Wilson. It must, of course, have been Polish, and in the second it had taken me to recognise the sound I had not been idle. Grabbing Boney's collar and the horse's bridle I was hustling my little menagerie into the thickest nearby undergrowth and scanning the clearing to check that there was no trace of my presence left on the ground. Of course such is my fortune that there in the middle of the clearing was a still steaming pile of horse dung that my mount had just left as it grazed. There was no choice but to dart back into the clearing, scrape up the filth with my hands and run back and throw it into the undergrowth. It took two trips and there was still a horsey smell over that particular spot, but as the lancers were sitting on horses themselves I did not think they would notice.

By the time I had buried myself back in the thick foliage with the animals, the voices could be heard quite clearly. From the sound of them, the Poles were relaxed, laughing and joking with each other like soldiers the world over. The voices were getting louder though, and I realised that they would pass close by. I crawled forward on my belly

222

to get a glimpse of them from between the leaves. There were around twenty in the group. They all wore blue tunics similar to those of the French with white cross belts and looked like other French cavalry apart from the tall lances with points that glistened in the sun and their helmets. Instead of the normal round tops, their shakoes finished in a square shape with points fore, aft and to the sides. They looked damned comfortable on their horses too which were all good quality, fast mounts. Slowly I shrank back into the foliage. I stayed still for a good five minutes to give them time to get away. When all was quiet again I emerged from the undergrowth keen to put some distance between me and those lances. I had put one foot up into the stirrup and was just bouncing to swing up when across the top of the saddle I saw two more lancers enter the clearing.

Quite why they were so far behind the others I never found out, nor at that moment did I particularly care, for their intentions were all too clear. With a shout of triumph they both spurred their horses forward with lances lowered to the horizontal. I realised instantly that I did not have time to mount and get away, by the time I could get settled in the saddle their lance points would be in me. I still had my hand on the reins and I pulled my horse to obstruct the path of the lancer to my left and ducked my head under the height of the saddle. The lancer to my right gave another shout, this time of delight as he saw his fellow blocked and me exposed to his approach. I reached down to grab my sword, but the lance tip was just a yard or two away with the Pole's face grinning in triumph as he judged which part of me to impale on his point. I realised that I would not have time to draw my weapon before I was skewered. In desperation I raised my hands to try and deflect the lance, with little hope of doing so given its horse driven momentum. But then just as I thought I was about to die, something grey flashed across my field of vision. Boney jumped and hit the lancer in the chest. The man raised his arms to fend off the snarling teeth from his throat. The lance point rose, its shaft hit me a glancing blow to the head, but then the lancer was alongside, with Boney still half in his lap, the dog's jaws snapping and growling. The lancer was reaching down trying to draw his sword but I grabbed hold of his right boot and hauled it up, tipping both man and dog into the dirt on the far side of the horse. That, I thought, would give Boney better odds and hopefully take one man out of the fight, but the second lancer was already wheeling around.

If Boney expected me to intervene further in his fight he was destined to be disappointed. I was grateful to him for saving my life but now it was every man and animal for himself. Staying in the clearing would be fatal and I darted into the nearest, thickest undergrowth making it harder for the horseman to follow. But from his higher vantage point the lancer could see my path, and he spurred his horse down a deer run in the forest. As I stumbled blindly through the bushes in panic, with twigs whipping my face, I could hear the thunder of hooves to my right. Then a lance point jabbed at me through the leaves. I twisted and turned to try and shake him off. I could hear more shouts from behind now as his comrades charged back to join the fray. By now I had lost all sense of direction and just stumbled from one clump of undergrowth to another, but whatever I tried my pursuer always seemed just a few steps behind. I was panting with panic and exertion and knew this could not last. The undergrowth was too thick to draw a sword, but I had the presence of mind to put a hand in my pocket and draw out one of my pistols. It was in the nick of time too, as when I flung myself around the next tree trunk the lancer was already there just a yard or two away, raising his lance to stab down at me over his horse's neck. Instinctively I rushed towards him so that I was too close for him to use the weapon, raised my hand and discharged the pistol into his chest.

We stared at each other. I was still panting but it seemed a moment of calm after frantic activity. Time almost seemed suspended as the smoke drifted slightly from my pistol muzzle and his horse moved several steps to the side. I remember he stared down at me with an expression of surprise. He was only young, just out of his teens I guessed, and he did not seem wounded at all. For a heart sickening moment I thought the pistol had misfired. Surely even I could not have missed at that range? Then slowly a small red dot appeared in the middle of his shirt. He looked down and we both watched it grow, it was quickly the size of the top of a cup. He looked up at me again then, his clear blue eyes locking onto mine, and then with infinite slowness he toppled from the saddle to land at my feet. I stood frozen for a few seconds more and then the sound of another pistol shot broke the spell. This one came from some distance back and was followed by the yelp of a dog.

I would like to say that I spared a thought for poor Boney, but I didn't, for now there seemed to be the sound of lancers crashing around the forest in all directions. I could hear several heading towards me so I turned and ran. I found myself in another deer run through the trees and hurtled down it as though the hounds from hell were on my tail, which they pretty much were. In hindsight, I think using the path must have saved me, for that way I was not moving foliage which would have given away my position. Gradually the shouting and crashing fell behind, but I did not stop. I must have run as fast as I could for nearly half a mile before I fetched up by a tree trunk, gasping for breath and retching from the exertion. I opened my mouth to breathe quietly, taking in big gulps of air as I strained my ears for the sound of further pursuit. There was still some shouting, but now it was distant and as I listened it did not seem to be coming closer, if anything it was moving away. I sat with my back against the tree and listened as the voices receded behind me. I waited for silence to settle again over the forest, but when the voices behind me had stopped I noticed a new noise, a very faint murmuring sound, this time from the opposite direction. I got up and walked forward towards the noise. I soon saw that I was approaching the edge of the forest and what I saw there took my newly recovered breath clean away again.

As I crept to the edge of the trees I had heard more distant voices ahead and I dropped to the ground and crawled the last few yards. I emerged from the middle of a bush and stared at the sight in the valley below. There, along a road at the bottom of the slope as far as the eye could see in both directions, were men. Thousands and thousands of them; the French army was on the move. They were heading west, towards the retreating British. Cavalry rode as pickets on either side of the army column. Just the men I could see matched the size of the British army but neither end of the army was in sight. I watched in wonder for a while and then it dawned on me that this lot were now between me and safety. Murderous Polish lancers to the rear and just about every French soldier in Spain to the front. There were trains of artillery, supply wagons, regiment after regiment of infantry, dragoons, hussars, even other lancers, but I could not see any Poles. It was an amazing sight and I must have been watching transfixed for around five minutes when I heard a twig snap behind me. I froze.

While I had been watching the French, had the Poles tracked me down? A bush rustled behind me; it was not the wind, someone else was there. With immense care I eased myself silently back into the foliage of the bush. I had not reloaded the pistol I had fired earlier but I still had a second gun in my other coat pocket. I eased the loaded pistol out and tensed as another twig snapped on the far side of the bush. I thought there was only one person, and as they had not yet found me I might still have the advantage of surprise. I stepped out of the bush, making as little noise as possible, and moved quietly around it to where I thought the intruder stood. With a leap I sprang forward, cocking and raising the pistol. There was no one there, and I had given away my position. I spun round in case someone was stalking me, only to find a pair of brown eyes looking at me with a quizzical look. Boney sat on the ground with his head cocked to one side.

'Hello, boy,' I called, reaching out to stroke him, but he turned his back on me and went to sit further away. He clearly had not forgiven me for running out on him after he had saved my life. 'Look, I had to run, the other lancers were coming back through the trees. We would both have been killed if I had stayed.' I know it made no sense talking to a dog, but let's face it, we have all done it when we think we are alone. I looked over the hound. There were some blood smears on his chest but no apparent wound, although he had a scorch mark on one flank with burnt hair, presumably from a pistol muzzle flash. We had both been fortunate, but unless we could out of here, our luck would soon run out. What I needed was a horse. Boney had done well to track me down and that gave me an idea.

'Come on, Boney, let's see if you can track down my horse.' The animal had run off when the lancers attacked, with luck it could still be roaming around the forest. I started to walk back down the deer run I had travelled down before, but instead of leading the way, Boney walked reluctantly behind. We had walked a fair way into the forest, and Boney was ignoring all my encouragement to find transport, when I heard a horse whinny. I froze. You get to recognise animal noises and it did not sound like my horse. Could the lancers still be patrolling the trees looking for me? On the other hand I needed a horse, so again I drew my loaded pistol. Moving stealthily through the trees I approached the source of the sound. It took several minutes to approach the animal without making a noise, but then suddenly I recognised a tree and realised that we were safe. I was in the little grove where I had shot the young lancer. He had fallen with his hand twisted in the reins. The horse had dragged the body a few yards to graze but the corpse acted like an anchor to stop it going too far.

I was surprised that his comrades had not found the body, but the woods were particularly thick here which was why I had run into them in the first place. Well, at least I had a horse, and that gave me a start. I could work my way back along the hills and hope not to run in to any patrols that the French were bound to send out to stop partisans attacking the outskirts of their army. The horse was nervous with a stranger and I was disentangling the reins from the dead soldier's hand when another thought occurred. An old drover had once told me that the best place to hide rustled sheep was in another man's flock. I needed to get past an entire French army and lying at my feet was a uniform of one of their allies.

The horse had pulled the corpse over onto its front. I could see that there was no exit wound in the back or blood on the blue cloth of the jacket. The more I thought of it, the better this idea seemed. I spoke reasonable French, but not as a native. I had been to Russia a few years before and heard enough Russians mangling French, the language of diplomacy, to approximate what people would assume was a Polish accent. I reached down to pull the jacket off the body; it was even roughly my size. Searching the pockets I found a stub of a pencil, a locket with some hair in it and some letters addressed to a Jan Zeminski from someone called Magda. I put them back in the pockets, they would add some authenticity if I was challenged. Transferring the pistols from my old coat I then stuffed that in the saddle bag of the horse. I found the lancer's helmet a few yards from the body. I had not seen my own hat since the windmill and this one seemed tall and ungainly. But it was certainly distinctive. I swept some dead leaves over the body of Zeminski to cover him up if anyone came looking for him, then picking up the lance I mounted up. Feeling faintly ridiculous I spurred the horse back down the deer run to the edge of the forest with Boney following on behind.

Reaching the edge of the forest, the scene was much as it had been before. Thousands of French marching west. I took a moment to gather the courage to carry out my plan. The thought of being among so many, disguised as a friend, was only slightly less intimidating than the risk of being found by them as an enemy. My biggest worry was running into more Polish lancers, as then my disguise would soon fall apart. I scanned the troops but could see no sign of their strange helmets among the cavalry screen, hopefully they were still searching for me over the hills. I took a deep breath and spurred my horse down the sunny slope into the valley. The main cavalry screen of hundreds of different horsemen was lower down the valley, some two hundred yards on either side of the main force. It made sense to ride alone if I could to reduce the risk of discovery, so I only rode part way down the valley. Then, with Boney loping alongside, I turned to ride parallel with the other horsemen.

For the first few hours it was ridiculously easy, I was half way between the woods on my left and the main cavalry screen on my right. With my distinctive Polish helmet and the tall lance resting in a cup on my right stirrup it was obvious which unit I belonged to and people let me be. The lance had a little red and white guidon flag at the point which would have made other Polish lancers stand out in the screen, but despite scanning regularly in all directions none were to be seen. All that morning I rode with the French army and spoke to no one apart from Boney. When I was not challenged I gradually increased my speed to start travelling slowly to the front of the giant column. For my plan to work I had to overtake it and get out in front to find the British. Some units stopped for a rest and for food at noon, but I pressed on. A cursory inspection of the saddle bags revealed trooper Zeminski had been expecting to find repast elsewhere as there was nothing to eat all. At least his canteen was half full of watered wine as the heat was making me drip with sweat.

'Hey, Polack!' I had been day dreaming of what I would write to Maria about her husband when the voice cut into my thoughts. For a second the word did not register and then I realised that the voice must be talking to me. I looked up and saw that a green coated dragoon had ridden part way up the hill towards me.

'Polack, come here,' the man shouted. He was middle aged with a big drooping moustache and sergeant's stripes on his arm. Zeminski's coat had no marks of rank, he was just a trooper, so I turned my horse towards him.

'Yes, sergeant officer,' I called back to him in halting French with what I hoped sounded like a strong Polish accent. He shook his head in resignation at my apparent misunderstanding of how to address a French sergeant.

'You are riding too close to the woods,' he shouted at me, clearly hoping that volume would add clarity to his words. 'Some of the partisans have rifles; they can shoot you dead from there. You understand rifles?' He mimed somebody shooting a gun and pointed to the trees. My look of shock as I realised that all this time I could have been killed by the partisans was all too genuine and he laughed at my evident understanding. 'And take off that shako, it is too hot for that,' he gestured to his own brass helmet that hung from a strap on his saddle. 'Our officer won't complain. Where is your unit?'

I had been prepared for this question. 'I am reinforcement sergeant officer.' The dragoon had started to ride slowly back to the column now and I brought my horse up to ride alongside.

'New in Spain are you? Well make sure you do not get your damn fool head shot off before you meet up with your regiment.'

'Yes sergeant officer,' I replied.

'It is sergeant, just sergeant. So what do you think of Spain, like Poland is it?'

I looked around, we were riding through a pleasant green valley with olive groves, abandoned farms and trees high up on the hill. 'Not like Poland but very nice,' I ventured.

The sergeant gave a snort of disgust. 'It is a stinking shit hole, you understand that? No probably not. It is a bad country, you understand?'

I gave a nod of comprehension.

'You cannot trust any of them, men, women and children. They all want you dead and will stick a knife in you or poison you any chance they get. Don't turn your back on them, lad. Even the whores would stab you with a blade as you stab them with your cock. Got a woman have you?'

'Magda in Poland.'

'Best place for her lad, don't bring her here. They kill French civilians as well as soldiers, they would treat Poles the same. Now come on down and ride with the rest of the cavalry.'

I followed him down the hill, but then he moved off to check on some other troopers so I continued to move along the line. I nodded in greeting to other horsemen I met but avoided conversation. Now I could see clearly the regimental numbers of infantry units, the size of guns and other elements of the army. I realised that if I did make it back to the British lines it would be helpful to have some idea of the force that was approaching. Reaching into my pocket I found one of Magda's letters and the pencil stub and I started to estimate the guns, regiments and equipment I had already seen. As I rode on I memorised regimental numbers and the calibre of cannon and then when few horsemen were about to see what I was doing I would scribble them on my list too.

I had a long stream of numbers on that letter by the late afternoon when I finally came up on the head of the army. There was more cavalry at the vanguard, including lancers, but none with the distinctive red guidon flag of the Poles. I slowed down as I would need darkness to slip through the lines. To rest the horse I dismounted and walked alongside an infantry regiment. They seemed confident and relaxed but I kept just far enough away to discourage conversation. I had been walking with them for nearly an hour when I was passed by mounted infantry officers shouting at their men to smarten themselves up. The men straightened their lines, did up buttons and put back on their shakoes. Clearly somebody important was coming. I moved closer to the marching men to get out of the way. As a humble trooper I thought it wise to put my helmet back on and mount up. A few moments later a curly haired general rode past with a gaggle of gaudily dressed staff officers. None of them paid any attention to the dusty men marching along the road. The group rode to the front of the column and disappeared amongst the mounted troops that spearheaded the advance.

'Do you know who that is?' asked a nearby soldier who had seen me watching the general.

'No,' I said dismounting again. 'I have just joined the army from Poland.'

'That's Ney. He will give the British some pepper.'

'Is Massena up there too?'

'Christ you are new here aren't you? 'Ere lads, this Polack was just asking if Massena was at the front of the army!' Several of them chuckled and shook their heads at my ignorance. 'No lad, Massena is not here. Neither would you be if you were over fifty and had the eighteen year old wife of one of your officers to warm your bed.' There were more ribald shouts at this and cries of 'lucky bastard.'

'You be careful,' warned one of his mates. 'When the girl tires of riding the marshal she dresses as a hussar and joins his staff. Don't you go making eyes at her or you will be sent off like her inconvenient husband.' There are few things soldiers like talking about more than the incompetence of their generals and women. With Massena they could combine both topics. He seemed quite a ladies' man with a string of mistresses and a penchant for issuing commands from his bedroom window. According to the soldiers' gossip he spent so much time locked away with his mistress, known as Madame X to avoid embarrassing her husband, that he was rarely seen at all. His men apparently had doubts that he had the energy to survive the campaign.

As we marched and talked I relaxed a little. It was good to enjoy the camaraderie of soldiers even if it was not the familiar redcoats. I was used to being disguised in armies; I had done it with three different forces in India. I knew enough to think before I opened my mouth and tried to keep the conversation on safe topics. A few times I pretended that I did not understand the French. When the conversation turned to women I described in my Polish accented French the attributes of the mythical Magda. I showed them the locket and then listened to their ribald suggestions as to whose bed she would be warming that night. For all I knew the real Magda could have been Jan Zeminski's aged aunt, but that afternoon her exploits as a lover became legendary amongst the half company I was walking with.

But as the army finally came to a halt late that afternoon it was clear that my welcome was over. Rations were limited and in a firm but friendly way they made it clear that they did not have enough to feed 'strays'. As a trooper I was expected to look after my own horse, so I watered him at a nearby stream, unsaddled him and left him hobbled to graze on the hillside. I had seen several large groups of men go up to the woods for firewood; those with axes taking plenty of armed guards to protect them from partisan ambush. We did not need the fires for warmth, but for light during the night. Boney also disappeared into the woods and came back a short while later with more bloodstains around his mouth, clearly having found some supper. I looked destined to go hungry. Another thorough search of the saddle bags, while keeping my red coat hidden, revealed only a small strip of food. Even now I am not sure if it was dried meat or old leather but it was all I had, so I spent the evening chewing and trying to swallow it.

As night fell the fires were lit all around the perimeter of the French camp and sentries were placed to shoot any intruders illuminated by the flames. There was the occasional shot and once the crackle of several shots, but these soon died out. They seemed to be due to nervous sentries. Those jumpy trigger fingers did not help my nerves as I judged it was dark enough to make my move. I had been sitting amongst two score of horses that were grazing on the hillside and quietly I now stood and returned the saddle to my mount's back. He stood patiently while I unhobbled him, and then taking his reins I walked him through the herd, making soothing noises at any of the other horses that seemed disturbed by our presence. I had been feeling pretty pleased with myself during the afternoon as I walked along chatting to the other soldiers. It had seemed a lot safer than trying to avoid the huge French army or risk encountering murderous bandits, suspicious partisans or vengeful Polish lancers. But now my plan was not looking so clever. I had to get past jumpy sentries and then disappear into the darkness where partisans would be looking for any stray French troops.

I had wrapped a blanket around my shoulders and across my chest to hide my white shirt front, and kept my helmet hanging from the saddle to reduce my profile. For the same reason I held the lance horizontally. I was fortunate that the night was once again as dark as the inside of a tar bucket. The moon was obscured by some patchy cloud, which was also blocking out much of the starlight. The only illumination came from the perimeter fires. I saw that they did not form a continuous line around a single camp for the whole army. Instead there were various circles of light around bivouacs for regiments and battalions. Reaching the end of our perimeter, I could see that there were two more circles of light ahead of me to the west. I was leading my horse through the last of the other hobbled mounts and straining my eyes into the darkness for the French sentries when I almost stepped on them.

'Look out!' called a voice from virtually under my feet, and three figures started to rise from the ground in front of me. That was all I saw before the blinding flash of a musket shot virtually in my face destroyed my night vision, while the ball only narrowly missed destroying my head.

'Don't shoot,' I yelled as I threw myself to the floor. I think I might have shouted it in English to start with but then remembered, 'Ne tirez pas,' and shouted that as well. A man fell on top of me and groped for my face and throat, but I managed to push him off and roll away shouting, 'I am Polish lancer, I am on your side,' again in my accented French.

'Are there any more of them?' called a voice.

'No just this one,' said another.

Feeling disorientated – I still could not see – my eyes were watering from the flash which still seemed reflected in my eyes. I reached up to feel my face to check it was not burnt.

'He is a Pole,' called the first voice. 'It is one of our army saddles and I can feel his helmet hanging from it.'

'Well, what the hell are you doing sneaking around at night then?' asked the second voice, giving me a sharp kick in the ribs to make his point.

I blinked and could just make out a slightly darker silhouette standing over me. 'I have a message for Marshal Ney,' I gasped, using an excuse I had thought of earlier. I reached in my pocket and pulled out the letter from Magda, and held it up as proof. It was far too dark to read but you could just make out the white square in the gloom.

'Well, you nearly got your damn fool head shot off. Don't you know better than to sneak around in the dark like a damned partisan?'

'I am Pole, new in Spain,' I replied, strengthening the accent so that I could pretend not to understand any awkward questions.

'What is it, corporal?' called a new voice from the main body of the army.

'Just some stupid Polack messenger that got himself lost, sir,' called back the man standing over me as he reached down to pull me to my feet. 'Ney is in one of those camps over there,' he said, gesturing to the rings of fire ahead. 'If you want to survive the night I suggest you go mounted with your uniform showing, and call out to the camp well before you get within musket range.'

Only now could I start to make out the features of the sentries in the darkness. They were three tough looking men; the one who had fired was busy reloading his musket. 'I am sorry,' I apologised haltingly, 'I did not see you.'

'That was the point,' snarled the second man. 'The bloody partisans like to sneak down and cut throats and steal horses. This way we can use the horses as cover to stop the bastards.' He pushed my helmet into my chest before adding, 'Now put that on and get out of here. We need to move because any partisan knows where we are now.'

I put on the helmet and then picked up my blanket from where it had fallen. 'Thank you,' I muttered, and if I sounded shaken then I damn well was. The shock of such an unexpected meeting had sent my heart rate soaring, but now I was starting to calm and my night vision was starting to come back. I climbed up in the saddle and was about to leave when I felt a hand grab my knee.

'You might be wanting this too,' said the second man sarcastically while handing me the polished black shaft of ash wood and shaking his head in dismay that a lancer could forget his lance.

I trotted forward a few paces as the corporal bawled at other nearby sentries that a single horseman was coming through. When I looked back over my shoulder at my former reception committee, they had already disappeared into the blackness. I sighed with relief. That, I naively thought, was the hardest bit over. Of course I had no intention of going anywhere near the rings of light ahead. I steered my horse slightly to the left to climb the slope. I would pass halfway between the woods to my left and the circles to my right and with luck nobody would know I was there.

Chapter 22

It was only when I was well out onto the hillside that I remembered about Boney, and then I was bloody furious. That damned dog must have smelt the French sentries and gave me no warning. Instead of helping out he had just slunk away. I was not even sure if he was still with me. I whispered his name out into the darkness. A few seconds later a familiar shadow flitted alongside.

'You bastard,' I hissed at him. 'I could have been bloody killed. Just because I ran out on you does not mean you can do the same.' The brown eyes glinted up at me. 'Do that again and you can bloody well fend for yourself,' I snarled angrily, but the hound just placidly strolled on alongside my horse. As my anger receded a new sensation took its place: unease. I was right at the forefront of the enemy lines. But it was not just one enemy, in my current uniform I also had the partisans to worry about. While the hillside seemed calm and peaceful in front of me, the hair on the back of my neck had risen, like some kind of primordial warning of trouble ahead.

I was not the only once sensing it, the horse's ears where twitching and now Boney was sniffing the air ahead. The perimeter of the forward French camp was some two hundred yards to my right while the woods were a similar distance to my left. I realised that if there was someone in the woods then I would be silhouetted perfectly in the flames of the guard fires. I kept the lance lowered to the horizontal to make less of a profile. Dark clouds covered much of the sky but there were a few dim stars showing and I did not want the guidon flag to be seen flickering in front of them.

My senses strained for any sign of people ahead. A forest is never silent. There were creaks of trees and the odd bark of a deer or call from an owl. Nothing certain to cause alarm, but somehow I knew I was being watched. There were the occasional shouts and calls from the French to my right too, but I could not see anything beyond the guard fires. The blazes at the perimeter of the French camp sent the faintest glimmer of flickering light this far out, but it was enough.

We were at the narrowest point between the French and the woods when it happened. Man, horse and dog saw and reacted at the same time. Amongst the faint flickering shadows ahead, one shadow moved without flickering. A black shaped seemed to rise from the ground some yards off to my right, then two more to my left. In response the man muttered, 'Oh Christ,' the dog growled and the horse reared and whinnied in panic. The horse was not alone in that emotion, but as I struggled to stay in the saddle, events moved on. There was a shouted challenge from my right as French sentries heard the horse, and more worrying were the thud of boots behind as I heard more people running down the hill towards me. By the time the horse's front hooves were back on the ground the shadows were moving towards me. Whatever happened, I was not going to be captured in French uniform by the partisans.

I stabbed my spurs back and urged the horse forward. Boney started barking and snarling as one of the shadows moved in front of him, and then the attacker to my right died from the slight movement of my wrist. It was an instinctive move on my part, I just moved the lance out to cover the man and the momentum of the horse and the man's running simply impaled him on the point. As I had held the weapon low I doubt the attacker even saw the razor sharp steep tip until it plunged into his chest. The shaft leapt in my hand as the man twisted to the ground. He barely made a sound, just a faint grunt and then a gurgling noise in his throat. Had I been trained to use the weapon I would have held on to the lance and wrenched it free as I rode past, but I let it go as I had far more to worry about.

Two shots now cracked out from the French on my right, to be followed instantly by several shots from the trees to my left. I realised I was stuck right in the middle of a partisan attack.

'Run you damned horse,' I urged, as I sensed the partisans trying to close round what they thought was an isolated enemy soldier. Fear seemed to attack the very marrow of my bones as I sat low in the saddle, almost paralysed with terror. Finally the mount began to pick up some speed as the black night seemed to explode with danger all around me. There was little I could make sense of in the flickering muzzle flashes, shouts and other sounds all around me, but all seemed exaggerated by the darkness and my vivid imagination into awful horror.

A crackle of more musket fire erupted from the French and I heard the balls buzz about me… just before I heard the whine of more balls from the partisans returning fire. There was a jolt to my head, but I seemed unwounded as the horse galloped on with me crouching over its mane. I had to get out of this trap. The French were likely to shoot me as a spy if I fell into their hands; while what the partisans would do to someone they thought was a Polish lancer did not bear thinking about. Then just when I thought things could not get any worse, they did. A crack opened in the clouds, illuminating the hillside with a sliver of moonlight. It was not a bright moon, but it was enough to show the shapes moving on the hillside. My only advantage before had been the cover of darkness, but now I was exposed to all.

There was not enough light to see colours, but what there was showed clearly a mounted man wearing a lancer's distinctive helmet, uniform coat and white shirt and britches in the middle of an attack by partisans who were dressed all in black. The French sentries had been warned by the previous camp that a rider was coming over. Perhaps they thought I had gone to investigate a noise and found more than I bargained for. In any event they set up a cry for me to turn right and ride towards them. Now the French camp was coming alive, more men were being called to arms and a volley crashed out from their ranks. I could see an artillery crew, only half dressed, frantically manhandling their piece to cover the attack and loading with canister. The artillery sergeant was shouting at me to get out of their line of fire; well, I was doing my best there.

Looking around to my left there must have been fifty partisans streaming down the hill, but now that they were revealed by the moonlight, I saw that they were hesitating. Their surprise raid had been ruined, firstly by me blundering into them, and then by the moonlight. Most of them were now falling behind but I saw one in front point a musket at me. Boney saw the movement too and sprang forward snarling loudly. The partisan faltered a moment too long, deciding between shooting man or dog, and then the muzzle flashed as he fired, missing us both.

Another volley crashed out from the French and then the crack of the cannon with canister. This time I did not hear the flight of balls. They were firing at the men behind me. Between the shooting I heard a forlorn cry in French of, 'Ride to your right, are you blind?' and then the sound of a bugle calling cavalry to stand to. The last thing I wanted was to be 'rescued' by the French, so I urged my horse on again and started to disappear into the gloom of the night. I took a last glance over my shoulder and could just make out several companies of French infantry advancing in line up the hillside to drive the partisans off.

I heard no more bugle calls and guessed the commander was not willing to risk a troop of cavalry riding about in the dark amongst partisans to save one lunatic messenger.

I rode at a full gallop at least a couple of miles down that valley before I allowed the horse to ease up, and by then it was blowing hard. Boney was still bounding alongside, panting but looking quite comfortable. He was the only one who was. My hands were still shaking slightly as I shrugged off the blue coat. The first thing I wanted to do when we stopped was to replace my French uniform with the familiar red coat of the British. I yanked the scarlet cloth from the saddle bag and pulled it over my sweat dampened shirt. Instantly I felt slightly safer. Now at least a partisan might ask questions before he tried to kill me. If necessary I could refer them to Rodriguez up the valley. I was sure he would vouch for me, if he still lived. I was going to throw the incriminating blue coat away, but it had been useful and I was not out of danger yet. It was possible that there were other French scouting parties that could cut me off, so having swapped the contents of the pockets, I stuffed it back in the saddle bag. I urged the horse on at the walk and then realised that I was still wearing the Polish lancer helmet. Reaching up, I took it from my head and then froze in shock. The top half of the helmet had been smashed in two by a musket ball that must have passed within inches of my skull. After offering up a silent prayer of thanks I hung the hat from a strap on my saddle.

As the grey light of dawn stretched across the sky I came across an abandoned village. I decided to rest for a while. Surveying back the way I had come with my glass there were no signs of pursuit and the surrounding hills looked quiet too. I was cold, tired and above all hungry, as I had not eaten anything apart from a strip of leather for over a day. While Boney disappeared to hunt I searched the houses and gardens for anything to eat. Everything of use to the enemy had been taken or destroyed. Fruit bushes had been chopped down and burned, and vegetables had been dug up so that now all was rotten or dried up. All I could find were a few tiny carrots that were so small they had been overlooked. I munched them greedily but they just served to remind me how hungry I was. Boney reappeared with a dead rabbit clutched in his jaws and I knew I had to have it.

'Come here, boy,' I called in a friendly tone, and held out my hand to him. He looked at me suspiciously but came a few steps closer. 'That's the way, good dog, come to your master, yes a couple more steps. Come and smell what I have in my hand…that's it,' I sprang forward and got a good grip on the rabbit before the surprised hound could react. There was a brief tug of war before I emerged triumphant with most of the prize. The head was still in Boney's jaws and the dog crunched down on it while giving me what seemed a look of hurt disappointment.

I can happily do the dirty on men like Hobhouse and Phillips, but I have to confess that I did feel a twinge of guilt at that look of betrayed trust. Not enough to give the rabbit back, of course, I was too hungry for that. I set to with my knife to skin and gut it before tearing down some of a cottage roof and thatch to make a fire to cook it. Boney watched me for a while and then disappeared. He returned a short while later with another rabbit, but this time he stayed a good distance away and watched me warily as he ate it. My breakfast was soon roasting over a fire. As I watched it cook I reflected that while I had threatened to abandon Boney the previous night, in reality I was more dependent on him than the other way round.

I have eaten in some fine houses in several countries, but there have been few meals that I have relished more than that half dog-chewed rabbit. I savoured every morsel apart from a particularly chewed bit around the neck. That I saved, and when I had finished I walked over to where Boney lay, and I tossed it towards him as a peace offering. Having given it a cautious sniff, he munched it down. He might be a 'dumb creature', but I had realised that he was useful to have around. You never knew when you might need another rabbit.

Chapter 23

I sat back against the wall of a cottage and must have dozed off, as I had not had much sleep for two nights. I awoke with a start to find Boney pawing my shoulder and the sun high in the sky. My first fear was that the French had caught up with me, but a quick scramble to the window showed that the valley was still empty. However when I reached for my glass I could just make out horsemen at its far end. It was then that I smelt burning, just faintly, but when I looked around to the west there was a column of smoke rising into the air. I remembered Rodriguez's warning about how to measure the progress of the French and wondered if they had somehow outflanked me. Within five minutes I was mounted and heading up through the trees. I thought about changing back into the French uniform as a precaution, but that was too dangerous with the risk of partisans about. We trotted on through the trees and then down a valley which seemed familiar. Finally at a crossroads, I realised where I was. I had passed this way before. We were close to Celorico where the British army had spent the winter, and judging from the direction of the smoke, it was Celorico that was burning.

Cautiously, I rode up the final hill before the town, using a copse of trees as cover so that I would not be seen. I almost sagged in relief when I saw what was happening on the other side of it. Celorico was burning, but it was men in red coats that were putting it to the torch. The irony was not lost on me that just a week before I had run out on this army thinking it was probably doomed. Now, thanks to a poisonous dwarf, vengeful lancers and cut throat partisans, I was back. I had slid out because I doubted that the British could beat the huge French army coming towards it. Having ridden with that army, I was more convinced than ever that the French would be victorious if met on level terms. Every French soldier I had met had been a veteran of earlier battles, and they had the skill and confidence of troops that knew what they were about. Now I would either have to put my trust in Wellington's mysterious plan or find another means to slip away back to Lisbon and a ship.

Most of the town seemed to be burning by the time Boney and I reached the outskirts. I saw a knot of officers trotting their horses around the far side of the town and rode to join them. My eyes were stinging with the smoke by the time I reached them and I was surprised to hear a familiar voice.

'Ah, Flashman, good day to you. Did you deliver your cousin safely to the bodyguard her husband sent for her?' Wellington did not seem the slightest bit surprised to see me appear through the smoke, and continued to stare about him to check that all buildings were now ablaze.

'Better than that, sir, I delivered her to her husband.' I thought better of adding that he was a malignant little runt, as Wellington was a snob when it came to titles. Most of his staff were of the nobility and half of them were his distant relations. My watering eyes stared at the man with his familiar plain blue coat. He seemed his usual brusque self, showing no concern for the massive army approaching his own. 'What are you doing here, sir?'

'I would have thought that was obvious. We are burning the town so that it will be of no use to the enemy. I have ordered all towns and villages here cleared of food. Did you come through any on your way back?'

'Yes, there is a village a few miles down the valley. I know that it does not have a shred of food in it as I was starving when I reached it.' The officers with Wellington snickered in amusement at the thought of a British gentleman scavenging for food. Most of them had their own country estates and had never been hungry in their lives. 'I managed to trap some rabbits and roasted them for breakfast,' I explained airily to quieten them.

Wellington, who hunted regularly with his pack of hounds, gave Boney a shrewd glance, but before he could say anything a tall staff officer I had not seen before sneered, 'Poaching is not exactly an honourable skill.'

'It is better than starving, Grant,' said Wellington sharply. 'Now, Flashman, we hear some of the French army is coming down the valley behind you. Did you see any of it? Is it their main force?'

'I have seen it and it is their main force.' Then, knowing that it would put the staff officers firmly in their place, I reached into my pocket and pulled out Magda's letter. 'I have made a note of most of the numbers of the infantry regiments and listed cavalry and artillery units that I saw, on the margins of this letter.'

Wellington was not an easy man to impress, but he looked genuinely stunned at the quality of my information. 'Good grief, you have done an excellent job Flashman. I had heard Marshal Junot was with Massena, but some of these regiments are in Ney's command. Is he with the main force?'

241

'Yes, he was commanding the advance guard. Massena is apparently occupied with a new mistress.'

'You cannot possibly know all of this,' exploded the tall officer called Grant. 'It is just gossip you have heard from the partisans. There is no way that you can make out regimental numbers on eagles and shakoes with a glass from the surrounding hills.'

'Grant,' replied Wellington irritably. 'Captain Flashman is very experienced in getting information for me on my enemies…'

'No, Captain Grant is quite right,' I interrupted, for now I saw an opportunity to enhance my reputation further. Having risked life and limb to get this information I might as well earn credit for it. 'You cannot read regimental numbers from the hillsides.' I reached into my saddlebag and pulled out the blue uniform coat before continuing. 'Which is why I acquired this and have spent the last two days riding with the French. I was able to see their regimental numbers because I was talking to the men wearing them.' Looking pointedly at Grant I added, 'I know Ney commands the advance guard because I saluted him as he rode past me.'

'Well done Flash,' said one of the other staff officers, and there were other cries of congratulation from the staff while Grant continued to look pompously stuffed.

'I admit I did not look through Massena's bedroom keyhole, so what he is doing with his mistress is gossip, but from the French army, not the partisans.'

'From what we hear of you, Flash,' chortled one of the staff officers, 'you would have stolen his mistress as well as a uniform if you had got close enough.' Most of the staff guffawed at that, leaving me to wonder what rumours about me were circulating.

'I take it you acquired your disguise from a Mr Zeminski?' enquired a smiling Wellington, holding up the letter.

'But sir, this is spying,' persisted Grant to Wellington. 'It is dishonourable behaviour, which is why both we and the French shoot those found disguised in our uniforms. How can you now condone this activity amongst one of your own officers?'

Several of the more experienced hands looked pityingly at the newcomer Grant before Wellington responded. 'Because Captain Flashman knows the risks he is taking. He is a brave man who saved my army from encirclement at Talavera and also provided me with great service as a spy in India. He knows he risks being shot, he was

242

nearly executed by rockets in India. But he does his duty to bring me information nevertheless.'

'Actually I was nearly shot this time,' I added, and held up the lancer's helmet. 'I was wearing this when it was hit by a musket ball as I rode away from the French through a night time partisan ambush.' There were more cries of admiration at that, and then they wanted to know how I had got the lancer's uniform in the first place. I gave a creditable story about how I had evaded an ambush by a squadron of lancers and killed one in the process, and felt well pleased with myself. If salacious stories of my time in the cathedral with Agustina were circulating amongst the staff, then accounts of me riding amongst the French would add a more martial air to my reputation.

The last of the soldiers who had been firing the town were forming up to march along the westerly road and the staff now also headed in that direction. Wellington called me over to ride with him, leaving the other staff officers to follow on behind.

'Take no notice of Grant,' he told me as we set off down the road. 'He is new and an inexperienced fellow, few people hold their honour more dearly than an impoverished Scotsman. You have done well, but of course I have come to expect that.'

'What happens next?' I asked him. 'You know the French will try to push us into the sea and they have the men to do it. My cousin told me that you have a plan. Will you tell me what it is?' I thought having done him such a service he could not refuse me, but I was wrong.

'She really did not tell you what it was?' he asked, looking at me. 'I can see from your face she did not,' he continued. 'I will personally show you the plan as you partly gave me the idea for it, but not yet. No, if the French are coming down the valley as you say, then we will first make a stand on the Busaco ridge.'

I knew Busaco; it was a tall escarpment across the road between here and Lisbon. It was several miles long and the French would certainly prefer to go over it than around it, but if we did stop them climbing over then they could easily outflank us. 'Won't the French simply go around us?'

'Eventually, yes. But I need a victory and I can have one at Busaco. The army has not fought for a year and it wants a battle. The politicians are also getting impatient for a return on the supplies and money they are sending the army.'

'But won't your plan give you a victory?' I asked, puzzled.

Wellington laughed. 'You will see Thomas, you will see,' he called, before spurring his horse onwards to ride alone. I went back to join the staff. While Grant ignored me, most of the rest were old friends. I told them what Wellington had told me and they were delighted about the prospect of a fight, but most were equally mystified as to what Wellington's plan was.

Chapter 24

Just over a week later I stood on the crest of the hill at Busaco. It was dawn on the twenty-seventh of September and already Wellington's arrangements for the battle had gone wrong. We had waited nearly a week for the French army to arrive as it had originally camped eight miles away, showing no intention of going further. During the time we were waiting, Wellington had built a road just behind the ridge so that he could quickly move his forces up and down it to meet any French threat, without the French being able to see where his forces stood. It was to be a classic Wellington defensive battle, the British army on the reverse slope of a hill safe from enemy artillery, only appearing as tired French columns reached the crest. What no one had foreseen was a thick fog which came up, near to the top of the crest. It completely hid the valley from us, but more importantly it would hide the French attacks until they were nearly upon the British line.

There are occasions when you can have too much planning. Countless times I have seen battles won on spur of the moment strategy, but for this engagement Wellington had calculated things to the last detail. Now the weather had made all the preparation obsolete. Everyone was feeling nervous. During the last week we had speculated on the French delay. Remembering the gossip of the French infantry, I had suggested that Massena's energetic mistress, Madame X, was keeping him occupied. This was laughed off as wicked speculation, but years later I discussed the battle with Ney and it turned out I was correct. He told me how he had been forced to shout the results of reconnaissance rides through the marshal's bedroom door. But all good things come to an end, and the exhausted Massena finally hauled himself from his bed. With his mistress riding alongside dressed as an aide de camp, he turned his attention to what were for him less strenuous activities, making war instead of making love.

We had seen the French army move to the plain in front of the Busaco ridge the previous day. Sixty-five thousand men build a lot of camp fires, and they had flickered during the night like the stars above them, until the morning mist had blotted them out. In contrast, Wellington had forbidden our army to light any fires that night, as he did not want the glow to give away our disposition behind the ridge. This explained why at dawn I was to be found pacing the crest, freezing cold with a cloak wrapped tightly around me.

'They are certainly busy down there,' mused Campbell who walked alongside me. We listened to the sound of bugles, trumpets and drums that the French were using to call their men to order, and the distant 'tramp, tramp,' of marching men.

'We can only hope that the fog is disrupting their attack as much as it is forestalling our defence,' I muttered grumpily. 'I am more worried that they might try and go around us while we cannot see them.'

'They won't do that,' said Campbell, confidently.

'Why not?'

'Because they are here to destroy our army. We are standing to give them battle and it will be a challenge their generals will be too proud to ignore. Their force is nearly three times the size of the British army here, and they discount the Portuguese, given their experience of the Spanish. They are not going to go round us when they think they have every chance of going through us and destroying our army.'

'Well, you are a ray of sunshine,' I grumbled. He was right though, the allied army was just fifty thousand. Half of those were British who had not fought since Talavera, and for many of those it had been their first battle. The rest were completely unproven Portuguese, whom the British had spent the last year training. Nobody was sure if they would stand. Meanwhile nearly every one of the sixty-five thousand men opposite were Bonaparte's veterans of countless campaigns and, as I had seen for myself, as tough as teak.

We fell silent as Wellington rode slowly towards us along the ridge with a group of his staff officers. He was complaining that he had been obliged to send a drunken commanding officer to the rear and I instinctively touched my brandy flask before remembering it was empty.

'Morning, gentlemen,' he snapped curtly to us as he moved on, and we touched our hats in reply. General Picton was riding alongside Wellington in what seemed to be a greatcoat over a night shirt with his night cap still on his head.

Captain Grant was among the other staff officers, and as he saw me he hung back a little so that he could speak out of earshot of Wellington. 'It is good to see you fighting in your own uniform Captain Flashman.'

I returned this greeting with an icy glare. If he thought he was going to provoke an intemperate remark that could lead to a duel he could think again. I had made enquiries and found out that he was a decent shot and swordsman. 'This must be your first battle, Grant. When you have been in as many as me you can give me advice.'

'It is not my first battle, I was on the Ostend raid in ninety eight,' he retorted primly.

I turned to Campbell. 'Ostend Raid? I was still at school then, was it a big battle?' I was pretty sure it wasn't or I would have heard of it.

'If I remember rightly,' Campbell's brow creased in concentration as he tried to recall the details, 'a storm blew up trapping the raiding party on shore and they were all captured.'

'We destroyed part of Bonaparte's invasion fleet,' said Grant hotly

'Burning a few barges is not much to show for at least twelve years in the army,' Campbell said to me before gesturing over his shoulder at Grant. 'He must have friends in Horseguards to keep him in comfortable billets. His regiment has recently come from Madeira.'

We both turned to a furious Grant as I confirmed happily, 'So apart from facing angry Madeiran fisherwomen this is your first proper battle then?'

'Cork brained fools,' he snarled before spurring his horse.

But he was not out of earshot before a laughing Campbell had added, 'I don't know, Flash, I hear those fisherwomen can put up a hell of a fight.'

The levity was gone a moment later when we heard a crackle of musket and rifle fire from the bottom of the forward slope. Our skirmishers, light companies and riflemen had been sent down the hill a while ago to slow the enemy advance, and now this noise indicated that they had made contact with the enemy.

'If only we could see what was happening down there,' said Campbell, staring into the thick fog. I listened for the direction of the shooting, but it seemed to come along the full width of the front and was steadily growing in ferocity. Campbell paced the ground, sniffing the air as though he could smell the French. He reminded me of Boney who seemed to have abandoned me the previous day. We were walking along the part of the ridge occupied by the Connaught Rangers and they had greeted Boney as though he was an old friend. I remembered that Byron had told me he had bought Boney from a Connaught man and the hound seemed to think he had returned home. The last I had seen of him, he was disappearing off with a soldier, who from his girth, was probably a cook.

I would not have been able to have him up on the ridge with me anyway. Wellington had forbidden any dogs up on the crest. Some thought it was to stop Avery's Brunhilde savaging any of our own side, but Wellington's excuse was that their barking warned the French where the British were standing. While Wellington wanted the French ignorant of our positions the fog had balanced the situation, neither side could see the other. I missed having the dog with me. Unlike Campbell, he would have been able to smell the approaching French.

I consoled myself with the thought that with the fog the French artillery were not wasting shot on the ridge, and considered what I would do when the French did attack. It was no accident that we were standing amongst Picton's division. He might be eccentric, but his men were more frightened of him than of the French, so they would stand and fight to the last. There had been some scandal a few years ago when Picton was accused of torturing some mulatto girl while a governor in the Caribbean. I had seen a drawing of the scene in one of the more scandalous illustrated news sheets during the trial. A beautiful half-naked girl hanging by her arms with Picton standing angrily over her. If she was half as beautiful as the drawing implied, then torture should have been the last thing on his mind.

The general was soon back from his inspection with Wellington, still wearing his ridiculous nightcap, not that anyone would dare laugh at him. He prowled around his men ensuring that all were ready to face the expected assault. Despite the disparity in numbers I was strangely confident. The most frightening thing at Talavera had been the guns, and here they were silent. I remembered the French columns advancing up the slope; we had beaten them back then and the slope was much steeper this time. The French were bound to be tired and disordered when they approached the summit. I thought that when they did finally appear, Campbell and I would go and stand behind the long lines of infantry out of their line of fire. We could watch the destruction of the columns and if there was a charge then the fog would at least cover my less than enthusiastic participation.

Looking around, I edged us over to stand in front of the Connaught Rangers, some of the wildest soldiers in the army. Most of them only understood enough English to get them through a parade, for the rest of the time they spoke Gaelic. If there was one regiment that loved to scrap it was the Rangers. When they were released to a charge they were only likely to stop when they reached wine or women and then there would be no moving them. Those are the boys I want in front of me, I thought. I could hear their muted murmuring in Gaelic as we stood near them and it reminded me of the Highlanders I had briefly commanded in India. I reached down and touched the gold sword, a reminder of those days, and then gripped the hilt as through the fog I heard the first distant shout of 'vive l'empereur.'

For a minute or two we heard nothing more, but then on the slight breeze we heard the distant thud, thud of French drums marking the time as the columns moved forward. Soon we could hear a faint crunching sound along with the drum beat and knew that tens of thousands of boots were moving towards us. While we could not see them, I could easily picture in my imagination the huge columns of men dressed in blue that were now marching up the bottom of the slope towards us. The few guns that we had placed on the ridge now crashed out, aiming blindly down the hill at the approaching men.

'It sound like there is a lot of them,' shouted Campbell over the noise of the gunfire. He was right; I could hear drums beating all along our front including some that seemed to come from directly below.

'How big do you think those columns are?' I asked, edging back slightly from the crest.

'Don't just stand there,' barked a voice from behind us. I turned and found myself staring into a pair of cold, flinty blue eyes under a nightcap. 'Get down that hill and help me get the light companies in,' ordered Picton. With that he walked past us down the hill, his coat still flapping to show his nightshirt, roaring for the officers of his light companies.

'Come on, Flash,' called Campbell with a grin. 'What a lark, eh?' and with that he followed Picton down the ridge, leaving me little choice but to follow.

As you can imagine, I did not go far. It made no sense to go into the fog, which formed a layer fifty yards below the crest. Our role was to rally the light companies – for that we needed to be seen. 'Light companies to the ridge,' Campbell and I bellowed at the top of our voices. Initially there was still a crackle of fire as our skirmishers attacked the approaching column, but gradually this died away and then in ones and twos, soldiers in red emerged from the gloom below. 'Form up over the ridge,' we shouted as they appeared. I knew that sound travelled further in fog, but the hairs on the back of my neck started to stand up as we waited on that hillside. The remorseless thump, thump of the drums and the march of feet was getting louder. I could hear shouts as rocks were dislodged on the hillside below, and scuffling as men moved around larger obstructions. It seemed as if at any moment the blue coated men would emerge from the fog below us.

'How far back are they?' I asked one group of skirmishers that came sprinting up the hill.

'A way back yet, sir,' called one, and I felt slightly comforted until his mate added, 'How do you know? That fog is so thick they could have been marching beside us.'

I was just about to tell Campbell it was time to get back, when over his shoulder three British officers emerged, walking calmly up the hill as though they did not have a care in the world. The one in the middle wearing a nightcap turned to me and barked irascibly, 'What are you still doing here? Get up over the ridge.' I did not need to be told twice. I started to run up the ridge before a voice barked behind me, 'Walk, gentlemen.' I fell back in beside Campbell, trying to walk calmly, while the ground almost vibrated with thousands of enemy boots marching towards my exposed back. I felt the first beads of sweat run down between my shoulder blades, but while moisture was appearing on my body, my mouth was bone dry. The noise of the approaching French was almost deafening now, and the sudden double beat of the drums and bellow of 'vive l' empereur' made me jump. There were thousands of voices and they were damn close. Suddenly the two staff officers who had been with Picton sprinted past on either side of us. I whirled round to see if the French had broken through, but all I could see was Picton, walking calmly behind us.

'Those gentlemen are running because they are obeying my orders,' he said to me as though I had accused him of inconsistency. He looked at Campbell, 'I know you, don't I?'

'Yes sir, Captain Campbell on Wellington's staff, and this is Captain Flashman.'

'Oh aye, I have heard of you too. You're the daft bugger that likes to dress up, aren't you?'

'Well...' I started, trying to think of what I could say to defend myself, but I got no further before he went on, shouting now over the noise of the enemy behind him.

'There will be no need of that today. The enemy are sending up huge columns and we either stop every single one or we are done for.'

'Surely we just have to stop most of them, sir,' Campbell was braver than me for arguing with him.

Picton pursed his lips angrily but then seemed to decide that Campbell deserved an answer. 'The French know when and where their next columns will hit our line. If one breaks through they will turn and attack those meeting the next column. You cannot do effective volley fire with a French bayonet in your back.'

We were nearly at the crest now, there were long lines of red coated men facing me lining the ridge, with officers closing gaps between them. To my right I could see two more cannon being set up to fire down the slope behind us. I looked over my shoulder and the mist behind us still showed no sign of the French, but then I heard shouting to my left. I turned and two hundred yards away the mist was suddenly getting darker, and as I watched the first French ranks emerged.

The head of the column was eighty men wide and I watched it almost transfixed. Rank upon rank was emerging from the mist, there seemed no end to them, but then the crest opposite its head was suddenly wreathed in smoke as the redcoats started their devastating volleys.

'Come on, Flash,' Campbell was pulling at my elbow and I realised with a start that I did not have time to watch this contest as a second column would soon be on us. We followed in Picton's wake as he passed through the red ranks, which shrank back as the general approached. An orderly was waiting with his horse and Picton swung himself into the saddle to survey his command. We stood behind the Connaughts; to our left was a Portuguese regiment in their green coats and to our right another British regiment, I cannot remember which. He nodded in grim satisfaction and then rode down the ridge to oversee the defence against the first column. The eighty men from the Connaught Light Company were resting from their climb, and gathered behind the other companies along the crest. I walked up to their officer.

'Are you sure another column will try to break through here?'

'Oh yes, we saw them forming up at the bottom.' He grinned at me before adding, 'Bloody thousands of them.' It was only then that I began to notice the sense of excitement in the men around me. I have stood and quaked amongst various nationalities waiting for an attack; stoic Scots, garrulous Welshmen, hard bitten Americans, icy calm Iroquois, I have even seen Zulu impis sweep in like a single animal, but I have never found a fighting force like the Irish. No nation on earth enjoys a drink or a fight more than them. There was a tension in the air amongst the Connaught Rangers that you could almost cut with a knife. It was as though they were gluttons and expecting a huge cake to be delivered to them. Even though we could see and hear a grim and bloody contest for the ridge just a short distance away there was not a hint of fear to be seen. For a windy beggar like me it was unnerving, but strangely comforting, to be amongst such confidence. They would take some breaking, I thought, and if they did break, well they would give me plenty of time to get well away. I realised I was being watched with benign amusement by another man on horseback, who grinned when he caught my eye. He had seen me gauging the mood of the men around me and nodded.

'They are magnificent aren't they?' he said, and judging from the uniform he was their colonel. Then he pushed his horse forward to stand in front of them. 'Connaught Rangers,' he called out, and the babble in the ranks fell silent. 'When the enemy appears we will stand here and fight them with volleys. No man is to charge until he is ordered. But when I do order it, I want you to chase those French rascals. Drive them down the hill.'

There was a cheer at that and the approaching French must have heard it, for their drummers gave the double beat and thousands of French voices called out in reply, 'vive l'empereur.'

The colonel just grinned and looked down at a soldier in the ranks. 'Sandy, give them a song to let them know the Rangers are waiting for them.' A plaintive voice started up singing in Gaelic, and within moments eight hundred voices had joined him. I have no idea what the song was about, but the man just in front of me had tears rolling down his cheeks with emotion a few moments later. The song included such a loud and passionate refrain that I noticed the Portuguese troops shrank back several paces, and they were on our side! The singing was only interrupted when there was a roar of triumph from our right. The colonel from his higher vantage point called out, 'The first column is breaking, lads.' A cheer rippled down the ranks and as it finished you could hear the distant calls for bayonets and the screams of panic from the trapped front ranks of the French as the blades moved forwards. Just like Talavera, I thought, and tried to reason with myself that this meant there was no cause for alarm. As if on cue the mist in front of the Connaught Rangers suddenly went dark.

The mounted colonel pushed his way back behind his men as the first French ranks appeared through the mist ahead. This column was also eighty men across and the centre of it seemed directly opposite where I was standing. Despite having climbed up a steep rock strewn hillside they seemed in good order and did not hesitate as they saw the Irishmen standing before them. The mist may have been an advantage

252

for us then, for I was to discover later that there were eleven French battalions in this column against just four battalions dressed in red and green facing them. Not that the Irish would have been dismayed, but the British and Portuguese on their flanks may have been hesitant to start to curl their line around the head of the column, as they were now doing, to create an arc.

'Fourth Company, fire,' called out a voice nearby, and the first volley from a third of the line crashed out. Around five seconds later came a second volley and then seconds after that a third crashed out. By then the men who had fired first were raising reloaded muskets to their shoulders. The devastating company volley fire I had seen at Talavera was being repeated with similar effect. The front ranks of the French tried to return fire while they continued to march forwards, but they were massively outgunned. I suddenly felt reasonably confident standing behind the massed red ranks. The French had to be winded after their long climb, and while there were thousands of them, only their front soldiers could fire. As the thought crossed my mind, a French lead ball passed through the brain of the man standing just in front of me. Blood and brains spattered my face and chest.

'God damn it,' I gasped, as I dashed the gore away from my eyes and involuntarily took several steps back.

'Steady sor,' said a voice behind, and I turned to see the Connaught Light Company arrayed in a double rank of forty men. I had backed into their sergeant who regarded me impassively as I spat out some blood that had got in my mouth. 'It looks like you have some oirish in you now sor,' he added, before glancing at the poor soldier who had been hit. He was now stretched out on the grass in front of me, his hands still gripping his musket as he had died. I looked beyond the sergeant at the Light troops who had fought in ones or twos on the hillside. They had to be tough, independently minded men to make it into the Light Company, so these were the toughest men from one of the toughest regiments.

Their captain was shouting at them to stay alert for trouble along the line as they were the reserve, but several of them impudently returned my look of inspection. They were not friendly stares. Some seemed amused at the reaction of the English officer to getting blood in his face and I heard some mutters in Gaelic. These were men of the west of Ireland, many of them tenants of English absentee landowners. They lived in poverty to pay their rents and that poverty had probably forced many of them to come and fight and die for the English. So there was little sympathy for English officers who got spattered with Irish blood.

I straightened up and turned towards the front. Looking along the line there were a score of dead and wounded now, lying on the ground or being helped to the rear. The front ranks of the French were faring a lot worse though, going down like skittles under the steady onslaught of volley fire. But for now they were still coming on, stepping over their dead and wounded to reach us and still returning fire. Some were even trying to reload as they marched, although they rarely survived long enough to complete the procedure.

'I say Flash, are you hit?' Campbell was next to me, staring at my blood soaked face and chest.

'No, it comes from some other fellow, a drop of the Irish if you will,' I laughed, trying to put on a brave front. It is a strange thing, but while I have a yellow streak a mile wide I always seem to attract the friendship of genuinely good and brave men. Campbell was by then one of my closest friends, but before him there had been Cochrane and Skinner and there were many more to follow. Few seemed ever to suspect my true character and, through disaster and mischance, I had normally suffered greatly to earn their respect. So while I did not care a jot for the opinions of the likes of Grant or Cam Hobhouse, I did greatly value my reputation amongst that band of brother officers. But there were times, like this one, when those lantern jawed heroes had no idea how much of a strain it was to maintain the pretence.

Campbell gave me a pounding slap on the back in reassurance, 'I'll bet there are a few bottles of powerful Irish poitin amongst the regimental baggage to help celebrate our victory, eh? Hello, what is this? They are spreading out.' He was staring through the recently created gap in the ranks ahead and I saw that while the head of the column was struggling to make progress, the sides of it were swinging forward like the wings of a bird. Now I realised why the Portuguese and British officers had been pushing their men forward to make an arc when they saw where the column had emerged. If the French could deploy their 'wings' they would bring many more guns to bear, and with their superior numbers the length of the wings could overwhelm us.

This was the critical moment of the engagement and everyone seemed to sense it. The French soldiers in blue, marching towards this maelstrom, gave a final bellow of loyalty to their emperor, and launched a determined effort to climb over their fallen comrades to close with their enemy. Men in the green of the Portuguese and the red of the Irish and British lost themselves in the automatic routine of loading, aiming and firing as fast as they could… and one British officer glanced over his shoulder to check where he had left his horse.

If the French broke through then the thousands of men below the head of their arrow would stream up the hill and we would be overwhelmed. There would be no chance to recover the situation with more columns on the way. But to do that the French had to get through the hail of lead that was now hitting three sides of the front of their column. Good troops could fire three shots per minute and as the battalion was broken into three sections that resulted in nine volleys a minute. I could not see the wing on the right but I could see the left, which had initially extended further forward. It got to within thirty yards of the Portuguese, but at that range the musket balls could penetrate several bodies and while the French were dying hard, they were still dying. I looked to my front and the Irish soldiers were firing like the well drilled machine that they were. Crash after crash of volleys smashed into the French ranks and now I could see that they were starting to falter. One of their eagle standards glinted in the early morning sun; it had not moved forward through the column. It was only now near the head of the formation because all the men that had been in front of it had been killed. As I watched it wavered, whether the man holding it had stumbled or been shot I could not see, but it seemed to stop. Then with a cry of 'retreat' from the French ranks the huge formation started to move back.

As at Talavera, when the French broke it was sudden. Collectively the column seemed to sense that it would get no further, and then it collapsed into chaos. The men on the wings broke first. They had fewer men behind them and where a second before they had been fighting, they were now running back down the slope. The movement spread to the centre of the column and men were turning, frantic to get back down the hill, pushing those in the way. On relatively flat ground this would have caused confusion with some still pushing up the hill from lower down the column. But on a steep slope it was disastrous. Those that had started to run soon found that they could not stop and crashed into those lower down, sending them flying. Others slipped and fell but most stayed desperately on their feet, and were soon running pell mell down into the valley and disappearing into the fog.

'Fix bayonets,' called the colonel of the Connaughts. The call was repeated down the line as the long blades were drawn and carefully fixed to hot musket barrels. Campbell and I drew our swords and showed ourselves eager to be unleashed, but only one of us was genuine in that emotion. I knew Campbell would be at the forefront of any charge. He was as fast as quicksilver over rough country and we had joked that there was mountain goat in his parentage. He would not expect me to keep up and with eight hundred screaming Irishmen there would be quite a crowd for me to get lost in. I looked down at the blood still covering me and decided that I would let them hurtle down the hill without me, and then I would feign a limp as I went slowly after them. A blood soaked and wounded Flashy, hobbling into battle despite his wounds; it would fit my reputation like port and cigars.

'Charge,' shouted the colonel.

'Charge, come on men,' called Campbell, already pushing through to the front and waving his sword in the air as eight hundred Irishmen, screaming more like clansmen warriors than British soldiers, launched off after him.

'Huzzah, forward you brave fellows,' cries the gallant Flashy, flourishing his blade in the air too, but only staggering forwards a few paces and watching the backs of the others recede before him.

Chapter 25

Before I had gone more than a yard I was aware of the Light Company men coming up from behind. The first few soldiers jostled past, but then I felt an arm lift me at my right elbow followed immediately another at my left. My feet were lifted off the ground and a voice called in my ear, 'Don't you worry sor, we'll help you down all right, so we shall.' With that I was carried off down the slope at an alarming speed, my arms in vice-like grips, my feet in the air and my sword waving futilely in my hand.

'Put me down you stupid bastards,' I roared, but they took no notice. The more I shouted and raged the more they laughed in delight. They swore afterwards that they thought they were helping the gallant officer meet the enemy, but it is my belief that they knew exactly what they were doing. Some had seen that the blood I was covered in was not mine and when I started to hobble away the evil minded villains saw straight through my charade. Laughing with glee they picked up one of their English masters and cruelly deprived him of his honest right to shirk his duty.

I realised this in the first twenty yards when they ignored my raging and a voice called in my ear, 'Come now sor, you don't want to miss the fun.' It was the blighter holding my right arm, but I didn't dare look round at him as I needed to see where I was going. My feet were touching the ground now but we were already going at such a speed there was no chance of stopping, especially in the middle of a crowd of men. The ground ahead was littered with wounded French soldiers and their dead, lying between rocks and boulders. One slip at this speed and I would be breaking bones all the way down the hillside. You could not help stepping on some bodies, and I remember one Frenchie screaming in agony as my boot punched down into his chest. Then we were into the mist, which now seemed thinner and lower than before. I could see that we were starting to catch up the slower Rangers lumbering down the hillside. On we went. Twice I nearly slipped and went down but was hauled up by the men at my elbows. At least two men in our group did fall, and as far as one was concerned, I suspect they do not call the speed we were going 'break neck' for nothing. The other screamed, yelled and bounced off into the mist.

God knows how far we had come when the ground began to level off and we heard increased shouting in front. The French were using some more even ground half way down the hill to try to stem their headlong retreat and organise a more orderly withdrawal. But through the mist we could see that the Connaughts were in amidst them and fighting amongst the rocks. As we ran up I saw a solid line of red coated backs in front of us fighting the French in front. Their line was broken only by a huge slab of rock, shaped like a wedge of cheese, which must have fallen from higher up the hillside and come to rest on this flatter stretch. They would have to stop now, I thought, but then one of the fellows with me shouted something in Gaelic and gestured to the cheese shaped rock that jutted out like a pier into the French lines. Instead of slowing down we were suddenly picking up speed again, the last of our momentum carrying us towards that huge piece of stone.

It took me a full second to realise what they had planned and then my guts were churning in terror. As their own comrades were between them and the enemy, the more homicidal lunatics of the Light Company had decided to use the slab of rock as a ramp from which to drop down on the enemy from above.

'Let me go you mad Murphy's, you will get us all killed,' I roared at them, and tried to wrench myself out of their grip. But my voice was lost in their renewed battle cries as they half ran and half hauled me up the ramp of stone. As we reached the top of the slope I had one glimpse of a sea of blue coated soldiers, before a hand in the small of my back pushed me into the air.

I was the first off the rock and any scream I emitted was lost in the yells of those that followed me. Campbell and others who had seen us charge up the rock assumed that I was leading this aerial assault rather than being its unwilling pioneer. It was a twelve foot drop to the ground below, but the area was tightly packed with French soldiers to break our fall. I had just enough time to look down at the startled face of a young French infantry man looking up, before I landed squarely on top of him with my stomach on his shako. He crumpled to the ground like the town drunk hit with a cudgel. A crowd of bodies started to follow me off the rock and onto the men around me. As I tried to disentangle myself from the flailing limbs my sword cut into the calf of a French infantry man who whirled round, bayonet raised. I can still remember those angry eyes glaring down at me above grey whiskers.

I was hemmed in by a wall of legs with nowhere to go. I desperately tried to get my sword up to parry the blow, but there was no need. My assailant was looking down at me when the poor devil should have been looking up. Another leaping Connaught Ranger landed bayonet first on his chest. The Frenchman and Irishman fell together, but only one got up with the Ranger tugging furiously on his musket to get the bayonet out of the French corpse. I tried to climb to my feet but was knocked down twice more, once from a glancing blow from yet another falling Ranger and the second time I was flattened by a stampede of French soldiers pulling back from the red coated troops.

There was pandemonium amongst the French now. Those behind the rock must have thought they were safe but they now pushed at those behind them to get away. The French front line started to dissolve as they realised that there were enemy soldiers to their rear as well as to their front.

Eventually I managed to stand and a strange hellish scene met my eyes. I was surrounded by a ring of Connaught men pushing their way out with bayonets into the French. They were all privates apart from the sergeant who had spoken to me back on the crest. The fog here was wispy and cold but it amplified the shouting of those around us. French voices screamed at those around them to move while other shrieks and yells indicated where the Rangers were now trying to push through as the French line collapsed.

'You bloody fool,' I shouted at the sergeant. 'You will get us all killed.' He just looked over his shoulder and grinned like some Barbary ape, for they were all mad on killing. The Light Company had come with loaded weapons, and now muskets banged and men fell around them. Firing into the blue throng you could not miss. Many of the French from the middle of the column were loaded too but found it impossible to level their muskets in the crowd, so initially the Irish gained the advantage. One of the Irishmen, swinging his musket like a club and yelling a challenge in Gaelic, charged alone into the blue throng. At first it opened before him, people falling over to get out of his way, but then he went too far. Bayonets stabbed into his exposed back and sides and he screamed his dying agony as the blue coats surged back to cut him off from the rest of us.

I looked up, I could just make out some of the Irish shakos of the approaching line in the mist but they were still some way off. 'Connaughts, for Christ's sake over here,' I yelled at the distant formation of men in red, but the French were still fighting that line and now that the Light Company men had fired their sporadic volley into those around them the French were closing back in around us too. There was not time for our men to reload so they just jabbed forward with their bayonets to keep the French at bay. As I watched, another redcoat went too far into those around him, and went down screaming from a bayonet stab in the belly.

'Keep in a circle,' I yelled at them, as I could see that we would only last a few moments as a group without some discipline. I grabbed the sergeant's shoulder and shouted in his ear, 'Keep them in a circle or we are all dead men.'

He glared round at me, but at that moment a musket banged and we were both spattered in more blood as the man next to him fell against us, shot through the chest. He looked down at the falling body and then reason seemed to get through to him. 'Steady lads,' called the sergeant. 'Get shoulder to shoulder, our boys will be through in a minute.'

It was desperate work. The Irish had to keep the French squeezed in or they would find room to fire their muskets, but if they spread out too far they left gaps in their line. So they pushed and shoved and danced back from stabbing blades if they could not parry them. The reach of a man with a musket far exceeded that of a man with a sword, so I pushed my sword tip into the hard ground at my feet and pulled out my pistols. I planned to save the shots for my personal protection and I did not have long to wait. A man to my left shrieked as a blade raked his arm. Dropping his musket he stepped back, and a Frenchman lunged into the gap. He was almost on me in a moment and I just managed to cock and raise the pistol in time. The point of his bayonet was just a foot away when I fired the pistol into his belly. In my haste I was not gripping the weapon tight enough, they are notoriously inaccurate, but at that range even I could not miss. The barrel swung up as it discharged and deposited a lead ball right between the soldier's eyes.

'Good shooting, sor,' called the sergeant, who had also swung round to cover the man.

'Shooting bedammed,' I snarled at him, 'watch your front, man.' There was no time to reload even a pistol and I dropped the weapon back in my coat pocket and cocked the second ready to fire. The men closed up to fill the gap left by the wounded Ranger and our circle slowly contracted. Glancing around there were more wounded on the ground at my feet and now there were just a dozen men standing.

One wiry little Irishman was in a desperate action on the other side of the circle. His bayonet moved with lightning speed as he fended off two attackers. In the second I noticed him a third managed to find the room to raise his musket and fire. How the devil he missed from that range I do not know. But not only did the little Murphy not even flinch, he darted forward in the musket smoke and managed to stab one of the attackers in the thigh. With a roar of rage, the Frenchman who had fired replaced the wounded man, and the Irish blade was darting about as fast as ever. The Rangers on either side were fully occupied fighting off Frenchmen of their own, and it was only a matter of moments before the little fellow would be beaten and then they would be through in earnest. It only took me two steps to cross our circle and then I was at the little bantam's shoulder. I fired my second pistol low into the body of one of his attackers. The distraction enabled the Ranger to catch the remaining one in the throat, he was faster that a Billingsgate fishwife with a blade, that one. He turned to look at me and I had thought he would show some sign of gratitude that I had saved his life, but instead it was a glare of irritation. He looked as though I had stolen food from his plate.

'I had them your honour,' he complained in a high sing song voice. Then he turned to the nearest Frenchman standing in the gap in front of him who was now trying to work out how to attack without standing on his fallen comrades. 'Will you come along now,' complained the little Ranger, 'we have not got all day.'

As I stood in the circle half paralysed with fear it seemed that my Irish comrades, despite being shot at and stabbed, were still enjoying themselves. Several were fighting with broad grins and taunting their opponents like the bantam. One great Paddy I now realised was even singing above the din of battle. They were fighting like terriers too and had managed to drive out the French between us and the rock so that we now only had to defend ourselves on three sides of a rough square. This freed up some men who were helping to hold the rest of the line, but it was still desperate. There was cutting, shouting, jostling and even the occasional shot all around me. With no time to reload and I dropped the second pistol in my pocket and darted across our little space to grab my sword, still sticking up in the dirt.

I felt impotent standing idle in the middle of so much activity. But I would not have been able to reach the enemy with my sword and would probably have just got in the way. Anyway, as another Irishman stepped back cursing with blood streaming down his arm, I was all too aware that despite the Irish love of a good fight, the line was a damn dangerous place to be. The wounded man stepped back into his place, holding his musket one handed. From the look on his face, even with one arm, I pitied the next Frenchman he faced. I decided I would stand at the back and look to stab at any Frenchman that broke through, while hoping our dwindling group survived long enough to be relieved. I glanced up again at the main Connaught formation coming towards us, it seemed a little closer but there were at least half a dozen French shakos between me and the nearest Connaught one.

For a brief moment I thought we would survive, as several of the French fighting the centre of our line suddenly stepped back and I wondered if perhaps they would follow their comrades further down the hill. But then I saw that I was wrong and we were doomed. Both armies put their tallest men in the grenadier companies, and into the gap created stepped the biggest French grenadier I ever saw. He was a giant of a man, holding his musket by the muzzle in one hand as though it were a child's toy. His mere presence was enough to encourage the other French soldiers, who threw themselves at our meagre line with renewed enthusiasm, confident that our end was nigh.

I was frozen in shock and horror for it was as though one of my nightmares had come to life; I had come close to being killed by a giant man in India. A huge Rajput warrior had nearly strangled me. That man had been shot and bayoneted twice and still he came onto to me. I vividly remembered him crushing my throat and feeling certain I was about to die. Luckily he took a bayonet to the groin and his grip finally relaxed as I lost consciousness. Ever since I had occasionally dreamt of the encounter and woken up sweating at the memory of his face. Now the grenadier seemed to smile directly at me standing in the centre of our group, and I could not shake off the absurd notion that the Rajput had sent this man to avenge him. Then the Grenadier looked down at the two Irishmen closest, the sergeant and another soldier who were watching and waiting for him. He grinned at them too and gestured for them to come at him. Damn me if the soldier did not step forward to take the giant on single handed until the sergeant pulled him back.

'Stay here Seamus,' shouted the sergeant above the noise of battle. 'You don't want one of the others to stab you in the back while you fight the big fella. Let him come to us.'

They did not have long to wait, for with a mighty roar the grenadier sprang towards us, moving with surprising speed, his musket butt just a fast moving blur above his head.

'Oh, Christ,' I muttered to myself, 'this is the end.'

The sergeant got his musket up to parry the swinging weapon but the wooden stock of the Brown Bess shattered as though it were matchwood. The iron barrel was torn away and still the Frenchman's weapon swung with sufficient force to knock the ambitious Seamus off his feet and send him flying into his comrades behind.

I was vaguely aware that Seamus had knocked down two of the Irishmen, and all three were struggling to regain their footing and fight off a reinvigorated French attack. Even though this was happening just a few feet away, I did nothing. I just remembering staring at this unstoppable behemoth and knowing with absolute certainty that this time I was about to die. The sergeant took two steps back, staring in amazement at the shuttered remains of his own musket as though he could not take in what had happened. Then, as the grenadier stepped through the gap he had created into the centre of our circle, the sergeant seemed to collect himself. Dropping the shattered stock, he moved to my right and snatched up a fallen musket from the ground. Staying crouched he launched himself at the Frenchman. The sergeant was fast and in too close for the Frenchman to swing his weapon, but the grenadier still had time to grab the muzzle of the sergeant's second musket and twist it from his grip. It all happened in a split second, but I realised that the Irishman was letting the musket go easily. He had not got to be a sergeant without learning how to fight dirty. Now he was close enough to the grenadier he swung his iron shod boot into a devastating crack on the Frenchman's kneecap. With a grunt of pain the leg gave way, forcing the giant down on one knee, but his free hand was already reaching out to grab his assailant.

As if waking from a dream, I came out of my brief trance-like state knowing instantly what I must do. With the grenadier looking away from me at the sergeant, I raised my sword and swung it round with every ounce of strength I possessed, knowing that my life depended on delivering a killing blow. I aimed for his neck and struck with a force that would have decapitated a lesser man. But the grenadier's neck was huge, with thick cords of muscle joining his head to his shoulders. The razor sharp blade bit deep and blood sprayed over me, but with a gurgling roar of rage the giant managed to haul himself back to his feet. With a sickening sense of déjà vu I knew that he still had fight in him.

I wrenched my blade free, opening the wound further, and stepped behind the man. His head lolled to one side, opening the deep cut in his neck, but he remained on his feet and moved quickly to face where

I had been. I saw the sergeant throw a punch at him, but for all the good it did he could have thrown flower petals. The grenadier ignored the Irishman while he looked for me. Frantically I stabbed at him again, this time in the back. I remember his uniform coat was stretched tight over his massive torso, but as I jabbed my blade towards him I must have hit a rib as the blade would not go in. I pulled my sword back for another thrust, but he started to turn once more. He staggered a step round, resting his weight on his good leg, and glared at me angrily. His lips curled into a snarl as he swung his musket round one handed, as though it were a giant club. I had no choice but to try and stab him again. This time the Damascus blue steel disappeared into the cloth. I had thrust up into the side of his massive chest, all the way until the hilt of the weapon was pressed against his skin. I was close enough to hear a slight hiss of air as the blade punctured his lung, and smell the mixture of sweat and gunpowder smoke from his clothes. I was pressed up against him now to avoid the weapon that was still swinging behind me. Once the blade could go no further I wrenched the hilt to twist the blade. The musket butt struck me weakly across the back as blood poured down my arm from the opened wound in his side. I stepped back, pulling out my sword, thinking now he must be dead.

He had not made a sound, but now looked down at me with an expression of surprise. There was blood dribbling down his chin but he stayed upright, and even seemed to heft the musket still in his hand slightly as though considering a second blow. With memories of that awful Rajput fresh in my imagination I rammed the sword blade into him once more shouting, 'die you bastard!' He just stared at me with glassy eyes as I pulled the steel out and stabbed him again and again. The rest of the battle was forgotten, everyone apart from that giant, which somehow in my imagination had become the creature from my nightmares. The fear and the terror of the last few minutes had taken their toll and now nothing mattered more to me than seeing that grenadier down and dead. I lost myself completely to the task. I have vague recollections of shouting at him to die every time I plunged my sword into his torso, and of that chest becoming soaked with his blood. He dropped down to one knee again but I kept on stabbing him. Finally my sword got caught in his ribs again and I was tugging at it, still shrieking for him to die, when someone was at my shoulder pulling me away.

'He is dead, sor,' whispered the sergeant. 'He is right proper dead thanks to you.' As he spoke the body finally toppled over, leaving my sword hilt pointing at the sky. I realised that there were tears in my eyes now and I dashed them away with my sleeve and looked about. God knows how long I had been there driving a blade into the Frenchman, but when I looked up the Connaughts were all about us and the French were in full retreat further down the hill. A sense of relief washed over me. 'I'll wager you're glad you did not miss the fun now sor, right enough' said the sergeant, grinning at me.

It took several seconds for this to sink in, but then the phrase, 'missing the fun' rang a bell. I remembered where I had heard it before. Then I understood that this was the cove who had grabbed my right elbow and carried me down the slope. 'You bastard,' I replied, as realisation dawned. Half of me wanted to punch him in his fat grinning face, but deep down the other half realised that in the last minute I had exorcised some demon that had been haunting me.

'Well I am glad you came sor, right glad, or that big bugger would have done for me.' The Irishman, still grinning, held out his hand and after a moment's hesitation I shook it. There was no point making an enemy now, not when the fighting was done, especially one that knows how to fight dirty. And anyway what could I have done, have him court martialled for stopping me from shirking?

Before I could say anymore, Campbell was pushing his way through the surrounding soldiers and he stopped in astonishment when he saw the giant corpse lying at our feet with my distinctive gold hilted sword sticking out of his side.

'Hell's teeth Flash, don't tell me you killed this brute?'

Before I could say anything the sergeant spoke up. 'Oh he did your honour, right enough. Tore into him like a wild thing he did.'

'Oh, he just backed into my sword,' I tried dismissively.

'Repeatedly,' said Campbell, grinning and looking down at the multiple wounds. Then his eyes were distracted over my shoulder and he muttered, 'Oh, would you look at that.'

We turned, and the first thing I saw were the still fleeing French, bounding uncontrolled down the second part of the hill. This time there were few Irish amongst them as the mist was now clearing. Only the most foolhardy lunatic would chase the French now, for two more huge columns of infantry waited at the bottom of the hill. As I watched I saw some French lancers were riding forward to dispatch any Irishman that made it to the bottom.

'No, not down there,' called Campbell impatiently, 'look along the slope.'

I raised my eyes and there, through the skeins, of mist were two more columns, several hundred yards away but climbing steadily up the incline.

Others had seen them too and in moments the call went out for everyone to get back to the crest of the hill. Campbell was already bounding up the slope, but I simply did not have the strength any more. My nerves were shot and I was exhausted. The sergeant was about to go after his men when he turned and grinned as I sat down on a rock amongst the dead and a few whimpering wounded that still lay on the level ground.

'Here,' he held out a flask to me. 'You look like you need it.'

I took a swig thinking it was brandy, and realised my mistake when it hit the back of my throat. In ancient times they had something called Greek fire, which was a liquid that burned everything it touched, it even burned on the surface of water. I felt as if I had taken a swig of the damned stuff, for my breath was taken away by the incendiary sensation down my gullet and into my stomach.

'What in the name of holy hell was that?' I croaked at the sergeant when I could get my breath.

Through watering eyes I watched as he came up and patted me on the shoulder with one hand and took the flask away with the other. 'That,' he replied, 'is poitin, a proper drop of the Oirish.'

God knows what was in the spirit, but by the time I could see clearly again I found my strength coming back. A glance down the slope showed that no French were coming back in my direction although I guessed they would do so presently to collect their wounded. My thoughts were interrupted by renewed volley firing further along the ridge, and I saw the first of the two columns we had seen make contact with the British line. The last of the mist was going now and I could see clearly the wings of the column trying to deploy and the curving line of the British preventing them. I tried to remember what regiments were along the line. Interspersed with the British redcoats were the unproven green and brown coated cacadores of the Portuguese army. Many of the British viewed them as inferior troops, but from what I had seen at Alcantara, I thought that they would take some beating.

Having retrieved my sword I staggered slowly up the slope. There was no point in rushing to get dragged into another desperate defence, even if I did have the energy. I was surrounded by the walking wounded and those helping them. It seemed strange, going for a stroll while a furious battle raged not far away, but I felt that I had more than played my part already. The noise of firing intensified as the second column engaged, with British cannon now also blasting through the tightly packed ranks.

I had fallen in with a rotund moustached corporal who staggered up the hill, puffing like an asthmatic walrus. Now, though, he stopped and pointed. 'Look sir, they are falling back.'

He was right. The first column we had seen was falling back and this was already having an effect on the second column. From our vantage point we could see the rear ranks of it start to move back down the hill. While we had not seen it, a third column further around the ridge had also advanced, straight into the weakest point in the line manned entirely by the inexperienced Portuguese. But the hours of drilling had paid off and they put up a rate of fire just as good as they rest of the line, sending that column packing too. I looked down the hill and saw the other two columns that had been waiting in the valley floor start to disperse. The French had decided to give up on the assault and find another way around our position.

I regained the crest of the hill just in time to see Wellington congratulate the Connaught colonel.

'Upon my honour Wallace,' he cried, 'I have never witnessed a more gallant charge than that made by your regiment.' Then he caught a glimpse of my battered frame climbing onto the plateau and grinned. 'Flashman, I might have known you would have been in the thick of it.'

The colonel was calling for three huzzahs for the general now, and as the men crowded round raising their shakoes and bellowing themselves hoarse, I stood back a bit. I was not part of this regiment and I still had no idea how we were ultimately going to beat the French. They had received a bloody nose with an ambitious plan of attack up a steep slope, but they would not make that error again. From now on they would treat us with more respect. I knew that they would not stop until we were back in our ships or in our graves. But before I could get too disconsolate something wet touched my hand. I looked down and saw two brown eyes looking back, and a tongue licking my blood-stained knuckles. Boney was back.

Chapter 26

Thanks to Campbell, by the time I returned to the mess tent I shared with other officers on Wellington's staff, everyone seemed to have heard of 'Flying Flash' and his leap from the rock. It cheered me up and I knew that it was the kind of story that would stick to my reputation. We celebrated our victory that night and heard that the casualties amongst the Portuguese and British were exactly the same, six hundred and twenty-six each, while the French were thought to have lost nearly five thousand men.

In the morning, the bulk of the French army was still camped on the plain before us but, as expected, we heard that French advance parties were scouting a route to our north. Both armies, though, rested during the day to allow time to recover from the battle. That night, with camp fires lit all along the ridge to fool the French into thinking we were still there, the British and Portuguese slipped away west. The next day we reached the city of Coimbra, and gave the citizens a rude awakening.

Wellington had been employing a 'scorched earth' policy, taking away all supplies and goods that could be of use to the enemy; the same tactic that the Russians would so successfully employ two years later against Napoleon when he marched on Moscow. The citizens of the frontier towns had cooperated, most were keen to get themselves and their possessions away before the French arrived. But the wealthy inhabitants of Coimbra had evidently expected Wellington stop the French at Busaco or for the whole of Portugal to be occupied by the French. Consequently they had made no preparations to leave.

It was a big city with its own university and other civic buildings. Two days were spent driving the citizens from their homes which were then torched behind them. A long procession of refugees, with every wheeled vehicle they possessed, struggled over the Mondego Bridge, mingling with the army and its own guns and supplies. It was a scene of chaos, with provosts desperately trying to maintain order and stop the soldiers looting. There was a large prison and an asylum in the town and their inhabitants were screaming as they watched the town burn, fearing that they would be burned alive. Eventually on the second day they were let out, so murderers and lunatics joined the throng. Some of the mad from the asylum seemed to prefer to stay in the burning town or take their chances with the French. I well remember seeing several of them, still dressed in nightshirts, shrieking in delight as they danced in the light of the flames.

The citizens could only carry so much with them and so, despite the best endeavours of the provosts, soldiers looted much of what was left. A blind eye was turned by many officers to the raiding of wine cellars in the larger houses before they were torched. Many a travelling officer's mess was restocked in that manner, and from the state of drunkenness in the army as it crossed the bridge, much more was drunk on the march. Some, though, tested the limits of the provost's tolerance. As we left the town on the other side of the river I remember seeing a sight that has stayed clearly in my memory all these years. A soldier, presumably drunk, had tried to loot from the city a full length gilt mirror. The provosts had hung him by the side of the road as a warning to others. But they had not hung him alone. They had strung up the mirror alongside him so that his last sight on this earth was his own slowly strangled face.

With the coast less than twenty miles away the army turned south towards Lisbon. Another evacuation seemed the best we could hope for now. I remembered standing in that church tower with Campbell so long ago and looking at the surrounding hills. Once the French got a foothold on those then the city would be indefensible. If Wellington really did have a plan then the time to use it was long overdue. Robert Wilson was back in London now and I could easily imagine the capital he would make of this. For all of Wellington's caution he had ended up where he started. Doubtless Wilson would also point out how close he had come to liberating Madrid with his tiny force before he was stopped, claiming it would have triggered a second rebellion.

Two days later and we were within thirty miles of Lisbon. I was considering how to get on one of the first boats to leave the city when a very young ensign rode up with a message for me.

'General Wellington sends his compliments,' squeaked the ensign whose voice had not yet broken, 'and he would be obliged if Captain Flashman would join him on a reconnaissance ride.'

I spurred my horse up to the front of the column and instead of finding Wellington worried and crestfallen I found him happy and jubilant.

'Ah, Flashman. You will recollect that I promised to show you my plan. Would you care to see it now?'

'So it is not too late?' I asked, astounded. 'I mean, sir,' I added hastily, 'that as we are so close to Lisbon I thought that the opportunity for this plan had passed.'

'No, not at all, now is the perfect time,' beamed Wellington, who did not seem the least offended by my lack of confidence.

'Could we come too sir?' asked Grant. It was then that I took in the faces of the other staff officers behind Wellington. Around half had a knowing smile on their faces but the other half were clearly bursting with curiosity like me.

'Of course,' agreed Wellington, who despite having a French army on the verge of trapping him against the coast, seemed in the best of spirits. 'But Thomas, ride with me, as you gave me the idea.'

We set off at a gallop and for once Wellington's habitual icy demeanour let him down. He was looking extremely pleased with himself and bursting to show off his plan. But he would not answer any questions as we rode, he just kept repeating that I would have to wait and see. When I did finally get to set eyes on his plan, I venture that my initial reaction was not what he was expecting.

'There, what do you think of that?' he asked as we breasted a rise and looked down on the valley ahead. I reined in and looked about. The most immediate thing to see was that the forward slope we had just reached had been cleared of trees. Various stumps could be seen protruding from the earth and judging from drag marks in the ground, the timber had been hauled off towards the hills in front. I stared about, confused, and looking at the other officers who were as bemused at me.

'You have cleared the bank sir?' I pointed out hesitantly, lost at how he could think this would stop the French.

'Never mind that,' Wellington almost exploded with impatience. 'Your glass man, on the hills opposite!'

We all reached for our field glasses and scanned the hills on the opposite side of the valley. They were the start of the hills of Torres Vedras, stretching from the lagoon at the mouth of the Tagus to the Atlantic coast. I followed the line of the road we were travelling on and saw that there was a new fort guarding the gap in the hills that it passed through, and then I saw hill forts on either side.

'You have fortified the pass,' I said.

'What else?' demanded Wellington, as though waiting for a dull child to understand a simple problem.

'There are more forts to the left,' called one of the staff officers.

'And to the right,' announced another.

I put my glass back to my eye and this time scanned the whole range of hills from the left to the right and for the first time I started to appreciate the immensity of what I was seeing. Nearly every hill top and every pass had been fortified. 'Good grief,' I breathed.

'Now do you see it?' asked Wellington. 'It was when you told me of Alcantara and how you fooled the French by using the hill as a wall. I needed a safe redoubt and here I have turned hills into the strongest possible walls.'

'But there must be dozens of forts along the line,' I exclaimed, astonished.

'One hundred and twenty-six, currently,' said Wellington, beaming with pride, 'and we are still building. Behind the line you can see here, there is a second line of forts. If the French manage to break through at any point we can trap them and destroy them.'

'But that many forts would take years to build,' protested one of the staff officers, who like me was struggling to take it all in.

'A single year,' replied Wellington. 'We have been using the Lisbon militia and conscripts but those that knew of the lines were not then permitted to join the army. It had to stay secret or the French would have tried to cut us off. Even Parliament does not know of their existence.' We rode forward, and the closer you got to the lines, the more impressive they were. Wellington explained how rivers had been dammed to create bogs, miles of walls had been built, tree tops had been dragged to block ravines and roads had been built along the lines so that troops could be moved quickly to meet any threat. Fields of fire had been cleared so that the French would be spotted the instant that they approached. 'Why,' continued Wellington, 'the Navy has even installed a telegraph system with signal towers that can send a message from one end to the other in just a few minutes. The army has been allocated places all along the line. Wherever the French appear, we will have the time and the means to have men ready to face them when they reach the lines.'

'But after the bloody nose we have just given them at Busaco, do you think they will attack us here?' I asked.

'I would be pleasantly surprised if they tried it,' replied Wellington. 'But no, I don't think Massena will be stupid enough to attack.'

'So we are set for a long siege,' I said. I was disappointed; I had been expecting a plan that involved destruction to the French, not just survival for the British forces. I remembered Cousin Maria had told me that Wellington's plan would use the advantages of the French against them, but this plan seemed wholly defensive.

271

The disappointment must have shown in my voice as Wellington looked at me and said quietly, 'Ride with me, Thomas.' He rarely used my first name, and normally only when we were alone. I had known him when he was desperate for his first victory, when he had shared his fears. But despite those intimacies I would have hesitated to call him a friend. He was notoriously remote to his officers, but now he seemed prepared to take me into his confidence again.

'You don't understand yet do you?' he asked, once we were alone.

'Oh, I understand that we can hold out behind those lines until hell freezes over, provided we are well supplied by sea, and the Navy can manage that easily.' I hesitated before adding a note of criticism of a plan he was evidently very proud of. 'It is just that I had expected a plan that would do more harm to the French.'

Wellington smiled. 'What do you think the French will do when they see these lines then?'

'Well, they will besiege us of course; keep us bottled up in Lisbon while they rampage all over the rest of the country.'

'Think about it, Thomas. How long do you think the French can keep an army in front of the lines? We have cleared the ground for miles of any food. If they try to get supplies from the rest of the country the supply columns will be raided by the partisans all the way here. And it will soon be winter, when the roads over the mountains will become impassable for wagons.'

'So do you think they will just turn around and go back to Spain?' I asked, puzzled.

'No, Massena has promised Bonaparte he will drive the British into the sea and destroy us. He would face disgrace if he simply turned around.'

'But if they cannot stay and they cannot go back to Spain, what do you think the French will do?'

'I expect quite a lot of them to die,' explained Wellington simply. He paused, grinning at my bewilderment before continuing. 'Massena will think he is besieging me, but in reality he will be the one besieged. He can stay in front of the lines for no more than six weeks with whatever supplies he has or we have missed. Then he will have to disperse his force across the countryside to stand any chance of them finding enough food to survive the winter. The cold, starvation and the partisans will then take their toll. While our army enjoys the shelter of Lisbon and plentiful supplies, the French will struggle to survive at all. Do you see now the harm these lines will do to the French?'

I sat back in the saddle as I took it all in. It was then that I started to realise the scale of the trap that Wellington had drawn the French into. I thought back to the people I had met recently and there seemed little doubt that he was right about the outcome. When I remembered the confident French army I had marched with in my lancer disguise, there had been not the slightest doubt in their ranks that they would be victorious. They were veterans who had beaten the best armies in Europe, and they were chasing down a British army that they had forced to run from Corunna just two years before. They would never accept that they had been beaten and simply turn around vanquished with their tail between their legs. Their emperor had commanded them to beat the British and they would stay until they had done so.

But if they stayed, I thought back to Rodgriguez and his partisans. There were countless groups like them now across Spain and Portugal and they would fall on the dispersed French like wolves. It would be a bitter and merciless conflict with appalling atrocities on both sides. Hunger and cold would add to the French deprivations, and all the while the British would sit safe, fed and warm behind their walls. In the spring when the British would emerge again, the surviving emaciated French forces would be in a pitiable state. The biggest French army in Spain would be destroyed and there would be nothing to stop us marching straight back into Spain.

'What the deuce,' I said as this sank in. 'This could be your greatest victory yet and you will achieve it while lying comfortably in your bed.'

Wellington grinned at me. 'Well if it is, Campbell tells me you know of two sisters in Lisbon who will also make it my most enjoyable victory. You will have to introduce me.'

Editors Epilogue

Despite being such a monumental undertaking, the lines of Torres Vedras were completed in almost total secrecy. Certainly the French had no idea of their existence until their forward scouts reported on the new hill forts as Massena's army advanced. The marshal found such a fortification so hard to believe that once again he forced himself out of Madame X's bed to go and see them for himself.

While Wellington was right in most of his expectations, he hopelessly underestimated the French foraging ability to stay before the lines. Instead of lasting six weeks as he thought, the French finally moved away from the region in March the following year. During that time both the French army, and to an even greater degree, the Portuguese civilians who stayed outside the British defences, suffered appallingly.

When the French army finally struck camp and tried to withdraw into Spain, their army was twenty thousand less than that which had stood at Busaco. In comparison British losses over that winter were negligible. The combined British and Portuguese army was now bigger than that of the French. But it was not just a matter of numbers, more importantly the morale of both armies completely reversed over that winter. The French arrived before the lines at Torres Vedras the unbeaten military masters, confident of victory and contemptuous of their enemies. Only slowly did they realise the nature of their predicament. At first they thought that the British were trapped, and after some probing at the lines they settled to their siege. Skilled at foraging food and extracting it from the populace which was left, initially all was well, but as winter set in food became scarcer and they were soon cut off from other French forces in Spain. Pride kept them before the lines long after others would have left. Soon every dawn brought gnawing hunger and the corpses of men either grown too weak, or murdered in the night. It was a wickedly harsh winter and once weakened by cold and hunger, disease also ravaged the French army. As thousands of men died and the rest struggled to survive, they were all too aware that the nearby British were well fed and tucked up in warm beds. When the French finally retreated their soldiers were half-starved scarecrows, in little state to fight and resentful that so many lives had been thrown away on such a fruitless gamble. The masters had been mastered.

In contrast, when Wellington's army had first arrived in Spain, many were inexperienced and those who had fought before had known mostly retreat, being chased out the previous winter at Corunna. Over the next two years they had known only victory; of course Cuesta would have pointed out that this was because they hid away from the French for much of that time. But they remained a fighting force, beating the French at Oporto, Talavera and Busaco, before watching the French struggle at Torres Vedras. Like Flashman, many of the British officers had been critical of Wellington during the retreat to the lines, and morale was low at the continuous retreating. However over that harsh winter, as half-starved French deserters recounted their experiences, they came to see the sense of his course of action.

It would be wrong to imply that life behind the lines of Torres Vedra was a bed of roses that winter. For the British soldiers and the Portuguese citizens of the city of Lisbon things were reasonably comfortable, but the city was also packed with thousands of displaced refugees, and for them very little provision was made. Some assistance came from churches and private charity but death and exposure carried off many thousands. The situation was, however, far worse for those Portuguese trapped outside the lines. In addition to coping with hunger and cold they faced torture and death from the French hunting for hidden food supplies that often did not exist or which had long since been consumed. While some Portuguese would have died in that harsh winter from natural causes anyway, it is estimated that fifty thousand Portuguese died that winter, the approximate size of either one of the combatant armies.

However, Torres Vedras was a turning point. While the British may have ended up where they started after two years fighting, when they left the lines they did not stop until they were fighting on the soil of France itself.

Flashman's adventures in Spain and beyond will continue in the next book.

I am deeply indebted to a variety of historians and sources for confirming many of the facts mentioned by Flashman in this account. These include the biographies of Wellington by Elizabeth Longford and Richard Holmes and most especially several books on the Peninsular War by Charles Esdaile. They confirm not only the broad sweep of the campaign and course of battles but also many of the incidental details mentioned by Flashman. This includes Wellington's reaction to the possible foundering of the ship taking him to Portugal, the contents of the despatch about Sir William Erskine, the account of Rigny, the resourceful French officer who masqueraded as a British agent, the murderous Catholic friar and other atrocities committed by both French and Spanish. They also confirm other anecdotal details such as the attempt by the medical corp major and some dragoons to 'liberate' nuns from a convent as well as the infantry soldier hung with his mirror at Coimbra. The diligent research to confirm that the jerez or sherry that the Spanish keep to themselves is vastly superior to that sold overseas under that name, was however conducted by the editor.

Charles Esdaile's books on the Peninsular War also confirm that the **Marquis of Astorga** was a proud and ruthless dwarf. While no mention is made of the marquesa there is a description of the marquis attributed to Lord Holland: *'The Marquis of Astorga was the least man I ever saw in society, and smaller than many dwarfs exhibited for money. He drove about with guards like a royal personage.'* He was president of the Junta of Granada and ruled with a firm hand. He put down one uprising by ordering cavalry to charge a small group of onlookers and placed infantry on every street corner.

John Downie

Downie was one of Wellington's commissary officers and a passionate supporter of the Spanish cause. He was of some personal means for largely at his own expense he did succeed in forming a regiment dressed in fashions dating back to late sixteenth century. He was also given the sword of Pizarro by the conquistador's family and there are accounts of him hurling this to friends across a river when he was injured and about to be captured. He was undoubtedly brave and lost part of his jaw in a bomb explosion. After the war he was given a pension by the Spanish crown and, as Flashman mentioned, was made governor of the castle in Seville. A contemporary account from a

British soldier of seeing his extraordinary regiment in the field is below:

'On the line of march this day, I saw a body of the Estremaduran legion; a corps raised, clothed, and commanded by a General Downie, an Englishman, who had formerly been a commissary in our service. Any thing so whimsical or ridiculous as the dress of this corps, I never beheld : it was meant to be an imitation of the ancient costume of Spain. The turned-up hat, slashed doublet, and short mantle, might have figured very well in the play of Pizarro, or at an exhibition of Astley's ; but in the rude and ready bivouack, they appeared absurd and ill-chosen. In the midst of our misery and discomfort, the same evening, we could not avoid laughing at the recollection of these poor devils, who, in their fantastic dresses, must have been exposed to the same violent storm which extinguished our fires, soaked our ground, and, forcing its way through our tents, drenched us to the skin.'

Sherer Moyle, Recollections of the Peninsula, first published in 1824.

The Defence of the Alcantara Bridge

Accounts of this battle are hard to find, largely for the reasons that Flashman mentioned: the antipathy between Wellington and Wilson, and because neither the French nor the Spanish had reason to recall the incident with pride. There is, however, the excellent first-hand account of the battle in A Narrative of the Campaigns of the Loyal Lusitanian Legion by Colonel William Mayne. You can find this freely available at the website of the Portuguese National Library or Biblioteca Nacional Digital. Not only does this cover the Alcantara Bridge defence, but it also gives first-hand accounts of various other events in the short but extraordinary existence of the Loyal Lusitanian Legion. This includes how the Legion held off a French force of ten times their number at Almeida during the winter of 1808/09, allowing the British to retain their foothold in Lisbon.

One of the delights in editing this book was to discover that the Alcantara Bridge still survives and looks exactly the same as it must have done in Flashman's time. There are plenty of photographs of it online and visitors to Alcantara can walk or even drive across this outstanding feat of engineering that is now nearly two thousand years old. The first span did collapse shortly after the battle and the British put in place a temporary repair in 1812. The bridge was not permanently repaired until 1860. The town of Alcantara remains on one side of the bridge, and you can still see the slope and bluff unchanged from when the Legion conducted their desperate defence of it.

Sir Robert Wilson

Wilson and Wellington were opposites in temperament, and as both men had very high opinions of their own abilities it was inevitable that they would fall out. Wilson viewed Wellington as high handed and overly cautious while Wellington considered Wilson reckless and dishonest. The title of Wilson's biography by Michael Glover, 'A Very Slippery Fellow', comes from a Wellington quotation dated April 1810. 'He [Wilson] is a very slippery fellow… and he has not the talent of being able to speak the truth upon any subject.'

Wilson and the Legion did come within seventeen miles of liberating Madrid while the French army was gathered to face Wellington at Talavera. But had Wilson succeeded it is likely that any liberation would have been short lived. The Legion only just escaped ambush and encirclement on its way back behind the allied lines.

During a long career as soldier and diplomat, Wilson saw action in a range of different countries. After an eventful war he was imprisoned briefly by the Bourbon government in France for helping a Bonapartist official escape from the death cell on the eve of his execution. In Britain he was dismissed from the army accused of inciting the household cavalry to mutiny. A more accurate description of his action was that he was trying to deter the soldiers from shooting into the crowd at Queen Caroline's funeral. Later he was reinstated, became a radical MP, and spent his last years as the Governor of Gibraltar. He is buried in Westminster Abbey.

Gregorio Cuesta

Cuesta is much maligned in accounts of the Peninsular War for being proud and arrogant and for his poor strategic and tactical understanding. He certainly did have all of those faults, but he was nearly seventy when the war started and struggled to adapt to contemporary tactics. His army was packed with unwilling recruits and incompetent officers, while he received very little in the way of supplies. His enemy was invariably better equipped with skilled and experienced troops and commanders. While he suffered a long series of humiliating defeats, given the interference from the Central Junta, rivalry from other generals and lack of support, it is perhaps creditable that he held his army together long enough to fight at Talavera. He made a valid point to Flashman in the carriage that while the British army had evacuated the previous winter, his army had fought on. It was to fight on for the next winter too, without its general, as the British sat peacefully in their winter quarters in Portugal.

Cuesta had an implacable hatred of the French, which it seems only slightly exceeded his dislike of the British, Spanish politicians and some of his rival generals. However his courage was beyond doubt. He did try and stop the retreat of his cavalry at Medallin, getting ridden down by both sides in the process. At Talavera he was humiliated by the inexplicable rout of his infantry in full view of his allies and planned the executions as described by Flashman. However he was extremely proud of the charge by the Royal Cavalry Regiment and its capture of the guns – which were second only to regimental eagles in terms of military trophies and a lot more useful. He sent glowing accounts of that part of the action to the Junta in Seville. While Cuesta was certainly in the gun emplacement to see the guns, in the interests of historical accuracy, it has to be pointed out that Flashman is the only witness to the fact that he nearly beat the attacking cavalry to the battery. Cuesta's abandonment of the British wounded to the French a few days after the battle was an unforgivable act to the British and if any had seen his charge they were unlikely to give him credit for it in subsequently written accounts.

Talavera

There have been many accounts of the battle of Talavera and Flashman's description aligns closely with the known facts. The first attack was aborted after the Spanish failed to appear. Despite planning the attack with Wellesley in some detail the previous day, Cuesta chose to stay in bed at the appointed time of the assault, refusing to be disturbed until Wellesley arrived in his camp. The most likely explanation is that he did not trust his allies to come to his aid. Whatever the reason, it denied the allies their chance of tackling Victor alone. Stung by British criticism he then marched the Spanish off on their own to attack Victor, and more by luck than judgement, escaped another catastrophic defeat before marching back to Talavera.

The skirmish before the main battle at Casa Salinas where Wellesley was nearly captured took place as described by Flashman, although he adds more detail on how the ambush was triggered. It was a sizeable action, dead, wounded and missing totalling four hundred and fifty men for the British.

One of the most extraordinary incidents at Talavera, or the whole Peninsular War, was the inexplicable routing of some two thousand Spanish infantry at the start of the main battle. It was witnessed by many including Wellesley, who was disgusted at the sight, but uncertainty remains over what triggered the event. Flashman was as close to it as anybody and even he is not sure, although the reasons he speculates are as good as any. Certainly after the appalling slaughter at Medallin, the Spanish infantry would have had a terror of French horsemen.

The battle was nearly lost by the British during the night time surprise attack by the French on the hill that formed the centre of the British line. As Flashman described, some of the forces that should have been the front line of any defence of the hill had been marched to the bottom, without warning the regiments behind. If the hill had been lost the British position the next day would have been untenable, forcing their retreat. However in a desperate night action the summit was regained by the British, enabling them to fight a robust defensive action the next day.

Flashman's account reveals that Wellesley was aware of Soult's approach that night whereas other sources suggest that he only learned about it the following day; but possibly Wellesley did not want to distract his army with this new challenge until the battle had been won.

The rotund general Flashman met on the slope during the night action and sat with on the hill the next morning was General Rowland 'Daddy' Hill. At a time when generals such as Picton and Wellesley commanded to a degree through fear, Hill was genuinely loved by his men for the care he took of them. He was sparing with their lives and was known to give funds from his own pocket to reward good service or aid the comfort of his men. His apparent interest in ornithology has not previously been noted.

The main events of the battle took place as described by Flashman. It was a classic defensive action of the type Wellesley, or Wellington as he became after this event, fought numerous times, making full use of features such as the reverse slopes of hills. The strange truce in the middle of the battle on the second day also took place, with various accounts of soldiers meeting and trading with the enemy while they drank from the stream. After repelling the French advances, the allies finally advanced with cavalry attacks on both flanks. The British attack from the north of the battlefield encountered an unexpected ditch which brought down many of the horses and stalled the attack. The Spanish cavalry charge from the south was far more successful, heading off enemy cavalry and infantry attacks while capturing the battery of guns.

As Flashman describes, the drama was not finished when the battle ended. Many of the wounded from both sides were killed when a fire swept through the battlefield, which had been fought on fields of crops and long grass baked dry in the July heat. Fanned by a breeze, the flames moved quickly, leaving little time to pull the wounded from its path. Some were rescued but many more were burned to death.

Ultimately while a victory for the allies, and a rare one for the Spanish, the battle was not strategically important. With Soult advancing behind the allied line, they risked being trapped between two large armies and a retreat across the Tagus was inevitable if they were to survive to fight another day.

Lord Byron

While it may seem fanciful name dropping by Flashman to include Lord Byron in a book about the Peninsular War, biographers confirm the details Flashman provides. When in London during 1808 he did stay at the Dorant's Piccadilly Hotel. In 1809, for reasons that were never entirely clear, until now revealed by Flashman, Byron and Hobhouse left London for a tour of the Mediterranean. They landed in Lisbon and travelled from there via Seville to Cadiz and on to Gibraltar to catch a ship to take them east.

Byron did meet Agustina de Aragon. Byron was so impressed by her story that he included a reference to her in his Childe Harold epic. The verses found by the doubtless long suffering Miss Tuttle for the old satyr to include in this book are from that work. Byron and Hobhouse then moved on to Cadiz and arrived there in time for the Talavera celebrations, having just missed them in Seville, showing that the timing of their journey aligns with Flashman's account.

Byron was known to be fond of dogs and even once vowed to be buried with a favourite hound. As Flashman describes, when Cambridge University pointed out that keeping a dog was against their rules, Byron retaliated by bringing a bear to university – something that Cambridge University rules unsurprisingly did not cover. The creature was kept in the university stable while Byron studied there. Byron was certainly impetuous in his decision making and it is therefore entirely possible that he would buy an Irish wolfhound from a Connaught soldier if the opportunity arose.

Agustina de Aragon

Despite being a national heroine, or possibly because of this, there are significant discrepancies in accounts of Agustina's life. There is very little biographical information in English but from what there is, various places claim to be her birth place and only the events of her later years are undisputed.

Some accounts suggest she married for love, and after her child died early in the war she and her husband went to Zaragoza. There, for the glory of Spain and guided by her Christian faith, she fired the gun that stalled the French advance on the city. She was then widely used as an example of Spanish Christian womanhood with various paintings of her including one by Francisco Goya, who grew up in Zaragoza. She escaped from Zaragoza after its capture and was paraded around Seville as a national heroine. Accounts state that she had a metal shield commemorating her achievement on her sleeve rather than a medal around her neck as Flashman recalls. However there is no suggestion that she was ever re-united with her husband and the Catholic Church seems to have taken a close interest in managing her image to ensure she upheld Christian values.

Other slightly more numerous accounts point out that she was a wild child and that as a teenager she used to frequent the gates of the barracks near her home. We can only speculate what she was doing there, bearing in mind that her family was poor and she needed to earn money. Many of these accounts also suggest that she was already pregnant when she married and was not at all religious. In these versions of her life she seems to have left her husband before the siege and gone to Zaragoza with her child to stay with a sister. There she met a man called Raul and she is with him when she fires the gun. These accounts have her child dying or being killed by the French after the siege or while she escapes.

All descriptions of her personal appearance indicate that she was a very attractive woman of twenty-three when Flashman met her. While his manuscript may appear to be an appalling defamation of her Christian reputation, some catalyst evidently occurred that enabled her to escape the Church's influence and become a successful guerrilla leader. Some accounts of her life state that later in the war Agustina left the guerrillas and went on to become the only female officer to serve with the British army in the artillery during the Peninsular War; achieving the rank of Captain at the battle of Vitoria. However Nick Lipscombe, author of Wellington's Guns and a leading authority on the Peninsular War advises that she definitely did not command a gun in the British army. After the war she married a doctor and settled down to a quiet life living in Zaragoza. She died aged seventy-one.

Visitors to Seville Cathedral today will see that in approximately the space where Flashman claims they stood, there is now a new tomb for the bones of Christopher Columbus. These were returned to the city in 1898.

Battle of Busaco

Again, Flashman's account matches those of his contemporaries, including descriptions of the night cap worn by General Picton. The British and Portuguese were in an extremely strong position and it says something about the arrogance and confidence of the French command that they thought they could beat the allies with a frontal assault.

The charge of the Connaught Rangers was one of the highpoints of the battle and various other sources mention Wellington's claim that it was the finest charge he ever saw. It was the first British action since Talavera over a year previously and like that battle it had little tactical importance. It was fought largely to give the army and the government a victory before retreat back to the lines. The French always had the option of outflanking the British/Portuguese position, which ultimately they did. Wellington was then forced to retreat as he could not afford to get cut off from Torres Vedras.

I hope you have enjoyed this book. If you have I would be grateful for any positive reviews on websites that you use to choose books to read.

Also by this author:

Flashman and the Seawolf

This first book in the Thomas Flashman series covers his adventures with Thomas Cochrane, one of the most extraordinary naval commanders of all time.

From the brothels and gambling dens of London, through political intrigues and espionage, the action moves to the Mediterranean and the real life character of Thomas Cochrane. This book covers the start of Cochrane's career including the most astounding single ship action of the Napoleonic war.

Thomas Flashman provides a unique insight as danger stalks him like a persistent bailiff through a series of adventures that prove history really is stranger than fiction.

Flashman and the Cobra

This book takes Thomas to territory familiar to readers of his nephew's adventures, India, during the second Mahratta war. It also includes an illuminating visit to Paris during the Peace of Amiens in 1802.

As you might expect Flashman is embroiled in treachery and scandal from the outset and, despite his very best endeavours, is often in the thick of the action. He intrigues with generals, warlords, fearless warriors, nomadic bandit tribes, highland soldiers and not least a four-foot-tall former nautch dancer, who led the only Mahratta troops to leave the battlefield of Assaye in good order.

Flashman gives an illuminating account with a unique perspective. It details feats of incredible courage (not his, obviously) reckless folly and sheer good luck that were to change the future of India and the career of a general who would later win a war in Europe.

CPSIA information can be obtained at www.ICGtesting.com
Printed in the USA
LVOW11s0314050914

402528LV00001B/46/P